PRAISE FOR SARAH BARRIE'S LEXI WINTER BOOKS

'Phenomenal. Lexi Winter is the gritty hero I didn't know I needed ... I'm now desperate for more.'
—Bestselling Australian author Nicola Moriarty

'Dark, gritty and filled with unexpected twists and turns, *Retribution* is brilliant and picks up to a relentless pace in the second half. Don't start reading this before bed ... there's no way you'll be able to put it down.'
—*Better Reading*

'Barrie has produced an impressive and fast-paced crime thriller with *Retribution*. Following complex protagonists across several compelling investigations, this is an awesome read that is guaranteed to keep readers on their toes.'
—*Canberra Weekly*

'This quick paced thriller stuns with many heart-stopping moments of danger, violence and destruction. Intense, fast moving and consuming, I was completely on edge while reading *Retribution*.'
—*Mrs B's Book Reviews*

'Dark, propulsive ... relentless and filled with unexpected twists and turns.'
—*The Australian* on *Retribution*

'Sarah Barrie at her nail-biting, heart-stopping best in this riveting novel of a flawed, gutsy heroine who emerges from a dark past to prey on the predators.'
—Bestselling Australian author Tea Cooper on *Unforgiven*

'A gritty, twisty journey of suspense. Recommended.'
—*Canberra Weekly* on *Unforgiven*

'If you like a read that keeps you on the edge of your seat, this addictive, suspenseful thriller is for you.'
—*Woman's Day* on *Unforgiven*

'There is drama and suspense aplenty in this gritty tale.'
—*Sunday Telegraph* on *Unforgiven*

Sarah Barrie is the author of ten novels including her bestselling print debut *Secrets of Whitewater Creek*, the Hunters Ridge and Calico Mountain trilogies, and a crime series starring Constable Lexi Winter. In a past life, while gaining degrees in arts, science and education, Sarah worked as a teacher, a vet nurse, a horse trainer and a magazine editor, before deciding she wanted to write novels. About the only thing that has remained constant is her love of all things crime.

Her favourite place in the world is the family property, where she writes her stories overlooking mountains crisscrossed with farmland, bordered by the beauty of the Australian bush, and where, at the end of the day, she can spend time with family, friends, a good Irish whiskey and a copy of her next favourite book.

Also by Sarah Barrie

Secrets of Whitewater Creek

The Hunters Ridge Trilogy
Legacy of Hunters Ridge
Shadows of Hunters Ridge
Promise of Hunters Ridge

The Calico Mountain Trilogy
Bloodtree River
Devil's Lair
Deadman's Track

The Lexi Winter Series
Unforgiven
Vendetta

RETRIBUTION

SARAH BARRIE

First Published 2022
Second Australian Paperback Edition 2023
ISBN 9781867287315

RETRIBUTION
© 2022 by Sarah Barrie
Australian Copyright 2022
New Zealand Copyright 2022

Except for use in any review, the reproduction or utilisation of this work in whole or in part in any form by any electronic, mechanical or other means, now known or hereafter invented, including xerography, photocopying and recording, or in any information storage or retrieval system, is forbidden without the permission of the publisher.

This book is sold subject to the condition that it shall not, by way of trade or otherwise, be lent, resold, hired out or otherwise circulated without the prior consent of the publisher in any form of binding or cover other than that in which it is published and without a similar condition including this condition being imposed on the subsequent purchaser.

All rights reserved including the right of reproduction in whole or in part in any form.

This is a work of fiction. Names, characters, places, and incidents are either the product of the author's imagination or are used fictitiously, and any resemblance to actual persons, living or dead, business establishments, events, or locales is entirely coincidental.

Published by
HQ Fiction
An imprint of Harlequin Enterprises (Australia) Pty Limited (ABN 47 001 180 918),
a subsidiary of HarperCollins Publishers Australia Pty Limited (ABN 36 009 913 517)
Level 19, 201 Elizabeth St
SYDNEY NSW 2000
AUSTRALIA

® and ™ (apart from those relating to FSC®) are trademarks of Harlequin Enterprises (Australia) Pty Limited or its corporate affiliates. Trademarks indicated with ® are registered in Australia, New Zealand and in other countries.

A catalogue record for this book is available from the National Library of Australia
www.librariesaustralia.nla.gov.au

Printed and bound by CPI Group (UK) Ltd, Croydon, CR0 4YY

*To everyone who has ever made
a life-altering mistake.
May you get that
second chance.*

CHAPTER ONE

Friday, March 4

Lulled by the gentle movement of the train, Daisy rested her cheek against the cool vinyl seat and stared out the scarred window into the darkness beyond. The carriage was quiet. Three other passengers shared the upper level space with her: a tired-looking fatherly type in a crinkled grey business suit and a couple of teenage Alice Cooper lookalikes more interested in their mobile phones than each other. She fought the temptation to allow her eyes to close. It had been a difficult day, one of many she'd had during the last year, and a bad night's sleep had left her drained of energy. But she needed to take care of things for her mum, so she'd get through it. That's just how it was. She yawned widely and stretched. Falling asleep and missing her stop wasn't an option.

The sharp slap of something hitting the floor brought her back to wakefulness. The middle-aged tradie in the vestibule downstairs picked his phone up off the floor, checked it, then typed something before returning it to a large gym bag at his feet. He crossed and uncrossed his legs before returning his gaze to the lower part of the carriage. He'd been staring in that direction each time Daisy's eyes had brushed past him.

He swiped an arm across the sheen of perspiration on his brow. It wasn't cold enough in the carriage to be wearing that heavy drill jacket zipped right under his chin. Whatever. Daisy yawned again, went back to gazing into the night.

The train's PA system declared the next station was Hawkesbury River. The train stopped and the opening doors blasted cool air into the warm space. They closed. As the train lurched back into motion, a shuffling noise drew her attention back to the vestibule. The tradie had gotten to his feet. He picked up his bag and walked down to the lower level of the carriage, eyes intent.

Daisy's skin prickled. A second ticked by, two, three, then a muffled sound of distress had her sitting straighter. A glance around showed the other three passengers hadn't heard. Or didn't care.

'No!' The woman's voice was tight. More words followed. Rushed, high-pitched. The man's voice was deeper, quieter. She couldn't make out what he was saying, but then the woman's loud, 'I'm not!' was quickly muffled. By force?

She should check what's going on. She got up slowly, crept towards the stairs and put her foot on the first step, the second. Her foot had just landed silently on the bottom step when the train's PA system sprang back to life.

'Next stop, Wondabyne.'

She scrambled back up the steps. The businessman in the suit gave her a curious look and shifted in his seat, cleared his throat and resettled. A well-built twenty-something in a hoodie and jeans came through from the carriage in front and stood at the doors. His eyes flicked around and down to the carriage's lower level. Remained bland.

Okay then. Maybe there was nothing to worry about. Daisy relaxed in her seat as the train rocked slightly, following the wind of the creek. Lights from a scattering of boats and a couple of houses across the water were all that competed with those of the station as it came into view.

Wondabyne. The tiny station sat between Mullet Creek, a tributary of the Hawkesbury River, and the steep mountainside of

Brisbane Water National Park. There was nothing more here than a few weird sculptures, a caretaker's cottage, a sandstone mine that rarely operated and a public wharf frequented by the handful of houses across the creek and the odd fisherman. It wasn't far from here to the busy town of Woy Woy, which was a few short stops away from the city of Gosford, yet Wondabyne gave off all the vibes of being in the middle of nowhere. Especially at night.

As the train crept into the station, her attention was drawn to a rowdy group of drunk, feral-looking campers on the platform who were picking up backpacks and sleeping bags in preparation for boarding. Daisy dragged her own backpack to her lap and checked it was still zipped tight.

'Doors opening. Please stand clear.'

The doors opened, flooding the carriage with noise from the campers. The guy that had moved into the carriage stepped off to greet them and help with their gear. The guard stepped out and barked orders, attempting to hustle the campers and their gear safely on board.

Gross. The carriage filled with the putrid odour of stale bodies and alcohol. She looked around, caught sight of the tradie in the heavy jacket stepping off the train, the smaller figure of a woman clutched tightly in front of him. She surged to her feet for a better look, but the guy in the business suit had gotten out of his seat and chosen that moment to step past her, blocking her view. 'Sorry, just going to change carriages,' the businessman muttered.

She fully understood why. 'After you,' she said over the general chaos.

She followed the suit down the steps, only to have the air knocked from her lungs as someone crashed into her from behind. 'Sorry,' a young man that smelled like a public toilet slurred.

'Excuse me,' she said in return, screwing up her nose as she side-stepped him.

'This is supposed to be the quiet carriage!' the suit complained to the guard.

'Sorry, sir, but it might be easier for you to move than for me to get this lot to shut up.'

The suit scowled then found a gap in the bodies still boarding and headed through the vestibule towards the doors between the carriages. Daisy stepped around two more men, hoping another gap in the fray would open up. She looked through the open doors but could no longer see anyone on the platform. The PA sounded again. *Shit*. Would everyone get out of her way!

Giving up, she shoved through the bodies and left the stale odour behind. As the doors closed and the train pulled away, she took a deep breath and told herself not to worry. Everything would no doubt turn out to be fine. Before long another difficult day would be over.

CHAPTER TWO

Saturday, March 5

'Lexi! Wait!' I hear as I charge into the gaping darkness of Woy Woy railway tunnel.

Nope. I am absolutely not waiting. I can run this little shit down, I know I can. The beam of my torch bounces erratically off the arched brick walls as I leap over one of two sets of steel tracks and smash through loose gravel, doing my best to keep said little shit in sight. My lungs are burning, both from the exertion of the sprint and the musty, stale air.

I should call out again, but I don't think I can talk and still breathe. My target isn't listening anyway. He's completely pumped on whatever he's taken and is kind of dance-running along the northbound rail line, his spray cans rattling as he haphazardly hits the wall with streaks of the same red and gold paint with which he'd decorated a nearby warehouse wall. I've seen the tag—a large gold crystal spearing from a stylised red G—in a few local spots. It's quite well done, but vandalism is vandalism.

I thought I could run this little shit down. Now I'm not so sure. I desperately need to stop and as he's showing no signs of slowing, I'm briefly tempted to leave him to it. He'll have to come back eventually. I'm not sure many trains run through here in the early hours of the morning. A pissed-off corner of my brain is telling me his untimely death via a speeding passenger train wouldn't be any great loss to society, but I'm not allowed to think like that. Now that I'm Constable Lexi Winter, a paid member of the New South Wales Police Force, albeit a probationary one, I'm supposed to value all life and risk my own to save the little shits of the world so they can live on and, in the case of the two we're after tonight, keep being little shits.

At least this one, along with the one my partner just caught, might spend some time behind bars. Last week they used some pretty impressive parkour skills to evade capture after beating a cop unconscious for trying to search them. I can safely say they either don't value or are incapable of higher learning. Because here we are.

The short, sharp warning sound of a train entering the tunnel echoes along the walls. Shit! I stumble to a stop, resting my hands on my knees to drag in air as I contemplate my next move. A small, blinding light bursts into view at the end of the stupidly long tunnel, becomes larger as the train approaches and the engine noise intensifies to a roar. That light illuminates the silhouette of the tagger now hot-stepping it back in my direction. The blast of the train horn sounds again and the squealing of brakes suggests the driver is doing his or her best to slow down, but it's not a quick process and the stupid little shit is still running down the middle of its same track.

'Fuck me.' I ignore my terror and force my jelly-legs back into action. I reach the little shit in a few more strides and yank at his arm, sending him stumbling out of the train's path and onto the southbound line. Despite the brakes, the passenger train hurtles past us with another ear-splitting blare of the horn. There's several seconds of wind that could kick your feet out from under you and those images I can now confirm flash before your eyes when you think you're about to die. Then it's gone.

My ears are ringing and my legs are unsteady as my heart struggles to return to its normal rhythm. Little shit has scrambled against the tunnel wall, staring at the disappearing train like a kid at a Christmas tree.

'Did you see that?' he asks in awe.

'How the fuck could you possibly think I missed it?' I snap. I draw in a few more much-needed deep breaths while I put myself back in the right headspace to resume being a police officer. We need to move before the next train tries to kill us.

'Get on your stomach!' I say, pushing him backwards onto the ground and rolling him over. I drop my knee into the small of his back and I'm met with little resistance as I pull one hand around his back, then the other, cuffing them together. I pat him down, checking for weapons, and pull a four-inch flick knife from his left pocket. I scramble off him and grab his arm. 'Get up. You're under arrest.'

'For what?' he whines, sounding about ten years old.

'You have the right to—'

'I haven't done anything wrong!' He attempts to turn his head to look at me, almost falling over his own feet in the process.

I continue my spiel as he continues his protests, and though his professions of innocence had started out whiny, it's not long before I hear aggression leaking in.

'Let's just get you safely out of here, okay?' I tell him in a tone reminiscent of a kindergarten teacher. I know how drugs can affect users, have seen many times how quickly addicts can go from chilled out to manic, especially if it's courtesy of methamphetamine. As I'm pretty sure that's what this one's on, I really need to keep him calm and moving back to Rico. I learnt a few self-defence moves at the academy, and I'm sure as hell a lot fitter than I used to be due to the program's medieval torture routines, but I've also seen how unbelievably strong and violent a teen on meth can be and I don't want to have to face that. 'Trains are dangerous.'

'Trains are dangerous,' he repeats and begins charging ahead so I have to jog-walk to keep a hand on him. Relief floods through me as we reach the exit and I hear Rico calling out.

'Here!' I shout and wave the torch around. Once out of the tunnel, I have no problem spotting him jogging towards us, but neither does little shit and it trips a switch in his drug-fogged brain. He knocks into me hard in an attempt to get free.

I lunge at him and we go down in a tangled, squirming mess on the track. There's a clang. I think it might be him banging his head on the rail, then I'm thrown off. He stumbles, finding it difficult to get his feet underneath himself with his hands cuffed. I grab his ankle and he goes down again, but somehow backwards, on top of me, pressing me painfully into the gravel.

Rico gets hold of him and his weight suddenly lifts. Little shit is yelling, swearing and spitting, then coughing as he's face-planted into the ground. Rico has him pinned, but it's taking some effort to keep him down. He looks back at me and I don't need the illumination of the full light of day to know he's pissed off.

'Seriously?'

I sit for a moment to recover then get up slowly and dust myself off. 'Have you got the other one in the car?'

'Yeah. Lexi, you were in that tunnel when that train came through!'

'No kidding.'

'And you took this one on alone after I told you to wait!'

'To be fair, I knew you were on your way.'

'Are you okay?'

'No. I'm not.' I'm not injured, but I'm covered in debris from our tussle. I brush at it uselessly. The uniform's not all that comfortable at the best of times, but now it's stupidly itchy. I untuck my shirt and shake it in an attempt to dislodge some of the grit and whatever was crawling on me. I can't see anything much in the dark. 'I have dirt in places dirt should not go.'

Rico's scowl almost becomes a satisfied smirk. 'Serves you right.'

I can't help but smile back. For a field training officer, Christian Rico is as good as it gets. He's likeable, considerate and has a sense of humour. At a year over forty, he's also built like a kind of modern-day Adonis. All six-feet-one of him is tanned muscle and dark good looks, which makes him easy on the eye from my perspective and terrifying to anyone considering taking him on. It's a win-win, given that during the last couple of months he's come between me and danger countless times.

'Get the fuck off me!' little shit screams as he thrashes around, but Rico keeps him down.

'Can I taser him?' I ask, only half joking as I find a piece of gravel in my bra and toss it.

'Let's see how we go,' Rico says, then to his captive, he says, 'Are you going to cooperate?'

'Yes! Fuck!'

'Okay.' Rico carefully gets him up. 'But one wrong move and she hits you with fifty thousand volts. Got it?'

'Where's Jason!' the little shit demands, and I do a mental fist pump. The kid has confirmed these are the two I was hoping they were: Jason and Aden Hamill of the very nasty Hamill crime family. Excellent.

'Back to the car, let's go,' Rico orders. I walk slightly behind them in case I really do need that taser, then move ahead as we reach the car to open the door for Rico to secure Aden next to his brother, Jason.

'This is bullshit!' Jason complains. 'We've done nothing wrong!'

'You seriously assaulted a police officer,' I say, dragging a twig from my hair before raking my fingers through the tangled black mess and twisting it back into a semblance of the obligatory bun.

'Prove it!' he demands as I slide into the front passenger seat.

'We have a witness, don't worry,' I tell him.

'You think that matters, bitch?' Jason spits. 'We're Hamills! You don't mess with us and get away with it!'

Ha. He didn't know the half of it.

'Settle down,' Rico orders.

'Not fucking likely! You better let us go or we'll send someone round to your place to mess you up, how's that sound?'

'Like another easy arrest,' I say, giving my shirt one last flap before doing up my seatbelt.

'Still uncomfortable?' Rico asks with a chuckle. 'I thought you were going to strip off out there.'

'Only those with breasts would understand. I'm going to need a shower when we get back.'

'You know, it could have been a lot worse.'

'Yeah, I could have shot the little shit.'

'Pig-bitch!' spits Jason.

Rico turns in his seat. 'I told you to settle down! You're not doing yourself any favours.'

'How about you give me a chance to bash your head in? That'd be doing me a favour. I will, you know. First chance I get!'

'It's never too late to use the taser,' I murmur.

'The boss is going to go ape shit as it is,' Rico says. 'I get in trouble too, you know. We're supposed to be out on a routine patrol in our own district.'

'These two bashed one of his best cops a week ago! Do you think he'll care what we're supposed to be doing?' I think about that and reply before he does. 'Maybe let's not mention the tunnel.'

'You'd rather he hear it from one of them?' He indicates the teens in the back. 'You've got fifteen minutes to come up with an acceptable spin on this, Winter. Start thinking.'

CHAPTER THREE

'I don't care what you thought you were doing!' the boss shouts at Rico as he attempts to explain. 'You allowed a probationary constable in your charge to chase an armed, violent, drug-affected offender into an active train tunnel!' His murky hazel eyes are wide, lips thin with tension. The angry colour that had started in Inspector Burns's cheeks moved up to hit his receding grey hairline. The infamous Burns flush. Combined with the always-blue suit he wore and his habit of huffing and puffing his way through his tirades, he'd earned himself the title the Tank, short for Thomas the Tank Engine. That kind of fits in nicely with tonight's little railway adventure.

Burns was most likely getting sick of dishing out these sorts of reprimands, but I was just as sick of receiving them. And it wasn't Rico's fault.

'Can we chill for a second, Tank?' I cut in. 'There was no *allow* about it. I just did it.'

Those slitted eyes turn to stare me down. 'The title is *sir*, Winter. And do you think I'm an idiot?'

I wonder if he wants the honest answer, decide I should probably play it safe. 'No, sir.'

'And have you been in my presence for the last two months?'

'Yes, sir.'

'Then is there really any need to cut in to state the obvious?'

'I suppose not.' I tack 'sir' on the end when his brow attempts to hit his hairline.

Burns's attention bounces back to Rico. 'You're going to tell me exactly how this came about.'

'We were following up on a tip-off that the two youths involved in the attack on Constable Hadley were in the location, sir.'

I look out the window of Wyong Police Station. It's still dark, though the sunrise can't be too far away. The roads are getting busier and the angry honk of a horn on the main road breaks the relative quiet. Wyong Police Station is one of three stations in Tuggerah Lakes Police District, which covers 820 square kilometres and serves a population of around 150,000 people. That information is only a small part of a diatribe of facts the boss seems to be inherently proud of. I can't even think it without hearing his voice booming it in my head. Sydney's got to have loads more people per district, but as he comes from a town in outback New South Wales that barely rates a dot on the map and is famous for sheep racing, I guess this is his own personal megalopolis. Other than when I'm copping the odd roasting, I generally enjoy being stationed here. It wasn't easy to get a posting on the coast straight out of the academy, so I was lucky.

'We went out to the area immediately as we wanted to ensure we were there in time to detain them,' Rico continues. 'We found them injecting what we believe was methamphetamine close to the tunnel entrance. They spotted us and bolted.'

Burns's eyes are back on me. He's looking at me the same way a weary, pissed-off parent looks at a toddler throwing a tantrum in a grocery store. I'm sure deep down he likes me. Deep, deep down. Somewhere. Because he hasn't kicked me out. Yet.

'While I was busy with one, Lexi continued into the tunnel after the other one.'

Burns's eyes return to Rico. 'Did you order her to stop?'

Rico hesitates, shoots me a weary glance of his own. 'Heat of the moment, sir. I can't remember.'

'Good save,' Burns says unappreciatively. His hand goes to his forehead. 'Winter, can you please explain to me what you were thinking, running into that tunnel?'

'The little shit's life was at risk. He'd loaded himself with drugs and gone bouncing down the tunnel like a whacked-out ballerina. If I hadn't pulled him out of the way of that train there wouldn't have been enough left of him to charge.'

'Winter, you're a probationary officer. Sergeant Rico is here to make sure you don't do stupid things like playing in railway traffic! You should be following his instructions, not making rash decisions and charging blindy into volatile situations on your own. You need to understand that the rules are in place for your own protection. Not that that's something any top-of-her-class-at-the-academy recruit should need to be told.'

As if I need reminding about the rules. Since joining the police force, I've never encountered so many. Whatever. I can't help the yawn, nor can I quite completely cover it.

The Tank fires up again. 'Am I boring you, Winter?'

'Only mildly, sir.' I mean, I don't want to be too blunt but the man probably needs to be reminded that only a year ago I survived the dual attentions of a serial killer and a sociopath. Burns looks like the top of his head might be about to blow right off. 'There's one other thing you should know,' I say before he can shout at me some more. 'The teens we brought in are Hamills.'

'As in ... part of the Hamill crime family?' He sits, takes several deep breaths and—oh hell, this is it. He's going to have a heart attack. 'Enough. I want the whole episode, in writing, on my desk by this time tomorrow.'

'Already done, sir,' I tell him almost smugly. Rico had wanted to make sure our versions of events were iron-clad identical, so despite my intense aversion to paperwork, he'd made me do it with him before fronting the boss. 'If I could just make a suggestion.'

'No.'

'Excuse me?'

'No, you may not make a suggestion,' Burns spits. 'Because I don't want to hear another word!'

Oh, for fuck's sake. 'Should I put that in writing too then, sir?'

Rico coughs. It was a gentle sound, nowhere near strong enough to cause his eyes to appear to pop out of his head as they were doing.

The Tank opens his mouth then rethinks whatever he was going to say, snapping his jaw shut. His beady stare moves between Rico and I for a moment, the heavy rise and fall of his chest suggesting he's striving for control. 'Get out of my sight, both of you.'

I want to, I really do, but now I have the Hamill twins, I need to make sure they go down. Tank has already got his elbows on the desk and his fingers at his temples. How much worse can it get?

'Yes, sir, but the Drugs and Firearms Squad would be interested to know we have the twins in custody. I could contact them for you—'

'No, Winter, you won't!'

'But—'

'I'm well aware of your connections to the big brass! But flashing those connections around is not a good look!'

My mouth drops open in disgust. 'Flashing? You think I'm—'

'Thank you, sir,' Rico says over my objection. 'We'll get out of your way.'

I'm being towed out of the room, Rico's expression threatening all sorts of things if I don't come quietly.

'Are you trying to get us on permanent desk duty?' he asks as we head out.

'I'm trying to do my job! There's an entire team of specialist police looking for any and every chance to build their case on the Hamills. They need to be told!'

'Look, we'll get the twins ID'd on the assault, charge them, then get them to spill their guts about the drugs. Once we have the evidence to call in the big guns, we'll let the drugs and firearms people know.'

'All that's doing is making a stupid concession to his little dick syndrome! They should be told *now*!'

'We have our orders, so let's follow them for now. Okay? Please?'

'Okay,' I huff. Because I've already got him into trouble this morning and he seems to worry more about that sort of thing than I do. 'But under objection. Seriously, what is his problem? That was a pretty epic tantrum over two successful arrests.'

We reach the break room and I head to the fridge and take out the sandwiches I'd tossed in last night, check the urn for water. It's half full and hot. Good.

'I doubt he's peaked yet.'

'Why?'

'You haven't been here long enough,' Rico teases, collecting his breakfast containers from the sink and stuffing them into his bag.

'Funny.' I screw the lid on the coffee I've made. 'What exactly did I say that was unreasonable?'

Rico's eyes gleam with fun. 'Nothing you weren't prepared to put in writing.'

My lips twitch. 'Well, if he won't let me speak …'

He leans on the table as he pins me with a desperate stare. 'Do you know how hard it is not to laugh? Can you imagine what would happen if I did? It's all right for you, probationary constable, but I'm a sergeant. Between the smartarse comments and those damn expressions you pull, I'm—'

'That's not fair! It takes every ounce of willpower I have most of the time just to keep my mouth shut! How can I help what the rest of my face is doing?'

Rico drops his head in defeat. 'If nothing else, we should get some brownie points for arresting those brothers. It's a real win to have them in custody over Hadley's assault.'

I pick up the coffee and sandwiches. 'Yay us, right?'

Rico walks me out of the station and down the front steps to the carpark. 'You want to get a hot breakfast?' he asks, glancing at my sandwiches and coffee.

'You and your big breakfasts. Are you trying to turn me into a hippo?'

'I helped you take down a couple of kids belonging to the most notorious crime family in the country this morning, *and* got roasted by the boss for it. That takes energy. You owe me breakfast.'

'Raincheck,' I tell him. 'I need to sleep.' Working the two nights, one day routine doesn't really bother me, and I'm not really all that tired, but I need time for another personal project I'm working on and there's never enough of it to spare.

Rico stops in front of his Jeep to dig out his keys. 'Then dinner tonight is on you. We'll spice things up and Menulog it to the station.'

'Oh, the extravagance. Fine. I'll shout you a burrito or something,' I promise and wave him off.

A moment later a shadow emerges from a sheltered corner of the building opposite. The man who approaches is elderly, his skin dark against the white of his hair and his tan-coloured coat. One arm of that coat hangs limp, nothing to support it. I've heard multiple stories about its loss, from a mustering accident in Far North Queensland to a croc bite in the NT. I'm not sure which—if either—to believe and I'm equally not sure he remembers which is true. 'You should have a proper meal with that young fella. He's a good 'un.'

'He is.' His previous relationship had lasted six years before the pressures of the job had ended it and he'd somehow managed to walk away on friendly terms. It didn't surprise me. That's the sort of guy he was. But I don't need a matchmaker; I'm not the relationship type. And I really like Rico, enough to not want to complicate things. Not that I'd ever tell him that. As far as he and everyone else at the station was concerned, I don't really like anyone. It's not that far from the truth.

'Still wearing the old jeans, Paddy?' I ask to change the subject.

'Yeah.' He pats the Target bag in his trolley containing the new pair I bought him because the others are falling apart. 'Saving these ones for a special occasion. That for me?' he asks, nodding to the food and coffee.

'You know it is.' I hand the meal over and he puts it in his trolley before handing me back an empty container and travel mug. I toss them in the car then lean back against the bonnet.

'Bit cold this morning. Looking forward to this coffee.' He blows into it, breathing deep before taking a sip. 'Thanks,' he says with a satisfied sigh. 'How was your shift?'

I shoot him a grin. 'I got to play with trains.'

'I like trains,' he says, placing the coffee in his trolley to start on his ham and cheese on rye. 'But last time you said you played with something you were trying to get yourself killed flagging down a bus to catch someone pinching underwear.'

My smile widens. 'Got to take the excitement where I can get it. Being dull would be murder on my social life.'

He wheeze-laughs and I worry again about the chest infection he doesn't seem to be able to shake off. 'You looking after yourself? Want me to get you some cold and flu tablets or something?'

'Nah, all good. I told ya—too much on the ciggies back when I could afford 'em.'

'But that sounds nasty.'

'Don't you be worrying any more about me, Lexi Winter. You're an angel.'

I raise an eyebrow threateningly. 'Anyone else tries calling me that I'll give them a black eye.'

'I know. You get going, get some rest.'

I slide into my car with a wave. 'See ya, Paddy.'

Before driving off, I pull a burner phone from the glovebox and turn it on.

I think for a moment, then type. *Looks like your grandsons have gotten themselves into a bit of trouble. You ready to play?* I hit send, turn off the phone. I don't need a reply. The Hamills know what they have to do.

CHAPTER FOUR

It was just after eight in the upper North Shore suburb of Hornsby, and the main road into Sydney wasn't letting Detective Sergeant Finn Carson through without a fight. He might have expected the chaos on a workday but this was a Saturday morning. The traffic was officially ridiculous.

He took a sip of the coffee he'd sacrificed a valuable five minutes to purchase and checked his watch. In a few hours, he needed to be back up the coast for his daughter's eleventh birthday party. It seemed like plenty of time, but he had a feeling it was going to evaporate. He was over playing homicide squad leader for his aunt, Inspector Rachael Langley, but he wouldn't have wanted her anywhere other than where she'd been this week. Rachael, along with Detective Inspector Craig Slavek, the head of one of the Drugs and Firearms Squad teams, had been in Canberra working with the Federal Police. They were there on a possible lead in their long-time number one case: Damon Vaughn, the child predator, murderer and all-out nasty piece of work who, with his associate Debbie Reynolds, had evaded capture last year by skipping the country. Rachael hadn't wanted to hand the case over but once it became international, that had been unavoidable. Finn was happy they finally had a break in the case, happy that Rachael had been brought in to collaborate.

'Body's not going anywhere,' Detective Jack Lincoln said from the passenger seat. Shuffling for space, he managed to get his shoelaces tied and stretched his legs out in front of him before starting on his tie. 'No point checking your watch every five minutes.' The six-foot-two rugby league and video games fan was in one of several pairs of identical black jeans with the standard white shirt—top button never fastened—and one of the blue ties he threw on only when he had to. He had skin a couple of shades darker than could be attributable to a tan courtesy of his Indigenous heritage and a ready smile. Even when he was dragged away from home at the most inconvenient times.

'We would have been here earlier if it hadn't taken you quite so long to get yourself out of bed this morning,' Finn said.

'It was occupied by someone worth stalling over.'

'I gathered. It's the only time you're ever late.'

Linc also possessed an undisputed gift with the opposite sex. He liked to play the field and play hard, and Finn knew he was unlikely to have heard the name of whoever Linc had been entertaining. But Linc also knew how to switch on and work a case, had a whip-smart mind and a sense of humour that managed to keep the rest of the team sane on the worst of cases. In the past year, two of Rachael's team had jumped ship, one to the Organised Crime Squad, another into retirement. Linc and 'Cass', Detective Sergeant Lisa Cassidy, had stepped in. It was a generally cohesive group. And a busy one. Despite the already overwhelming number of cases his team had on their books, one week out of six they remained on call for any homicides that came through, and yet again, it seemed his team had drawn the short straw. He could only hope this one turned out to be straightforward, or by some miracle, not a homicide after all.

'You might stress less if you give it a go,' Linc suggested. 'I know a few ladies who'd be interested.'

'Too many murders, not enough time …' Finn muttered. He hadn't dated anyone seriously since his divorce almost four years ago and didn't have any plans to dive back in.

'Rachael's back Monday, right?'

'That's the plan.'

'How did she enjoy working with the Feds?'

'I haven't really had a proper catch-up with her.'

'So no exciting leads to report on the famous case then?'

'All I know is Vaughn and Reynolds were in Bangkok ten days ago, but they've disappeared again.' The frustration in his voice didn't do his feelings justice. The fact that the man who had attempted to do unspeakable things to his daughter was still breathing free air kept a burning rage simmering in his gut.

'Man, I wish I'd been on that case. How's the computer whizz going?'

'You mean Lexi? She's come out of the academy recently and is posted at Wyong.'

'I'd love to meet her. Abused child turned prostitute turned computer-hacking vigilante turned police officer. That's quite the journey. She must be pretty kickarse.'

'She's lots of things.' He sent Linc a half-smile. 'She doesn't really fit into any one category.'

'So she was as crazy to work with as everyone said?'

Finn thought for a moment before answering. 'Her sense of right and wrong is more important to her than following the rules, so that made life interesting more than once, but if you're ever backed against a wall, you want her in your corner.'

'Good to know.'

'If we find out Vaughn and Reynolds were in Bangkok for the purpose of sneaking back into the country, the team will be reinstated, and Rachael will pull her back in. If you work with Lexi, you can trust her. But you might have to think outside the box occasionally to keep up.'

'I look forward to it,' Linc said with a mile-wide grin.

'Yeah, by all means try that charm on her.' Finn didn't bother to hide his smirk. 'There it is.'

As he managed to finally crawl his way to within sight of the crime scene, Finn waved his badge out the window and a constable on point duty somehow manoeuvred enough traffic out of the way to let him through. He pulled his car up behind one of several police and other emergency vehicles clustered around the construction site and got out. As he went to do up his jacket he noticed the stain. Shit. He'd managed to spill coffee on his white shirt. He swiped at it, happy to see that fastening his jacket hid it from sight, then looked around.

The project was wedged between a couple of office buildings and outgrew them by two extra floors. Five storeys of scaffolding, green mesh wrapped around its exterior, and brown brickwork to the bottom of the third storey. A large banner announced this was a Latimer Developments project.

'Hey, Carson!'

Finn looked around and sorted through the myriad people milling about until his gaze landed on a solidly built officer in a blue forensic suit. 'Nick, how's it going?'

Nick Meyer, the long-time crime scene investigator, nodded at Finn's coffee. 'Be a heck of a lot better if I had one of those. Body's up there.' He pointed a finger skywards. Finn's eyes followed, but he saw nothing more than flapping mesh.

'Cause of death?'

'Impaled.'

'Who found him?'

'One of two guys that live in an apartment across the road spotted him over his Weet-Bix just on sunrise. Got a much better view from up there.'

Finn saw two men in the direction the detective had pointed. One young and skinny, all wide eyes, nerves and perspiration, the older one looking calmer, though his hand was unsteady as he lifted a coffee cup to his lips. 'Young guy found him?'

'Yeah. How'd you guess?'

'Looks like he's about to lose that Weet-Bix. Do we have an ID on our victim yet?'

'Not yet. Steve just arrived. I've got a couple of guys rigged up to move the victim—ah, there they are,' he said as, above them, two men in full safety harnesses hugged the side of the building. 'They'll cut him loose and bring him in when they're given the go-ahead.'

'Any idea what happened?'

'Looks like the victim either fell or was pushed from the top floor. The safety mesh has caught him, but he's slid down it then fallen two storeys down, onto scaffolding. My team is all up there. You ready?'

'Yeah, thanks. Reckon it could have been an accident?'

'Love your optimism,' he said.

'Let's go,' Linc said with a slap on Finn's back. He charged ahead with an admirable amount of enthusiasm. Finn heard a wolf-whistle and noticed a couple of women checking Linc out as they were herded past the crime scene. Linc noticed too, giving them a wink before grabbing a suit and pulling it over him. 'You coming or what?'

'Yeah.' Finn got ready then stepped hesitantly onto the lifting platform. It didn't look solid enough. 'Is this thing safe?'

'I hope so,' Linc said, giving it a shake.

'Who's in charge of this place?' Finn asked Nick, holding on as the platform went up. He really hated heights.

'As you no doubt saw, a mob called Latimer Developments. Don't know any more than that at this stage.'

'Is Cass up here yet?' he asked.

'You really think you can keep her away from a dead body? I've known that woman for six years and she still believes she needs to be on scene early to make sure I don't miss anything.'

'She's certainly a perfectionist.' Cass was not only a perfectionist but also the professional conscience of their team. The kind of cop who very rarely lost an argument—she should have been a lawyer—and excelled at convincing people to do what she wanted them to: by the book, following the rules. Right now, Finn noted as the lift stopped with an alarming jolt and they stepped into organised chaos, she was frowning at the clumsiness with which the body, complete with sawn-off scaffolding rods, was being brought in.

'Careful!' she and Steven Van Zettan, the pathologist, barked in unison.

Finn stepped onto the concrete floor. 'Morning,' he said.

'Finn. How's it going?' Van Zettan said. He stood up, raising his lanky surfer's frame from the victim. As usual, a few wisps of his blond hair refused to be tamed and poked free of his coveralls.

'Hi, Finn,' Cass said, stretching her back as she straightened.

Finn looked down at the body. Rigour had set in, leaving it in a stiff and awkward pose. The victim's hair was short and neat. He wore a collared beige shirt rolled at the sleeves, blue jeans. Pen in his shirt pocket, short leather work boots, vest, no hard hat, but it had perhaps come off in the incident. Metal rods protruded from his abdomen and neck, abrasions covered his face. 'Odds it was an accident?' he asked Van Zettan.

Van Zettan's eyebrows lifted as he continued to study the body. 'Cases piling up on you by any chance?'

'Something like that.'

'I'm afraid I doubt it.' Van Zettan examined the victim's face. 'I don't think all of these injuries line up with the fall. I believe it more likely this gentleman was involved in a rather serious tussle prior to death, the evidence of which may well be two floors above.'

'Does he have any ID on him?'

Van Zettan nodded at the bulge in the victim's back pocket and removed a slim brown wallet. He flicked it open, revealing a driver's licence in a clear window. 'Jeremy Latimer.'

'Latimer?'

'Looks like someone's knocked off the boss,' Linc said.

Finn looked at the floors above, decided he wasn't getting close enough to the edge to see anything worthwhile. 'He fell two storeys?'

'Scaffolding on five looks like someone's gone through it,' Nick said.

'I've sent two technicians up there to gather evidence,' Van Zettan added.

'So what else have you got for me?' Finn asked.

'Body temp and rigour suggest he's been dead approximately ten to twelve hours. That puts his time of death at somewhere between six and eight last night. The height and direction of the fall allowing for the interference from the mesh barrier seems consistent for a man of his estimated size and weight impaling himself as he has. But you know I won't give you anything official until he has been more thoroughly examined.'

'Yeah, of course. Thanks.'

'I'll head up those couple of extra floors and look around,' Cass said.

'I wouldn't mind a look either,' Finn said. Then, when she pulled a face, 'Relax, Cass, I won't touch anything.'

'I've heard that before.'

'I'm still the boss, remember?'

'Less than forty-eight hours to go,' she reminded him as though handing him a particularly exciting present, before stepping onto the lifting platform.

It would help if he couldn't see how high they were. After another bump, he stepped gratefully onto the top floor and kept back from the edge. Cass, on the other hand, headed straight for the broken scaffolding, stopping short of the investigator dusting for fingerprints.

'There's blood here. Spattered around,' she said, pointing. 'Partial footprints, smudged prints …'

'Sounds like Steven was right about that tussle,' Finn said. He got as close as he dared as, apparently satisfied, the fingerprint technician collected her things and left them to it. He studied the rails. 'Looks like the iron buckled.'

'Or the joint failed. See here?' Cass said, pointing.

'Or both.' He edged closer and gave the scaffolding a shake. 'It doesn't seem all that solid.'

'Do you know what "don't touch anything" means?' Cass said.

'They've got their fingerprints and photos already.' Finn pulled his phone from his jacket as it rang. Linc. 'Yeah?'

'I spoke to the security guard. He said cameras record at the entry and exit points. That's it. Nothing up there. His company is preparing the footage for us.'

'Great. Would you mind going over to the building opposite, doing a door knock to those few apartments? It might be a good idea to find out if anyone else saw or heard anything while it's still early enough to catch them at home.'

'No worries.'

'You ready to head down?' he asked Cass. 'We need to find next of kin ASAP. I'm surprised the media aren't here already.'

'Got it.'

His phone rang again. 'I'll meet you down there,' he told Cass before answering. 'Ava! How's the birthday girl?'

'Hi, Dad. You know it's actually tomorrow, right?'

'Like I'd ever forget. But it's party day! Is everything okay?'

'Yep. Just checking you're still coming at six?'

A tug of guilt pulled at him that she felt she had to make sure. The job so often messed with their time together. 'Absolutely. Wouldn't miss it.' But there was a pause long enough that he knew something was bugging her. 'But that's not why you called. So come on, what's up?'

There was a long huff. 'Mum wants to surprise everyone with the news tonight and I'm not supposed to say anything, but she and Louis are getting married.'

He acknowledged the punch to the gut, though he wasn't sure what that was about. They hadn't been a couple for a long time and he knew the decision to split had been the right one. Perhaps it was more about what could have been. But there was anger there too. Did Vivienne really have to hijack her daughter's birthday party for her own celebration?

'Dad?'

'Sorry, sweetie, just working. Oh, well that's good news, right?'

'Yeah, I'm so excited. NOT. I've already told Mum I'm not calling him Dad.'

'Why would you? You've already got the best one in the universe.'

That drew a chuckle. 'Yeah and the engagement ring she got from you is heaps nicer than the stupid one he gave her.'

'I'm sure it's lovely,' he said, chewing on a grin. He'd never encourage the attitude Ava had towards Louis but he could enjoy it privately. He was human, after all.

'Aunty Rach messaged. She and Ed are definitely coming. Lexi can't. She's working,' she added, sounding disappointed.

Ava had invited Lexi? How did she even have her number? He hadn't seen Lexi himself since he and Rachael had headed down to the police academy to congratulate her on graduating. Top of her class, after all that shit she'd been through. Some people were unstoppable. That was what, two or three months ago? He should call her. 'I'm sure you can catch up another day. Sweetie, I have to get back to work. Don't worry about your mum and Louis. It'll all work out. You have a great day and I'll see you tonight, okay?'

'Okay. Bye, Dad, love you.'

'Love you, too.' He put the phone away and got his head back in the game. He needed to get this sorted if he was going to keep his promise to Ava and be there on time. As far as he was concerned, Rachael couldn't get back to work fast enough.

CHAPTER FIVE

Rachael Langley sat at the Parramatta café enjoying morning tea and one of the last quiet moments she would have with her partner, Homicide Commander Superintendent Ed O'Hanlon, for the foreseeable future.

'You really didn't have to come in the morning after you returned home,' Ed said, finishing his coffee and shifting in his seat.

'It's perfectly fine,' she said. 'The sooner I get back to work, the better.' She brushed some crumbs from her grey suit. 'If the couple of quick phone calls I've managed to Finn are anything to go by, he's over playing boss and being a team member down.'

'You're telling me,' Ed said with a grimace. 'And I can fully understand why. I'm going to have to do something about your team's caseload.'

'I wish I had more to tell them about our progress this week. I'd love to let them know Debbie Reynolds is back in the country.'

'When you work with the Feds, you work by their rules, you know that.'

'I know. And I know they're right. With the ties the Hamills have, we can't be sure there won't be a leak somewhere along the line. If they discover we've found out about Reynolds, we've lost our slight upper hand. And if he's not already back in the country, Vaughn won't risk following her.'

'But as soon as he does, you can put a strike force together, get Vaughn back where he belongs. Once we get hold of him, he'll never see the free light of day again.'

'Yep.' Rachael finished her coffee. 'But for now, it's back to wading through the regular caseload.'

'In which case—' Ed popped the last of his muffin into his mouth and dusted his hands, '—I've got a hell of a mess to get back to in there, too. Let's go.'

While they waited to cross the road, Rachael looked at police headquarters. The building had a modern design, comprised of two towers of nine and thirteen levels, with a three-storey atrium and enough good outdoor spaces for the occasional breath of fresh air. The security surveillance system and blast-resistant facade were both state of the art. The podium screen artwork highlighted the building with blobs of bright colour, designed to mimic the patterning of DNA X-rays in forensic science. Headquarters was as familiar to her as her own home and, all in all, it wasn't a bad place to be based between cases.

She was welcomed by several people as they entered the building, so it took longer than expected to reach the eighth floor housing the Homicide Unit. As the lift opened, she prepared herself to embrace what would be controlled, or not-so-controlled, chaos. Homicide was working over one hundred cases, and there were always hundreds more unsolved and waiting for review. It kept everyone busy.

The unit comprised mostly half-walled sections, or 'pods', giving each team their own working area. Meeting rooms provided space for morning briefings and interviews. Glass-walled offices were reserved for higher-ranking officers. Rachael entered her office and dropped her purse on her desk. She kept the space sparse of personal touches. Two photos greeted her on the filing cabinet. One of her and Ed, one of Finn and Ava. An ivy plant someone had given her a few months ago hung from a filing cabinet, limp but healthy enough, its long branches reaching for the floor. She sat at her desk and absorbed the quiet energy. She was back. She should probably see who else was in.

She walked out to her team's pod and spotted Cass at her desk, staring thoughtfully into her computer monitor. Beside her was a scattering of roughly written notes, beyond that a picture of her family in a dark wooden frame. The only other adornment was an extra-large refillable coffee cup Rachael knew would contain at least half of a low-fat iced coffee. Cass never bothered with hot drinks because they inevitably sat on her desk until they were stone cold. Her cream-coloured suit was spotless and crease free. Rachael wasn't sure a crease or a stain would dare come within twenty feet of Cass. She admired her coworker's attention to detail. How the woman juggled that sort of perfection and a young son, she'd never understand. Cass was a tough-as-nails cop and a soft-centred mush pile of a mother, the type that would turn up for work ignoring serious illness or injury but take a day off in a heartbeat if her child needed her. Something else Rachael admired about her.

She'd never gotten around to having kids of her own, had jumped headfirst into parenthood after her sister had died and she'd taken her nephew Finn in. She wasn't sure she ever really developed the knack for it, but they'd both survived so she supposed she can't have been a total failure.

Cass glanced up as she came closer. 'Rachael! Welcome back! What are you doing here?'

'My conscience wouldn't let me stay home when we've got so much on. I hear you all had an early call-out?'

'Yes. To a construction site in Hornsby. Looks like the victim was involved in some sort of physical altercation before falling or being pushed from the building. Got hooked up on some construction rods. As of half an hour ago, Finn and Linc were heading out to inform the next of kin.'

'Okay. So let's get a board set up.'

'Already on it,' Cass said, snatching her coffee from her desk before winding her way out of the pods to their regular briefing room. The name Jeremy Latimer was written on the whiteboard above a photo and a list of details. Cass took a sip of her iced coffee and placed it on the table that ran almost the length of the room. 'We have our victim, Jeremy Latimer, owner of the Latimer Developments company, forty-six-year-old resident of St Ives, married to a Carole Latimer, father of one, no criminal record. The altercation took place on Friday afternoon. There's no witnesses that we know of, but we do have incoming CCTV. Police crime scene investigators and Van Zettan's team were still on site last I heard. I've prepped something for the media liaison.'

'Sounds like it's all under control.'

'Of course. Oh, sorry,' Cass said when her phone vibrated in her pocket. 'That's Finn.' At Rachael's nod, she answered her phone. Rachael saw a pained expression cross her face before she reassured Finn she would take care of it and ended the call. 'Apparently the security guard told Carole Latimer about her husband's death before Finn and Linc could reach her. Finn just fielded a hostile phone conversation and Mrs Latimer is on her way here to demand answers over her husband's death. She should be arriving at any moment, but Finn's still about fifteen minutes out.'

Straight back in the deep end. 'Okay. Would you mind making sure we have an empty meeting room ready? Have some refreshments and tissues organised.'

'Of course.' Cass hurried off.

Rachael went back to her office to call Finn. She needed more details if she was going to handle this.

Carole Latimer was barely five foot two in heels, with a slight frame, a stylish auburn haircut, expensive silk suit and expertly applied make-up currently streaking her cheeks from her tears. 'Someone *murdered* my husband?' she wailed. 'It wasn't an accident?'

'We can't be sure until the investigation is further underway,' Rachael said kindly. 'However, the evidence does suggest there was an altercation prior to your husband's death that may have led to his fall.'

Carole sniffed, her face closing into a frown. 'An altercation with who?'

'We don't know that yet.'

'Then why aren't you out there finding whoever did it!' she shrieked, sitting straighter.

'We're working on that right now. In the meantime, you could help by providing us with all the information you can that might be relevant.'

'I can't believe this. This is real. This—he's really dead.'

'I'm afraid so. When was the last time you saw or spoke to your husband?'

Carole shrugged helplessly, shook her lowered head. 'I spoke to him about … eightish yesterday morning, I think.'

'Was he his usual self?'

'Well, he didn't throw himself off the building, did he!'

'I'm simply establishing if there were any indications something might have been wrong. If he might have been worried about anything, upset with anyone?'

Carole leant forward and snatched another tissue. 'He wasn't upset, he was fine! I mean, surely he would have told me if he thought anyone might want to kill him? And I certainly don't know of anyone who would want to.' She blew her nose loudly.

'When he didn't come home last night—'

'I didn't know my husband didn't come home! I've been on one of my monthly women's retreats.'

The door opened and Finn came in. 'Sorry.'

'Mrs Latimer, this is Sergeant Finn Carson.'

'Nice to meet you,' Finn said. 'I'm sorry for your loss.'

'I was just saying the first I knew Jeremy was in any trouble was when I got the call from the security company.' A hint of steely anger appeared in her face. 'It's a hell of a way to find out your husband is dead.'

'I apologise for that,' Finn said, taking a seat. 'We did attempt to reach you as quickly as possible. I appreciate you coming in.'

Carole nodded. 'I'm afraid I'm not at my best at the moment. I shouldn't be rude. It's not your fault. I'm sorry.' More tears followed and Rachael waited quietly for her to compose herself.

'Mrs Latimer, would you happen to know which of your husband's work colleagues might be best able to assist us with any enquiries linked to the worksite or the business in general?'

'If you want to know about what was going on with the business, you should talk to our project manager, Mark Bradley. He takes care of everything.'

Finn jotted the name down. 'Do you have a contact number for Mr Bradley?'

Carole shook her head again. 'It will be in Jeremy's phone.'

'There was a phone located at the scene but it was badly damaged.'

'Oh. Then I'll have to get it from the office.'

'Thank you,' Rachael said. 'We'd appreciate it if we could also take a look at your husband's computer. It might provide a clue to why this has happened. We'll also need a list of the employees who were on site yesterday.'

'Okay.' Carole lifted her hands, palms up in helplessness. 'I don't know what to do. What should Mark tell the workers? When can they get back to work?'

'I can't answer that yet, I'm sorry. The whole building is a crime scene. Possibly a few days,' Finn said.

'I see.'

'Thank you, Mrs Latimer,' Rachael said gently. 'Cass, would you mind taking care of Mrs Latimer and collecting those few things?'

'I'm not sure where Jeremy left his laptop. I'll find it then have my secretary drop it in along with the employee records.'

'We appreciate that.'

'Mrs Latimer, would you come with me, please?' Cass asked. 'I'll show you out.'

As the door closed on the women, Finn relaxed back in the chair. 'Odd reaction, the whole "but when can we get back to work"?'

'A bit, yeah. But everyone deals differently. She's grasping for normality. It's a form of denial. You know that.'

'Yeah, I guess.'

'Where's Linc?'

'He's gone to the security company's office to organise access to their CCTV.'

'Excellent.'

'Yeah, also, hi. I can't say I'm not relieved to see you, but what on earth possessed you to come back in early?'

CHAPTER SIX

The chatroom conversation on my computer is not really holding my attention and I check the phone on the desk for the umpteenth time. I absolutely have to get ready for work but I haven't heard from my informant, Lochie, since we arrested Jason and Aden, and I need to know he's okay. He always answers my texts at this time of the afternoon. Always. So why hasn't he?

I spin around in my chair to look at walls covered in photos and string lines, dot points and police reports. I've turned my boring beige spare bedroom into a home office devoted to finding Damon Vaughn and Debbie Reynolds. Their faces stare back at me from pride of place above my computer.

My real target is Vaughn, the sociopathic narcissist who'd teamed up in prison with Thomas Biddle, aka the Spider. The Spider had offered Vaughn all the money and notoriety he'd collected over his long reign as the most feared child predator in the country, in return for one thing. Me. He'd already made my childhood hell but I'd fought back, I'd ended his reign, and he'd wanted a final shot at me before the cancer he'd been riddled with caught up with him. He'd failed, but my rescue cost us the chance to catch

Vaughn and Reynolds, the psycho former cop who'd helped him carry out his plan. I get why the Federal Police had taken over the search, but that didn't mean I had to stop looking for them. At least unofficially.

Despite having his own dark web channel where he continues to rape and murder for profit, Vaughn leads a seemingly ghost-like existence, impossible to track down. But there's one chink in his armour: his travelling companion, Reynolds. Pretty much every squad in the force has been after her disgusting excuse for a family, the Hamills, at one time or another. Early intel told us she was in touch with them, using the family's overseas contacts to stay hidden, before we lost them altogether. So, as I need to find her to find Vaughn, I've launched a full-scale cyber war on her arsehole family.

I turn to a pyramid stuck on the back of the door containing all the Hamills' names and faces. I've ranked them from most important at the top, to least important at the bottom and the plan is to work my way up, taking them out one by one for as long as I have to until Raymond Hamill gives up his estranged daughter.

Raymond is on top of the pyramid, the long-reigning king of illicit drug production and weapons deals on the east coast. He and his wife Lena spawned seven sons and a daughter, all chips off the old block. Two sons are dead, one of a drug overdose, the other in a gangland killing, and another, Charlie, is doing life in prison for murdering his wife, so I'm left with four sons in play: Adam, Robert, Elias and Karl. I've stuck Adam, the favoured son and business manager, on line two alongside his mother Lena, the love of Raymond's life. That leaves Robert, Elias and Karl on three. Line four is a mishmash of grandchildren—Elias's sons Jason and Aden, and Robert's daughter Josie—and a few useful Hamill associates. Underneath those is a line of less important names that probably aren't going to be helpful, but might be—you never know.

I pick up a red texta and slide my chair forward to put a cross through Jason's and Aden's names.

A phone pings and I jump at it. Lochie. 'Well, finally!' I tell the screen in real relief.

Where have you been? I demand.

Hiding. I heard the police arrested the twins. Was that you?
Yeah.
So I might be okay. I might be able to get out.
You still need to be careful. This is not finished.
Do you think it would be safe to see my parents?
I don't know. It would be safer to go to the police, trade them info for some help.

They might put me in jail! I can't handle anything else. Then after a short pause, *I'll think about it.*

Be careful, I type, because I don't know what else to offer without thinking it through. He doesn't have a clue who I really am and I can't risk anyone finding out, so the help I can provide is limited. *Let me know what you decide to do.*

I sigh, get up, and drop the phone into my bag in case he gets back to me. I know how scared he is of the Hamills, and of being on the wrong side of the police. Lochie's way too good a kid to have gotten caught up in this. He just wants to go home, see his mum and dad and go back to uni, have a normal life. But he's only one of the many kids the Hamills continue to target. Kids from loving families who are sweet enough and naive enough to be easily manipulated, and scared enough to do what they're told. He's desperate for all this to be over, but Jason and Aden's arrests don't make him safe. Not yet. Because there's plenty of Hamills still out there, and once they've dragged you in, they never, ever let you go. A quick check of the time tells me I'm ten minutes late.

Fuck.

Eight minutes later I force my hair—it really would be easier to cut it short—into submission as I power through my front door, still putting together my uniform while juggling my dinner under my chin. I'm hit immediately with a blast of thumping bass emanating from the house across the driveway. Trevor and his two welfare-bludging roomies like to play loud eighties music so the Parkhursts, my not-so-friendly other neighbours, finally have someone to spend their time harassing other than me. Of course, now that I'm a cop, the Parkhursts mostly leave me alone. I'm pretty sure they still harbour doubts though. Maybe I'm dressing in the uniform each time I go out to fool them.

'Afternoon, Lexi!'

Ah, shit. As usual, Trev and his mates are camped out on their tiny strip of front lawn drinking beer in fold-up chairs. An esky and a garbage bag sit at their feet, their windows wide open to let the music spill out. All three seem addicted to elastically challenged trackies and shirts unable to contain ample middle-aged-plus bellies. The plumpest one farts, sending them into momentary hysterics.

I can't believe I used to think my old neighbour Dawny was annoying. I briefly wonder how she and Desmond are doing. If they're enjoying their fugitive-style existence.

'Off to work?' Trevor obviously hasn't bothered with his hair today. The greying, thinning mess is sticking out at all angles.

'As usual your powers of deduction defy belief.' I drop my dinner onto the driveway in my hurry to open the door. Shit.

Trevor scratches his head and stretches both arms above him with a yawn. His shirt rides up, exposing yet more ew. 'I love that sense of humour,' he calls back. 'Seriously, where have you been all my life?'

'I probably wasn't born yet for the first half of it.' I check the lid on my dinner. It's still intact so I pitch it across the car to the passenger seat and fall in. 'Bye, Trev.' I don't have time for their shit today. It's not like I'm never late, but after this morning's drama, I feel more inclined to be on time. For Rico's sake if nothing else.

I deliberated a lot about filling Rico in on what I was up to with the Hamills. He's out there taking the risks with me, so he probably deserves to know. But getting him tangled up in all this is only going to get him into trouble, because he couldn't not try to help, and everything is so dangerous. One wrong word, one wrong move, one wrong keystroke and the Hamills will work out who I am and where to find me. And I know what happens to people who are caught messing with the Hamills.

I ignore the mock salutes of the three amigos as I drive away. It occurs to me to wonder if Jason and Aden have been charged yet. I hope they get prison time. There are worse places they could end up, like back outside a railway tunnel pumping that shit into their bodies. Not giving them a chance to deal that night had to mean there'd be a lot more kids not pumping it into their bodies, either.

Something about that nags at me until I realise what it is. I know they had a backpack with them but I don't remember checking it in. Where was it?

My stomach sinks as I realise it might have been left back at the scene. Maybe that's why Aden ran into the tunnel. To ditch it. To make sure I didn't see him dump his stash or stumble over it. 'Damn it!' I thump the steering wheel with the heel of my hand, call myself an idiot. I need to find those drugs. Then I tell myself not to worry, Rico had no doubt got it.

I remember to slow down at the speed camera—just—and even with a quick Macca's drive thru for a clubhouse chicken meal, I park with a minute to spare.

'Evening, Paddy!' I huff as I get out. I don't know why I'm breathless, I've been sitting in the car. Psychology is weird.

'Hi, Lexi. How's it going?'

'Great,' I say, handing him his Macca's. 'But I'm in a hurry!'

'No worries. Thanks for dinner! Did you make sure they took off the tomato?'

'Tomato free, my friend!' I reassure him as I cross the carpark and take the steps two at a time. I compose myself at the door, walk through like I haven't just gone for gold in the fifty-metre sprint. I greet the cop on the front desk slightly breathlessly, swipe in and head down the hall.

Rico, as usual, has beaten me to work and, as I enter the room, looks me up and down with a half-grin. 'Someone's on a mission.' He leans back and links his fingers behind his head. 'Tell me, young Jedi. How are you planning on pissing off the boss this shift?'

'Never once has that required planning. And I still don't get the *Star Wars* references.'

'I'm telling you, we're going to have to start bingeing movies. It's not right.'

'Yeah, yeah, did you pick up a backpack?' I ask.

He immediately looks concerned. 'Inside or out?'

'No—no one's trying to blow up the station. That I know of. I mean, the twins had a backpack.'

'Are you sure?' he asks, looking more relaxed.

'Yes! I remember seeing one of them swing it onto their back as they took off but I'm not sure which one it was.'

'I didn't get it.'

'Damn it! I think that could be why Aden ran into the tunnel. He was miles ahead of me, but then he ran back. Why would he do that unless he was dumping something he didn't want us to find?'

'The vein full of meth and the train heading straight for him might have had something to do with it.'

'We need to go back and find it.'

Rico rubs his forehead. 'Okay. Maybe. We'll see if we can clear a return trip with the boss, but I've already copped another spray about being reckless and I'm supposed to remind you the paperwork is mounting.'

'I hate paperwork.' I flop into my chair.

'Hence why it's mounting.'

'I suppose at least while the twins are in custody they're not going back to get their bag. We've probably got some time. If we grill Aden over it— What?' I ask, because Rico has a look on his face that I know means he's preparing for battle.

'The witness to the attack on Hadley refused to ID them,' he says with a long sigh. 'She gets off the train there alone every evening and is frightened of reprisal.'

'She ... really? They bashed a cop! How could she be less frightened with them out on the street than behind bars?' But I already know the answer. She's no doubt been paid a visit by one of Raymond Hamill's thugs.

'I don't really know. But the Hamill lawyer apparently swept in not long after we left and demanded they be released.'

'They're out?' *Shit*. This is not good. Lochie doesn't know. I need to warn him.

'Without that testimony we've got nothing except the minor graffiti damage and a personal use drug charge. That's fine and release.'

'Son of a bitch!'

Rico sits up straight, looking past me. 'Okay. Just ... Stay calm.'

'Too late! I nearly died catching that little fuck nugget and they both walk? There's a whole team in the drug squad dedicated to bringing down the Hamills and we had two of them with the drugs they're allegedly producing and dealing in their systems! The squad would have found a way to hold them!'

'Problem, Winter?' Burns asks from behind me. His tone is a degree or two below freezing.

I spin around, still fuming. 'What do you think? You let them go!'

'Thanks to your witness refusing to cooperate, we had no choice but to release them, and we don't bother the drug squad with news we've had a couple of teens brought in on very minor charges because some family relations are on a watch list. Talk to the witness again and change her mind. We need them on the assault.'

'We might have something else, sir,' Rico says. 'We believe there's a backpack containing a commercial quantity of drugs still at the scene. If we can find it, that could be enough to drag them back in and hold them while we talk the witness around. We'd like to go back to the tunnel to retrieve it.'

'Request denied.'

'You can't just leave it there!' I burst out. 'The twins will go back and get it!'

'Rico, my office. Winter, be smart and shut up. Take over out front and be glad I didn't take your little rant personally.'

I have my mouth open to argue when Rico makes a 'don't you dare' face and follows the boss out.

I close my mouth but the vitriol continues to roll in my head as I storm out to the front desk, where a tired-looking constable coming off day shift is more than ready to leave. I'll go get the damn backpack after my shift. Assuming that's not too late. Now the little shits are back on the street, they'll no doubt make it a priority to collect their stuff.

I send Lochie a message, letting him know the twins are out and that it really would be handy if he would please tell me how he contacts Jason. He's been reluctant to because if they do catch him again it'll get him in even more shit. Last time he tried to escape they bashed him senseless. I'm hoping we can now agree that this time he'll be dead if they find him, and that he needs to load me up with every chance to prevent that from happening.

I don't get a reply and I reluctantly decide I should probably get that paperwork Rico was on about under control. I busy myself for the next half-hour, taking my mood out on the computer keys until the front door opens and a young woman comes in. She's slightly built with long fair hair falling freely around her shoulders. Her T-shirt doesn't look warm enough for the weather outside but it's a nice brand, is accompanied by some new-looking cargos and Havaiana thongs. Student, I'm guessing. Maybe from the local TAFE. She chews her thumbnail as she approaches and looks me over nervously.

'Hi, can I help you?' I ask as pleasantly as I can, considering.

'I don't know. Maybe.' She laughs anxiously. 'I'm not sure.'

'You seem a bit upset. Are you in any trouble?'

She smiles, sort of. 'No, I'm sorry. I'm not making sense. Last night I was on the train coming home from the city and I saw something. I kind of dismissed it at the time. It was late and I was tired ... but anyway, it's been worrying me all day, so I thought I should check, you know. In case.'

'Okay, let's back up. I'm Constable Lexi Winter. And you are?'

'Daisy—Mackenzie.'

'Great. Nice to meet you. So you were on the train from the city. What time was this?'

'It was the 11:48 train from Central. There was a guy. I think he may have taken someone off the train against her will.'

'Why don't you tell me exactly what you saw?' I ask, and listen as she takes me through a pretty bland story.

'Anyway, he looked like a construction worker of some kind. I can describe them both if you like.'

'Okay, but first of all, did you see or hear the guy hurt or threaten her in any way?'

'No. But they were arguing.'

'Did you hear what they were arguing about?'

'No, it was muffled. Then when the train stopped it was noisy, a bit chaotic. There were campers and the guard got off the train to yell at them.'

'So the train guard was on the station? Did the woman call out to him or anyone else for help at any point?'

'I don't know. I don't think so.'

'Did you see a struggle? See her try to get away from him?'

'No. But I only got a glimpse once they were off the train.'

'So what makes you think she was forced off?'

'The way he was holding her so close, I guess, I don't know. It just ... It didn't look right.'

'Okay. What station did they get off at?'

'Wondabyne.'

I do a quick check to be sure and shake my head. 'Nothing's come through about a train incident or a missing woman today. I think the best thing for me to do would be to take down your contact details, then if something comes up we can talk more about it. Is that okay?'

'Yes. Of course.' I take her details and she smiles, a little more relaxed. 'Thanks for not making me feel like an idiot. I was having a shitty day yesterday and convinced myself I was probably building it into more than it was but ... just in case, you know?'

'You're not an idiot for caring when you see something that looks off and reporting it. A lot of crimes are solved by seemingly insignificant pieces of information. I'll be in touch if anything pops up. Thanks for coming in.'

'Okay, thanks.'

Only seconds after she leaves, Rico comes in behind me and taps me on the shoulder.

'Let's go.'

'Go?' I race after him. 'Where are we going?'

'Shoplifter. Woolworths, Westfield.'

'Oh, how interesting.'

'You can go back to paperwork if you prefer. Who was that?'

'Who was who?' I ask as we head down to the lower level where the patrol cars are parked.

'The woman you were talking to.'

'Oh. She thinks she might have seen some guy force a woman off a train last night. They might have been fighting but she didn't see him threaten or harm her. There was a guard on the train that stepped off onto the station but the woman didn't scream, didn't alert him or anyone else on the crowded platform that she was in any sort of trouble. What am I supposed to do with that?'

'Take her details in case anything crops up.'

'Did that. What did the boss want you for?'

'To ask me more about these drugs we think we might have left behind. And after a quick chat with Brisbane Water Police he's given the okay for us to go back to the tunnel with another car to search for the bag.'

'Oh, finally some sense!'

He unlocks the car and I get in the passenger seat, pull my seatbelt on.

'Under the condition you stay with the cars while I go into the tunnel with other backup,' Rico says before starting the car.

'What! Why?'

'Boss's orders. He would prefer not to have you back out there at all except we'll be on patrol together at the best time to organise it.'

'The best time would be now, in case the twins haven't been out there yet.'

'Transport for NSW will temporarily close the tracks for us later tonight once it's quiet enough not to interrupt train services more than necessary.' He turns the car out of the gates and we head through the evening traffic towards Tuggerah.

'That's stupid!' I huff. 'The drug squad would be up here with the lines shut in a heartbeat. They'd probably want to be the ones conducting the search.'

'You've got your orders, Winter. That's it.'

'Here we go with the orders again. I hate cops. Always have. How the hell I ended up in this uniform …'

'Let me guess, someone dared you?'

'No,' I say unappreciatively. It hadn't been a dare, just a push from the right people at the right time. 'Rachael and Finn suggested the idea during the Spider case. I'd never considered it before then, but the work we were doing was … I don't know … Exciting. Challenging.'

'And you got hooked on it.'

'It was Ava that made my mind up.'

'Ava? Oh, yeah, the kid you saved.'

'Finn brought her to see me after she was rescued and it hit me. She was alive and safe, at least partly because I'd been able to help her.'

'Ah. So it wasn't the chance to catch bad guys that convinced you to join the cops, it was the chance to help the victims.'

'As corny as that sounds. Besides, I needed some job or other pretty quick so …'

'So you joined the cops.'

'I barely had the "why not" out of my mouth and Rachael had me fast-tracked for recruitment.' I shrug. 'It all happened so quickly.'

'And here you are, a year later, relegated to general duties probationary constable after bringing down the country's worst child predator with some of the best in the business. No wonder you get frustrated.'

'I get frustrated because of how often the rules stop us from doing our jobs properly. And there's so damn many!' Because we're nearing the shops, I decide I'd better ask, 'So, what is the shoplifting about, anyway?'

'Baby formula.'

'Baby formula.' I swear under my breath. You expect people stealing are going for the big stuff—cars, smart TVs, jewellery—but the truth was it was most often about trying to access basic supplies. 'Someone's broke and trying to feed their kid and we have to go over there and play the bad guys?'

'Yeah, I know,' he says, turning into the shopping centre carpark, 'but if she's that desperate, she needs help. Maybe this way we can get her some.'

CHAPTER SEVEN

Kylie Clarke, seventeen-year-old mother of Tyler Clarke, was about as big and dangerous a criminal as I'd expected. Pregnant as the result of a one-night stand, kicked out by her family and struggling to get welfare payments sorted out—the boy refused to come to the party with any child support—she was desperate enough to try and sneak a tin of S26 out in the canopy of her second- or third-hand pram.

By the time we'd arrived she'd been a complete mess: red face, tears and exhaustion painted all over her overwhelmed young features. She'd never been in trouble in her entire life, she told us over and over. But her milk never came in and she needed to feed her baby. At least the Woolies manager dropped the charges after I bought her the damn formula, along with a few other small essentials, and Rico managed to put Kylie in touch with someone who could help, but she was so terrified they'd take little Tyler off her that she was reluctant to officially accept any.

After a little woman-to-woman chat, I'm pissed off enough to have convinced Rico to call in on daddy dearest. He's not entirely sure it's necessary, but here we are in the pretty rural suburb of

Yarramalong hoping to find the guy and give him an inspiring talk on parental responsibility.

'It's the one on the left,' I tell Rico, and he slows before turning up a steep driveway. The headlights sweep around the property, showing off tidy, post-and-rail paddocks framed by massive bare-branched trees waiting for spring. At the top, the driveway becomes a neatly gardened roundabout which sets off a sprawling white colonial-style cottage. Sensor lights spring to life, illuminating a gazebo that links a granny flat in matching style to the main residence. Outside that sits an electric blue modified Commodore.

'Doesn't really match the ambience of the place, does it?' I ask Rico and climb out of the car.

'I very much doubt it's Mum and Dad's car.'

'And I very much doubt this little arsehole, or at least his family, can't afford child support.' I pull on my jacket because there's a cool breeze—and besides, it's my favourite part of the uniform—then I walk to the front door. Knock.

'For all the difference it'll make, this is really a job for social services and the courts.'

'So you said.'

'They're not home!' comes a young male voice from the granny flat.

I follow it to the kid's front door. 'Hi, are you Oliver?'

Now he's looking more suspicious than annoyed. He's noticed the car, the uniform. 'Ah ... why?'

'Because if you're not, that's not your car and we'll have to seize it,' I make up.

'Of course it's my car! Who said it wasn't?'

'No one, just establishing your identity. So, here's the thing. You need to start taking responsibility for Tyler and pay some child support.'

'Ty—'. His eyes go round. 'This is because of that Kylie bitch, isn't it? Man, it's not my kid!'

'He, Oliver. Not it. He's a child not a baby goat. His name is Tyler, and as you're the first and only guy Kylie has ever slept with, that makes it likely he is yours.'

Oliver walks around in a few small circles, huffing and puffing and shaking his head like he can't quite believe how badly he's being persecuted. 'She's full of shit.'

'I'll admit she's hazy on the details. One minute she was drinking a Coke you poured for her at that Easter weekend party last year, the next she was feeling pretty out of it, only barely remembers the act, then she's waking up way too many hours later wondering how it all happened. Now, I'm going to give you the benefit of the doubt and say she was just really, really tired that night, because otherwise, I'd have to think you laced her drink with something and that would be a crime. A serious crime. Do we want to go there?'

His face is red and outraged and he's jiggling on the spot. 'It's not my kid!'

'Then you won't mind doing a paternity test so we can get this all sorted out.'

His fists clench. 'I'm not doing it! Forget it. She's a liar!'

'Do you know what happens if you refuse, Oliver? You'll end up in court being ordered to take one. If you refuse in court, you're pretty much implying you know you're the father and the court can then declare you Tyler's daddy regardless. Either way, you can't ignore a baby and hope it goes away.'

'When are your parents getting home?' Rico asks.

Something shifts behind his eyes that clearly says he's about to lie. 'Not for a few days. They're away.'

'Right, we'll wait.' Rico leans against the patrol car and crosses his feet at the ankles, folding his arms.

'I said a few days!'

'You've got to understand, your credibility is pretty low at this point,' I tell him.

After a quick internal debate, Oliver throws up his hands. 'Fuck this, I'm outta here.' He climbs into his car.

The Commodore roars to life, then thrums down the drive and out onto the road with a spin of its tyres.

'Oh dear,' I sigh dramatically. 'That could be an expensive tantrum.'

'Get in,' Rico orders. 'He's going to kill himself, or someone else.' Rico turns down the drive and catches up to the Commodore, turns on the lights and a few seconds later, follows it off the road.

Oliver is straight out of the car, slamming the door. 'What now?'

'You or me?' Rico asks.

'Oh, absolutely me,' I purr, and approach Oliver's car. 'Can I see your licence, please?'

'Why?'

'Just your licence please, sir.'

Oliver mutters something under his breath, then, in a fit of temper, fumbles getting it out of his wallet, drops the wallet, tries again. Several more curses later, I have his licence in hand.

'Why'd you pull me over?'

'Often leave your driveway in that sort of a hurry? Sounded like a burn out.'

'Get stuffed! It was not!'

'And your exhaust sounds a bit loud. We think it might be over the legal decibel limit.'

'Seriously? Prove it!'

'Hmm. Actually, now I get a better look, is there a problem with the shocks, too? Your car seems to be sitting a bit low on the road here. We should probably get out the wheel of doom, Rico, take a look.'

'Agreed.' Rico removes the measuring wheel from the patrol car and walks to the back of the Commodore, crouching down to slide it underneath. 'Tyres are looking pretty bald and, uh oh,' he says when a rasping sound clearly suggests the measuring wheel is hitting the underside. 'Afraid there's no hundred mill ground clearance on this one.'

'Shame. Can you see a P plate? Because there doesn't appear to be one on the front.'

Rico takes a look. 'No. Not that I can see.'

'I—I was pissed off at you lot hassling me! In a hurry. I forgot, look.' He pulls them out of the glovebox.

'Yeah. I'm afraid they don't meet legal display requirements from inside the car,' I tell him.

'Oh, fuck this—you're picking on me!'

'You're not making it difficult,' Rico says. 'This car is a turbo. You shouldn't be driving this—even if it was roadworthy—until you're off your P plates.' Rico heads back to the patrol car to write tickets while Oliver snarls at me. I smile pleasantly.

'Ouch,' I say when Rico returns. 'That's a lot of fines. How are you on points?'

'I …' His eyes widen as he looks over my shoulder at approaching headlights. 'Oh, you've got to be shitting me!' he explodes as a car slows then pulls over ahead of us. A well-dressed couple step out and hurry over, looking concerned.

'What's happened?' the man asks.

'Dad, they're picking on me!' I can't quite make out if Oliver's more incensed at us or worried about getting in trouble from his parents, but he suddenly sounds a whole lot younger and more whiny.

'Mr and Mrs Goodwin?' I ask.

'That's right,' Mr Goodwin says while his wife stares with annoyance at the car she so obviously has very little love for.

'Nice to meet you. We're just making sure your son is safe. Unfortunately this car is unroadworthy, and we don't need any more teenage fatalities on country roads. Especially young fathers.'

Whatever else Mr Goodwin had been about to say vanishes as the glare he was sending his son turns to blank disbelief. 'Young what?'

'It's bullshit!' Oliver whines.

'I'm sure Oliver will fill you in, but in case he, ah … forgets anything or you're interested in finding out more than he is, here's the card for the social services officer who'll be handling the case. Have a good night.'

Rico waits until we're back on the road before he says, 'Maybe the young father part was a bit much.' Though I'm pretty sure there's a smile lurking there somewhere.

'They're his legal guardians!'

'You can't be a hundred per cent sure Kylie's telling the truth.'

'Oh, I'm sure. I'm equally sure he's sure, or he'd get that test to prove what a liar she is. And to get out of trouble with his parents. What I would have liked to do is search his flat for date-rape drugs. Hopefully with some support, Kylie can be convinced to make a formal statement.' And speaking of drugs … I glance at the time. It's just after ten.

'You late for something?'

'That backpack is going to be gone.'

Rico is prevented from answering as a job comes through on the radio. There's a brawl outside the railway station at Wyong. All cars in the area are requested to attend.

'Feel like breaking up a fight?' Rico asks.

'Guess it'll pass the time.'

'That's the spirit.' He responds to the call, is told there's several other units en route. 'Must be big,' he says. 'Don't be a hero, okay? Stay with me, follow the training.'

I glance out the window as the dark roads of Yarramalong are left behind and the bright lights of Wyong illuminate the car. '"Don't be a hero" is about the least likely thing anyone is ever going to have to say to me.'

'Yet I happen to remember hearing you kicked that Vaughn guy senseless during the Spider investigation.'

'That wasn't heroic. That was panic.'

'I meant to ask actually. The boss said you were carrying on so much about the Hamills because that Debbie Reynolds from the Spider case is related to them. How can she be the daughter of a crime boss and not have that flagged when joining the police force?'

'Because legally she's Debbie Reynolds, adopted daughter of Mr and Mrs Reynolds of Avoca. Debbie was Raymond and Lena Hamill's last child. She was born when Lena was in prison doing a stint for assault and possession, which was to be followed by a drug rehab period. As Lena wasn't in any state to look after a baby and Raymond wasn't interested in raising a daughter, they signed away their parental rights to avoid further prying into the family by the cops and social services.'

'That should have been a good thing.'

'What no one knew was that Lena Hamill had tracked Debbie down once she turned eighteen and convinced her to rejoin the fold. Her role in joining the cops—we can only assume—was to shield the family business from any avoidable investigation.'

'Good parents are everything.'

'Tell me about it.'

'So I'm guessing the Hamill family are being watched very closely.'

'Right. And the more we learn, the worse these people get.'

'Why doesn't that surprise me? Oh, here we go,' he says, turning down a lane behind the local pub. 'This looks like fun.'

CHAPTER EIGHT

By what Finn was happy to call a small miracle, he walked into the go-kart building right on time. Inside was filled with music and excited, happy noise. Just about all of Vivienne's family and a lot of parents and friends of Ava's had already arrived and every table in the party area was decorated in purple tablecloths and filled with food, drinks, presents and people. Some of those presents were huge. He placed his own small gift among them and hoped it stacked up.

'Hello, Finn, how are you?' Vivienne's mum Eleanor asked. She was about the only one of Vivienne's family who spoke to him.

'Hi. Well, thanks,' he said, exchanging a kiss on the cheek. 'Yourself?'

'Oh, it's all a bit loud and energetic for me, I'm afraid.'

'Ah, you're kidding me,' he said, speaking loudly to be heard over the general chaos. 'From what I remember, you can keep up with anything.'

'We're all getting older, Finn. Arthur's not here. He's in the hospital recovering from a hip replacement.'

'Wish him well for me, would you?'

'Finn, you're on time,' Vivienne said, appearing in front of them.

'Surprising, isn't it?'

'Dad!' Ava barrelled into him.

'Hi, happy birthday, sweetie.' He lifted her off the ground and hugged her, spinning in a circle before releasing her. 'I popped your present on the table.'

'Thanks! You remember Lizzy and Kara?' she said, dragging her friends forward.

'Yeah. Hi, girls.'

Both girls said shy hellos before giggling. 'Come on,' Lizzy said to Ava, dragging her away. 'We'll miss our turn!'

'You have to watch me race, Dad!' Ava shot him another big smile then ducked back through a gathering of parents.

'Bit hard to compete with the friends today,' Vivienne said.

He didn't consider it a competition but he nodded. 'You've put on a great party for her.'

'She and four of her friends had a sleepover last night, went horse riding this morning then out for lunch, then spent hours in the salon getting pampered for the party. I can't wait for it all to be over.'

'Wow, that's … a lot.'

'Too much, if you ask me,' Eleanor said. 'You're trying to keep her happy since you and Louis …' At Vivienne's glare, her words faded.

'Hello, hello,' Rachael said, appearing with Ed. One of Ed's arm's was firmly around Rachael's shoulder and the other hand held a pink gift bag. 'Where's the birthday girl?'

'Waiting for her turn to race. No, scratch that, she's seen you,' Finn said.

'Aunty Rach! Ed!' Ava gave them both a hug. 'Thanks for coming.'

'Happy birthday!' Rachael said as Ed handed her the present.

'Thanks!' Ava's face fell marginally. 'I'm not allowed to open presents yet. It has to go on the table.' She ran off to put it there. 'I'm next. Want to watch?'

'Sure.' They moved to the railing that separated the track from the party area and watched Ava climb in her go-kart. A moment later she and a friend were laughing as they raced a couple of laps, finishing in a dead heat. Finn took photos, enjoying her fun.

'Excuse me, everyone.' Finn recognised Louis's voice and turned. 'I don't want to hold up the party but today is a bit of a double celebration. Vivienne and I would like to let you know she said yes last night, and we're officially engaged.'

Cheering and clapping erupted as family and friends gathered around to congratulate them.

'Did you know about this?' Rachael asked.

'Ava told me this morning.'

'How does she feel about it?'

'Meh.'

Ava ducked her way through the crowd and back to them. 'Did you see?'

'Sure did. You handled that kart like a pro! Hey, I want a photo with the birthday girl,' he said.

'I'll take it,' Rachael said, using her phone to get a couple of shots before Ava's smile dropped. Finn followed her gaze to where Vivienne was showing off her engagement ring.

'We haven't even had the cake yet. Jeez, Mum, make it all about you,' Ava grumbled.

'Aw, come on, it doesn't matter,' Finn said brightly. 'This is a great party!'

'Yeah, I guess.' Then brighter: 'Lexi messaged me to say happy birthday.'

'Of course she did,' Rachael said. 'I'm sure she would have loved to have been here.'

'Yeah, I know.' The big smile came back. 'She could have pretended to be Dad's girlfriend so he didn't have to turn up on his own.'

'Ava!' Finn objected with an uncomfortable laugh.

'What? Remember Mum's face when she was at your place that day? She still asks me about her sometimes.'

'Then she knows Lexi's not my girlfriend.'

Ava's face twisted. 'I might have let her think she was.'

Rachael laughed loudly before dragging Ava in for another hug. 'We'll have to go and see her one day, okay?'

'I see her all the time.'

'Huh?' Finn asked.

'We FaceTime.'

'You FaceTime Lexi?' The two had hit it off when they'd first met and Lexi saving Ava's life hadn't hurt the bond that he knew they'd begun to share. But he'd had no idea about the FaceTime. He doubted Vivienne did either.

'Yeah. She's awesome. She showed me her gun.'

'She's awesome because she has a gun?' he asked. 'I have a gun.'

'Which you won't show me.'

'Because guns aren't toys.'

'And if I was three, I'd nod solemnly and say *yes Dad* in awe.'

He couldn't help but grin. 'But you're not three, are you? You're eleven going on thirty. Hear that sarcasm?' he said to Rachael. 'She even sounds like Lexi.'

Ava shrugged. 'She's cool.'

'Who's cool?' Vivienne asked, joining them.

'Doesn't matter,' Ava said, confirming Vivienne probably didn't know about FaceTime with Lexi.

'Finn, have you got a minute?' Vivienne asked.

'Sure.'

'Why don't we grab a drink?' Rachael said to Ava. 'Got any lemonade?'

'Okay.' Ava gave her mother a suspicious look as she led Rachael and Ed away.

'Congratulations,' Finn said.

'You don't look surprised.'

'Should I be?'

Vivienne's face reflected disappointment. 'She told you, didn't she?'

'Is there any reason why my daughter shouldn't talk to me?'

'I asked her to keep— No. Of course not. Is she ... okay about it?'

'You don't know?' he asked, failing to keep the disbelief from his voice.

'She doesn't say much.'

'Have you asked?'

From the look on her face and the change of subject, she hadn't. 'Look, so yeah, we're getting married. We want to buy our own house. We both want a fresh start. But that means I'll need my share of the money from ours.'

His stomach sank. His mother's house, the only thing he had left of her. He'd moved them both into it when he and Viv had gotten married. The divorce and fifty-fifty split of their possessions had meant he'd faced selling it, but he'd found the money to rent his little flat and let Vivienne stay in the house with Ava to put off selling it for as long as he could. This was always going to happen.

'Okay, no worries,' he said. 'I've still got a few months left on the rental but let me talk to the bank. See what I can do.'

'The thing is, there's this house we really like. We don't want to miss out on it.'

'Hold up,' he said, taken aback. 'You've already found a house? How long have you been looking? Why didn't you tell me this earlier?'

'It's only a couple of streets back from the beach,' she said, ignoring his questions. 'You know how much Ava loves the beach. I need the money as soon as possible. The faster we get the house on the market, the better.'

Finn banked his temper. 'I understand that, but I need time to try and organise the finances to keep it. You know how much this house means to me, Vivienne. A bit of a heads up would have been handy.'

'Oh, grow up, Finn! It's just a house.'

He set his jaw against the bitter retort. 'Not to me.'

'You're making Dad sell the house?' Ava asked from behind them.

'Ava, go talk to your friends,' Vivienne snapped.

'But it's Dad's house! Mum, I don't want to move!'

Vivienne looked around as though worried they were drawing attention. 'We'll talk about it later, Ava.'

Ava looked directly at Finn. 'Dad?'

'We'll get this sorted, don't worry,' he said as calmly and quietly as possible. 'Go have fun.'

'Why are you even doing this now?' Ava asked Vivienne. 'You've already turned this into an engagement party, now you're ruining what's left of it!'

Finn knew exactly why Vivienne was doing it now. She'd been hoping she could drop this on him in an environment where he couldn't make a fuss about it. And now, by the look on her face, this whole scene was all his fault.

'Thanks, Finn,' Vivienne said under her breath. 'Thanks a lot.'

'Yep,' he said to himself, 'my fault.'

Rachael joined him as Vivienne strode away. 'She wants to sell the house?'

'Yeah.' He caught Ava staring so he forced a smile back onto his face. 'I'll figure something out.' He waved at his daughter and pointed to where her friend was beckoning her to the karts. Then he leant against the barrier to watch them race.

CHAPTER NINE

I sit higher in my seat to get a better look as we approach the scene. All hell has broken loose in the carpark behind the pub in the form of a swarm of drunken young idiots. Police cars are blocking off both ends of the lane and a handful of cops are busily breaking up fights while more are holding others back. One's making an arrest. Rico crawls to a stop behind another patrol car.

A woman in front of us whose dress has ridden up in all sorts of places wobbles on heels and yells encouragement to a heavy-set type whose white shirt is stained with blood, only one button still holding it together. He manages to throw off his attacker and get a punch in at the angry thug's jaw before rugby tackling him. They bounce off our car before falling to the ground.

'Bunch of young hothead guys, a few girls on the sidelines. So what is this over? Girlfriends? Drugs?' I ask Rico as he prepares to get out.

'At this point it doesn't matter,' he says with his serious, assessing-the-danger face on. 'Stay with me and do as I say, okay?' He comes around beside me, moves a drunken loudmouth away from my door so I can get out of the car.

The woman in the riding-up-everywhere dress wobbles over and I can see her make-up's as dysfunctional as her dress and something has been spilt down the front of her. She's maybe sixteen.

'Hey—you guys. Hey! Youse have to listen to me. Tell them other cops they're arresting the wrong guy. That's my man they've got and he was just trying to help me out. It's the other guy they need to get.'

I spot the guy she's talking about now in cuffs, being ordered to stay seated on the kerb by another officer. He's not being particularly cooperative. 'Okay, how about you take a step back for a moment for us, please, miss, while we sort this out,' Rico says.

We move off but the woman's skirting along at Rico's side and grabs hold of his shirt.

'Nah, nah, you've gotta listen!'

'Hey, why don't you talk to the constable?' Rico instructs, prying off her fingers. Then to me, he says, 'Take her out of harm's way and see if you can make sense of what all this is about.'

I know that's his way of finding me something relatively safe to do but I can't say I really want to jump into the mass of seething bodies out there, so why not? 'Sure.'

'Why won't he talk to me?'

'Because Rico has important wrestling-type stuff to do, and grabbing hold of his shirt is not the best way to make friends. What's your name?'

'Jacqui.'

'Okay, Jacqui, why don't we go talk over here?'

'But—'

'Over here.' I guide her back to the car and out of the swing zone as two more patrol cars pull up. A few brawlers run off, shouting. We might be making progress. 'Okay,' I ask her, my eyes mostly still on what's going on in the carpark. 'What happened?'

'I was hanging out over there, right, minding my own business,' she slurs, pointing to the back of the pub, 'when these, these … shitheads come out and start hassling me and asking what I charge and shit. And they don't believe me, right? They don't listen when I tell them I'm not a hooker. So they keep at me and so I have to call my boyfriend out of the line for his beer, right?'

'I see,' I say and grimace as Rico dodges a swinging fist before getting another random arsehole under control. I send him a silent cheer.

'Yeah. He has to come outside and tell these shitheads to piss off, so then they, like, start this big commotion. So my boyfriend, he's got no choice, right? He has to get his friends to give up their beers and come out and help get them to leave me alone. And then the next thing it's just, like, totally out of control and it's not his fault. He was trying to get them to go away, so he called his friends and they called their friends and it went to shit. Like, epically.'

'I'd call this pretty epic. So you were hanging out, dressed like that in a pub carpark by a dark alley, smashed off your face in the middle of the night. What is that, some sort of hobby?'

'Course not.'

'Were you buying or selling?'

'What?'

'You tell me. Pot, dope, smack?'

She sways on the spot, eyes skywards. 'Maybe I was after an upper. I asked the guys if they had anything I might be interested in. That's when they got all nasty.'

I'm still keeping a pretty close eye on everything going on around me. There's an ever-increasing line of brawler butts on the kerb and a lot of the crowd has dissipated but a few diehards are still going at it. One cop resorts to pepper spray as he wrestles someone away from his weapon belt. Another guy goes down.

'Right, well, I'd like to know what you thought was gonna happen.'

Jacqui's face creases into an indignant scowl. 'Listen, lady, I should be able to hang around as drunk as I like wearing whatever I like at any time of the night in whatever carpark in whatever neighbourhoods I want to. And those bastards should know they've got no right to touch me!' She's slurred the words but honestly I'm impressed she got the details mostly right. The final fighters are broken up. Angry explanations are being yelled at officers.

'Why aren't you saying anything?' she asks after a minute.

'Because I agree with you.'

'Oh.'

'But back in the real world, I'd still like to know what you thought was going to happen.'

Rico jogs over, a lot more dishevelled than when he left. 'I think I've got the story from the other guys. They're saying they mistook her for a prostitute. They didn't actually touch her, but they did make some suggestive comments. Do you agree with that?' Rico asks Jacqui.

'Yeah. Filthy-mouthed shitheads! I was scared!'

'Yeah, I can imagine. The one you smacked in the face with your purse isn't pressing charges.'

'Pressing charges? I should be pressing charges!' Jacqui stumbles, her ankle rolling.

'Is that something you want to pursue?' Rico asks.

'Nah, just need to get home. Feel sick.'

'Can we call you a taxi?'

'Got no money left. Was supposed to get home with my boyfriend.'

'Unfortunately, your boyfriend's going back to the station to cool down,' Rico tells her. 'Where do you live?'

'Kariong.'

Rico and I exchange glances. 'We can't leave her here,' I say. 'Not with so many of those guys still lurking around.'

Rico eyes Jacqui dubiously. 'Are you going to promise not to throw up in my car if we take you home?' he asks.

'Yeah. Probably.'

'All right,' he says and opens the rear door. 'Get in.' Then to me, he says, 'Keep an eye on her. I'll make sure we're good to go.'

The trip to Kariong is relatively silent, though Jacqui still possessed enough functioning brain cells to lead us to her house. 'It's the next street on the right,' she says.

'No problem.'

I look at the time. It's after one. Only an hour until we're due at the tunnel. 'Hey, I wonder if our backup is on track?'

'Good question. Let me check.'

'That's it there!' Jacqui says, thrusting an arm between us to point to a tidy house and garden. 'Mum and Dad's place.'

'Take her in, would you?' Rico suggests. I know damn well Jacqui can find her own way to the door. I also know he doesn't want me anywhere near the radio while he's talking to the boss if things haven't gone to plan.

'Okay, Jacqui, let's go!'

By the time we reach the door the porch light is on and a well-rounded woman wrapped in a dressing gown is standing, hands on hips, behind a screen door. Her stance is strong, but her expression reads worry and disappointment.

'Evening!' I say pleasantly. 'We've just given Jacqui a lift home. There was a bit of an incident in Wyong and her boyfriend got caught up. Nothing to worry about.'

'I'll bet,' the woman says, looking her daughter up and down as she opens the door. Jacqui goes in without a word. And—scratch worry and disappointment—up close, the woman's expression is helplessly sad. 'Is it just alcohol this time or has she taken a pill?'

'Fortunately, she wasn't able to source any pills tonight.'

'That's something then. Thanks for bringing her home safe. It's not like you police don't have enough to do.'

'It's no problem. Have a nice evening.' I feel for the woman, but I can't get back to the car fast enough. 'So?' I ask as I slide in.

'Still good to go. Our backup is out on a domestic dispute but they're hoping to meet us on time.' He checks his watch. 'We can get a coffee beforehand.' He starts the car and pulls away from the house. 'Rail security will be waiting at the gate to let us through. Once the other car arrives, we go in.'

'We're probably too late, but if not, if we run into them, there's a chance this could be dangerous. Don't forget who their family is.'

'What's this?' he asks in mock surprise. 'A complete change of tune?'

'No, I'm just saying—'

'Hold up. This is organised. These two little shits bashed one of my best mates. You think their name scares me? They've probably already collected anything they left behind or aren't going to risk coming back for it. On the slight chance we run into them I'm pretty sure four fully armed police will be enough to handle it. Don't you think?'

'Of course I do.' But I'm also thinking maybe I should have gone over Tank's head and spoken to Rachael. 'But I have to stay with the damn car, remember?'

'True. You know, if you're scared …'

'Shut up and get there faster,' I say, unimpressed.

CHAPTER TEN

Sunday, March 6

'So ... they're not here and it's ten past two,' I say. Sitting in a deserted carpark surrounded by locked-up warehouses in the early hours of the morning isn't my idea of fun, and with nothing to entertain me but watching moths and beetles crash into security lights, I'm getting antsy. Besides, the clock is ticking.

'I know.' Rico gets on the radio, discovers the other car is still ten minutes out. At least. 'Give me a minute.' He gets out and relays this information to the guard waiting in his own car, before coming back and poking his head in the door. 'Apparently this is not good enough.'

'Someone's on a power trip,' I mumble.

'I think he's probably cold. And pissed off he's been dragged out here in the middle of the night. On a weekend.'

'So what now?'

He looks around. Other than the warehouses, there's nothing to see but the railway gate illuminated by our headlights and the darkness of the tree-studded mountain beyond it. No movement, no sound. He gets back on the radio. 'Boss, we're here with rail security. We've been here for fifteen already. The other car is at least ten minutes out. No sign of our POIs. The trains are now being held up. We're not winning friends with Transport for NSW. Can we go in and check for this bag?'

There's a long silence before we get reluctant approval.

'Imagine that,' I say. 'I get to go in after all.'

'Yeah.' Rico snags his jacket from the back seat and pulls it on. I do the same. It's cold and the wind is blowing. 'Let's hope these drugs are in here,' he tells me, and waves at the guard before starting the short walk along the lines to the tunnel. Bushland envelops us on both sides and our torch beams highlight the portal. Its heavy brickwork is framed by pillows of clinging moss and sprays of dripping ferns, their tendrils reaching out as though to beckon us into its gaping mouth. I point my torch at the depths within and the light disintegrates into the complete and impenetrable darkness. It's eerie. I hesitate.

'Want me to go first?' Rico offers.

Embarrassing. 'Why?'

'Could be dangerous, remember?'

'They've stopped the trains.'

'It's not the trains I was thinking about,' he says in a dramatic whisper.

I ignore it. 'We haven't seen or heard a trace of the twins.'

'Not them either.'

I sigh and play along. 'What then? The tunnel monster?'

'You jest,' he says in that same teasing tone, 'but do you know how many people have died in here?'

'Ah ... great. Why didn't I realise how creepy this place was the first time?'

'You were too busy chasing a dickhead and dodging trains. Now it's all quiet and spooky.'

I hear something tear through the undergrowth of the steep bank beside us. 'Whatever that was isn't dead.'

'I wasn't kidding, though,' he says, walking inside, torch bouncing off the curving walls as he talks. 'There's been deaths in here dating back to 1917. Once an entire work gang was run down. The line was strewn with body parts afterwards.'

'Don't make shit up.'

'I'm not! I read it this morning when I was looking up how long this damn tunnel is.'

'So how long is it?'

'One-point-six-nine kilometres.'

'Yep. That's long.'

'There are more tunnels connected to it somewhere and an ammunitions tunnel above us. That was built during the war to blow the tunnel if the Japanese tried to get through.'

'Fascinating.'

'Yeah, and when they built the tunnel there was an entire town near Wondabyne Station. There're a few remnants left if you look hard enough, apparently. Even some graves.'

'Don't care.'

'Whoa!'

'Whoa what?' I spin around. 'Rico?' Nothing. Where the hell did he go? Where could he go? It's a tunnel! I take a few quick steps back in the direction we came from, then nearly faint as he pounces from a safety recess in the wall.

'Boo.'

'Drop dead, dickhead,' I say with a laugh. Something comes over the radio. It's garbled and disjointed.

'You catch that?' he asks.

'No. It's probably our late backup.'

'There's not enough reception in here. I'll run back a bit, flash the torch around so they know where we are.'

'I'll keep looking.' I watch him jog back towards the entrance and suddenly feel very alone. Talk of ghosts aside, this is a long, black, disconcerting space. I point my torch everywhere: on the ground, along the walls. I keep walking. How far in had I chased Aden? I was sure I hadn't come this far, but I had been running, so maybe ... And then my torch beam bounces off something red and I jog to where it sits. Yes! It's the backpack.

'Bingo!' I pull on some gloves and open it up. Inside is a commercial quantity of what I'm betting is methamphetamine bundled into neat little sachets. I zip the bag back up. 'Hey! Rico!' I call over my shoulder. I'm not sure how far it is back to the entrance, but I'm pretty sure he should be able to hear me in the echoing tunnel. 'I've got it! I'm coming back!'

A noise echoes back at me from the exit as I stand and turn around. A tinny rattle like pipe bouncing off pipe.

'Rico!'

He doesn't reply. Why can't I see his torch? Has he gone all the way back to the car to meet the others? If so, what made that noise? More uneasiness settles over me. I try my radio and get static. The sound is suddenly too loud in the eerie, enveloping silence. I get moving, half expecting to see a decapitated spirit float out of the darkness. The hairs on the back of my neck prickle. 'Don't be stupid,' I say out loud. Damn Rico and his ghost stories. But my pace speeds up. Where *is* he? If he jump scares me again he's history. Assuming I don't die of a heart attack first. Another victim of the tunnel.

'Come on, Rico. It wasn't funny the first time!'

As the blackness of the tunnel finally ebbs into the more natural darkness of moonlight I spot a figure lying across the tracks. What the hell? My power walk becomes a sprint.

'Hey! Rico, is that you? Are you okay?' Maybe he tripped. He really better not be pulling another prank. 'Rico. Hey.'

My torch beam hits his face. His head is a bloody mess. My heart seems to stop in my chest. I drop straight to my knees. On the way down, I hear the whoosh of something by my left ear, feel the crack of it graze my temple. I fall sideways, drop the torch. As I reach for it, I feel the impact of a boot in my ribs. The air leaves my lungs as another boot under the jaw forces my head back. For several seconds the world is nothing but pain.

I gradually become aware of the sound of footsteps running back into the tunnel, a crunch, crunch, crunch in the gravel. I lie there, breathless and stunned into immobility. Another few seconds go by before I attempt to move. Rico. I drag myself over onto my side. Ow. Gritting my teeth, I crawl to the torch, get it in my hand. Rico is still just lying there.

'Hey, hey. Rico, are you okay?'

I shine the light right in his eyes but he doesn't complain or squint. He's alive, though. I can see the pulse beating in his neck. A voice comes over the radio. It's our backup. Do we need assistance? I manage to relay something but I'm not sure it makes sense.

Rico moans quietly as his head lolls. I shift to cradle it so I can better hold some pressure on the wound. It would be useful if I could stop shaking. There's so much blood. Nothing feels solid under my fingers.

'Hang in there, okay?' I tell him. 'Help is coming.' Within seconds I hear the shouts of the second lot of cops coming towards us, see their torches. 'Hear that?'

His eyes move around, stop somewhere near my face but I'm not sure he's seeing me. I swallow back a panicked sob.

'Tears.' It's not much more than a breath.

I manage a weak laugh. 'This is top secret, but I'm not completely heartless.' Then louder to the approaching cops: 'We need an ambulance!'

'It's coming!' a female voice shouts as she comes into view, a shadowy figure behind a torch.

'You're going to be fine,' I tell Rico as reassuringly as I can. But I hear the catch of a breath, its long release, and when I look into his eyes I know he's not. And never will be again.

CHAPTER ELEVEN

'Detectives are still out at the scene searching for our POIs,' Inspector Burns told Rachael as he led her at a clip down the hospital corridor. 'Losing one of our own is always a tragedy, but Rico was such a highly valued and experienced officer. It's devastating.'

'Of course.' The fact that Lexi had been brought to a ward from the Emergency Department was worrying Rachael. She would have been released if there were no serious injuries.

'Most of my officers are with forensics,' Burns continued. 'I've been running through the details of the incident with Constable Winter.'

'And how is she?'

'Lucky to be alive.'

'But why has she been brought here? What are her injuries?'

'One of the kicks she received to the head gave her a mild concussion. The ED is busy and she had to be put somewhere to await the results of the X-rays of her ribs.'

'I see.' Relief swept through her.

'She's managed to briefly explain the events of the evening, but we'll have to go through things more formally once she's discharged.

She'll be suspended from duty of course, while an inquiry into the incident is undertaken.'

Rachael stopped. 'What exactly did happen out there, Burns?'

He sighed. 'Winter and Rico carried out two arrests in the location the night before. A couple of drug dealers bashed one of our officers last week and somehow Winter found out they were going to be in the area. She and Rico took it upon themselves to pick them up. Unfortunately, in the ensuing chaos, they failed to collect an item of evidence relating to the drug offences before leaving the scene. Winter realised this prior to the start of last night's shift and the two decided they needed to return to collect it. I agreed on the condition Rico enter the tunnel with two more experienced officers during a lull in railway traffic when it was easiest to have the tracks closed.'

'Why not Lexi?'

'I didn't want her there at all! Winter has very little policing experience and makes rookie mistakes. She chased an offender into the railway tunnel the night before and almost got herself hit by a train, so I decided she should stay with the car. This is exactly the tragedy I was attempting to avoid.'

'But she went in anyway?'

'Unfortunately the backup was delayed. There's only so much time Transport for NSW can shut down the tracks for and with no POIs apparent, I agreed to let them go in. They located the bag but were separated and attacked attempting to leave with it. That's all I know so far. She's in there,' he said, pointing to a doorway.

'Thank you.' Rachael's eyes skimmed over three other patients, then was drawn to a curtain at the far end of the room. She heard Lexi's voice and a deeper male voice, presumably a doctor or nurse.

'Lexi? It's Rachael.'

'It's okay. Come in,' Lexi said.

She stepped past the curtain, found Lexi sitting on the edge of the bed, a doctor standing nearby. No emotion showed on Lexi's face, but she could see the fatigue, the strain and the nasty red circle on her temple. Lexi held an icepack under her jaw.

'Well, you took a beating,' Rachael said, attempting a smile. 'How's the other guy look?'

'I wish I knew. Bastard got me while I was bent over Rico.'

'I'm sorry about your partner,' Rachael said sincerely. Then to the doctor, 'Rachael Langley.'

'Mitchell Ford.'

'Anything serious or does it just look spectacular?'

Ford checked with Lexi, who nodded her consent. 'No fractures, but bruising and a mild concussion. She's going to need to rest for a few days. Some meds for the pain.'

'She's in the end bed,' Rachael heard Burns say from beyond the curtain. 'But you can't go in there until Inspector Langley and the doctor—'

'Stop me.' Finn's voice, short and sharp. Then, 'Lexi?'

'Here.' Lexi's body sagged a touch. 'Did you wake anyone else up?' she asked Rachael.

Rachael shook her head. 'Just Finn.' She was going to need help with what had to happen next, and she'd known Finn would want to be involved.

He slipped through the curtains. He greeted them both, then said to Lexi, 'How are you holding up?'

'Okay.' Lexi adjusted the icepack and flinched.

'I thought some drug dealer hit you.'

'He did.'

'Looks more like it was the train,' he said with a sympathetic smile.

'I'll leave you to it,' the doctor said. 'Lexi, we can discharge you as long as you have someone to keep an eye on you for the next twenty-four hours or so. Okay?'

'Yeah. Thanks.'

'Thanks, doctor,' Rachael said as he left them alone. She needed to get Lexi out of here. She was holding up, but the strain on her face was prominent. Losing a partner, watching him die in front of her, was going to take a lot longer to heal than bruising.

'I guess you want to hear what happened?' Lexi asked.

'I've been briefed.'

'Great, then can we move on to how we're going to find the little shits?'

'One step at a time.'

'But—'

'I'll head down to the scene,' Finn said. 'Check it out, talk to Steven and the crime scene guys. Anything they should know?'

'I'm sure they already know by now but the guys they're looking for, they're part of the Hamill family—Jason and Aden.'

The Hamill family, Rachael thought with dread. She'd have to contact Detective Inspector Craig Slavek. The drug squad would need to be brought up to speed, along with her team. 'Lexi, why would you go after Hamills?'

'I was going after their stash.' Lexi closed her eyes and dragged in a deep breath. 'The pair beat up one of the constables from our station, but when we brought them in, the witness wouldn't formally identify them, so they walked. They'd dumped some drugs in a backpack in the tunnel during the arrest, and finding the bag was our best chance of bringing them back in on charges while we convinced the witness to change her mind. We waited for the other cops but they were held up. We had a guard a hundred metres from the tunnel back at the gate, there was no sign of the brothers. We were given the okay to go in.'

And you're so, so lucky you're not dead. 'But you know how dangerous the Hamills are. You should have called me.'

Lexi's eyes flashed. 'I told Burns to contact the Drugs and Firearms Squad right from the get-go. I told him they'd want to handle it. But Burns didn't want the big guns called in because he didn't think we had enough to warrant it. I'm supposed to do things his way, Rachael. I can't call you and complain every time a superior officer disagrees with me. If I'd been doing things my way I would have safely had those drugs in hand hours before all this happened. But no. I followed orders and this is what happened.'

And there at last was some emotion. Hopefully the shock was wearing off. 'Okay. I understand.'

'It's not okay!'

'Did you actually see who attacked you?' Finn asked. 'Do you know for sure it was the twins?'

'No. We were searching the tunnel when something came over the radio. Rico went back to the entrance to try and make it out and I kept looking because we didn't have much time. I found the bag, took it and left. I got to the end of the tunnel and found Rico on the ground. Something struck me from behind. Whoever it was booted me a couple of times, grabbed the backpack and took off. But the night before, when we arrested them at the tunnel, Jason had specifically promised to bash Rico's head in at the first opportunity. And who else would have known where those drugs were? Who else would have been after them?'

'Right,' Rachael said, anger brewing in her chest. 'Okay, let me talk to Burns again then we'll get you home.' She stalked out of the room. Of all the stupid bloody things ...

She almost strode right past, finding him in a small, otherwise empty waiting room, phone in one hand, a styrofoam cup of instant coffee in the other. 'A moment?' she asked when he ended the call.

'Yes?'

'You had two Hamills in custody and Constable Winter made a point of telling you the drug squad would want to talk to them. Would you mind telling me why no one was informed?'

His face closed up in a scowl. 'Due to a witness backing out of a formal identification over the assault we had nothing to hold them on. I certainly wasn't going to drag the squad in on the possibility there *might* have been a bag and it *might* have contained drugs. If we'd found it and it was as Rico and Winter had assumed, then of course I would have contacted the drug squad with the evidence. But as it stood I couldn't justify it.'

Rachael held on to her temper. 'A couple of teens might not appear to be all that dangerous, but those teens are part of a large, well-structured organisation that's been responsible for multiple deaths. It was absolutely warranted for a specialist team to step in for that recovery operation. Constable Winter—'

'Constable Winter does not run my station!' Burns snapped, tossing his cup into the bin with force. 'Frankly, I'm sick to death of having my every decision questioned and being told how to do my job by a probationary constable!'

'I see,' Rachael said coldly. 'Then would you say this tragedy is the result of inexperienced policing or your ego?'

His fingers went to his temples as he made a visible attempt to calm down. 'It wasn't like that. I just didn't see—'

'You should have!'

'Don't make this a witch hunt, Rachael. I know about the connection between you and Lexi. Turner might have deserved what he got,' he said of a detective that had been forced into retirement due to poor conduct during the Spider case, 'but I'm not Turner. Hindsight's a fabulous thing, but I made a reasonable decision at the time.'

'You keep telling yourself that. I'm taking Lexi home. I'll be in touch shortly to take over this case.'

'You know, Turner called it right,' he said to her retreating back. 'You really are a hard-headed bitch, aren't you?'

'Not at all,' she said, pausing to look back at him. 'But I do have a couple of decades of experience seeing through testosterone-fuelled bullshit.'

'How are you really holding up?' Finn asked Lexi. Sitting there injured, pale and shaken in a hospital gown that swamped her, she looked too fragile to survive what she'd just been through. But he knew her better than that. She'd rally that ironclad will of hers. She'd get past this.

'It all happened so fast,' she admitted. 'I didn't follow my training. I should have checked. I should have looked around before I dropped down beside Rico. If I had, I might have caught whoever did it instead of sitting here wasting time.'

'Your first thought was your partner's safety. It's a hell of a tough situation. Don't beat yourself up about it. We'll get them.'

'If they've run home, maybe. Otherwise, I doubt it. Not with their connections.' Her face reflected bitterness. 'But I will.'

'So,' he said. 'What's your first move?'

'I had a life before all this cop stuff. On the streets, dealing with people that would never talk to police. I can find them. But I have to do it out of uniform, on my terms.'

'Look, I get it. I do. And it's going to take a while before everything feels okay again—'

'I told him to drop dead! Right before he headed back down that tunnel. I was joking but …' She pressed her fingers to her eyes and dragged in a ragged breath.

Ah, hell, guilt on top of trauma. 'You couldn't have known,' he said gently, sitting beside her. 'Do you really think he'd have taken you seriously?'

'No. But it doesn't make me feel any better.' She stared at the floor as a tear dared to escape. She swiped at it angrily. 'I was useless.'

'Lexi, there was nothing you could have done.'

She shook her head and when she turned back, her face was set, determined. 'Whatever. I can do something now.' She handed him the icepack, gingerly slid off the bed and swayed a little as she found her balance. He bet she had a killer headache. 'I need to get out of this gown, go home. Then I'll head out to some of the places I know these sorts of guys like to hang out, ask around in case anyone knows them. Say I'm after some of their stuff. Or something. I'll figure it out.'

'Great idea. Can you walk in a straight line?' he asked, getting close enough to grab her if she keeled over.

'Home. A shower. Some painkillers. New me,' she said.

'And what happens if you're lucky enough to stumble upon these two idiots?'

'Do I really have to tell you?'

'Seriously. They yell cop and those old friends of yours might suddenly be a lot less friendly.'

'I'll risk it.'

'I won't.'

Rachael returned. 'Right. You're coming with—what?' she asked, looking between the two.

Lexi had once threatened to stab Finn with the bluntest knife she could find. She had that look on her face again.

Finn cleared his throat. 'We're discussing where to from here.'

'The incident will be investigated while Lexi takes some time off to recover.'

'Oh, I don't think so!' Lexi said.

'Why don't you get dressed,' Finn said and gestured for Rachael to step out of the room with him. 'Rach, you know as well as I do she's not staying out of this. She's already planning her next move.'

'Of course I know that. But right now I'm going to take her home, make sure she gets some rest. We'll go from there.'

'You talked to Burns?'

Anger filled Rachael's face. 'Burns knew he had Hamills. Craig Slavek's team should have been here tonight. I dared point that out and now we're anything but best friends.'

'He probably wanted to present it as a done deal, and if it didn't pan out, spare himself the embarrassment.'

'I agree. I appreciate you going to the scene. Let me know how you get on. Then I need you to get back to the city and give the team the heads up on this. I need to talk to Craig. His team's extensive knowledge of the family could be useful, and as all this is tied in with the Hamill drug operation, he'll probably want to work it with us. This case will take priority with the team. As soon as we have a plan of attack, I'll let you know.'

CHAPTER TWELVE

'Here we are,' Rachael says.

With effort, I drag my eyes open and realise she's pulled into my driveway. I'm not sure what time it is but sometime between leaving the hospital and the short ride home, the sky has gone from a dark blue to shades of sweeping pastels. She's taking a look around. There's not much to see. Home is stuck on the end of a row of unimaginative, eighties-build townhouses. An identical set line the opposite side of a narrow drive. Behind the complex is a wall of thickly vegetated mountainside that seems reluctant to let the morning light stream through.

'Oh, thanks.'

'I haven't been here for a while. Have you heard from Dawny?'

'No, she was in a terrible accident, remember?' I respond automatically, though we both know she wasn't. She and her husband Desmond are on the run from police over her husband's outstanding warrants, and no doubt enjoying every minute of it. 'I now have these fabulous new neighbours who like really, really loud music, which annoys the Parkhursts more than I used to.'

'Good for them.' Then, when I don't immediately move to get out of the car, she asks, 'Okay?'

'Yep.' But I'm not okay. My head is pounding and my legs feel like jelly. Every tiny movement of my ribs feels like a hot poker going through my side. My stomach is flipping and churning and my vision is blurry at best. I'm not sure if it's the injuries or the drugs but my body is demanding quiet and darkness. Sleep. How can I sleep while Jason and Aden are still out there? Rico's last moments flash in my mind and the ache in my chest is crippling. I thought I hated the Hamills before. I was wrong. *This* is hate. I'm going to bring the entire fucked-up family down.

But first I have to get out of the car. I work the door handle and swing one leg carefully, then the other. Ow.

'Keys?'

'Bag.'

Rachael grabs my bag from the back of the car and rummages through it until she finds them.

I count to three and take a deep breath before pushing to my feet. The world spins again. 'So what are we going to do next?'

'You're going to get some rest,' Rachael says.

'I mean about finding the twins!' I don't quite mean to bark it out, it just sort of happens when my ribs bite at me as I move towards the door.

'Is that what you were talking to Finn about?'

'I said that if they've gone to ground locally, I might be able to find them through the contacts I made when I was on the streets.' Rachael unlocks the door and I walk inside. 'He thought that was a bad idea. I disagree.'

'So do I.' Rachael puts our bags on the kitchen counter and fills the kettle under the tap. 'I think whatever helps find these two is something we should look at moving on. But right now, you sleep.'

'I'm not tired,' I lie.

'You're well beyond tired. You're just too upset to realise it or too stubborn to admit it. You're running on adrenaline and painkillers.'

'But while I sleep they have hours to get further away.'

'They can run, but we'll catch up.'

'We?'

'It's what I do, isn't it?'

'But you're not officially back on duty yet.'

'A cop was murdered and you were injured. You think I'm going to let anyone get away with this?'

'I guess not.'

'We'll get them, Lexi.'

I lean on the kitchen bench. 'The boss ordered me to take time off, but I don't think he can. It's not mandatory to take time off under these circumstances.'

'No. But then again, he's legally required to ensure that all officers under his command are physically and emotionally fit for duty, so technically, he can. I don't think he's going to want to see you back in under three months.'

'That's ridiculous! I need to—'

'Hold on! This is a cop killing. It's out of Burns's hands and firmly in ours. Every officer on the coast is searching for the twins as we speak, but if we don't find them fast I'd like you working with us to track them down. So, until the investigation into the incident is completed, you're off duty. But as the senior officer inviting you onto this case, I'm prepared to assess your fitness for duty immediately after that.'

'Thank you.'

'*Assess* it. If I don't think you're up to it, you're still out.'

'As if—' I take one look at the set features and decide to change tack. 'Thanks. What are you going to do now?'

'Talk to the inspector in charge of investigating the Hamill drugs and weapons operations. If these two have been dealing, he'll want to be involved and he might have some ideas on where those boys could be.'

I edge onto a stool. 'There's no question they're dealing. And they're carrying enough to supply other dealers. I have a contact who's been buying from them for months.'

'Something else he'll be interested to hear. I think the first step will be to get someone over to the Hamill home to see what else we can find out.'

'Can't we go?'

'I'm not sure how much you remember, but the Hamill family live in several different homes on a large property southwest of Sydney. The whole place is a fortress.'

'Yeah, I know. I remember.'

'I've been reliably informed by those who have dealt with them in the past that, depending on what mood they're in, you'll be greeted graciously or told via intercom to piss off if you don't have a warrant. If you do get inside, it's vest on, and for all the social niceties they might throw at you, the situation can escalate very quickly. Every word has to be measured, precise. They know how to play the system. There's only a few cops we send in and they're highly trained in negotiation.'

I nod slowly. I know this. They get away with it mostly because they're too smart to do anything then and there. They wait, they hire people, they get their enemies when they least expect it. Dozens of horrible deaths have been attributed to the Hamills but most have been unable to be proven.

I get back on my feet and slowly cross the kitchen for some water. As I fill my glass I notice a small amount of blood in the groove of my fingernail. Rico's blood.

'Lexi?'

I stick my hands under the tap. Scrub them clean. 'I'm fine.'

'I'm going to set up in your kitchen, work from here for a while.'

I turn around to frown at her. 'You don't need to do that.'

'You need to be kept an eye on. Doctor's orders. You're swaying on the spot. Go and rest.'

'You don't need to manage me,' I grumble and cop one of Rachael's bossy stares.

'I don't want to see you again for at least eight hours.'

'Fine.' I'm too tired and sore to argue so I stagger off to do as I'm told.

CHAPTER THIRTEEN

By the time Finn walked into the Homicide Unit at nine with an armload of coffees, he felt like he'd already put in a full day's work. He forced back a yawn as he reached the meeting room where the team were waiting and pushed through the glass door. 'Morning.'

He'd only just placed his tray down when a scrunched-up piece of paper bounced off his head.

'That's detention for you,' Linc said with a smirk. 'Late again.'

'Been up since three, have you?' Finn asked with a yawn. 'Because I have.'

'Thanks, Finn,' Cass said with a frown at the ball of paper. Cass was one of the few women Linc couldn't quite get wrapped around his finger, probably because most of his power over the women in his life came from sex appeal, and as Cass was well settled with a wife and child, she wasn't into him. 'Was it a call-out?'

'Yeah. So here's the thing. There was a murder up on the coast a few hours ago.'

'We've got *another* case?' Linc said with a groan. 'Surely one of the other teams can take it.'

'He was a police officer. The partner of a friend of mine,' Finn said. 'Lexi was lucky enough not to die but she copped a beating and her partner had his head smashed in. Died in her arms.'

'Lexi?' Cass said. 'As in the ex-prostitute vigilante?'

A shot of anger hit him. 'As in the woman who was not only vital in solving the Spider case but who risked her life to save my ten-year-old daughter from a sociopath bent on drugging, raping and murdering her. The one who's been through more hell in her life than you could dream up. The one who wouldn't sink low enough to judge another person based on a shitty start to life and what they had to do to survive.'

'Ah, yes, the smart one,' Linc said brightly, diluting the tension in the room.

'Shut up, Linc,' Cass said.

'Oh, look, she can talk with her foot in her mouth.'

'Okay.' Cass lifted her hands in truce. 'What are we attacking first?'

'Rachael's talking to Detective Slavek about the next steps. The two suspects are part of the Hamill family and have been dealing in the location, so this is going to be a joint investigation. Until we hear more, we'll continue with the Latimer case. Anything new?'

'I've got an update on the CCTV footage,' Linc said, pulling it up. 'No vision of the altercation, unfortunately. But we knew that. Cameras are pointed at the entry and exit points on the ground level. We can see the workers arriving around seven thirty, a lot of hard hats exiting and entering around lunchtime, fast forward to the end of the day and most of them can be seen leaving between three and five thirty. The only person who enters the site close to his estimated time of death is Jeremy Latimer himself.'

Finn took a look at the grainy black and white footage. 'So our murderer was on site since lunchtime at least.'

'Yeah.'

'That reduces the chance it was someone outside of the company. If our POI is an employee, he shouldn't be too difficult to track down.'

'You'd think, wouldn't you? Jump to a half-hour from the time Jeremy arrives and two of the three last workers on site leave, heads down in their phones, then a few minutes later this guy emerges, also head down, but fast and facing away as though he's deliberately dodging the cameras. We don't have faces for any of them.'

'Okay, so it's a process of elimination. Find out who was on site that day, cross-check them against those we can identify from the surveillance and figure out who's left. Do we have the employee files?'

'They just came in,' Cass said, 'along with Latimer's laptop. The employee files contain photos, so identifying the ones with the faces on screen shouldn't be a problem.'

'You could also try using the dimensions of that entry frame to get an approximate size of the guy we're looking for,' Finn said to Linc. 'And I want to talk to everyone who was working Friday afternoon regardless of whether they'd left before Latimer's arrival. We need to get a feel for what was going on in that workplace, especially any recent rivalries or altercations. Someone has to know something.'

'I'll find out, start making calls,' Linc said.

'Great. Where are we on forensics, Cass?'

'Steven's got a backup of post mortems to deal with but he's going to push Latimer up the list and try and get to him tomorrow. Initial forensic results taken from the crime scene should start trickling in by tomorrow afternoon or Tuesday morning if we're lucky.'

'Then let's get to work.'

'How many left?' Finn asked Linc as yet another Latimer employee left the construction office. Carole Latimer had allowed them to use it for interviews, but so far, every worker they'd spoken to had seemed more upset they might be out of a job than that their boss was dead. And on that point, no one seemed to know anything.

'Just one,' Linc said. He went to the doorway. 'Dale Morton?' Then, 'Please come in.'

'Thanks for coming,' Finn said.

'Yeah, great way to spend a Sunday arvo.'

'Sorry about that. We have a few quick questions and we'll let you get on your way, all right?'

'So Latto's dead and you wanna know if I know anything?'

Finn nodded. 'That's the gist of it.'

'I got to work at seven thirty as usual, went across the road for KFC at lunchtime, should have clocked out at three but the damn scaffolding wasn't cooperating and me and a mate had to hang back, change some over. There's been a few problems with it and because Latto was on site, I thought I'd mention it. So I was headed up from the floor below but when I reached the lift I could hear him having a go at someone on the floor above. Latto's pretty well known for his shit temper, so I reckoned it'd be better to leave it. No point copping the punch for someone else pissing him off.'

'Do you know who was with him?'

'Nah. Why would I? Anyway, me and my mate Cruz went to the pub instead.'

Linc shuffled through the paperwork and nodded, which told Finn the stories lined up.

'You say Latimer had a temper,' Finn said. 'Would you mind telling us a bit more about that?'

'Yeah, not much to tell. He was fine as long as you did the work. But if you slacked off or mouthed off too many times there was a good chance you'd be done. I've heard a few rumours about him knocking one or two workers on their arses over the years, but that's all. Nothing serious.'

'Were you one of those one or two, Mr Morton?'

'Huh? Nup.' Then his eyes widened. 'You don't think I knocked off Latto?'

'These are routine questions. So you didn't recognise the voice of the person he was arguing with?'

Morton shrugged. 'The radio was blaring. Makes it hard to tell, you know? Might have been the boss. Guess, thinking back, I assumed it was.'

'Mr Latimer isn't the boss?'

'Well, yeah, but he's Latto, the owner. He kinda swans in and out, keeps a bit of an eye on things. Our site boss is the project manager, Mark Bradley, he's the one in charge of running the build.'

'And what's Bradley like?'

'I've worked on builds with Bradley for coming on eight years. I woulda said he was mostly pretty chill. Fair. Not recently, but. He's been a bit stressed out, a bit mouthy at the boys. They've all been making jokes he needs a good shag, ya know?' He smiles but it drops when it's not returned.

'So he's been acting out of character for how long?'

'A couple of months, I suppose. Dunno if Latto was on his case about something but he's been uptight a lot. Don't go telling him I said nothing, though. I don't want to be getting in shit.'

'Of course not. Thanks for your time, Mr Morton. We'll be in touch if we have any more questions.'

Linc let him out and sat back down. 'Mark Bradley's the only POI that hasn't been identified leaving on CCTV.'

'Then we need to find Mark Bradley.'

CHAPTER FOURTEEN

The ache hits me first, the dull, then, as I move, not-so-dull throbbing that has me wondering what's going on. I open my eyes and squint against the daylight. The clock says it's close to four in the afternoon. What? A blissful moment of confusion then it all falls in on me again. Rico. Grief snatches the breath from my lungs as the memory floods back. I want to sink back under the covers and never come out. But that won't be happening. I can't catch Rico's killers from here.

I struggle to sit up and tell myself the soreness will work its way out as I move around. My face feels heavy and painful, but nothing is spinning. The nausea is gone. I do my best to shake off the dregs of sleep and the crying jag I hadn't been able to stave off last night when scenario after scenario had run through my head with a hundred different ways Rico's death could have been prevented, torturing me with what ifs until exhaustion had finally won out.

I take a few deep breaths, make them steady. I need to find the Hamill twins.

I sit on the edge of the bed for another minute while I toss possible strategies around in my head, then I move stiffly to the bathroom and allow myself a few minutes to stand under the hot spray of the shower and take in my bruises. When a plan begins to materialise I get out, get dressed and go into the office to boot up my devices. I'm steadier now, focused. I check on Lochie first and—yes! He's given me Jason's number. At least, the one linked to the phone he uses for making deals. I open my desk drawer and slip out the cheap prepaid phone I've designated for this purpose. I turn it on, think about what to say, then, satisfied with my plan, send Jason a message.

While I'm waiting for a reply I log in and out of the various online identities I'm using to collect dirt on the rest of the Hamills, swapping servers and bouncing my location around from place to place as an extra measure to ensure I'm not easily tracked.

A few of my involuntary informants are online, the sort that hang out in dark web chatrooms and forum sites, keeping each other up to date about rival dealers, dodgy police intel, arrests, releases, buyers and sellers. Deals are made, along with the odd gang-related death threat. The gossip is often gold. Today I've found some talk about a drug lab raid in Newcastle, some closer-to-home low-rung ice dealer copping a beating and a warning to a local graffiti group that the cops are closing in on them. It's nothing useful, nothing that gives me any hints as to where the twins might be.

I glance at the phone again. Jason's still not talking. 'Come on, fuckwit!' I mutter.

While I'm waiting, I decide to check in on his grandfather. I pull the phone labelled 'Raymond' out of my top drawer and turn it on. I've had a reply to my last message.

Benny Tillman

Am I supposed to know who that is? I turn off the phone again and google the name. There's a couple of news reports mentioning Benny Tillman's death. I click on the first one. TILLMAN SLAIN IN GRUESOME GANGLAND ATTACK. There's a photo of a human brick wall, bald head covered in tattoos. He's wearing a bikie jacket, jeans and the expression of a pissed-off Incredible Hulk. 'Mildly scary.' I read on. The fact someone, I'm gathering a Hamill someone, managed to take down this small planet, somehow containing him long enough to torture him before finishing him off, is kind of morbidly impressive. But what's it got to do with me? General 'leave us alone' threat?

I remotely log into the police network to see if I can get any further information, and oh—here we go. No, not so general. Tillman had considered himself some sort of glorified bounty hunter. Word had gotten around just prior to his murder that Debbie Reynolds had become his latest target. The police suspect Hamill involvement in the murder but, as usual, can't prove it. I check out the crime scene photos. Ew. Nasty. He'd lost a few fingers, some teeth. They'd gouged out an eye. Most of the rest of him wasn't very recognisable. The medical report found the fingers, teeth, one eye and a few other appendages had been removed prior to several more nasty events that had—eventually—led to his death. My stomach is churning. No matter who that guy was in life, it's hard not to feel for him.

Message received, Raymond. For a second, the image of me in the same position transfers from my mind to the screen. My stomach does a definite lurch.

'Don't be stupid.' I won't end up like that. I turn the phone back on.

One less competitor. You're making this easier for me. I send the message and switch off the phone.

Contacting Raymond and telling him that I intend on taking his family down piece by piece until he hands over Debbie has, up until now, left me with a gnawing worry in the pit of my stomach. I've been counting on the one million dollar police reward on Debbie's head and my ability to remain anonymous to open the field of potential suspects. But Rico's death has left me somehow numb to the risks. All I feel is angry, determined and like I can't get it done fast enough. This family has destroyed one too many lives. It's game on.

'What's all this?' Rachael says from the doorway.

I flinch in my seat. She's still here? Or is she back?

'Hi. Um, yeah.' I casually wave a hand at the walls. 'It's everything we had on Vaughn and Debbie before the Feds took over.'

'And some they've learnt since?' There's a question there, because she knows what I can do with a computer. But I'm not answering it.

You're not allowed to hack into or in any way spy on the Federal Police and I'm not incriminating myself more than these walls already have.

'Only if they've learnt it since I did.'

Rachael smiles at that as she scans a wall. I take the opportunity to slip the phone back into the drawer. Now is not the time to freak her out again.

'This is an incredible amount of work.'

'I don't want to miss anything.'

'Clearly.' Then, her attention back on me, she says, 'How are you feeling?'

'Fine.'

'You'll get a call in the next couple of days from the police psych offering you some counselling. You should—'

'You never told me what happened in Canberra.' I change the subject. I'm not steady enough to talk about Rico yet, and there's no way in hell I'm talking to some police psychologist.

'There's not much to tell,' she says. She steps to the pyramid, studies it. 'So what's with all this general Hamill research?'

'I've been familiarising myself with the family. We know they're the most likely to know where Debbie is. Find Debbie, find Vaughn. So I'm doing what I do—scraping up as much on them as I can, hoping it will lead to something useful.'

'Given that's the case—' she shoots me one of her direct stares, '—did you know who you were going after the first time you went into that tunnel?'

I shake my head. 'I put some feelers out online to find out who bashed Constable Hadley. General consensus was it was two guys who usually sell meth by the tracks down at Woy Woy. I did also know the Hamill twins were dealing somewhere on the coast, but not where. The guy I met online who was buying from them was nervous about telling me and once you push these guys too hard or seem too interested, they bolt—or come looking for you. So, no, I didn't know for sure it was them until Aden demanded to know where Jason was during the arrest.'

Rachael processes that. 'Okay. So why have you put them all in a pyramid?'

'To get a handle on the structure of their organisation.'

'At the top you've put Raymond. Makes sense. Second row ... Lena, Raymond's wife, and Adam, his son. Why this one son on this line?'

'Because Adam's second-in-command. He answers to his parents. Everyone else answers to him.'

'How do you know that?'

'It's common knowledge to anyone who deals with them.'

'And you've made contacts who deal with them.'

'Tentative ones, yeah, like the guy who tipped me off about the twins.'

'Okay, so third row contains Raymond's other sons Karl, Robert and ... Elias.'

I'm impressed. 'I didn't realise you knew so much about the Hamills.'

Rachael's brow lifts. 'I have to find those twins, so I've been taking a more detailed look into the family while you've been resting. Fourth row, the grandkids Jason and Aden, and Josie. That's Robert's daughter, right?'

'Yeah.'

'And these other people on four? They're not Hamills.'

'Hamill employees. Names often associated with the brothers. The last row below are lower-level associates of one sort or another. Minor dealers, mostly. Red crosses mean they're out. Either dead or locked up.'

Rachael nods slowly, taking the spare seat in the corner while still studying the board. 'There's a few missing. Wives, cousins ...'

'I'm only interested in their core structure. The main players who are most likely to have contact with Debbie.'

'Does the drug squad have this information?'

'I wouldn't have a clue. I'm just a lowly probationary constable on general duties, remember? All this is personal research. Aside from anything else, I need those Hamill associates on the streets for now. They're feeding me useful information.'

'Hmm. And the grand plan is to do what with all this? Hope someone will give something away?' Her eyes return to the walls, to my monitor, my face.

'The grand plan is to force the Hamills into giving up Debbie.'

'How?'

'By finding every piece of dirt I can on everyone on the pyramid so we can take them out from the bottom up. I want to kick the legs out from under their organisation until King Raymond has nothing left to bargain with. Except Debbie.'

'I get it. But all this is unnecessary. The Drugs and Firearms Squad are working with the Organised Crime Squad on the Hamills. The Federal Police are handling Debbie and Vaughn.'

'Yeah and every day Vaughn's out there, another kid is getting hurt or killed for profit. Are the Feds even close?'

'They're running an outstanding investigation. They're making good progress, Lexi. Trust me.'

'What progress?'

Her face tightens slightly as she turns around. 'Detective Slavek and I were invited down there simply to answer questions. We were privy to bits and pieces of information that enabled us to collaborate with them on the best way to move forward. But until it's made official, that information has to remain confidential.'

Rachael's shutting me out? I admit I'm probably a bit hair-trigger this afternoon but it pisses me off. 'When it's official? When the best chance I have of finding them has already been blown?'

'Lexi,' Rachael says as though pandering to a sulking toddler. 'Have a bit of faith in the rest of us good guys, okay?'

I sigh because she's right and I probably deserved the tone. I know she most likely wants to tell me but can't. That her integrity is at stake; that she could lose her job.

'Yeah, of course. Sorry,' I say. 'I'm just a bit raw, I guess.'

'You've been through a hell of a traumatic event. You haven't even had time to begin processing that yet and you're trying to catch Rico's killer, take down a major organised crime family and bring an international felon to justice on your own.'

I manage a smile. 'So what's your point? I'm not going to sit here doing nothing. I'll go insane.'

Rachael smiles too and gets to her feet. 'Okay, what you do with your spare time is up to you. If you want to spend it gathering intel on the Hamills, then go for it. But I expect you'll hand over anything useful you find so I can share it with the relevant teams. You're not a one-woman show anymore.'

'Got it.' I push myself out of my chair and the pain that grabs me in the ribs has me hissing in a breath. I follow Rachael out to the kitchen, lean on the counter and wait for the aching to calm down. Rachael pours me a glass of water and places it on my table along with my painkillers.

I gingerly sit. 'Thanks.'

'I'm sorry I can't talk to you about the Federal Police investigation,' she says, sitting opposite. Rachael's laptop and a bunch of paperwork is spread out between us, a cold coffee mug and phone beside it. She must have been here the whole time. 'But I can fill you in on ours. We sent some specialist police around to talk to Elias and his wife, Leila, about Jason and Aden. Unsurprisingly, the family isn't feeling very cooperative today. They're not letting us in and they're not telling us where the twins are.'

'Do you think they made it home?'

Rachael shakes her head. 'There's been a car parked outside the residence since last night. If either boy tries to get in there, we'll pick them up, but we believe they're still up here on the coast somewhere, hiding. They're likely lying low until all this calms down.'

'Well, that's something.'

'You should go lie down again.'

'No, what I need is a coffee. I've got stuff to do.'

'Such as?'

'I have to go pay an old friend a visit.'

'Today? Why?'

'Because I feel like a catch-up? *And*,' I add because she's clearly waiting for the rest of it, 'it just so happens that if anyone knows where Jason and Aden are, this old friend will.'

I'm waiting for the expected lecture so I'm surprised when she simply says, 'You should eat something first.'

The thought of food has my stomach somersaulting. 'Maybe later.' I eye her suspiciously. 'No lecture about staying out of it? Resting? Nothing at all?'

'No law against you visiting an old friend.' Rachael grabs her keys. 'We'll get you that coffee—and food—on the way. Where am I taking you?'

I don't know what's gotten into her, but I'm not going to argue. 'Wyoming. But you can park near Gosford Station and I'll walk from there.'

'Why?'

'Because this friend doesn't like cops.'

'And you're asking me to let you go in alone. In your current state.'

'He likes me,' I reassure her.

Rachael's eyes roll as she heads for the door. 'Let's go.'

'Don't know 'em. Nup.'

It was the answer I'd been expecting, but I wasn't giving up yet. Juicey was known as such for his habit of swallowing, sniffing and injecting anything he could get his hands on. He knows everyone in the business and often does them favours in return for his next hit, so it made sense to see him first. I wouldn't like to guess how old he is; he's looked fiftysomething forever. Jamaican by birth, he's got a scrawny, greying Rastafarian thing going on, his Bob Marley shirt as old as he is and his impressive dreadlocks partially covered by some sort of brightly coloured crocheted headwear. His residence is a dingy granny flat at the back of a row of old houses I'm not surprised to see are set for demolition, behind an out-of-business used car dealership. I briefly wonder where he'll go when they bulldoze the place. I can't picture him anywhere else.

'Come on, Juicey,' I beg, leaning against the wall because I don't want to risk sitting on the ancient, smelly lounge.

'Where you been all this time, anyways?' he asks, lighting a cigarette.

'Around. Surviving.'

'I reckon I remember you stuck to pot. Why you after meth?'

I hadn't mentioned which drug the teens were selling, so now I know he's holding out on me. 'I'm not after the meth, I'm trying to find the guys selling it.'

'What for?'

I wince at the movement of pulling my wallet out of my pocket. As I shuffle through, a twenty-dollar note peeks out the top, joined by another, then another. I see Juicey's head lift to get a better look. 'I need to talk to them.'

'Who you workin' for?'

'Me.'

'That why you come in here all beaten up? C'mon, who put you up to it?'

'Okay, you want to know why I want them, because this,' I say, indicating to my face, 'is their fault.'

'So you're selling for someone else? They've scared a few people off with those sorts of bruises lately. I don't need to go getting involved in no turf wars. I'm not goin' back to jail. You heard that guy Lochie that was workin' for 'em got a target on his head?'

Panic shoots through me. 'No. Why?'

''Cause he wanted out and was told no. Next thing the twins are sprung. Hamills don't like it. Reckon he tipped off the cops. I'm not going back to jail for killin' no one else. Not even to save his life. That's what I told him when he came round wantin' help. Did give him an address to squat at—wanna help a bit, ya know? He's a nice kid. But he was talkin' 'bout running to the cops for protection. Kinda proves he's guilty. Dead for sure now if the cops don't do somethin' about makin' him disappear.'

Fuck. I hope he's okay. 'You don't need to be involved in anything.' I count out a hundred, wave it at him. 'I was never here.'

He snatches the cash, takes another look at the pictures I brought with me of the twins and their tag. 'Dunno where the twins are. But the tags don't belong to them. That's just advertisin'.'

'Advertising?' As he's still staring at my wallet, I pull out some more cash.

'Where you can pick up the meth. Hamills' cook's been doin' this new thing, 'cause competition round here's been gettin' a bit tough. So their dealers use this tag to let buyers know where to come get Crystal Gold. You hang round that spot and you're wearin' somethin' red, T-shirt, bracelet, bandana—anything—they're gonna approach you. You show 'em the cash, you get the goods.'

'Wait. The Hamills have men dealing this stuff all over the coast?'

'Oh, yeah. The twins do the peninsula. Someone else got the north run. Though I heard that's not been goin' so well the last coupla weeks. Jason and Aden had to go up there last week then nearly got caught by some cop. Had to rough him up a bit.'

That's why the tags had been found from one end of the coast to the other. It suddenly made so much more sense. 'You sure you don't know where they are right now?'

'Nah. But it shouldn't be too hard to find out,' he says, staring at my wallet again.

'Thanks,' I say, shoving another fifty at him. 'And hey, there's more where that came from if you can track them down for me.' I shudder a bit on the inside as he snatches at the rest of my grocery money. 'You got somewhere to go when they knock this place down?'

'Yeah,' he says with another long draw on his smoke. 'Got that place I told Lochie about, or Millsey's got a spot for me swag at the old packing house if I need it.' He's staring at the cash like it's Christmas. I hope it's not all in his arm before nightfall or he won't be finding anyone.

'Soon as you track them down, let me know, yeah? You got a phone?'

He hesitates. 'Got access to one.'

'Great.' I spot a Keno pencil and scrawl down one of my numbers on the back of a nearby magazine.

'It'll cost ya another five hundred. And don't come runnin' back here when they're after your head. And no telling tales or it'll be me that comes after ya.'

'Yeah, yeah, you old softie. Thanks.'

I walk down the road and head for Rachael's car, but in a round-the-block way to make sure he's not snooping and following me. As I limp along I send Lochie a message. Unless the cops have got him safe somewhere he's going to need urgent help.

When I finally reach Rachael's car I take one more glance around before manoeuvring myself into the passenger seat.

'How'd you go?' she asks, obviously relieved to see me.

'The tags are about the meth, not the brothers. They're an advertisement for a drug they're producing called Crystal Gold. I've heard a bit about it online, just hadn't made the connection. There's at least one other major dealer working for the Hamills who's responsible for the north end of the coast. He and the twins are supplying the smaller dealers, and the tags let people know where to buy.'

'So it's a big operation. I was under the impression the Hamills imported their drugs.'

'So what next?'

'I drop you home. I went along with this because we both know you would have gone the moment I left, but from now on you stay home and rest. Deal?'

'Deal,' I agree easily enough. I have plenty of work to do from there.

'I'm going to take this information back to headquarters, pass it on to the drug squad and make sure my team are on top of taking over Rico's murder.'

'Great. Um ... can you look into someone for me?'

'Sure. Who?'

'That guy I was telling you about that got me the info on the twins has gotten himself into trouble with the Hamills. He was trying to get out and it wasn't going well. Apparently he went to see the local cops but I don't know what happened after that and I can't reach him. If he's back on the street with the Hamills looking for him, that's about as bad as it gets and I need to help him.'

'What's his name?'

'Lochie Ballard.'

Rachael notes the name down. 'I'll see what I can find out.'

CHAPTER FIFTEEN

Monday, March 7

'Burns should have informed us,' Detective Inspector Craig Slavek told Rachael. His dark hair sat straight up off his face, like he'd shoved his hand through it more than once that day, the usually mild expression in his dark eyes replaced by glinting annoyance. 'You had every reason to have a go at him. I pointed that out when he called yesterday to tell me why he was right and you were wrong.'

'That'll make you about as popular as me,' Rachael said, sitting back in her chair.

'He was trying to cover his arse, plain and simple. He's a good cop, but he made a bad call. He'll have to wear it.'

'Agreed. I think he underestimated the Hamills. If our information is correct, Jason and Aden were dealing on the southern end of the coast and another POI is handling the northern end. The product is called Crystal Gold and the tags associated with selling points have been located from one end of the coast to the other.'

'We knew about the Crystal Gold. We're on it. But you found all this out how?'

'Lexi has a contact. A few, I think. She hasn't stopped looking for Vaughn and Reynolds since the task force was put on hold. She's not letting it go.'

Craig grinned. 'She really is a Rachael Langley protégée.'

'Oh, no. Lexi Winter is very definitely her own person.'

'She's got some impressive computer skills. I ran into her at the academy. So what's she thinking?'

'She's looking for Debbie Reynolds for the same reason everyone else is. If she finds Reynolds, she'll find Vaughn. Take a look at this.' Rachael opened her phone and showed Craig a photo she'd taken of Lexi's pyramid.

Craig examined the photo. 'She's got a good take on the Hamill hierarchy. She put all this together herself?'

'Yeah.'

'Mind sending me this? I'll check it against what we have.'

'Sure. The crossed-out names are dead or in custody. Know any of the others?'

'You mean other than the Hamills? Yeah. A couple.' He increased the image size over some names. 'This Lochie fellow spoke to a couple of my officers about the Hamills.'

'That answers my next question. Lexi was hoping to find out what happened to him.'

'Local cops brought him down saying he had information and wanted witness protection. We talked to him. He said he knew the twins were dealing meth and where, but courtesy of Lexi, we already knew that and there wasn't anything else of the sort of value that warranted witness protection so we cut him loose. Wrong move?'

'I have no idea.'

'It's just that there's been a bit of pressure on the Hamills, whispers going around that someone's causing them some trouble. That's not unusual, but this time they're jumpy about it. He didn't seem the type to be causing it.'

'You think it's because of the million-dollar reward we put on their daughter?'

'It's possible. There's been a couple of unscheduled family meetings recently and some major cracking down on security.' He went back to studying the pyramid. 'This guy here, Lee Crouse, is interesting. We suspected Hamill involvement but his death was put down to a failed robbery on a bikie gang member. I wouldn't mind chatting to Lexi about him. This one over here that she has down as Crowley, is Ray Crowland. He was found dead yesterday with a bullet in his head and enough nasty injuries to suggest he was tortured before being shot. One of the other homicide teams handled it, passed it on when his name popped up in our database.'

'Lexi mustn't know about Crowley yet. He's not crossed off.'

'A few more of these men I don't know. Bring her in. We'll compare notes.'

'She's having some time off. It might not be for a few days. And ...'

'And?'

'I refused to discuss my information on the Feds' case,' Rachael admitted. 'I'm not sure how helpful she'll feel like being.'

'That's not your choice to make; she knows that.' The amusement in his eyes surprised her. 'But if she doesn't want to come in and talk to me, tell her to let it go.'

'Really? Why?'

His grin just got bigger. 'Never mind. If anything comes up on the twins, or there's any chatter about the murder, I'll be in touch.'

'Thanks. I sent Cass and Linc down to collaborate with the local detectives over Rico's death earlier this morning because I wanted to attend the autopsy. The local detectives have been doing everything they can, but you know what it's like. No one dobs, no one opens their mouth when it comes to the Hamills. And there's no witnesses, no luck with any CCTV. We found the murder weapon at the scene but there's no prints. We're still waiting on forensics to see if anything turns up for DNA.'

Craig got out of his chair. 'Don't stress. You'll crack it, and I understand Lexi's not going to be ready to go back to work yet, but I really would like to have a quick, informal chat to her as soon as she's up to it. The Hamills have been getting away with too much for too long. This could be a real chance to bring down a few more members of the state's number one crime family.'

She frowned. 'But didn't you just tell me to let it go if she didn't want to come in?'

He chuckled, confusing her further. 'No, I told you to *tell* her to let it go.'

Finn knocked on the door. 'Sorry, Craig. Rach, have you got a minute?'

'She does,' Craig said, stepping to the doorway. 'I'll let you get back to it.'

She followed Craig's departure with a quizzical look.

'How'd the autopsy go?' Finn asked, taking a seat.

'No surprises. Massive head trauma,' she said. 'Looks like our POI waited for Rico to walk out of the tunnel then attacked him from behind. There was some serious force attached to the blows. Steven said the first blow cracked his skull, the second and third blows left him no chance of survival.'

'Lexi said Jason Hamill had threatened to bash Rico's head in, but why kill him?'

'I guess they didn't want to risk him warning Lexi. Besides, they're Hamills. They're not known for empathy.'

'And the catch-up with Craig?'

'He's pissed off Burns didn't let him know about the twins. He sent a couple of his guys who regularly deal with the Hamills out to try to talk to them again. He believes Leila and Elias are inside but they're not showing their faces. They got their lawyer to provide a statement to the fact they don't know where the boys are. He hasn't issued a search warrant because he's ninety-nine per cent sure the boys aren't in there, and the shitstorm it'd cause would be a nightmare, but he's got twenty-four-hour surveillance on the property and anyone coming and going.'

'Right.'

She stood and stretched her arms, rolled her shoulders. 'So, the Latimer case. I hear you've got a suspect?'

'Actually that's why I came in. Between the CCTV and staff interviews we've worked out our likely POI is Mark Bradley, the project manager. He's married to a Kirsten Bradley. His residential address is a property owned by Kirsten's mother in Blue Haven. No luck contacting either of them on their mobiles, or the home's landline, so I'm going to run out there this afternoon before heading home, check it out.'

Rachael grabbed her bag. 'I'll come with you. I have to stop by Lexi's again and try to convince her to talk to the drug squad.'

Finn looked surprised. 'I'm sure she'd be keen to be involved ... No?' he asked at the look she sent him as they reached the elevators.

'Oh, she's keen to be involved all right. You should see what she's got on the Hamills. But she's not happy I couldn't let her know what the Feds shared and you know how she likes to work on her own. Besides, I'm trying to get her to take at least a few days to recover.'

'How was she feeling yesterday?'

'My definition? The full emotional and physical wreck. Hers? Fine. She had me run her out to some dodgy spot in Wyoming. Except I had to wait a couple of k's down the road in the car because her friend doesn't like cops. She limped the entire distance, pumped up on painkillers. She survived and the guy gave her some good info on the Hamill twins, so overall it was a success. I'm worried about her though. She's living on adrenaline and has all these big plans for taking down the Hamills.'

'She was never going to fall in a heap. That's not Lexi. Hopefully a few sessions with the police psychologist will— She's not going to do it, is she?'

'How about *you* try and make her go?'

'Bad idea.' His phone rang as they stepped into the lift and he answered on speaker. 'Yeah, Linc, what's up?'

'There's some problem out at the construction site. A building inspector is demanding access.'

'Demanding?'

Rachael caught Finn's questioning glance and nodded.

'All right, we'll sort it out.' Finn ended the call. 'I wonder what could be so important?'

'*If* it's important,' she answered. 'This guy wouldn't want to be wasting our time.'

It took forty minutes to reach the site and the man Rachael assumed was the inspector didn't look impressed. The security guard, however, looked nothing but relieved.

'Inspector Rachael Langley,' she said. The site inspector straightened from where he'd been leaning on his car, extending his hand for the shake. 'This is Sergeant Finn Carson. What can we do for you, Mr?'

'Ellis. From the Australian Building and Construction Commission.' He flicked open his wallet and flashed his credentials. 'I'm attempting to follow up on a complaint about workplace safety.'

She exchanged glances with Finn. They'd been dragged out to the building site for this? 'I'm sure you'll understand, Mr Ellis, that a murder investigation takes precedence over a building inspection.'

'It has to do with the scaffolding, inspector. We believe the company may deliberately have been using inferior materials on site. Your victim fell through and was impaled on scaffolding, wasn't he?'

Gotta love the news. 'I'm afraid we can't share the exact details of the investigation at this point, Mr Ellis.'

'Where did this complaint about the scaffolding come from?' Finn asked.

'I couldn't possibly say.'

'Excuse me?' Finn asked sharply.

Ellis began to look uncomfortable. 'It's against regulations. But in any case, I really don't know. You'd have to contact the office. They may or may not be able to help you, due to our privacy act. I'm simply carrying out instructions.'

'Okay, then perhaps you could contact the complainant and have them call me. If they refuse, I'll go through a judge and have them talk to me anyway. How's that sound?'

'Like a much better idea from the perspective of me keeping my job. So can I go in?'

Finn glanced at Rachael.

She considered the request, decided the information could prove important enough to warrant it. 'Okay. Take him up.'

'All right then,' Finn told Ellis. 'We'll head up on the condition you stay clear of the taped-off areas and don't touch anything.'

'No problem.'

Rachael watched from the ground as photographs and notes were taken on each level before both men headed back to the ground, where the contents of a shipping container were examined.

'Thank you, detective, that's all I need,' Ellis said when he was finished.

'Did you find anything?' she asked.

'I have to check my findings against the specific complaint before I can tell you for certain, detective. In the meantime, I'll contact the complainant and let them know you've requested their assistance.'

'Thanks.'

Ellis nodded and went back to his car.

'Could he have been less helpful?' Finn said.

'He needs to keep his job. There's a line, I guess. If we don't hear from the company by tomorrow we'll chase it up. If there is something illegal going on here, we don't want to miss it. For all we know, inferior scaffolding could be what got Latimer killed.'

'Yeah.'

'Come on, we still need to get to Kirsten Bradley's house.'

CHAPTER SIXTEEN

'You're only telling me this now?' My sister Bailee is on the phone and she's pissed off I didn't tell her about Rico's death straight away. 'You should have called me from the hospital!'

'Why? There was nothing you could do. It was all police and stuff. Then I needed some time to just hang at home and *not* talk about it for a while. Besides, I know you had your friend's hen's night on. I'm fine, honestly.'

'You might not be if I could get my hands on you. I'm coming around later to see for myself how *fine* you are. I'll have to bring the kids.'

'I'll be here,' I promise. The phone on the table beside my elbow pings and I take a hopeful look. Jason has replied to my message. I snatch it up. 'I have to go; that ping was work.'

'I thought you were having time off?'

'Yeah, which is why I'm home getting messages. See ya!' I end the call before she carries on and check the message.

None till Friday.

So they're still dealing? So much for hiding out. These Hamills seem to think they're invincible. But what if the cops get too close before Friday rocks around and they bolt? I don't like it. I put some pressure on.

Come on, man. I'm desperate! I type, my leg jiggling impatiently while I wait for an answer.

You'll have to wait.

Fuck that. *If I want to keep Lochie's clients I need this! I was at the pickup point last time and you never showed!*

Yeah, well. Something came up.

Yeah, it was Rico and me, you arsehole. I see Rico lying on those tracks, his head a mess. The anger spurs on my resolve. I'm going to catch these arseholes. *This* is the best way to deal with Rico's death. Not by talking to police psychologists and discussing feelings, but by keeping things moving. By making the Hamills pay.

I'll pay double! I have the cash. Look. I attach a photo of a shoebox full of bundled cash Dawny left me for emergencies. I make it tiny, so he has to click on it in order to see it properly. As soon as he does, the spyware I attached to the photo goes to work, copying files from his phone and sharing them with my computer. The Hamills use a special messaging app for all this stuff, so the police can't see what's going on if they get hold of their phones, but I cracked that months ago.

As I take a look at the content, another minute ticks by without a response. Then, *Hold on.*

I wait while he sends a message to someone simply saved as D, before also forwarding mine. Another window pops open on my screen as my photo attachment is opened a second time. 'Yes!' I murmur happily as files from the second phone upload. It doesn't take long for me to realise that this phone belongs to his father, Elias; D must be for Dad. Jason's asking him what to do. I save everything to go through as soon as I have time.

Jason is told to make the meeting for three thirty, to message the other clients for four. Make it worthwhile. He's going to hit me up for double then sell to his other regulars anyway. Who cares.

Okay, Wednesday morning. Three thirty. Same place, Jason confirms.

Perfect. I'm going to have these little bastards back behind bars before the end of the week and I can now link Elias to the Crystal Gold business.

I've been doing more digging. For a while it was popular to dye meth blue due to a rumour largely started by a television show that stated the blue stuff was more pure. However, pure meth isn't blue. When it's totally without contaminants, it's colourless. Science aside, the blue trend died down after a lot of people had less than impressive highs.

But from the chatter around this gold stuff, it's the best on the market. I've got to surmise it's only a matter of time until every meth cook out there adds the same food colouring to whatever contaminated crap they're selling and the gold trend dies too. Maybe I should start a pool on what colour will take over.

Thanks.

You don't have the cash, you die.

Won't be a problem.

'I'm gonna get them, Rico,' I murmur, picking up my phone to call Rachael. I get her voicemail so I let her know I need to talk to her. I'm not putting anything more specific in a message.

I check Raymond's phone next. I forgot to check it after snapping at Rachael yesterday. Stupid. Under my taunt about having one less competitor Raymond has typed: *Four. They all thought they were smart. They were all just like you. Now they're dead.*

He's had four other people killed for trying to track down Debbie? He's got to be making that up, but ... what's he so worried about? They're all poking around here and she's in hiding overseas. Or is she? Could she be back? Coming back? Could that be it?

Something about his words stick in my head. My eyes move to the image of Vaughn on the wall. Vaughn had prided himself on being smart. His image blurs into a memory.

Sharp, burning pain sets fire to my scalp as my head is jerked back by my hair. 'You think you can outsmart me? You think you're smarter than I am?'

I can see the flashing of coloured lights bounce faintly off the fence, then turn brighter as the sirens get louder. As he taunts me, he pulls my hair back even harder. The words in my ear are hazy compared to the excruciating pain.

His breath is hot against my cold face, his beard scratches my ear. 'I know everything you do. Always. Don't ever think you can outsmart me.' He uses his grip on my hair to catapult me into the brick wall. 'I'm smarter.'

I shake myself out of it. Raymond had been Vaughn's boss and mentor before he went to prison and met the Spider. I suppose it makes sense they're equally as vain and brutal. I'm guessing those four he had killed all ended up much like Benny Tillman. I hadn't really considered there'd be much competition. But having others out there is all the better. Too much pressure might mean protecting Debbie is no longer worth it.

I decide I may as well not waste any time diving in. With a few keystrokes, Elias's whole criminal world opens in front of my eyes. Too easy. Though I guess, as it's taken a year to get to this point, it hasn't been *that* easy.

It's obvious this phone is used for business only. The contacts list is short, but interesting and—yes! Adam's number is listed. The phone hierarchy seems to loosely mimic my pyramid. Each rung on the ladder only has a contact for another contact one step above them. Jason has his father, Elias has Adam. I wonder if I can use Elias to contact him. Whether he, too, would be stupid enough to open a photo file.

Knocking drags me away from the computer and I'm not impressed. I'm on a roll and I hate being interrupted when I'm making progress.

It's Rachael.

'What, did you teleport?' I ask as I open the door. Finn is behind her. 'Hi.'

'We're on our way to check out a location on another case. I was on the phone when you rang, got your message.'

'Want a coffee?'

'Maybe just a cold water. Thanks.'

Finn's looking at me as though I might be about to burst into tears or something.

'I'm fine, thanks,' I say, and walk to the fridge to pull a jug from the shelf.

'It would be perfectly reasonable not to be.'

I ignore the comment and pour the water into two glasses before carrying them to the table. 'You may as well sit,' I add, earning a smirk and a 'gee, thanks' from Finn.

'I spoke to a friend in the drug squad about your pyramid,' Rachael tells me, taking a glass.

'Thought you might,' I reply, not really surprised.

'And about Lochie.'

'And?' I ask nervously.

'He spoke to the police, but they turned him loose. He didn't have anything strong enough for witness protection.'

'They what? Rachael, he needs to be off the streets!'

'I didn't make that decision. But find him and I'll see what I can do. And there was another guy from your bottom row ...' Rachael scrolls through her phone. 'Crowley. He was murdered yesterday, so you can cross him off.'

'I heard he was sampling a bit much of the merch. Maybe that did it.' But my mind is on Lochie. Where is he? At the squat Juicey mentioned? How am I going to find out where that is?

'And another on your bottom row, Lee Crouse. His death doesn't appear to be related to the Hamills.'

I rub my fingers across my eyes. Focus. 'Yeah. The break and enter gone wrong conclusion is bullshit.'

'Catch me up?' Finn asks.

'Underground chatter is Karl Hamill sent Lee in with another standover man to collect drug money and their bikie victim fought back—put a hole in the poor kid.'

'You knew him?' Finn asks.

'Only online. He was okay.'

'He was working for the Hamills,' Finn says as though that in itself was enough to question my read of him.

'That doesn't mean he deserved to die!'

'I'm not saying he did,' Finn said reasonably, 'but he got himself into it, right? He knew what he was doing was wrong.'

'Don't go there,' I growl. 'I've heard it all before. They're lowlifes, bottom feeders, pond scum. Whatever. I know some do this shit because that's exactly what they are. But I've been talking to a lot of these guys for months and the majority of the ones I've befriended aren't bad people. The Hamills infiltrate high schools, universities, clubs, they gatecrash parties and they pass out free meth so these kids become hooked, become dependent on it. Then they get them to break the law for a regular supply, to deal or whatever. These kids are in over their heads, their lives ruined before they have a chance to figure out how it's all happened. If they try to leave or don't do what they're told, they're dead.'

'And that's what you're worried will happen to Lochie?' Rachael asks.

I nod. Sigh. 'Lochie was introduced to meth last year at a uni party by a Hamill arsehole posing as a student. He was studying hard, tired, was told a few hits wouldn't hook him, just give him a boost to get all that study done. He didn't have many friends and this arsehole pretended to be the best one he'd ever had. He was hooked in no time, then they cut his supply, forced him to start dealing for it. He was a smart, friendly, happy eighteen-year-old university student one minute, a meth-addicted Hamill slave the next. His parents found him one night, comatose in a gutter outside Woy Woy pub close to his dealing post. It took months at a residential facility to get him through detox. He was home two days and the Hamills found him, beat the shit out of him and pumped that shit straight back into him, threatened all sorts of things if he didn't keep dealing. With the twins locked up, he thought he could make a break for it, but then we let them go and he's petrified what they'll do if they track him down. I told him to go to the police. He was scared they'd lock him up but he trusted me enough to do it. Now you're telling me they turned him away.'

'Okay, that's—I take it back,' Finn says with more sympathy.

The helpless anger rises in my stomach again. 'It has to stop. These people are monsters.'

'There's a lot of people working on that,' Rachael reminds me. 'We need to work on finding Jason and Aden.'

'Yeah, done that,' I tell them.

Rachael's glass stalls at her lips. 'What? Where?'

'I've got them pinned down for a meeting on Wednesday morning, early am. That's why I called you.'

'That's close.' I can see Rachael's mind ticking over the details. 'How'd you do it?'

'Jason thinks I'm keen to take over from Lochie. I sent him a message telling him I needed meth ASAP. He finally got back to me just before I called you and gave me a when.'

'You have his phone number?' Finn asks.

'I have *a* phone number for him.'

'Why didn't you say something? We could have tracked it.'

'Well, I would never have thought of that,' I say, widening my eyes in mock astonishment. 'The phone's never on long enough.'

'But you've been in direct contact with Jason,' Rachael presses. 'Digging into their lives is one thing, but contacting them, engaging with them, that's something else entirely.'

'Damn straight it is, and much more efficient.' Then at her stricken look, I say, 'Don't stress! I didn't exactly invite them over for coffee. I'm working under multiple aliases and taking every precaution. Besides, you said that if I wanted to continue my little investigation into the Hamills while being forced to take this time off, that was fine and you'd appreciate it if I shared anything useful. Which I am. So you're welcome. I mean, I'm not quite handing the twins to you on a silver platter but it's pretty damn close.'

Finn clears his throat. 'And you said she wouldn't want to—' Rachael's glare shuts him up.

'Okay,' Rachael says, expelling a long breath, 'okay, you win. For now. We can make this work. I'll take this information back to headquarters, then first thing in the morning you can talk to a friend of mine who's working on the Hamill case. Not to work the case,' she warns, 'just to fill him in on the details.' She drains her glass and checks her watch. 'We have to get going. We're chasing another investigation.' She looks at Finn, who nods and gets to his feet.

I follow them to the front door. 'Good luck.'

'Thanks. I'll pick you up at seven. Don't talk to any more Hamills until we sort this out tomorrow.'

CHAPTER SEVENTEEN

'You really told Lexi she could do her own investigation into the Hamills?' Finn asked Rachael as he guided the car through a warren of suburban streets on their way to the Bradley home.

'I thought she was just information gathering. I thought it would give her something to do to take her mind off Rico's murder and keep her safely hidden away while she recovered. I certainly didn't realise she was a couple of texts away from doing business with them!'

'I don't know how you could have possibly believed any of those things.'

'Yes, I should know better. But under the circumstances I thought a bit of autonomy would be okay ... as long as she was staying put and sharing.'

'Staying put being your main objective,' he guessed, and turned off the main road into a residential area where a mix of weatherboard and brick homes sat quietly, bordered by bushland.

'Should be the next street on the left,' she said.

'Got it.' His phone sounded so he hit the bluetooth connection. 'Carson.'

'Detective?'

'Sorry, yes, can I help you?'

'My name is Gavin Westlock from Newborne Construction. I was asked to give you a call regarding my complaint against Latimer Developments.'

'Ah ... yes. Thanks for calling.'

'I was under the impression I wasn't given a choice.'

'Well, I appreciate you not making us chase you up.'

'The complaint was made over their use of unsafe building materials. You see, the scaffolding is the former property of Newborne. Without bogging you down in too much detail, we purchased the scaffolding as T6—6061 aluminium, the strongest, most suitable aluminium for scaffolding. However, this is not what was provided. The aluminium we received was an inferior grade unsuitable to comply with Australian safety standards. After a lengthy battle with the international company involved, they refunded us and I later found out through a mutual contractor that Latimer Developments were using the same scaffolding on one of their sites.'

'So you're suggesting Latimer purchased and used that scaffolding on the Hornsby worksite knowing it was an inferior grade of aluminium?'

'I know it. I went over there on Friday morning to take a look. They were unloading more scaffolding from one of the shipping containers marked with the same company name and order number.'

'Did you approach Mr Latimer about this?'

'I called him Friday afternoon after Mark Bradley caught me poking around and threatened me. Jeremy didn't answer so I left a message stating my concerns. I don't bow to threats, detective, which is why I then contacted the ABCC. They're putting their workers' lives at risk. I might add that the ABCC have confirmed that I was correct.'

'Did you know Latimer very well?'

'Only in so much as competitors know of each other. We rub shoulders occasionally.'

'How would you describe him?'

'A careful man, with a very good head for making a profit.'

'One who'd deliberately cut corners?'

'If he did, he was generally much better at covering his tracks. I was honestly surprised he was using that scaffolding.'

'And what about the manager, Mark Bradley?'

'I'm afraid I haven't had any prior dealings with him. But judging from his attitude, I wouldn't be surprised if he cut corners wherever he could. My suggestion would be to put some of their other construction projects under a microscope. That will tell you more than I can.'

'I might just do that, thanks. We appreciate your time.' Finn ended the call. 'Looks like we need to do some digging into Latimer Developments.'

'If Bradley had purchased the inferior scaffolding without Latimer knowing, then Westlock complained to Latimer, that could have caused friction. Possibly the altercation that killed him.'

'Solid possibility.'

'There's the house. It's the white one on the right.'

Finn pulled the car over and they got out. The house was a modest single-storey residence backing onto Wallarah Creek. An easy-care garden was neat and tidy and surrounded by a simple black rail fence.

Finn whistled, clapped. Called out. 'Doesn't look like there's any big angry dog coming out to eat us,' he said, before opening the gate for Rachael.

'Let's hope not.' She went to the front door and rang the doorbell. 'It looks all locked tight.'

'Yeah.' Finn covered his eyes from the sun and attempted to look through the window. 'All quiet.'

Rachael rang the doorbell again. 'Did you hear that ring?' she asked.

'Maybe it's broken.'

She tried knocking. The door swung open against her fist. Her eyes met his in warning before she stepped back slightly from the open doorway. 'Mrs Bradley?' she called out. 'Police.'

Nothing.

'Mrs Bradley?'

The sound of something falling had Finn drawing his weapon. 'I'll go first,' he said, stepping cautiously inside.

They made their way down a hall to a small kitchen. Another sound—scraping. Finn spun around the corner, spotting a fluffy ball of brown and white fur chewing its way into a bag of cat biscuits it had knocked from a shelf.

'Damn. Hey, it's just a—' As it looked up from its biscuits, Finn made out two enormous eyes, a kind of squished-in alien face, little ears. 'Wait—what is that?'

Rachael stepped around him. 'It's a cat, Finn.'

'Are you sure? It looks like one of those things that turn into Gremlins when they get wet.'

'It's a Persian. They're supposed to look like that.'

'Huh.' He got a better look as the cat walked daintily towards him with its tail high, long coat flowing, copper eyes locked on his. It meowed. It was pretty but— 'Do you think it's friendly?'

The cat turned sideways, rubbed the length of its body against his leg and began to purr.

'I don't think it's about to gnaw your leg off,' Rachael said dryly. 'I wonder where its owner is?' She wandered away to check out more of the house. Finn decided he may as well help the cat out and feed it. 'You're a nice cat, aren't you?' He slid a hand along its back as it ate.

'Finn.'

'Yeah, I know. Back to work.'

'Finn,' Rachael said again, this time more urgently.

Damn. Something was up. He followed the direction her voice had come from, through a bedroom and into an ensuite.

Rachael was staring at a pile of bloodied men's work clothes. 'Looks like Bradley came home for a shower,' she said.

He looked around. 'There's more blood on the sink and on the shower door.'

Rachael stepped cautiously out. 'Let's not disturb this any more than we already have.'

A sound from the front of the house caught their attention.

'Hello?' The voice was female and tentative.

'We're police,' Rachael called, before going down the hall to find a woman near the doorway anxiously peering in.

'Oh, wow,' the woman said with a hand over her heart. 'I thought someone had broken in. Scared me.'

'And you are?'

'Alison Ambley, Kirsten's sister. Why are you here? Is this about Kirsten?'

'We came to talk to her, found the door ajar and were concerned for her safety.'

Alison chewed on her lips, worry marring her features. 'So am I. I haven't heard from her since Thursday. I came to see if she'd gotten back yet and to check on the cat.'

'I gave it some biscuits,' Finn said.

'Thank you. I appreciate that. If I get too close I start sneezing.'

'Is it unusual for your sister to take off?' Rachael asked.

'Well, yes. But everything's been a bit volatile lately. I wasn't too worried because she'd said she was planning on taking a few days away. The only thing is she was supposed to call if she did, and she hasn't.'

'Volatile?' Rachael prompted.

'Between her and Mark—her husband.'

'How do you mean?'

'They were having problems.'

'Let's step outside,' Rachael suggested. 'We can chat on the veranda.'

They sat at a pretty outdoor setting overlooking the creek and a small private jetty where a motorboat rocked gently.

'So your sister and her husband weren't getting along?'

'They were fighting a lot,' Alison said, staring down at her fingers. 'Mark was having an affair. She was sure of it, but he kept denying it. So they'd fight and he'd drink. He was always shitty, yelling, swearing, standing over her. Until a few weeks ago, he and Kirsten used to look after my three- and four-year-old boys every Sunday afternoon for a couple of hours so I could get stuff done. Sunday afternoon was always movie afternoon with Uncle Mark. They looked forward to it. But I had to stop that because of how he was behaving.'

'Do you know if he was ever physically violent towards Kirsten?' Finn asked.

'I don't think so, but I know she was becoming scared of him. Said she thought he might hurt her in one of his drunken rages.

Then a couple of days ago she found a phone, not his regular one, in the pocket of one of his jackets. It had lots of conversations going back months with a bunch of disgusting messages and photos from a woman, proving he was cheating on her. So on Thursday night she called and said the next morning, while Mark was at work, she was going to pack up some of her stuff and take off for a few days, think things through before confronting him. She wanted to be sure in her own mind of what she wanted to do, what was going to happen next before talking to him again. She was going to keep hold of the phone as proof in case it went bad. But she was supposed to call me when she got there, let me know where she was staying and when she'd be back.'

'And you've tried to contact her?' Rachael asked.

'A million times. I'm not getting any answer. You don't think something has happened to her, do you?'

'We don't know anything at this stage,' she said.

'Then why are you here?'

'We're trying to locate Mr Bradley over a different matter. It's a serious one, I'm afraid. Do you have any idea where he might be?' Finn asked.

'No, I couldn't say.'

'That's okay. But I'm afraid we're going to have to ask you not to go back into the house until we've had some specialist police out here.'

Alison's eyes filled with tears. 'You think he's done something to her. Oh my God.'

'It's too early to say what's happened yet,' Rachael said kindly. 'But we're looking into it, okay? We'll find out what's happened.'

'Thank you.'

Rachael patted Alison's hand. 'I'll get some details and be in touch. We'll lock the house for the time being. It's probably better you take the cat. With our people coming and going it might escape, and we can't say how long it will be until you can come back.'

Alison's already worried expression intensified as she shook her head. 'Oh, I can't take it home. Like I said, I'm allergic. I'm not sure what to do with it.'

Finn opened the door to his apartment and put the box on the floor while keeping the door open for Rachael. 'Okay, cat,' he said, lifting the lid, 'welcome to your temporary accommodation.'

The cat raised his head high, sat up in a move that had Finn thinking of a meerkat, then lithely hopped out of the box. After a quick assessment of his surroundings, he slunk out of the room and hid under Finn's bed.

'You're welcome.'

Rachael laughed. 'He'll get used to the arrangements.'

He didn't need the cat. He wasn't supposed to have a cat. But until they found someone to take care of it, the cat was his. He'd left a note on the kitchen bench to let Kirsten know if she happened to come back. But he had a bad feeling she wasn't going to.

Rachael unpacked the bag of things they'd brought back for the cat. Finn had just sorted the litter tray, which he decided was probably going to be the worst part, when his phone rang. It was Vivienne. Great.

'Hi, what's up?' he asked, forcing some brightness into his tone.

'I wanted to see if you'd done anything about the house yet.'

'Viv, you only told me on Saturday. I'm in the middle of two high-priority cases and it's Monday. What am I going to have done?'

'That's okay. I have a realtor who can pop over for a quick look this afternoon.'

'You what?'

'I told you, Finn, we need to move on this. On the phone the agent was really positive about us getting a good price. Family homes this size are difficult to come by in this area and Louis thinks if you tidy the garden up a bit—maybe take out the big tree in the backyard—we might push the figure up quite a bit more again.'

He envisaged the backyard, the old paperbark tree his childhood swing had hung from. It stung to think of chopping it down. Was he being overly nostalgic? Maybe.

'So I was hoping you might have some time to come round and do that gardening?' Vivienne continued.

'Look, I'll do what I can, okay? I'm not putting it up for sale until after I've spoken to the bank. I might have some time this week, but I can't promise anything.'

He glanced at Rachael, who had stopped texting. How many times had she stretched finances almost too tight to ensure the house was there for him? He wanted to keep it, damn it.

'Don't be silly, Finn,' Vivienne scoffed. 'You can't afford that sort of loan. I'll make sure I get two agents out for a couple of opinions on value and let you know what they say. But I'm telling you now, it's worth a heap. Maybe we can sign with the best of the two agents in the next couple of days? Can't hurt to get things underway while we're tidying up.'

'Sure, Viv. After I speak to the bank.'

He ended the call and sat heavily. She was probably right about the loan. He was living almost totally week to week as it was. The repayments on top of the rent he was locked into on his apartment for another six months were probably going to be too much. He put his head in his hands and rubbed his eyes. What did he need with a four-bedroom home on a big block anyway?

'She's pushing the house sale,' Rachael guessed.

'Yeah.' As though in sympathy, the cat emerged to rub against Finn's leg and he absently stroked his back. 'You hungry?' The cat sat and blinked at him and he decided there was interest in the big brown eyes. 'I suppose I should feed you. Again.'

'Don't give him too much,' Rachael said. 'I don't think you'll like the outcome if you upset his stomach.'

'Yeah. Right. Sorry, cat. Maybe later. What's with the texts?'

'Craig's not going to be in the office until tomorrow afternoon. I'll message Lexi and reschedule that meeting.'

'You know, it might not hurt to play facilitator between Lexi and Burns at some point. She is going to have to go back to her regular job sooner or later and this is Lexi—she won't hold back.'

Rachael blew out a breath. 'I like the idea but I don't suppose you want to do it?'

Hell, no! Then much more reasonably than the tone in his head, he said, 'She'll pay more attention to you.'

'Ha. Chicken.' Some of what he was feeling must have been reflected on his face, because her expression softened. 'What are you going to do about the house?'

'I don't know that there's much I can do, other than go along with the sale.'

'You can't get finance?'

'I haven't had a chance to try yet.'

'Come on, then.'

'What?'

'You need to talk to the bank.'

'I need an appointment.'

'So call. See if anyone's available.'

'But the case.'

Rachael already had her hand on his front door. 'Finn, you need to know where you stand with all this. It won't take long. Do it now.'

CHAPTER EIGHTEEN

True to her word, Bailee had dropped in, complete with Chinese takeaway and both her kids. Now she's grilling me over Rico. 'I don't know what you want me to say!' I tell her. 'It sucks. It does. But the best way I know how to handle it is by finding his killer.' I scoop up another mouthful of fried rice. The kids had decimated their dinner in the first couple of minutes and were busy building forts in the lounge room with every bit of furniture and blanket I own.

'You have to talk about it,' Bailee insists. 'You can't keep going like it never happened. It'll catch up with you.'

'So let it. Later. I'm not discussing this anymore.'

'Yeah, because it's too hard, right? You don't want to acknowledge—'

'Oh for fuck's sake!' I complain, the heel of my fork hand hitting the table with a loud bang. 'How about this. I *acknowledge* the shitload of anger lodged in my chest over what they did to Rico and I *want* it there. I *need* it right where it is to help me catch these arseholes. Satisfied?'

'You're using your anger to attempt to keep going,' Bailee says with a knowing nod that has my teeth grating. 'But—'

'But nothing! I haven't survived the life I've lived by talking to psychologists. I know what's best for me.'

Lucy, Bailee's three-year-old daughter, skips in, her blonde curls bouncing around her cherub face. 'Aunty Letsi, cupcake time?'

'Of course,' I say, relieved at the interruption. I take the lid off the pack I'd defrosted when I knew they were coming. I keep a stock of such things to prove to myself I'm a half-decent aunty. Lucy and her five-year-old brother Kai have been eyeing them off since they arrived an hour ago and I'm surprised it's taken them so long to get around to asking. I put the cupcakes into plastic bowls.

'Can we eat them in our fort?' Lucy asks.

'Sure.' What's a few crumbs, right? How much mess can they possibly make with one cupcake each? They're having fun.

Lucy takes the bowls and disappears into the blanket entrance.

'Do you have to feed them sugar?' Bailee asks.

'I'm their aunt, it's my right. Besides, you fed them takeaway.'

Bailee sighs and rolls her eyes but I know she doesn't really mind. 'It's just that none of us is getting a full night's sleep at the moment.'

'What's up?'

'Lucy has decided she's scared of being alone in the dark.'

'Ah. I'm guessing she's not scared of being alone in the dark, she's scared of *not* being alone in the dark.'

'Yeah, okay. Right. Anyway, she's got it stuck in her head that you catch monsters because of a conversation Kai told her he overheard so she doesn't believe me when I tell her there's no such thing.'

I catch Kai and Lucy peeping out of the corner of the blanket, covertly listening. 'Of course there's monsters,' I tell Bailee. 'There's plenty out there.'

'See!' Kai tells Bailee, bursting out of the hiding spot with a wide-eyed Lucy in tow.

Bailee pulls a face at me, which I mirror before waving Lucy over. 'Hey, sweetie, tell me about this monster.'

'It hides under my bed.'

'What noise does it make?'

Lucy thinks about that for a second, then makes a kind of creepy, creaky noise.

'Ah, yeah, that'd be a Springomonster.'

Lucy crawls onto my lap and tucks her legs underneath her, her expression endearingly serious. 'What's that?'

'They're teeny tiny monsters that hide under beds and make a really creepy noise to try and trick you into thinking they're big and scary.'

'Teeny tiny?'

'Mmm hmm.'

'Do they eat kids?'

'Well, here's the thing. It's not really about eating kids. It's about power. Springomonsters pretend to be big and tough so they can bully you out of bed and have your warm snuggly blankets all to themselves. So I need you to do something for me. When they make that scary noise, I need you to make a bigger, scarier one.'

'Why?'

'Because we don't let monsters who think they're bigger and scarier than us bully us. We never let the monsters win. I bet when you make that bigger, scarier noise you'll see what a coward that Springomonster really is.'

'Ooh.' I can see her eyes starting to light up.

Kai comes closer, edges onto the chair beside me.

'What kind of noise?' Lucy asks.

'If you were a bigger, scarier monster, what noise would you make?'

Lucy and Kai both try a few out, then Lucy comes out with a creaky, hissy, raaaarrr sound that makes me wish she hadn't done it right in my ear.

'Great! That'll do it! If you make that noise when it turns up, it'll run away and hide.'

'Really?'

'Mmm hmm. But sometimes they don't give up easy, so you have to keep making it too hard for the monster to win until it stops. Because the secret is—' I lean in to whisper, '—if you're not scared of them, they lose all their power.'

'Ooh.' Lucy and Kai exchange the sort of glances that suggest I've given them the key to life itself. Maybe I have.

'Thanks, Aunty Letsi!'

Lucy slips from my lap and she and Kai run off chattering and making monster scaring noises.

'Thanks. I think,' Bailee says, smiling.

'Tick of approval from the child psychologist. Nice.'

'You sure know a lot about monsters.'

'Like I said, there's plenty out there.'

'Are you working with Rachael and Finn again to catch yours?'

'I'm supposed to be taking a few days off. Right now it's more of a keeping me in the loop situation.'

'Keeping an eye on what you're up to, you mean.'

'Undoubtedly.'

'When's the funeral?'

I sag a little bit. 'Rico's father is in defence. He's on some overseas mission. They're going to wait until he can get back next week.'

Bailey nods sadly. 'You're going, right?'

'I hate funerals.'

'Everyone hates funerals. It's closure. You should go.'

'Yeah, it's going to be some big police deal. Of course I'll go.'

'Good. And if you change your mind and want to talk about it …'

'Yeah, nah. I told you, I just need to catch these guys.'

'Hmm.'

'You know, Rachael makes the exact same noise.'

'Hmm,' Bailee says again. This time with a smile.

After another hour of chaos I wave them away then go inside to tidy up. I stop in the lounge room and sigh. My fault. Bailee had insisted I let the kids pack up their mess but Lucy had fallen asleep and Kai was tired and cranky so I'd given her the 'don't be silly, they're tired, blah blah' argument and here I am.

I pull apart the fort, fold blankets, right furniture, then pull out the vacuum. I'm not sure what Bailee was worried about. There can't be much cupcake in either child with what's left in the carpet. Note to self: Never again.

Once it's clean, I get back to what I'd begun when Rachael and Finn had appeared: taking a proper look at the contents I copied from Jason's and Elias's phones. I grab my Jack Daniel's and close myself in my office.

I find mostly messages, pick-up times and locations, quantities and payments. All sorts of case-building fabulousness against Jason, but not much else. Elias's phone is more enlightening. A check in his images shows drugs, screenshots of some large money transfers and … I click on a video. The camera is looking through a car windscreen as it approaches a guy running along a dirt road in the dark. The car's speed increases then dramatically slows. The guy looks around. He seems kind of familiar. He's frightened, and it looks as though he's running for his life. There's a laugh from inside the car a moment before it speeds up again and ploughs into him. This is followed by a sickening series of bumps before the car stops, reverses. More wavering of the camera as the car bounces back over their victim. I hear an argument.

'That's done it.'

'Get out. Make sure.'

'Man, you do it.'

'I'm driving the fucking car. Where's your balls? We need to be sure. Give me the phone and get out!' The phone is snatched away then pointed back through the windscreen at the bloody figure sprawled on the road in front of them. I hear a car door open. Close. Elias Hamill comes into view, leans over the body, then looks back at the camera.

'He's not dead!'

'Then fucking finish it! Hurry up!'

Elias looks around as though reluctant. Then he jumps, his foot coming down on the guy's head. Again. Again.

The faint beams of twin headlights in the distant darkness has the driver telling him to hurry up, get in. Elias jogs back, takes the phone. The driver gets moving, running the victim over one last time before speeding away.

'You get that?'

'Yeah. We've got the proof. No more Wilko.'

'I'll send this to—' The video stops.

Well, that was unpleasant. I sit back, scrape my fingers through my hair and take a long deep breath against the rolling in my stomach. Wilko? Had to be Brent Wilkinson. Of course. I hadn't seen or heard anything from him for a couple of weeks or more. No wonder. I get the date, check the police computer for the incident. All it tells me is that he's dead. Suspected drug-related hit.

I find a news story on the incident. Parents want closure and the perpetrator brought to justice. But there's no suspects. I feel for them. They seem so normal. Just two people who'd wanted better for their son. They were aware he was tied up with drugs, but they also claim he was trying to get out, get clean. 'Same old story,' I mutter. The video had been sent from Elias to Adam. I don't know who the driver was. Regardless, I've now got video evidence of Elias committing murder and implicating Adam. And it makes me wonder if I've been too quick to assume it was Jason or Aden that killed Rico. Could it have been Elias? He is Jason and Aden's father. They stuff up, he goes back to fix it. Or the guy Elias was in the car with? Who was that? He seemed pretty comfortable with violent murder.

I shove my chair back from my desk because it somehow seems easier to breathe the further I am from the video I just sat through. They're all as bad as one another. I take a large swallow of my JD, then I slide my chair back in and continue to dig. Maybe there's something here that will give me more information.

CHAPTER NINETEEN

Tuesday, March 8

My phone buzzes just after five am but I'm already awake. It has not been a restful night. I had a nightmare of Rico dying in my arms every time I drifted off. Late night messages woke me, then blurred into a compilation of Brent Wilkinson getting run over and over while his parents looked on.

There is way too much shit going on in my life.

Sick of tossing and turning, I drag myself out of bed and check my phone on the way to the kitchen for coffee. No new messages from Lochie. I scroll back through the ones from last night.

I think they've been reading my messages! I had to get another phone before I could get back to you.

Are you okay?

No! What am I going to do? They've got everyone looking for me. They've got a reward out on me!

Where are you?

I can't say. It's too dangerous.

I'll come and get you.

Then you might get hurt. They're everywhere.

After that, no amount of messaging had gotten a reply. I send another quick message asking if he's okay.

Still no reply. Shit. What if something has happened to him? How many more young people and their families were going to have their lives completely screwed up by the Hamill family? I set the kettle to boil and toss a spoonful of instant into a mug along with a dash of milk that I manage to slosh onto the counter. I feel like I'd be better off with a swig of JD but I mop up the mess and, when the kettle has boiled, pour the water into my mug with more care.

I'm worried sick about Lochie but I can't get the faces of Brent Wilkinson's parents out of my head. They're suffering. At least with this video evidence I can give them some closure. I just need to figure out the best way to do it.

I take the coffee into my office and rock back on my chair as I ponder what to do. The movement reminds me that I'm far from healed, and I gingerly move the chair into its proper position.

Okay, focus. The hit was on Adam's orders, but as the organiser of all things criminal, I need him to stay in the game to help me topple the rest of his brothers. I can't give him up yet. So Elias will be the next to go down. He was the one who killed Brent. If he gives up who was with him, more the better. Two for one. If he gives up Adam—no, he'd die before doing that. His life wouldn't be worth living.

I have my hand on my phone to call Rachael when another one pings. It's Lochie. I get a *Yes at the moment* answer to my earlier check-up. My relief is very real.

Back to Elias. I need to get this video to Rachael. My thoughts wander back to Lochie's predicament, and I have an idea. Meeting with him is beyond risky. But I have to get him somewhere safe. I can't leave him out there.

I text Lochie. *You had me worried. I need to see you.*
Why?
I've got something for you that will get you that witness protection.
What?
It's a video. Where are you?

There's a long pause. Long enough that I don't think he's going to reply. It gives me time to start on getting Mr and Mrs

Wilkinson that closure. I'm down to three unused phones. This is not a cheap exercise. I plug one of them in and write Adam's name on it while it starts up. Once I'm in I attach a small section of the video, add a message and send it out to the number I got from Elias's phone.

Hey Adam, you might want to know this video has been leaked.
Who the fuck is this?

I honestly hadn't expected an answer so it takes me a minute to catch up. *Someone who knows you ordered the hit, that you had the video taken as proof.*

A longer pause this time. Then, *What do you want?*

I want payback for Brent Wilkinson. I want Elias rotting in prison for his murder.

Fuck off.

Your choice. The video is headed for the cops. If Elias hands himself in, you're off the hook. He doesn't, I turn over the proof you ordered the hit. Oh, and say hi to Raymond for me.

You're the little fuck who wants the reward on Debbie, aren't you? Listen, dumbshit. You wanna keep those big balls you think you've got? You drop this or I'll fucking get you! I'll track you down and you'll be fucking sorry!

'Yeah, yeah,' I murmur, ignoring the nasty and genuinely disturbing threats that follow.

I turn off the phone and get up to shower. When I return, Lochie has texted me an address. I check the time again, tell him what I'm wearing so he'll recognise me and ask him to do the same. I promise to be no more than half an hour and hope this, too, falls into Rachael's loophole of no law against visiting friends.

I find the house at the end of a very long, very quiet street on the dark side of the mountain in Narara. The houses are old and the nature strip is mostly a dumping ground for rubbish that the garbage collectors must forget on a regular basis. Assuming they ever come down here.

I do a U-turn and park in front of a house that looks ready for demolition, while I check out the address across the road from the safety of my car. It's a single-storey fibro, long grass, broken fence, looks abandoned. There're a few cars parked out the front that don't look like they've moved in years. In my head, the idea of doing this in broad daylight had seemed safer. Now I wish there was some darkness to hide in.

I reluctantly get out, walk down the opposite side of the street until I'm a few houses past the one I'm after, then cross the road and turn back. Everything's still quiet. Should I knock? I decide to peek in the side window by the gate first.

My heart just about jumps out of my chest when a hand goes over my mouth and I'm dragged with a thump to the ground.

'It's me!' Lochie hisses.

I can't reply due to the big stifling hand. Besides, I'm still trying to breathe courtesy of the now thrumming pain in every damaged part of my body.

'Get off!' I finally manage.

'Shh! They're in there!'

We must have made some noise because the screen door crashes open and two built types in balaclavas come out slowly, look around. One has a sawn-off shotgun dangling by his right leg.

My heart is pounding louder than my breath is coming out. We're not very well shielded from sight but we're both too scared to move in case we make another sound. Across the street another door bangs and a guy appears with a big dog on a lead. The two in Lochie's house retreat just inside the front door.

'Now,' I whisper and shake him off, then move as quickly as I can towards the car. I hear him behind me, nearly trip when his long, lanky frame bumps into me in what I guess is an attempt to make me go faster.

We get across the road without incident. I have a hand on the car door when I hear, 'Hey!'

That same clang of the front door tells me the masked men have spotted us. I look for the guy with the dog but he's vanished. Lochie leaps the corner of the bonnet and dives into the passenger seat. I fumble to get the car started as I see one of the figures bearing down on us at a loping run. The car kicks to life and I flatten the accelerator. I hear the thud of the guy's fist on my boot but I'm leaving him behind.

'Who was that?' I demand.

'I dunno! Deadbeats after Raymond Hamill's reward maybe.'

'They look a bit more serious than deadbeats,' I say with a glance in the rear-vision mirror. The second man had reached the first on the road. 'What was that place anyway?'

'Just somewhere I've been hiding out.'

'The place Juicey told you about? Who else knew you were there?'

'Uh ... my mate, Crowley.'

Another glance as we round the corner show the men running towards a car. Fuck.

'Crowley's dead.'

'Huh?'

'Murdered.'

'Oh, shit! They got to him. Must've been tortured into dobbing me in. Poor bastard.'

Another glance back has my mouth drying up as a tan-coloured Falcon chases us down. I reach an intersection with a giveway sign but keep going and hope for the best, my eyes squinting as I expect something to hit us. When nothing does, I speed up again.

'You need to go faster!' Lochie says, his voice a jumble of nerves.

'I'm doing my best!' My poor little car is not meant for speed. I go out of my way to get onto the nearest main road where there's multiple lanes, lots more traffic and, if I'm lucky, a highway patrol car.

'Okay, we're good,' Lochie says. 'They've stopped.'

'Are you sure?'

He takes another look. 'Yep.'

'Right.' I ease off the accelerator and relax in my seat, snatching my first real look at Lochie. He's too skinny, no question, but he's remarkably clean and tidy for a teen who's been hiding in a squat. His light brown hair is brushed, just a little overgrown. He's shaved recently, and his warm brown eyes are clear of any sign of substance abuse and currently locked on me with curiosity. I could see this kid at uni. See him in a graduation hat. I'm going to make sure he gets that chance. 'Well, that was fun,' I tell him, for something to say.

'Can't get my head around it. You said your name was Sam. I thought you were a guy.'

'Excellent.'

'I get it. Of course you wouldn't want anyone to know who you are. Thanks for coming to get me. Where are we going?'

'Right now, as far away from them as possible. Are you absolutely sure they're gone?'

Lochie takes another long look out the back of the car. 'Yeah, I reckon.'

'Okay, then give me a minute.' I get my bearings, change lanes again so I can turn off towards where we're supposed to be headed. 'Look in the centre console.'

He pulls out a thumb drive. 'What is it?'

'Your ticket to witness protection. That's a video of Elias and another guy killing a dealer.'

'Truly? Who's the other guy?'

'I don't know.'

'If they're killing someone, it's probably the Butcher.'

'The who?'

'Karl Hamill. The violent one I was threatened with.'

'Karl Hamill is called the Butcher?'

'Yeah. The cops don't know half of what he's done.'

Neither do I. 'So tell me about him.'

It takes me twenty minutes to get to Gosford Police Station because I don't dare take him to Wyong, and he's still not finished telling me Butcher tales when we get there. Karl Hamill is one genuinely fucked-up human. 'Okay, I'm going to drop you off here. You've got proof of a murder this time. You tell them you have it, that you have absolute proof Elias killed Brent Wilkinson and that you'll hand it over in exchange for protection.'

He takes a deep breath and suddenly looks so, so young. 'Okay.'

'If they ask you to testify against the Hamills in court over the drugs, you'll have to.'

'Sure.' He hesitates. 'How do I say I got the proof of the hit?'

'Tell them … tell them you got it off another Hamill associate. They'll want to know who so you'll have to tell them you forgot his name. You were off your face or something. Whatever. They can't prove otherwise. Just don't bring me into it.'

'I couldn't anyway. I don't even know your real name.'

'It should stay that way. Good luck, Lochie.'

But he doesn't get out. 'What?'

He stares down at his hands. 'I'm still worried I'll go in there and they'll charge me for dealing for the Hamills. But I know I wouldn't have survived out there another day.'

He's probably right. 'Don't worry about it.'

'Why do you care? I mean, I know you hate the Hamills, but why did you do all this for me? Why'd you risk your life like that?'

Because you're a good kid, because it's not fair, because you've lost everything, because everyone else thinks you're as bad as they are but I know you're not, because your parents love you and you deserve more time with them, more life ... The becauses keep coming. In the end I settle on, 'Let's just say I know what it's like to be stuck in a fucked-up situation. You should get going in case those two bastards have been sneaky and followed us.'

'Thanks,' he says. He gazes at me with the kind of intense gratitude that has me swallowing down a sudden lump in my throat. 'Thank you so much. I'll never forget what you've done for me.'

'You're welcome. Good luck.' My phone rings but I wait until Lochie's out of the car before answering. It's Rachael. 'Yeah, hi,' I say, watching Lochie go inside.

'You promised me you'd stay home. Where are you?'

'I know. Sorry. I found Lochie. I figured out a creative way of sharing some info I dug up with the cops so I dropped him at the station with it.'

'Great on Lochie, but what do you mean—actually, never mind. Can you meet me back at your place in fifteen minutes?'

'Ah, I don't have lights and sirens on this car, but I'll do my best. Why? You said we weren't on until this afternoon.'

'Meeting with Burns.'

Ugh. 'Why?' I ask yet again, this time much less happily.

'Just a courtesy chat, really. He needs to know that once you've had some time off you'll be assisting us. I also think it would be a good chance for you two to meet—calmly—because at some point you'll be going back to work with him.'

'Yay, I can hardly wait.'

'We'll head straight from there to headquarters for that chat with the drug squad and I need you to share everything you've got on the Hamills and ... probably how you got it. So bring your laptop and any other research, okay?'

'Double yay.'

I hear her sigh. 'Just get here as fast as you safely can.'

'I'm on my way,' I say and end the call. I take one more look around. All clear, so I turn on the ignition and resign myself to the day ahead. I absolutely do not want to talk to Burns, but at least going into the station will give me a chance to get Paddy a meal.

CHAPTER TWENTY

'Are you ready to go in?' Rachael asked when Lexi didn't get straight out of the car. Lexi had made it back home in twenty minutes and had made an effort with her wardrobe, changing into a nice pair of black business pants and a blue silk shirt. So here they were, on time and looking the part. She just had to get her through the door.

'Well?' she prompted.

Lexi shrugged. 'May as well get it over and done with.'

By the sounds of things it wouldn't hurt to have a little pep talk first. 'Great, and look, I know you're not a big fan of Burns at the moment ...'

Lexi's eyes stayed fixed on the windscreen. 'On a sliding scale where one is mildly annoyed and ten is I'd unplug his life support to charge my phone, he's a solid twelve with me right now.'

'But it wouldn't hurt to show a little understanding and respect.'

'I'm here, I'm dressed. What more do you want?'

'He's already copped it from Craig and me, he's aware he made a bad judgement call and he's not expecting you to be here, so I'd like you to cut him some slack.'

'We'll have to see how it goes. He got Rico killed.' A muscle worked in her jaw.

'I guess that will have to do. Let's go then.' She led Lexi inside, saw the constable on the front desk jump up to let them in and wondered what might have been said through the grapevine.

'I'm just going to dump these in the fridge,' Lexi said and came back a moment later without the pre-packed sandwiches she'd found time to buy on her way home. 'Okay, after you.'

Rachael knocked once on Burns's door, then stepped through at his greeting.

'Inspector Langley. Welcome.' In contrast to his words, Burns's tone was cool and his features darkened further when Lexi stepped in behind her. 'Winter. You are supposed to be taking time off.'

'Constable Winter will be assisting homicide with some ongoing enquiries,' Rachael told him.

'For goodness' sake, inspector! Constable Winter needs proper time to rest and heal!'

'I'm all rested and healed, thanks,' Lexi said dryly.

'This is not a good idea,' Burns said, ignoring Lexi. 'He was her partner! She shouldn't be involved in this investigation.'

'Oh for heaven's sake, Frank,' Rachael said. 'You know as well as I do she's going to go after these men. She may as well be assisting us.'

Burns's face reddened. 'If that's the case she's not a police officer, she's still a vigilante!'

'Oh, you'd want to hope not.' Lexi's voice dripped venom as she stepped around Rachael. 'Because as a cop, I have to put up with your shit but as a vigilante, I don't. Rico's dead because you wanted to show me how big your balls were and the only thing stopping me from making you pay for that is my badge!'

'Okay, that's enough.' Rachael stepped calmly between them. 'This is an emotional time for all of us. Especially the two of you. You're both feeling Rico's loss. We need to try and stay calm and focused and—'

'You need to consider very carefully how you speak to me, constable!' Burns said.

'Oh, believe me, I consider every word!' Lexi shot back. 'Want to hear some more?'

'And what that means for your career!'

'My care factor might be higher if you hadn't gotten Rico killed!'

Rachael made a silent plea for strength before stretching her arms out to keep them apart. 'Both of you—stop!'

'She needs to apologise for speaking to me like that!' Burns barked.

'And he needs to admit that if he'd notified the drug squad, Rico would be alive and this wouldn't have happened!'

Burns's mouth opened again then closed. He sagged. 'I know that, Winter. I fully believed at the time that I had chosen the correct course of action. I knew the family were flagged but I didn't want to go higher without the necessary evidence to warrant it. I ... underestimated the threat.'

Rachael watched as multiple emotions crossed Lexi's face. Finally, she said, 'I don't know why I thought hearing that would make me feel better. Because it doesn't.'

Burns stared down at his desk, Lexi at the wall.

'Yelling at each other won't bring Rico back,' Rachael said.

After another uncomfortably heavy silence, Lexi huffed out an angry sigh. 'Fine. Rico's death is on the Hamills. They need to pay for it.'

'Agreed,' Rachael said. 'Now, if that's settled? Burns, your team did a great job with the immediate investigation into Rico's murder. We'll keep you in the loop with any progress.'

Burns nodded once and said quietly, 'Thank you.'

Rachael gestured for Lexi to step out of the office in front of her. 'Well done making peace with Burns,' she said as they walked back to the entrance. 'That'll make things a lot easier when you come back.'

'The guy on the news last night! It was him! The one I reported!' The words travelled clearly from reception.

'You filed a report with us?' the constable out front asked calmly. 'Let me just look up—'

'I want to talk to the lady that was here last time! She already knows what I'm talking about!'

Lexi frowned and sped up. 'I know that voice.'

'Who did you speak to?' the constable continued.

'Um, it was ... I wrote it down ...' The young woman in front of the reception desk shuffled around in her bag then pulled out a purse and dug out a card from inside. 'Winter. Constable Winter. I need to talk to Constable Winter!'

'It's okay, all good, Fletch, ta,' Lexi said, slipping through the door then, 'Hi … Daisy, right?'

Daisy surged forward so rapidly Rachael readied herself to stop her.

'The guy on the news! He's the one from the train! The one that got off with that woman at the station. I told you he was creepy! He killed her, didn't he!'

'The man you reported on Saturday when you came in was on the news?'

'Yes! He was on the Channel Seven news! Don't you know? They said the cops are looking for him!'

'Okay. Let me find out a bit more. Give me a moment.'

'Hi there,' Rachael said. 'I'm Inspector Rachael Langley. Daisy, was it?'

'Yeah. Why?' Daisy asked.

'Thanks for coming in.' She pulled up a photo of Bradley on her phone and showed it to Daisy. 'Could I ask you to take a quick look at this picture? Is this the man you mean?'

Daisy's eyes widened. 'Yes! That's him!'

'Fabulous. Would you mind coming with me? I'd really appreciate it if you could take me through what you saw. Lexi, you can sit in. I'll catch you up.'

'So, I gather you caught on,' Rachael asked Lexi after farewelling Daisy from the station.

'Yeah. A lead in the other case you're working. That's great.'

'I need to call and update everyone.'

'Okay. Oh—wait.' Lexi disappeared into the break room before reappearing with a travel mug and the sandwiches she'd brought in. 'You may as well make that phone call. I'll meet you at the car.' She headed for the door.

Not likely, Rachael thought, wondering what she was up to.

She watched Lexi cross the carpark and approach the back of a building. A homeless man emerged from the shadows, leaning on a shopping trolley. Rachael followed as far as the nearby cars.

'Was wondering what had happened to you,' the elderly man said to Lexi. 'That face looks sore. Have I gotta beat someone up for ya?'

'Wouldn't be a fair fight,' Lexi said, handing over the coffee and placing the sandwiches in his trolley. 'You'd smash them. How's that cough?'

'Meh, what cough?' He sipped his coffee and coughed. It might have been funny if the cough didn't sound so terrible. 'It's no big deal. But serious, though, that's some nasty bruising.'

'Just another adventure.'

He wheezed again and put the coffee down so he could open his sandwiches. 'My favourite,' he said, taking a mouthful.

'You're welcome. Hey, listen, I'm not going to be around much for a while. You going to be okay? Need some money or something?'

'I'll be fine. Who's your friend?'

Lexi turned and, spotting her, scowled. 'That's Rachael. A very bossy, very nosey police inspector who was supposed to wait inside.'

'That right?' Paddy said with a chuckle. 'Hi, Rachael! I'm Paddy.'

'Nice to meet you.'

'I've got to go,' Lexi said. 'I'll see you when I see you. Look after yourself.'

'Bye, Lexi, thanks again. Bye, Rachael!'

'Bye, Paddy,' she called and copped another frown as Lexi came back.

'I told you I'd catch up.'

'And here I was thinking how good it was you hadn't lost your appetite. That's a nice thing you just did.'

'I make sure Paddy gets a meal whenever I'm on duty. It's no big deal.'

'Maybe not to you. I'm guessing it means a lot to him.'

Lexi shrugged. 'It's just a meal.'

'Why do you get so embarrassed about being nice?'

'I'm not embarrassed and I'm certainly not *nice*.'

Rachael couldn't help but smile at Lexi's perplexed expression but didn't say anything further until they were in her car. 'So, you ready to talk to Craig?'

'Oh, that's right, you want me to share *my* information,' she complained lightly.

'Okay,' Rachael said with a sigh. 'Craig said if you didn't want to come in I was to tell you to let it go.'

Lexi's expression froze, then her eyes hit the roof of the car. She huffed out a laugh and a 'bastard' as she flopped back in her seat.

'Excuse me?' Rachael asked.

'This Craig you keep referring to is Detective Inspector Slavek, isn't it?'

'Yes. Why?'

'Never mind. I'll talk to him.'

Fascinated, she wanted to delve further but her phone rang.

'Hey, everything okay? How'd you go?' Finn said when she answered.

'Yes, all good, I was held up by a witness who has come forward with a sighting of Mark Bradley. She saw him on the late train to Newcastle on Friday night. He got off at Wondabyne Station just before midnight. He sat alone, but when he got off he had a woman with him the witness has identified as Kirsten Bradley and she looked scared and upset.'

'Wondabyne? Why would he take his wife off the train in the middle of the night at Wondabyne?'

'I don't know. I wondered if maybe they were running, but where can they run to out there? Have Linc request CCTV both from Hornsby and Wondabyne stations that night. And there was a guard on that train who got off at the station briefly. He was busy with some drunk campers getting on but he might have seen or heard something useful.'

'Right. I'll track him down. Oh, and Carole Latimer is dropping in to pick up her husband's computer. Do you want to talk to her about the scaffolding?'

'It wouldn't hurt to have a quick chat, see if she knows anything. If I'm not back, you take it.'

'No problem. See you soon.'

A million thoughts rushed through Rachael's mind as she took the turn onto the main road.

'Fill me in?' Lexi asked.

'Why?'

'Because if you're going to ponder it all the way to headquarters I may as well ponder it with you.'

'Okay ... Our POI is Mark Bradley.'

Lexi reached for her laptop and phone. 'Go on.'

'What are you doing?'

'Research, of course.'

The team were at their desks when Rachael walked into headquarters an hour later.

Linc spotted her first. 'Hey, I heard you had a productive morning?'

'We certainly did. Did you request the CCTV?'

'Yep, expecting someone to get back to me at any moment.'

'How about you, Cass, where are you up to?'

'Jeremy Latimer's computer doesn't help us much. I have a calendar that can shed some light on his day-to-day movements dating back a while, some mundane business emails, staffing records, notes on events like conferences and other business related travel ... but there's nothing that could help us with the events leading up to his murder.'

'Assuming Bradley is responsible for Latimer's death—and we haven't proved that yet—the only motive we have is an argument that perhaps got out of control after Latimer discovered Bradley's purchase of inferior scaffolding. When we find Bradley, we need to have something ironclad to present to him that's going to convince him that we're on to him, that he'd better start talking. What do we need to make that happen?' Rachael asked.

'To start with, I'd like access to the company records in order to get a clearer picture of Bradley's role within the business,' Cass said, 'and find out if Latimer could have been privy to the scaffolding purchase.'

'Okay,' Rachael said. 'Have you checked for any emails between the pair? Anything to suggest there was any friction between them recently?'

'I didn't find any emails between Latimer and Bradley.'

'Surely that's strange?'

'Now that you point it out, yeah. Maybe he deleted them as he went.' Cass looked at the computer again. 'There's nothing in his deleted items folder but there might be a way to find out if any have been permanently deleted.'

'He would only do that if he had something to hide. Right, Lexi will be here in a sec. Let her take a look. She'll have some ideas.'

'Lexi's here? Why is she involved?' Cass asked in surprise.

'She's here to talk to Inspector Slavek about a possible lead in Sergeant Rico's murder, but she's got a good head for untangling computer problems so you should use her. She won't mind. We ran into Neutron in the foyer so they're catching up. Won't be long.'

'It's fine, thanks. I'll ask Neutron.'

'He was on his way out. Is there a problem?' Rachael asked.

'The problem is I don't think an inexperienced cop with a questionable history should be here at all, let alone helping me do my job,' Cass said.

'Well, don't hold back,' Lexi said as she joined them.

Rachael had to close her mouth against the involuntary groan. 'Lexi, this is—'

Lexi held up her hand. 'I know who she is, and I think we can agree the polite introduction ritual is redundant now, yes?' she said with a pointed look at Cass. 'Let's skip it.'

Cass's face had turned from annoyed to wary, staring at Lexi as though ... waiting for something? Rachael wasn't sure—sometimes she found Cass hard to read. Then the moment was gone as Lexi turned her attention to Linc.

'Jack Lincoln,' Linc said, leaning past Rachael to give Lexi his best smile and shake her hand. 'Call me Linc. Welcome.'

The overenthusiastic greeting had Lexi's gaze flicking to Rachael before she smiled back at him at least partially in amusement. 'Hi. Thanks.'

'Rach,' Finn interrupted after a ping had him checking his phone. 'Carole Latimer is on her way up. I'll catch her at the lift and take her into the meeting room.'

'Thanks, Finn. Talk to her about the scaffolding and buy me a few minutes, would you?' Then she turned to Lexi. 'This is Jeremy Latimer's computer. We're trying to establish whether or not he was complicit in the scaffolding purchase and thought there might be something in his emails. But we can't find any between him and Bradley, which seems odd. Could you check for any permanently deleted files?'

'Excuse me …' Lexi said, sliding into Finn's chair before slowly extending her arm towards Cass and moving the computer across the space between them like she was dealing with a dangerous animal. Linc chuckled, then turned it into a cough.

Once the computer was in front of her, she opened it. 'I can only recover one email at a time, not complete folders, so it might take a while if there's a few …' She concentrated on the screen. 'Or none. No deleted emails to or from anyone.' Lexi closed Outlook and checked the rest of the content. 'Are you sure this is his computer? Other than a stack of easily transferable work data, there's nothing. No personal photos, no emails to do with his life outside of the office, no Google search history … it's like someone's handed you a reasonably clever prop.'

'To throw us off?' Rachael said.

'Off what?' Cass asked. 'Carole handed it in and she's next to clueless about the business.'

'Hey, you don't need an inexperienced cop with a questionable history helping you do your job,' Lexi reminded her, then said to Rachael, 'I have an idea. Want to hear it?'

'Tell me as we walk.'

'Nice to meet you, Lexi,' Linc said as they retreated.

'Is he for real?' Lexi asked.

Rachael rolled her eyes. 'He's a genuinely nice guy who uses humour to play peacekeeper. Cass snapped at you so he'll take it upon himself to make up for that. He's a bit too used to women falling all over him for his own good.'

'Huh. Could be amusing, I suppose. Hey, I never ran into Cass during the Spider case, did I?'

'No, why?'

Lexi shook her head. 'I don't know. Nothing. Now about Carole Latimer …'

Rachael stepped into the meeting room where Finn and Mrs Latimer were talking. She greeted the woman with a smile and took the seat next to Finn as she slid the computer across the table.

'Is that mine?' Carole asked.

'Yes,' Rachael said. 'Thank you. Unfortunately, there wasn't anything of any real value on it in relation to the case.'

'The detective has been filling me in on the scaffolding issue. I hope you're not suggesting Jeremy put the entire project and his men at risk by ordering scaffolding that wasn't safe. He wouldn't do that!'

'We're not accusing your husband of doing anything wrong,' Finn said. 'We're simply trying to establish if Jeremy was aware that Mark had purchased it.'

'I'd guarantee he wasn't aware of it! Is that what you think they were arguing about the night my husband was killed?'

'We don't know.'

Some of the fight went out of Carole Latimer. 'Jeremy trusted Mark with all our ordering and payments. That was his job. He oversaw everything. He seemed so good at what he did.' She dabbed at a couple of tears. 'It would make sense my husband would want to confront Mark when he found out about it. He wouldn't have stood for it. Should I contact a lawyer? Am I going to be liable for anything?'

'We can't advise you on that,' Rachael said. 'But none of your workers were hurt. This is all about getting to the truth of what happened to your husband.'

'Well, I think it's pretty obvious, isn't it?' Carole said bitterly. 'Jeremy called Mark out on the scaffolding, Mark killed him and took off!'

'We're doing everything we can to track Mark down. When we find him, we'll give you some answers, Mrs Latimer.'

Carole Latimer stood and clutched the computer. 'I appreciate that, detectives. I really do need to get back to the office. I have staff scrambling to pick up where Mark left off and I have a funeral to plan.'

'Yes, we understand. Thank you for coming in,' Finn said.

'Oh, one other thing,' Rachael said. 'Due to our investigation into Mark Bradley, we're going to have to take a close look at the business he did through your company. I know you aren't too involved and I don't want to put you to any trouble, so I'll send a couple of my detectives out to find what they need. I'm sure your secretary will be able to help them. Rest assured, Mrs Latimer, if Mark is responsible for your husband's death and damaging your company, he will pay for it.'

Carole stilled, her hand on the door. 'Oh, um. All right … Could we make it tomorrow?'

'It really would be better to jump on this. Is there a problem?' she asked, seeing a flicker of distress in the woman's expression.

'No. Of course not. Later this afternoon will be fine.'

Rachael nodded. 'Thank you. But I can send them over straight away. Do you need assistance finding your way out?' She caught Finn's questioning look. She generally insisted someone accompany any visitors to homicide back to the foyer.

'No, I'm fine,' Carole assured her with another sniff. She walked out and Rachael watched the hallway as Lexi followed the woman.

'What was all that about?' Finn asked when they were alone. 'And where was Lexi going?'

'We're not sure Mrs Latimer's above board.'

'I think I missed something.'

'Let's head back to the others and I'll catch you up.'

Linc and Cass were still at their desks and glanced up as Rachael and Finn reappeared.

'How did you go?' Linc asked.

'Not sure yet,' Rachael said.

'Is Lexi coming back?'

'Yeah. And Linc, we're in the office,' Rachael said. 'At work. Remember that.'

Linc suppressed a smile. 'Got it.'

'What do you mean, not sure?' Cass asked.

Finn dropped into his chair. 'Apparently we're *not sure* Mrs Latimer is being straight with us.'

'Lexi and I did some research on the Latimers on the trip down here,' Rachael told them. 'Mrs Latimer's been telling us the business is her husband's thing. She talks as though she knows nothing much about it, but that's not true. She spoke at the 2017

Australasian Builders Convention. She lectured on women in the construction industry, where she covered the responsibilities of her role in her company and it wasn't all scripted. She painted a very different picture to the one she's portraying now. She ...' Her words petered out as Lexi reappeared. 'Anything?'

Lexi nodded. 'She's in the end stall of the ladies' room, firing out instructions at a million miles per hour to someone called Gabby.'

'That's the secretary,' Finn said. 'She was the one who let Linc and me in on Sunday to do the interviews.'

'She's telling her to delete files on some laptop in Jeremy's office, and to remove some of the folders from the filing cabinet. I think you've got a small amount of time to get there before she does because it sounds like Gabby wasn't in the office. Carole was pissed about that. Kept telling her she had to hurry.'

'Right. Finn, Cass, head straight over,' Rachael said. 'Linc, see if you can fast track a court order for us to seize everything in that office.'

'On it,' Linc said. Then catching sight of someone behind Rachael, he nodded in greeting. 'Inspector.'

CHAPTER TWENTY-ONE

'Craig,' Rachael greets Inspector Slavek, spotting him a moment before I do. Then his eyes land on me and he grins widely. 'Elsa!'

'Fuck off,' I groan. I'd had no idea who 'Craig' was when Rachael had first mentioned him, but the message to 'let it go' had been a dead giveaway. Damn academy nicknames. He'd hummed the stupid song under his breath every time I was within hearing distance during the module he ran on organised crime. It had frustrated the hell out of me. Even if it was kind of funny. He'd stirred up all the recruits in one way or another, made them feel comfortable in the class, but in a way that had him not losing any respect. And everyone had worked their arses off for him. Including me.

'Glad you came,' he says, still grinning. 'Shall we head for my office?'

I think Rachael might actually be speechless. The look she sends me is not warm, but I follow her to Craig's office, mentally shifting between cases. How Rachael keeps track of more than one or two at a time is a complete mystery to me.

'Take a seat,' Craig offers, gesturing to one of two chairs opposite his.

I remove my laptop bag from my shoulder then sit next to Rachael as he moves around the other side of his desk.

'So, Lexi, good to see you up and about.'

'Yeah, thanks.'

'We've had your friend Lochie back with a rather important piece of evidence against Elias Hamill,' he says.

'That's good news. I hope Brent Wilkinson's family won't be kept waiting too long for some closure.'

'You know what? Straight away I thought, I bet Lexi knows something about that. And look at that. You do. The best part is, he can't remember who he got it from.'

Smartarse. 'What can I say? He's forgetful.'

'Maybe you should have come up with a pretend benefactor for him.'

'Maybe I should just throw your "let it go" right back at you.'

His nod carries a smirk as he sits back and gets comfortable. 'Rachael tells me you've been keeping a close eye on the Hamills. That you might have some information we don't and vice versa. So. I'll show you mine if you show me yours.'

I can't help the pained expression. 'The thing is, inspector, despite what Rachael may have told you, I'm not sure there's anything you can show me that I haven't already seen.'

His expression turns to mock indignation. 'And I was so looking forward to seeing yours.'

'It'd blow your mind.'

'Are you two quite finished?' Rachael says. I can't tell whether she's amused or horrified. 'Lexi, the inspector is willing to share confidential information with you.'

'Well, at least someone is,' I shoot back at her. 'How do you know I haven't already seen it?'

'Because it's confidential.'

'Never stopped me before.'

Craig's expression turns serious. 'I've heard that about you. We've been working for years on this. We know more than you might think.'

I don't want to appear too excited—he might change his mind—but I'm desperate for every scrap I can get. Still, I have to make sure. 'Lochie's getting that protection?'

'Done deal.'

'All right then, I'll play. Who's the second guy? The one who was driving the car.'

'Voice analysis suggests it's Karl Hamill.'

'The Butcher.' Lochie was right.

'Yeah. AKA the Butcher. He's responsible for the majority of all the nastier cleaning up the Hamills do from time to time,' Craig says.

'If you know this, why don't you have him in custody?'

'We can't find him. There's several warrants out for his arrest but he stays off radar and no one with half a brain in their head will risk crossing him to tip us off.'

'And you know about the Crystal Gold?' I ask.

'The latest manufacturing effort by the Hamills. They were importing from the Middle East until the supply got intercepted one too many times. It was costing them millions so they decided to make their own. They've been dealing for years but they've shifted their stomping grounds and had a shake-up of branding and procedure so we're catching up. We know they have several chemists on their books importing the raw ingredients for them. We're in the process of tracking them all down and we've had someone planted as a customer on the northern end of the coast for a couple of months now. He's been buying off the guy who buys from the Hamill dealer. That's as close as we've gotten so far. It's a work in progress.'

'So you knew about the tags, the red clothing, all of that?'

'We did.'

I glare at Rachael as though it's somehow her fault I've been doing all this extra catch-up.

'I haven't been involved in the drug investigation,' she says. 'That's why you two need to talk to each other.'

'Lexi, how did you find all these people?' Craig asks.

'They're a well-known crime family with lots of contacts,' I say as though it's obvious, because really, it is. 'They weren't difficult to find.'

'But all the people connected to them?'

I shrug. 'I befriended friends of friends of friends and infected computers and phones with remote-access software so I could monitor conversations between their friends and their friends and so on. I created dozens of different online profiles so I could pretend to be whoever I needed to be in order to reel in the ones that were useful and gather more. Then I dug in. Kept track of the interesting people they talked to, the conversations they had online. Chatted back. Learnt from there.'

'That's a massive undertaking for one person. How much time have you put into this?'

'After the strike force was put on hold, I didn't really stop.'

'Along with the academy workload and the assessments you're still completing as part of your probationary training.'

'I don't sleep much.'

'Okay,' Craig says, linking his fingers behind his head. 'What do you know?'

'Raymond makes the big decisions but otherwise hands over the running of everything to Adam. Adam manages everything but he's very much hands-off. Robert Hamill runs the weapons deals, Elias runs the drug operation and Karl is the standover arsehole who tortures people.'

'We know this. What else have you got?'

'I know how and where they're recruiting kids and how they're controlling them. I know that Lee Crouses's death wasn't a break-in gone wrong, I know people the twins are likely to run to if they can't get home and I have eyes on the street looking for them as we speak.'

'And the twins are still dealing. That's interesting. Rachael said you've got something lined up with Jason for tomorrow night.'

'It is and it isn't. This family thinks they're untouchable. But yes, I do. I'm supposed to be picking up some Crystal Gold.'

'Keep talking.'

'I contacted Jason and told him Lochie had split, that I was taking over his patch and that I had all his buyers depending on the Crystal Gold that never turned up last week. That if I was going to take over I needed to keep the clients and they didn't want to wait until the weekend. After checking with Elias, Jason agreed to meet me at three thirty tomorrow morning on the condition I pay twice the regular price. Then Elias told Jason to contact the other regular dealers in case they wanted to buy while he was there.'

'How do you know what Elias said to Jason?'

'I sent a thumbnail picture of the cash to Jason to prove I was legit. He clicked on it to see it better. It had spyware attached which downloaded when he opened it.'

'So you got into Jason's phone.' Craig leans in expectantly. 'And Elias opened it too?'

'That's how I got the video. So what now?'

'So we'll need that information. But back to this meeting. You think both twins will be there?'

'That's how it generally works.'

'And they're expecting a few people to turn up.'

'After me, but yeah.'

'Handy. I can put someone in the field close by as well as others in hiding. I know your team is slammed, Rachael, and there's a drug takedown involved so we can use my guys. We'll bring them in on the murder *and* drug charges.'

'Sounds like a plan.'

Craig's gaze shifts back to me. 'Feel like a field trip?'

'Seriously?' I ask. I look at Rachael expectantly. 'Is that internal investigation into Rico's death going to get in the way?'

She sighs. 'I don't think so. It's pretty cut and dried. But,' she adds, turning to Craig, 'she's technically on leave.'

'So we reinstate her. She's too valuable an asset to be sitting at home.'

Rachael's not looking comfortable with the idea, but I want to do this. I want to look these little assholes in the eye when the cuffs go on.

'Even if we do, she can't go into that situation,' Rachael says. 'They'll recognise her.'

'She won't have to interact with them,' Craig says. 'She'll wear a listening device and as soon as she spots them she'll say the word and we'll move in. She'll fit in, she knows what to expect.' Then finally, to me, he says, 'No pressure, though. If you need more time or you think seeing them again will be too painful we can—'

'It'll be fine,' I say. 'I'll wear a hoodie to hide my face. It'll be cold, no one will think twice about it.' Because I can see Rachael's still dubious, I add, 'I *need* to get them.'

'I know,' she tells me, and blows out a breath. 'So okay.'

'Let me pull the team together,' Craig says, getting to his feet. 'We don't have long to organise this.'

CHAPTER TWENTY-TWO

Finn put down the last box of evidence he'd lugged up to homicide from the Latimer Developments office. Cass had everything spread out over the length of their meeting room table with the overflow stacked on the floor. This was going to take them days. 'Okay, that's everything,' he told them.

'You busy?' Linc asked hopefully.

'As much as I'd love to help …' Finn's phone pinged. Perfect timing. 'I have to go talk to the train guard who was on duty when Bradley was spotted with his wife at Wondabyne. Rachael's bringing him up.' He grimaced as several loose pages fell from a folder to the floor. 'Good luck.'

He closed the door behind him in time to see Rachael coming out of the lift, talking to a man close to retirement age with a round belly and a pleasant expression.

'Finn,' Rachael said. 'This is Noel Wheeler. Noel, this is Detective Finn Carson.'

'Nice to meet you,' Finn said with a handshake. 'Thanks for coming in.'

'This is an impressive building,' Wheeler commented as he was gestured into another room to take a seat. 'Guess you guys deserve a bit of nice space with what you put up with every day.'

'Thank you,' Finn said.

'Can I ask what's this about?'

'Last Friday night,' Finn said. 'You were working on the 11:48 train from Central Station to Newcastle.'

Wheeler nodded slowly. 'Sounds right.'

'We were hoping you might be able to help us with our enquiries into an incident at Wondabyne Station.'

Wheeler chewed on his lip, his gaze sliding sideways. 'Bunch of drunken idiots? Campers. Drunk as skunks. Stank. Been hiking. Got lost and were late coming in.'

'Yes, that's the incident we're referring to,' Rachael said. 'While all that was happening, two passengers got off the train. Did you see them?'

Another far-off look was accompanied by a shake of his head. 'Other than the regular guy who hops off there, I only had the one other request to stop from the young man hoping we'd pick up his hiking mates.'

'The regular guy,' Finn said, showing him a photo of Bradley, 'is this him?'

'Oh, yes. That's the one. He and a … ah … mate like to go fishing out there every Friday.'

'He told you that?'

Wheeler shrugged. 'We've shared a quick word or two on occasion. Just long enough for the train to pull up and him to get off, you know.'

'And when this man asked you to stop at Wondabyne, did he seem in any way agitated or upset?'

'I don't think so.'

'And you didn't see if he was accompanied by a woman? Can you be absolutely sure?'

Wheeler stared into space. 'I might have, but I was busy with getting the drunk lot safely on the train. Wasn't really paying attention to anything else. I do know I checked up and down the line before we pulled out and ... actually ... maybe I did see a woman on the station, come to think about it.'

'Could you describe her? Could this have been her?' Rachael showed him a picture of Kirsten.

'Ah ... I can't be sure, sorry.'

'That's okay. So to be clear, this man,' she said, pointing to the photo, 'has gotten off the train at Wondabyne every Friday night that you know of to go fishing with another man he meets by boat?'

Wheeler bit back a grin. 'Ah, never said man.'

'He was meeting a woman?' Finn asked. 'How long has this been going on?'

'Oh, couldn't tell you. I've only been on that route for twelve months or so. Reckon he was there at least that long.'

'Okay, what about the woman he was meeting? Could you describe her?' Rachael asked.

'Ah, lightish hair, I think, slim build. I only got one half-decent look at her once a while back. It's always dark and she's pretty covered up—on the water at night, you know, so can't tell you much more than that.'

'And was the woman you just described waiting for him on this particular night?'

'Oh, yes. I remember that because I always look for the boat, smile to myself, you know?' A worried frown wrinkled his forehead. 'I hope there's no trouble coming from this. We're not timetabled to stop there on request at that time of night, and some drivers won't. But if we leave someone on the station they're there all night. Being an all-stations service it's not really holding anyone up much to stop. And we do fairly regularly get other passengers jump on and off through the night. Fishermen, local residents—especially the railway caretakers' kids after an evening in the city. Can I ask what this bloke's done?'

'We just need him to help us with some enquiries.'

'That's code for it's top secret, right?' Wheeler said conspiratorially. 'I always wondered what it would be like to be a detective. I like all the crime shows on the television. Did you ever watch *Criminal Minds*? One of my all-time favourites.'

'A few episodes,' Rachael said, smiling. 'Thanks for your time, Mr Wheeler. We'll be in contact if we need to speak to you again, but in the meantime if you think of anything else ... ' She handed him a card.

'Detective Inspector. Impressive title. You must be pretty important.'

'Just busy,' she said, making him laugh. She thanked him again for his time and Finn showed him out.

He found Rachael back in her office. 'That was a useful conversation.'

'A weekly Friday night rendezvous with another woman on the way home from work is one thing,' Finn said, 'but to then take Kirsten out there?'

Rachael shook her head. 'I don't know, Finn. I don't like it. We need to hurry up and find this guy.'

'We've alerts out in all directions and if he touches his bank account, we'll know where and when. He's not getting far.'

Rachael checked her phone when it pinged. 'Linc has something for us.'

Linc and Cass were watching his laptop screen when Finn and Rachael joined them. 'I've got some CCTV footage,' Linc said.

'That was fast!' Rachael said. 'I thought you'd be elbow deep in Latimer files for days.'

'We've barely scratched the surface,' Cass said. 'But the footage came through quickly because Linc's on remarkably good terms with the woman in charge. We prioritised it.'

'The human rule book doesn't approve,' Linc said with his signature wicked grin, 'but Leonie and I have drinks on occasion.' He turned his laptop slightly to give them a better view. 'Okay, so here we go. We've got no footage from Wondabyne Station. CCTV was monitoring, not recording. I do have a recording from Hornsby, though. You can see both Mark and Kirsten get on the train at Hornsby. It looks to me like Kirsten is nervous. She's doing a lot of looking around before getting on the very last carriage. Skip ahead a couple of minutes—' another picture appears on the screen, '— Mark appears and has a brief word to the guard before getting on.'

'That lines up with what our witness said about them travelling separately,' Rachael said.

'So he leaves the worksite at six fifteen, gets to the station and on the train roughly six hours later?' Finn noted. 'I wonder what he was doing between murdering Latimer and getting on that train?'

Cass pointed to where Bradley stood on the platform. 'Shopping? He's carrying a decent-size bag. Perhaps he was packed up to bolt.'

'Why would he pack up to bolt, then drop home again for a shower?' Finn said with a shake of his head.

'Did we contact the caretakers at Wondabyne?' Rachael asked.

'Currently on the Gold Coast on holiday,' Linc said.

'Damn. So all we have is the guard and the train passenger's accounts. Okay, we know Kirsten was supposed to be taking a few days to sort herself out before confronting Mark and that changed. Why?'

'Perhaps something on that phone she found made her aware of the Friday night rendezvous,' Finn suggested. 'She could have been trying to catch him out, hence the argument the witness heard.'

'But then what? We need more footage. I want to know if he or Kirsten got back on another train that night.'

'I'll request more CCTV from the stations closest to their home,' Linc said. 'See what I can find.'

'Great. Cass, it's too dark now, but we need police on the ground at Wondabyne first thing in the morning searching the area. Can we also get a police vessel organised to visit all the local residences and marinas? A woman on a boat at that time of night in that location suggests to me she lives close by. We need to ask around.'

'Yep, I'll get it sorted.'

'Great, then call it a day. I think we've got a few long ones ahead of us between working this and Sergeant Rico's case. On that, Lexi will be assisting with the Rico investigation.' When Cass's head shot up in surprise, Rachael added, 'She has some valuable intel we're going to be working from. Finn, my office?'

Finn followed her in and closed the door. 'What's up?'

'I meant to ask if the bank got back to you.'

His shoulders dropped. 'Yeah. Loan approval's not a problem based on my equity in the house and my wage, but with also having to pay for my flat and child support and the rest … It's just stretching things too far.'

'What if I—'

'Stop right there. I appreciate it, but if I can't do it myself, I'm not doing it.'

'So you're going to let it go?'

'I'm sorry, Rach. I know what you went through to hold on to it for me. I'm going to go talk to another couple of lenders, but if nothing changes, then I'll have to.'

'Don't be silly. I won't lie and say there's not a part of me that wishes you didn't have to sell, but that's how it is. You're going to have some money behind you with the sale so that's got to be a good thing.'

'Yeah. I might put it towards something smaller and more affordable. Get out of the renting cycle.'

'Great idea,' she said with enthusiasm, though he wasn't sure it wasn't forced.

Cass knocked on the door. 'Water police will have a boat out at Wondabyne first thing.'

'I'll go with them,' Finn said. 'Take a look around myself.'

'Sounds good,' Rachael said and checked the time. 'Go home, it's getting late. Would you mind dropping Lexi off?'

'Of course not. She's still here?'

'I left her with Craig. They're developing a plan of attack for tomorrow. I'll message her.'

He was missing something. 'What's happening tomorrow?'

Rachael's fingers rubbed at a frown on her forehead. 'That drug pick-up Lexi has arranged with Jason Hamill. Craig's keen for Lexi to play a role, so we're going to the pick-up location with a few cars in the early hours to see if they show.'

'You're letting Lexi go?' Finn asked in surprise. 'They've seen her. And you trust her to come face to face with that piece of shit and not do something understandably stupid?'

'I'm not thrilled about it but she says she can do it. As to the rest, it'll be dark, she'll be dressed appropriately and wearing a hoodie. We'll have carloads of cops ready to pounce if the twins show up. They're not going to get close enough to recognise her. Even if they do, it'll be too late to do anything about it.'

'But why take the risk at all?'

'Because she has all the information she needs to blend in if any of the other buyers talk to her. She knows how this works. None of us can fit in like that.'

'Do you need me to be there?'

Rachael shook her head. 'No, let's stick to the plan for now. There she is.' Rachael gestured as Lexi stepped out of the lift.

'Rachael?' she said. 'There's a couple of minor tweaks to the plan.'

'Come in. Won't be long,' Rachael promised Finn.

Linc wandered over to stand with him. 'Man, how did you get any work done with that sort of distraction?'

'What distraction?'

'Lexi! During the Spider case.'

Finn frowned. 'Lexi wasn't a distraction, she was an asset.'

Linc shook his head in disappointment. 'You really are a eunuch. I had my suspicions …'

'A what? Oh, cut it out. And back off Lexi. She's not falling for it.'

'I was actually trying to mend some fences. Cass can be a total bitch. I wanted her to feel welcome.'

'I wouldn't worry. Lexi can more than hold her own and I doubt Cass's opinion matters very much to her.'

'Message received. What's going on in there?'

Finn ran him through what Rachael had told him.

'I might stick around, wish her luck.'

'Sure. While you're waiting there's plenty more Latimer files to wade through.'

Linc's grin flashed. 'I'm gone.'

Lexi's phone pinged as she got into Finn's car and she took it out of her bag. 'Linc's a persistent little thing, isn't he?'

'He's messaging you?'

'Wishing me good luck for tomorrow. I've known the guy for five minutes and I wasn't even that nice to him.'

Finn set his jaw. 'Let me know when he gets on your nerves.'

'You mean when I get tired of the hot, womanising, charmer facade?'

'You think he's hot?'

'He is. And he knows it. I know some egos come with a nasty streak, but I've got him pegged as a big teddy bear who just enjoys who he is a little too much.'

'That pretty much sums him up perfectly.'

'At least he's friendly,' she said, her tone cooling.

He caught her meaning. 'Cass's a stickler for rules and order, that's all. You don't work the way she does and she doesn't like it, but she doesn't have any reason to not like you personally.'

'I'm sure I'll help her come up with one.'

He couldn't help but laugh. 'We've all been on the receiving end of the human rule book and honestly, you probably intimidate her. She had some sort of moment when you walked in earlier.'

'I thought maybe I'd seen her somewhere before. Maybe she recognised me too.'

'You spent a lot of time here during the Spider case. She was in another squad but you might have crossed paths. And look, she'll see what an asset you are. In the meantime, don't feel you have to put up with any crap, but don't antagonise her either, please.'

'I haven't!'

'Go on,' he prompted.

'Go on, what?'

'You wanted to say, "I haven't ... yet".'

'Well, no points there, that's a given.'

As they reached a section of road lined with shops and takeaway outlets, Finn yawned. 'You want to drive through for a coffee?'

'Nah, it'll keep me awake. I need an early night.'

'What time is Rachael picking you up?'

'Two thirty.'

'I hope you know what you're doing.'

'I'll be fine. They won't know who I am until after they're cuffed.'

He chuckled. 'I still remember Neutron's reaction when you put on the prostitute outfit to catch the Spider.'

'Yeah? I remember yours,' she said with a slight smirk before looking out the window.

That tied him up for a second or two. 'Just be careful, okay?' he said more seriously. 'It might be harder than you think, coming face to face with them again.'

CHAPTER TWENTY-THREE

Wednesday, March 9

The knock on my door comes at two thirty sharp. 'Yeah, I'm coming.' I check my appearance one more time. Ripped skinny jeans, a black shirt that wouldn't provide nearly enough protection from the early morning cold, but a battered, hooded jacket over it that should. A bit of cheap jewellery, loose hair that mostly covers my face and a hood over a red baseball cap. I doubt very much either twin will put this me together with cop me in the dark before the million police hiding in the bushes surround them.

I walk out of my room and accept the coffee Rachael has brought. 'Thanks.'

'You look the part. If you're ready, we should go.'

'Yeah.' Once outside I do my jacket up against the cold night air, then regret it as I climb into the warmth of the car. The coffee is hot but I take a few brave sips, hoping the caffeine will kick in. 'So where's Craig?'

Rachael does up her seatbelt and as the engine springs to life a new blast of warm air hits. 'Briefing his team. They'll be in position by the time we arrive.'

'Right.'

'Can I ask?'

I glance at Rachael. Her lips are twitching. 'Can you ask if you can ask what?'

'You, Craig, the Elsa thing?'

I groan. 'Everyone at the academy had a nickname. I'm Winter, so *Frozen*, so Elsa.'

'Got it. Still, we don't tell inspectors to fuck off.' Her phone buzzes. 'Can you check that?' she asks as she turns out onto the street.

'Speaking of Craig. They're good to go.'

'Excellent.'

'Hey, why is Finn's ex showing you a picture of a house?'

'Don't read all my messages!'

'It's right below the other one. I tapped it accidentally.'

Rachael clears her throat. 'It's probably the house she just bought. I think she's trying to keep me onside because things are a bit tense.'

'So Viv's moving out? Great. Finn can have his place back.'

'No, unfortunately. Vivienne needs him to sell it to fund the new house.'

'Oh, no! Really? He loves that house.'

'Viv and the new love interest just got engaged. They want to start afresh in their own place—understandable—and she needs her share of the house in order to buy the one they want, which is also totally reasonable.'

'I hear a but.'

'But they decided all this, found the house they wanted and told Finn at the last possible moment. Finn would have bought her out but he needed six months to clear the lease on the apartment and she hasn't given him any time or warning. She and Louis have taken out an expensive bridging loan to secure the new place so they need to sell his place immediately.'

We stop at a red traffic light as a lone car turns out of a side street. It's the only other car I've seen on the road so far. 'That sucks. Can't he refuse to sign or something?'

'Legally tricky. He could stall but that will cost money in court fees and he's trying hard not to have any massive arguments with Viv for Ava's sake.'

Silence falls while I sip my coffee. It's not fair. I have nothing against Vivienne, but I do have a problem with the way she treats Finn.

We speed towards Woy Woy and before too long are headed down the winding hill that leads to the area of mismatched industry and wasted space near the pick-up point. I spot a small group of teens smoking by the tagged wall of the storage park.

'See them?'

'Yeah.' Rachael drives on past and parks far enough down the road that they won't see me get out, but not so far I can't sprint for the car if I have to.

'There's two other carloads of cops. They've been sitting in parked cars for a couple of hours. Craig was going to plant himself as a homeless guy in a sleeping bag somewhere near the spot you suggested.'

'Got it.' I'm guessing one load is in the black van I can just make out, its windscreen dewy and fogged up.

'Keep your head down and don't approach too closely. You're there because you know the deal. That's it. As soon as either of the twins turn up, you let us know and walk away. Craig's team will be on them in a heartbeat. Turn your listening device on.'

I check it. 'You know, I used to think these were the big clunky contraptions everyone in the movies got caught wearing.'

'Not anymore.' Rachael gets on the radio and sure enough, though the place looks all but deserted, everyone is in position. Watching and waiting.

I get out, close the door quietly. It's freezing. I blow on my hands and glance around, begin trekking back down the road past dark and silent houses until I reach the carpark of the small industrial area.

I see a figure in a sleeping bag and assume it's Craig. He's tucked up against a building where he has a good view but no one can sneak up on him. The three guys and one woman I'd spotted as we drove past are off to my right and in the dull glow of the nearby security light they look like they've had a bit too much meth in their time. The biggest guy has a red cap on. They've got to be waiting for the dealers. I wander around just far enough away, deliberately keeping my face in a phone. One guy finishes a beer and tosses the empty bottle into the small creek behind the fence. It lands with a loud plop. They're taking a pretty good look at me as they check their phones and generally muck around. I can't hear what they're saying.

Ten minutes pass, twenty. Then it's almost four. Where are the twins?

The group approach. I remind myself there's a few carloads of cops nearby as well as the one pretending to be asleep in the sleeping bag ten feet away.

'Who the fuck are you?' the big guy asks.

'None of your fucking business,' I answer in the same tone.

'I'm making it my business!' He moves in too close and stands toe to toe with me. 'So who are ya?'

I should probably shut up. But living on the streets gives you a pretty good gut feeling for these types. I've got this one pegged as all bark but I have to hope my radar hasn't dulled. 'What the fuck do you care?'

'I don't like not knowing who's hanging around!'

'Oh, there, there, princess. I won't hurt you.' His friends chuckle and I can see he's going to try and save face so I add, 'I'm taking over from the other dealer, Lochie, you know, the one who's been buying and selling ten times what you're getting. That makes me pretty damn important to the Hamills, so you might want to back the fuck off.'

They all look at each other then do back off a bit. Ten more minutes pass. I scratch at my arms, hope I'm coming off as desperate for a hit. Another lone figure turns up, head in his phone after checking us all out. Another of the guys that was supposed to meet with this lot? Or another cop?

The original four down a few more beers and, after a quick glance at the newcomer, don't seem interested in asking questions. A regular, I decide. Time ticks slowly. Next check tells me it's half past four, then quarter to five.

Eventually the girl calls out, 'You got the message they were coming, right?'

'Yeah,' I say.

'See!' she says as though it's a point of dispute. 'I'm not the only one.'

'Then where the fuck are they?' the big guy asks.

'Fuck,' the new guy says.

'What?' the big guy asks with enough aggression to put me back on edge.

'Got a friend with a police radio,' the loner says, looking up from his phone. 'Some dude got smashed by a train at Wondabyne earlier. Cops are there. What's the bet our gear's all over the tracks?'

My mind is racing. Wondabyne? 'You really think it's one of them?' I blurt.

'That's where they pick up, right?' He's looking at me, suspicious.

'Dunno. I used to get my stuff from Big D in Gossy,' I say, dragging up a name from the past. 'This is my first pick-up.'

'Right.' Then, with another look around, he says, 'Fuck this. I'm gone.'

I hang around, still looking hopeful, until the others follow suit and wander off. I give it another five minutes after I'm sure they've gone, just in case. Then I head back to the car, get in.

'You catch all that?' I ask before realising Rachael's already on the phone. She holds up a finger in a 'hang on' gesture. I hear her thank someone and tell them we're on our way.

'Yes. They pick up at Wondabyne and someone's been hit by a train out there,' she says, answering my question.

The sudden appearance of a dirty face surrounded by heavy black clothing two inches from Rachael's window gives me a start. Then I realise it's Craig.

'Got ya,' he tells me, startling Rachael in the process. 'Can we confirm there's a victim at Wondabyne?' he asks.

'Yep. I was just on the phone to the police on scene. The victim was wearing a red hoodie, so there's a good chance random drug addict guessed right.' Then to me, 'Do you want to come out there with me? Otherwise I'll have someone run you home.'

'As if you need to ask,' I tell her, and think about what we've learnt. 'So it's gotta be a hike, right, from here to Wondabyne? If they're using the trains, then why not just pick up from Woy Woy?'

Rachael opens a map on her phone. 'It is, following the walking trail, but not if they follow the tracks around. And it's much more secluded between there and here than Woy Woy Station for dealing.'

'Okay, so we should walk it.'

Rachael's brows shoot up. 'I'm not walking through a train tunnel at five in the morning just so we can experience it for ourselves.'

'If one of them has been hit by a train, where's the other one? What if he's hiding out close by?'

'Then he'll have to emerge somewhere,' Craig says. 'As dead people are your thing,' he tells Rachael, 'you should head straight out to Wondabyne. I'll clean up here, organise a search for our second POI.'

'Yes, okay. I'll let you know what we find.'

Craig jogs away towards a couple of members of his team waiting nearby. Rachael's staring into space.

'What?' I ask.

'It's pretty coincidental.'

'What is?'

'Wondabyne. A tiny little station where nothing ever happens. Now we have two cases linked to it.'

'Like you said, it's secluded. It could be criminal central for all we know.'

Rachael's phone blares and she answers.

As I sit back and wait, it occurs to me to wonder which twin is in pieces on the tracks. I can't dredge up much sympathy. Thinking about the twins has my mind wandering back to their father, Elias. I wonder if Adam has convinced him to turn himself in over Brent Wilkinson's murder yet.

CHAPTER TWENTY-FOUR

A heavy fog was rising from the water, making visibility poor as Finn wound his way through the mountains. Every now and then the cloud opened up, revealing the pretty scenery of the M1 motorway. It was a drive he generally enjoyed but right now he was busy fielding a delicate issue with Ava.

'He's not my dad!' she said over the phone. 'How come he gets to tell me what to do?'

'Well ... because he's an adult and when you're in his care you need to do what you're told so you're safe and ... stuff.'

'How is making me clean my room keeping me safe? How come he can tell me I lose PlayStation time if I don't do what he says?'

'Come on, Ava. You should keep your room tidy anyway. Louis shouldn't have to threaten you. Isn't that your mum's rule too?'

'I want to live with you!'

'You can't, sweetie. We've been through this. Besides, I'd still expect you to keep your room tidy.'

'But it was bad enough when he visited. Now he's going to be here all the time and he's all bossy all of a sudden. I hate this! I don't even like the new house.'

'Aw, come on, that's not true. Your mum said you love it.'
'They love it.'
'It's right near the beach.'
'It's further away from you. And I like *this* house.' Finn could hear Vivienne speaking in the background. 'I've got to get ready for school. I love you, Dad.'
'Love you too, sweetie.'
He ended the call and swore under his breath. He didn't like the idea of someone else disciplining his child either, but he had no reason to think Louis was in any way unreasonable. Ava was going to have to learn to live with it.

His phone rang. Rachael. 'Morning. How'd everything go?'
'Not quite to plan.'
'Is everyone all right? Lexi?'
'Fine. The twins didn't show, but someone in a red hoodie got hit by a train just prior to pick-up time. From what's left of him, there's a good chance that it's Aden Hamill.'
'Ah, crap.'
'Yeah, I know. Too quick.'
Finn huffed out a laugh. She was generally a very reasonable human but not when it came to people she cared about being attacked. 'And the other one?'
'Not sure. We've got men on the mountain searching. Want to guess what station?'
'Seriously, Rach, it's really early.'
'Not when you've been up since midnight. Wondabyne.'
'You've got to be kidding. You still want me out there?'
'Yeah. Where are you?'
'About five minutes from the jetty at Mooney Mooney.'
'Great. Water police are waiting to bring you across. I'll get them to drop you here then take off and handle the door knocks.'
'Okay, no problem. See you soon.'
He took the off ramp and drove under the motorway, saw the police boat bobbing gently on the water as he entered the carpark that bordered the wide stretch of the Hawkesbury River. The area was dotted with cars and campervans. Even in winter it was a popular spot. He parked near the wharf.

'Morning,' he said to the two police on board.

'Sir.'

He stood for the quick trip along the river. There were worse ways to spend an early morning than coasting along the water, though the wind held a decent bite. They cruised between Spectacle and Long islands to where houses perched on the hillside at Cogra Bay, before taking the turn under the railway bridge into Mullet Creek. The railway line came into view, tightly hugging the shore in parts and stretching out into the creek between juts in the mountainside in others, creating a series of small lagoons as it snaked towards Wondabyne Station.

Finn spotted the jetty, the small grassy clearing containing the caretaker's cottage on the far side of the tracks, and the tall sweep of the sandstone mine up the dense mountainside nearby. A figure caught his attention. Lexi was walking along the rail line in his direction. He waved, but intent on something, she didn't look up.

On the sparkling, choppy water ahead, several boats watched the events. A police boat bobbed gently at the jetty, sharing space with a smaller boat with no apparent driver. Rachael was on the station, speaking to two forensics officers. Shielding her eyes from the sun, she spotted Finn's approach and strode out to the jetty to meet him.

'Forensics are finishing up. What's left of our POI is on its way to Steven and the rail line's reopened.'

He heard the sharp whine of a motor and looked up to see a drone hovering over nearby bushland.

'I'm sure enough it's Aden, so we're looking for Jason. No sign as yet, though,' Rachael said. 'And no drugs. We've got men at the ends of the trails out of here and a couple more hovering at the other end of the tunnel where Lexi was meant to meet with them, but after something like this, he's probably long gone.'

'So we're a bit late to preserve any possible evidence of any crime being committed by Bradley out here,' he said, watching the last of the forensic officers cleaning up.

'I alerted the police out here as soon as I could, but they'd been traipsing all over the area for a good half-hour by then. Anything they did find will be logged.'

He scanned the water. 'We've got a few spectators.'

'Yes.'

'Who's the boat on the jetty belong to?'

'I don't know. I'm guessing someone who lives on one of the local waterfront properties. Maybe it's tied here while the owner trains it to and from work or something.'

He walked onto the tiny railway platform, looked around. 'There's the cameras, a panic phone. The guard was off the train, on the station. Kirsten had a few options for alerting help.'

'If it was a straight-up argument with the husband she might not have thought she needed it. I don't know. Until we find Bradley, we're just guessing.'

'Where was Lexi off to?'

'Lexi?' Rachael looked around. 'I don't know; did you see her?'

'She was walking along the train line back in that direction,' he said, pointing south.

'That's not a walking track! The trains are coming through again, albeit slowly. She shouldn't be out there.'

He had to agree, noting the lack of any real room between the lines and the water. 'I'll go find her.'

'I'll call—'

'Nah, the way she was walking, she's on to something. I want to go see what it is. You know she won't come back until she's ready anyway.'

'Be careful!'

He followed the line around a bend to where the tracks temporarily stretched away from the mountain to form one of the small lagoons he'd seen on the way in. There was still no sign of Lexi. How far had she gone?

'Lexi!' he called out.

'Yeah, I'm up here!' he heard from somewhere in the thick green void of the mountainside. He saw her footprints in the muddy bank on the lagoon. Shit.

He reluctantly followed them, skirted the worst of the mangrove-clogged silt, stepped around a boggy mess of rubbish that looked like it had been there longer than he'd been alive, and brushed at several spiky shrubs as their twigs caught on his jacket. 'Where?' he called again, trying not to be annoyed.

'Up here!'

He moved a few more branches, looked up, and spotted her standing on one of several large rocks that overlooked the lagoon and creek beyond. 'Why?' was all he could think to say.

'Come over.'

He'd been afraid she was going to say that. He found a narrow trail that in no way protected him from the clinging vines and low scrub he encountered as he made his way around.

'I'd heard the two cops with the drone mention some old miners' cottages used to be out here,' she said as he got closer, 'and I wondered if any still stood. If there could be any kind of shelter for Jason to hide out in. But there's just a lot of rubbish and some old building supports.'

'So why did I have to—'

'And this thing up here.'

'Damn it,' he grumbled when she disappeared again. He didn't mind bushwalking, but he did object to doing it in his work clothes.

'Just here.' As Lexi spoke he saw the man-made wall and rusted valve peeking out of a wet muddy mess.

'What is this, some sort of dam? Why would it be out here?'

'You're asking me? How would I know?'

'Must be something to do with the railway,' he said. 'What's on top of it?'

'The reason I made you trek up here. Take a look.'

'That's weird,' he said. Someone had painted a section of the wall a soft pink. A bunch of flowers sat on top. The white roses with some sort of greenery were wrapped in red tissue. Quite fresh, maybe two or three days at most. Dew had dampened the paper, making it soggy, its colour leaching into the pink wall. A few candles at various stages of melted stood alongside. 'There's a graveyard of dead bouquets behind me,' Lexi said. 'Looks like this has been going on for a long time.'

'It's like some sort of memorial site,' he said, checking out the dead flowers. 'I'm not sure it's relevant to our case if it's been going on that long, though.'

'No, but come on, who doesn't want to check out something creepy in an abandoned something or other in the middle of the woods?'

'It's not the woods, it's the bush.'

'It's always the woods in horror movies. And you were already here, so …'

'Yeah okay, kinda cool,' he admitted. And definitely creepy. 'We should get going.'

'Lead the way.'

'Yeah,' he said, eyeing the best way out. 'You can fill me in on your morning as we walk back.'

CHAPTER TWENTY-FIVE

'The twins were picking up from the station?' Finn asks me as we leave the skimpy trail and walk single file along the rail line.

'That's what one of their clients told me this morning.'

'They come in by train and get off here? Why?'

'Probably because it's nice and secluded.' I can hear a train coming in slow and we step as far off the tracks as we can to let it crawl past. 'If one of them has gone in front of a train he was probably as smashed off his head as he was when he went dancing down the tunnel last time. Why do these guys do any of the shit that they do?'

'Addiction, power, greed, selfishness, complete self-absorption …'

'Ooh, why do I feel like a certain ex-wife might be coming into play here?'

'What? No. Maybe. Sorry. Got a few things on my mind.'

'Yeah, like the fact she's selling your house out from underneath you.'

'Bit of warning would have been nice, that's all,' I hear him mutter, before it occurs to him to ask, 'How do you know?'

'Do you really think you can keep a secret from me?'

'I'm not sure ASIO could keep a secret from you.'

'You're probably right.' I grin and watch my footing as we trudge around the final bend in the line to Wondabyne Station. Forensics is loading equipment into the police boat.

Rachael spots us and hurries over. 'What happened to you?'

'I heard a couple of cops say there used to be some miners' cottages a bit further south. I wanted to go check out if there were any potential hiding spots for Jason.'

'The council knocked them all down a few years back.'

'Yeah, it's all rubbish. There's signs someone's been out there pretty recently but no evidence it was either of our POIs.'

'Lots of people hike the trails around here,' Rachael said.

'I don't think that's it,' Finn said, but left it at that.

'Cass has spoken to the train driver,' Rachael tells us. 'He said the victim was one of two men fighting near the tracks. They were behind the platform. He didn't see them until it was too late. One either stepped back from a punch or was shoved. Driver's pretty traumatised.'

I watch the police boat creep away from the jetty. 'Ah ... how are we getting back?'

'They're going to run the forensic guys back to the carpark then they'll cruise around talking to all the people on the boats out here until I call them back. See if they saw anything useful or they're just rubbernecking.'

'I want to get a better look around this station, maybe the caretaker's cottage. Did you say the occupants are away?' Finn asks. As Rachael replies, the two walk away.

I yawn and, feeling a bit achy again after my hike, I decide to stay put. It's been a hell of a morning. I wander out onto the jetty and sit, staring into the water. A few minutes pass. I hear footsteps moving with purpose as they come towards me. Too heavy for Rachael. Finn, I assume, but when I glance up as the footsteps get closer, a man in a hooded jumper is walking to the end of the jetty.

Where did he come from? No train has stopped here this morning. He gives me a casual nod and steps into the small boat that's been tied to the jetty since we arrived. Interesting timing. The police boat has just left and Finn and Rachael have disappeared. Intentional? I can see why he wouldn't worry about me. In my street kid clothes I look much more like a hiker or casual visitor off one of the fishing boats on the creek than a cop.

I look for Finn and Rachael but I can't see them, so I check this guy out again as he unties the rope from the pylon. I catch a glimpse of his face, see a stream of tattooed tears running from the outside corner of his eye down his cheek.

Tears.

Rico had said tears.

My stomach flips. What if the comment hadn't been about me? What if he'd been trying to tell me who had attacked him?

I realise I've frozen, eyes stuck on those tatts, and the guy attached to them is staring at me with hard, cold eyes. Fuck. I scramble to get to my feet but I'm too slow. Before I can run he grabs a boat hook and swings it at me. I yell out as the slap of it slams me into the water.

The cold envelops me. It takes a moment to figure out up from down then the boat propeller kicks in too close to me and I push my arms out and kick my legs to send me backwards, out of the way. I push up for air but my sleeve has caught on something. I exhale sharply at the unexpected jolt. I fling my body in all directions trying to get free from whatever it is I'm attached to. Something shifts. I feel the bump as it rises level with me then I'm staring as two cloudy eyes gaze sightlessly back at me from a damaged, discoloured face. The body it belongs to hovers inches from me, hair floating around the face, reaching out to mine, surrounding me with death.

There's no air left, only agonising panic. There's an explosion of sound as the water thrums chaotically from behind me, then two hands are ripping my jacket from my arms. I scream noiselessly as the action opens a gash in my arm, turning the water red, but I shake out of it, kick, and feel myself dragged to the surface.

The first lungful of air has my head spinning. I drag in another, then another as I continue to flail around.

'I've got you,' Finn says quietly and calmly, keeping my head above water and swimming us to shore. 'You're okay. Just breathe.'

I can't control the shaking or the racking coughs. I need to throw up. To tell him. Did he see? Did he see *her*? I try to speak but it comes out as a raspy squeak.

I can hear Rachael shouting orders then more splashing as she crashes into the water to help us out. But all I can see is that face. I barely have the energy to move my limbs as I feel the smooth rocks of the shoreline under me. Finn helps me onto the jetty and, stupidly weak and still coughing, I curl into a ball. I'm freezing. I feel like I've run a marathon. And still that face …

The police boat pulls up. Rachael is calling for a blanket, a first aid kit. Then she's ordering the boat back out on the water. As my senses start to return I can feel my upper arm is throbbing. I look at it, see warm blood oozing from it. Doesn't matter. 'Dead. She's. There's a …' I get onto my hands and knees and crawl to the edge of the jetty. Look over. I can see the tips of the hair trying to creep to the surface.

'What's she saying?' Rachael asks.

'She got caught on whatever was used to weigh down the woman in the water,' Finn tells her. 'We need divers down there.'

Rachael's eyes go wide before she peers over the edge. 'Kirsten?' she asks.

'Can't tell,' he says, removing his soaked jacket and shoes. 'Maybe.'

'She was right there,' I murmur. 'Staring at me.'

Rachael puts the first aid kit down and gently draws me back. 'We need to wrap that gash on your arm. Turn around.'

I do as I'm told and lean against the pylon. My body seems to weigh a ton. Then I remember. 'The guy on the boat!'

'We're after him,' Rachael tells me, wrapping my arm. 'We were over near the caretaker's cottage when we heard you call out. We saw you hit the water. Do you know who it was?'

'He had tears.'

'He was crying?'

'No, that's not it,' I say in frustration through my chattering teeth. 'The last thing Rico said to me was "tears". I thought he said it because I was upset he was injured but he might have been trying to describe his attacker. That guy on the boat had tears. Tattoos.'

Rachael exchanges glances with Finn. 'I'll let everyone know. You two get dry.' She fastens my bandage and gets to her feet. 'And we need to get you to a hospital. You're going to need stitches.'

'And antibiotics,' Finn says, after talking on the radio. 'That body down there is in bad shape.'

Understatement. Those dead, staring eyes refuse to budge from my mind. I wonder if I'll ever not see them again.

CHAPTER TWENTY-SIX

Rachael read and re-read Craig's text message as she took the lift to the eighth floor. He'd been sidetracked. Elias Hamill, Jason's father, had turned himself in to local police. Her foremost question was why. Yes, Lochie had handed in the video showing Elias beating Brent Wilkinson to death, but why not just disappear? Craig was on his way to collect and question him. She would have liked to have been in that interview room, but this morning's incident had taken up half the day and she had her own work to do.

She strode through the meeting room door and found Cass and Linc waiting. 'Morning,' she said. 'Anything new?'

'Yep,' Cass said. 'We brought Carole back in as you asked and questioned her. Apparently she panicked after learning about the scaffolding. She was terrified that on top of losing her husband she'd lose the business. She was full of tears and remorse. Said she didn't think she could handle anything else. We told her she'd committed an offence by attempting to hinder the investigation but I wanted to leave it to you as to whether we charge her or not.'

Rachael shook her head. 'Nothing was destroyed and I want to try and keep her onside—for now. Let her think she's safe while we figure out what's really going on.'

Cass nodded. 'Also, I got hold of Latimer's and Bradley's phone records. I haven't found anything of interest as yet. I also searched their social media. Neither Latimer nor Bradley are particularly active on social media so there's nothing but Kirsten's social posts have been full of depressing memes of late about relationship problems and self-help quotes, that sort of thing.'

'Okay. It was worth a shot. Linc?'

'Yeah, first up, how's Lexi doing?' he asked with a pointed glare at Cass.

'Last I heard from her she was fine.'

'She's been attacked twice in less than a week. Been immersed in water with a dead body. She's fine?'

'It's her favourite word. Finn's taken her to the hospital to get a gash in her arm checked out.'

Linc grinned. 'He got to play hero.'

'I'm glad he was there. We were so far away when she went in the water. Then she didn't come back up.' She grimaced. 'He moved fast, thank God.'

'If you get a chance, pass on my best wishes.'

'Will do.'

'It's great she's okay,' Cass said. 'I might not agree she should be here but I wouldn't want anything to happen to her.'

'Big of you,' Linc said.

'Don't start, you two. Linc, CCTV?'

'Okay, so I've found footage showing Bradley getting off at Warnervale Station at 3:30am. No Kirsten but we now know why.'

'Okay. Let's move on to Rico,' she said, going to the other board. 'So as you know, this morning's operation that should have led to the arrests of the twins was interrupted when Aden Hamill was struck by a train at Wondabyne Station, possibly after being pushed into the train's path. The train driver gave us a description of the man responsible that matches with that of the man who knocked Lexi in the water while trying to escape the scene. Before he died, Rico mentioned tears to Lexi. This man wears tear tattoos on his face. Lexi did a rough sketch.' Rachael took the pen sketch marking the location of the tears from her bag and put it on the table. 'Under the circumstances, I'm going to make a relatively safe leap and suggest the man who killed Rico, the man who killed Aden and the man who attacked Lexi are one and the same.'

'Yeah, but who is he?' Cass asked.

'That's what we need to find out. Crime scene investigators have swept the area, and water police are going out to continue to door knock and talk to locals.'

'I'll run the tears tattoos through the police database,' Linc said, studying the sketch. 'Hopefully something will turn up.'

'And if possible, organise for CCTV to be recording out at Wondabyne at all times in case Bradley or our mystery POI return for any reason, or anything else goes on out there.'

'Will do.'

'Cass, prepare a statement and get in touch with the media. We need Bradley's face on the news, on social media. We need to appeal to the public for any information they might have.'

'Yep.'

'And if that isn't enough to keep you busy, we need to keep churning through the Latimer files. Let's get moving. I'm off to attend Kirsten's autopsy.' Rachael raced out before anyone else could hold her up. She called Finn from the car. 'How's everything progressing?'

'I'm finally dry,' he joked. 'But my suit's never gonna be the same. I threw my shoes out.'

'They were sacrificed for a good cause. How's Lexi?'

'She rang Bailee to pick her up from the hospital and ordered me to get lost and dry off.'

'I'm sure she was grateful.'

'Yeah, I know. She gets shitty when people fuss over her. She was making noises about coming in if you needed her.'

'I'll message her and tell her to stay put. I know I'm starting to sound like a broken record but she needs to rest and I can't see this autopsy being done until well into the afternoon. I don't need her. She can come in and debrief tomorrow if she must.'

'Any news on our boat guy?'

'He disappeared. I've got more boats out on the water and Linc's going to run the tattoos through the system.'

'Okay. He and Cass are juggling a lot. I'll get back in there and lend a hand. See you soon.'

She ended the call and a few minutes later pulled up at the Forensic Medicine & Coroners Court Complex. Inside the autopsy suite, Kirsten's body lay on the stainless steel table, the decay already dehumanising what had been a lovely woman.

'Morning, Steven.'

'You're keeping me busy, Rachael.'

She lifted her hands in objection. 'I'm not killing them.'

'No, but I'm blaming you anyway,' he said. 'Surf has been looking good the last few mornings but you keep insisting I do your autopsies.'

'You're the best.'

'It's a curse.'

She rubbed her hands together to warm them against the chill of the cold, clinical space. 'Any blood results from the samples taken from the clothing we found at Bradley's home?'

'We found traces of Bradley's own blood and another male I still have to cross-check as Latimer. That's it. I've taken a quick look at your train disaster.'

'Already?'

'As soon as he came in. Well, most of him. Human bodies and trains are not a good combination. It'll make a good teaching opportunity. My new assistant is about to get her first chance at putting together a human jigsaw puzzle.'

'New assistant?'

'Sorry!' A young woman charged into the room. Willow slim, with dark hair tucked neatly away and dark eyes in a delicately featured face. 'My lecture ran late.'

'This is my new assistant, Kenja Mei. Kenja is in her last year of forensic science at Sydney University. Kenja, this is Detective Inspector Rachael Langley.'

'Pleasure to meet you,' Kenja said.

'Likewise. And congratulations. You must be doing very well.'

'Excitingly talented, top of her class by a mile,' Van Zettan said, 'and still can't seem to manage to be anywhere on time.'

'I really am sorry, the—sorry,' she petered out when Van Zettan sent her a silencing look.

Rachael gave her a wink. It wouldn't take her long to realise Van Zettan was all bark, no bite.

'Right. Shall we begin?'

CHAPTER TWENTY-SEVEN

Thursday, March 10

I wake to the sound of someone letting themself into my house and my mind swims with possibilities. Bailee? Rachael? Aliens? The way my life is going at present, nothing would surprise me. I've got to take back all my spare keys.

I drag myself out of bed and by the time I'm almost at my bedroom door, Bailee has appeared in its frame.

'Hi,' she says. 'How are you?'

'Absolutely fine,' I lie. 'You didn't need to come back this morning.'

'I wanted to check on you and bring you some breakfast.'

It's on the tip of my tongue to tell her I can get my own breakfast, but she's here and being helpful and I don't want to hurt her feelings, so I do my best to smile. It's not her fault I've woken up in a bad mood from my fast-compounding injuries. I must have rolled on my stitches twenty times during the night. It's my favourite sleeping side. Not that I did much sleeping. I still haven't managed to shift the image of those dead, cloudy eyes from the back of my eyelids or the accompanying sick feeling from my stomach. 'Thanks. Just let me have a shower and I'll be right out.'

'Don't get your bandage wet.'

'I'll manage.'

I walk into the bathroom and lean heavily on the vanity. Fuck. I take a few deep breaths, reminding myself I can breathe. It's over with. I have work to do. I need to shake this off.

When I emerge a few minutes later, Bailee is hovering by a contraption I think could be a juicer and a shopping bag of green stuff she must have brought with her. She's roughly chopping a vegetable I can't name.

'What's that?'

'I've been making smoothies for breakfast every morning. This one is full of antioxidants and superfoods.'

The face I pull is genuinely horrified. 'Bailee, the only time I eat anything green is if someone misguidedly puts lettuce on a burger.'

'I know,' she says, unimpressed. 'Which is why you should try this.'

I poke at the shopping bag and, nup, can't name anything. 'What's in the paper bag?' I ask, spotting it under a mass of green leaves.

Bailee sighs and tosses ingredients into the blender. It whirls to life. 'Backup.'

I wasn't sure I wanted to eat, but my stomach grumbles so I pull it out, ignoring the slap of her hand. It's a ham and cheese croissant. 'Thank goodness for backup,' I mutter, taking a bite. I flick the kettle on and sit at the table with my breakfast to watch in equal parts horror and fascination as Bailee pours a thick green concoction into a glass.

She puts it in front of me. 'Try it.'

'I will. Post croissant and coffee.'

'No, you won't.'

'You're absolutely right.'

Bailee rolls her eyes but I can see the smile at the edges of her mouth. She takes the smoothie back and sips it.

I check my phone and see a message from Craig. Elias is in custody. The news helps lift my mood.

'What's that about?' Bailee asks.

'Work.' The kettle clicks and I make a coffee. Change the subject. 'How's the monster thing going?'

'Great!' Bailee says with way too much mock enthusiasm. 'Lucy wakes us every night and lets out these bloodcurdling monster screams. Sometimes multiple times. I'm sure our neighbours think she's possessed.'

I manage a grin into my coffee. 'But is she scared of the monster?'

'No. She's setting traps with Kai to try and catch it. She wants to be like Aunty Lexi.'

'Oh, your tone says it all. How terrible.'

Bailee chuckles. 'Not only is it not terrible, if she doesn't catch this thing soon I'm sending her to live with you. I value my sleep.'

'You know I have the perfect solution, right?'

'Please, enlighten me.'

'Buy her a new bed frame. One that doesn't squeak. She'll think she's conquered the monster, gain a little self-confidence and you'll get your peaceful nights back.'

'You really are a genius. I'll do it today.'

I don't think she's kidding. A phone sounds in my office so I get in there fast and pick it up. Lochie. Shit, I forgot to turn the phone off. And what the hell has gone wrong? 'Yeah?'

'Hey.' The voice is low, almost a whisper.

'Is everything all right? You're not supposed to be talking to me!'

'I know. I borrowed the cop's phone for a sec. He won't notice.'

He's got to be shitting me! 'Why?'

'Because I didn't think to tell you when I saw you and now I'm feeling bad about it.'

'Tell me what? What are you talking about?'

'I have a friend who got roped in kind of like I did. His name's Luke Stubbert. Goes by Stubby. He's been in longer than me and when a couple of Robert Hamill's guys got knocked off they pulled him in to the weapons side of things. He looks like a big tough guy but he was scared, really scared. I told him I'd met someone online who was keen on bringing down the Hamills and that you were helping me get out. I'd promised him I'd see if you could help him too. I can't break that promise. I couldn't live with myself if something happened to him and I didn't try. Please.'

Robert Hamill. I wasn't close to getting near him yet so this is too good an opportunity to miss. And if I can help someone else escape this shit, I'm in. 'Tell me where to find him,' I say, snatching a pen and notebook from my top drawer. 'I'll talk to him myself.'

'Thanks. You ready?' Lochie rattles off a chatroom and online alias as well as a couple of places Stubby likes to hang out. 'So that's that. The police talked to my parents for me. They even said once the Hamills drug operation is taken down I should be able to go back to my life. Uni, all of it.'

He sounds so damn relieved. So happy. 'That's great. Now get going! No more contact.' I hear a voice in the background of the call and it sounds pissed off.

'Gotta go! Thanks!' The line goes dead.

'Goodbye, Lochie. Good luck.'

I hope he doesn't get into trouble for that phone call. I've got to respect his determination to keep a promise. To care. He really is a good kid. I slide the phone and my scrawled notes into my top drawer—remember to turn the phone off this time—and head back to the kitchen. Bailee's still sipping the green goo. I pull a face at it then gratefully finish my coffee.

'I've got it,' Bailee says, springing to her feet at the knock on my door. At least this someone doesn't have a key.

A moment later Finn is standing in my kitchen. 'Hey, how's it going?'

The concern on his face bring yesterday's events straight back into focus. I just got the woman's dead face out of my head for two seconds and there it is, front and centre again. I could strangle him for that. 'All good.'

'Would you like a coffee, Finn?' Bailee says.

'Nah, I'm fine, thanks.' His eyes move to the dressing on my arm. 'How many stitches?'

'Six. It's nothing.'

But the pained expression remains. 'Sorry about that.'

I stare back in disbelief. 'You jumped into a creek contaminated with putrefying human remains and saved my life. I got a scratch. I forgive you.'

'Well. When you put it like that …'

We exchange grins.

'Have you heard anything?' I ask.

'This morning? Not much. They're looking for the guy with the tear tatts. That's all I know so far.'

'Poor woman.'

'Yeah. Did you know I've got her cat?'

'You've got a dead woman's cat?'

'I've been minding it, hoping she'd turn up alive. The sister said it'd have to go to the pound otherwise. She's allergic. Now I'm not sure what to do with it. Anyone want a cat?' he asks, looking between me and Bailee.

'Why would I want a cat?' I ask while Bailee shakes her head.

'It's very pretty and friendly ... and well behaved.'

'Sounds like maybe deep down you'd like to keep it,' I say.

'I'm not supposed to have pets. Also, litter trays are revolting.'

'Way to sell it. Does the sister know you found Kirsten?'

Finn's expression saddened. 'She was informed last night. She's sure Bradley's responsible.'

'How come?' Bailee asks.

'Marital issues.'

'And he couldn't just ask for a divorce?'

'Apparently not. So anyway,' he says to me, 'Rachael thought you might want to come with me to headquarters this morning.'

'Yeah, that would be great.' I glance at my old jeans and tee. 'Give me a sec.'

I reemerge in some office-worthy black pants and one of the muted silk shirts Bailee helped me pick out. I still feel a little odd in them, but whatever. Rachael had seemed to approve of the last outfit and I've thrown most of my old wardrobe out. There's not much call for skimpy dresses in my new line of work.

Bailee is washing out her blender but stops and wrestles the hairband from my hand as I try and roll my ponytail into a bun. She has it secured in seconds.

'Thanks. Sore arm and all that.'

'All good. Take care!'

'No more diving with dead people?'

'Making it a joke won't make it any easier to deal with,' Bailee says.

I pull a face and grab my bag. 'See ya. Go get that new bed!' I close the door behind us and head for Finn's car.

'You seem very pleased to get to work,' he says, climbing in beside me.

'Yeah. Bailee was trying to make me have some sort of gross green smoothie. Tried to sell it as full of antioxidants and superfoods. I'd rather clean your cat's litter tray.'

'It's not my cat. You look good in that stuff.' He adds, 'Very professional,' when I look at him like he's grown another head. 'And Bailee's only trying to help.'

'I know. But she's doing my head in. Hold on,' I say when my phone rings. 'Hello?'

'You still looking for that kid?' Juicey whispers. ''Cause he's here.'

'Yes! I'm coming. Thanks.'

'Bring the cash!'

'Of course.' I end the call, trying to remember where the nearest ATM is.

'Problem?' Finn asks, already slowing the car in case he has to turn around.

'How much money have you got on you?'

'Maybe a hundred. Why?'

'That's not enough. We need to get to Gosford. Stop at an ATM on the main strip. But we need to be quick.'

Finn changes direction onto the Central Coast Highway. 'Mind filling me in?'

'Working on a tip from an old ... friend. He doesn't work for free.'

'There's rules for paying informants.'

'I know.'

'If you did, you wouldn't suggest we—'

'Top of the academy, Finn. Top. There's rules for everything, I know. I'm surprised you don't need a permit to go to the toilet on duty. Do you want Jason Hamill or not?'

His expression is suddenly serious. 'I'll call for backup.'

'You do that, he's gone. No backup. Trust me.'

'That's funny.'

'And go faster.'

'There's rules on that too, you know,' he grumbles.

'Then live dangerously or let me drive.'

'Both those options involve living dangerously. And we're telling Rachael about this.'

'Sure,' I agree, digging into my wallet to see what notes I've got. Two fives. Pathetic. 'Once we've got him.'

The look Finn shoots me is pure disbelief. 'Oh, I'd just love to explain that to her.'

'She might tell me I can't do this. And then I can't do this.'

'What happened to living dangerously?'

'Living dangerously was about driving faster, not crossing Rachael! This is strategy.'

'Strategy? Like proper police strategy?'

'Yeah. Tried that. It got Rico killed,' I say, finally shutting him up. 'There's an ATM at that servo over there.'

'I'll get you the cash,' he says. 'But we're still calling Rachael.'

CHAPTER TWENTY-EIGHT

Finn looked out the windscreen dubiously. So far he wasn't a fan of this idea at all. They were parked in an abandoned used car lot that bordered an industrial development. There was a row of dilapidated houses on the next street over that were set for demolition. It was a lonely, desolate space and Lexi was planning on meeting Jason Hamill there. And she wasn't letting him come with her.

'Okay here's the thing,' she said, counting out the five hundred before rolling and pocketing it. 'In anywhere between a few seconds and a few minutes, Jason is going to come tearing out of the hole in that fence at lightspeed.'

He checked out the old paling fence belonging to the third house in the line. It was warped and eroded with age. Bright graffiti covered much of its surface. In the middle of the space, several boards were missing and yet more had been kicked out, forming a messy, triangular hole that hinted at an overgrown backyard beyond. Above the fenceline he could see part of a rusted tin roof. 'We need more cops,' he said.

'Look, we called Rachael and she okayed it. The backup you wanted is going to be two streets away.'

'Reluctantly okayed it, and I think you may have misrepresented the situation here.'

Lexi sighed and looked at his groin with a frown.

He immediately shifted uncomfortably. 'What are you doing?'

'Wondering if you still have your balls.'

'Of course I do! We need more cops *because*—' he leant on the word, hoping to give his point extra credence, '—if anything happens to you, I'm stuck out here waiting for Jason.'

'You worry too much. Besides, first sign of a cop car and my source will never trust me again.' She got out, closed the door then bent down to look in the window. 'You're going to catch him. Got it?'

'Is he going to be armed?'

Her gaze returned to his nether regions with a small smirk.

'It's a reasonable, manly question!' he objected.

'I can't tell you, but he's about to be on the move again. It's now or never.'

He looked back at the fence and assessed his chances. If he stood against it, he could most likely grab the kid as he ducked through before he could use any weapon he might have on him. He hoped. He wasn't worried about being injured, but they couldn't afford to blow this opportunity to catch Jason.

'How do you know he'll come this way?'

'Because it's the only way to get in and out of this place. The front door doesn't work and the industrial fencing runs along the front.'

'And you're sure you want to go in there alone?'

'It's not the first time,' she said. 'I've got this! Just be ready.'

He could only hope so. He got out of the car and, when she ducked through the fence, he waited, ears straining for any sign anything could be wrong. One sound from Lexi and he was going in.

There was no sound from Lexi, but within seconds Jason Hamill was crawling through the hole, awkward in his rush to escape. Finn dropped both hands on Jason's hoodie and hauled him around, spun him face first against the fence. 'You're under arrest.'

Lexi came through a few seconds behind. 'Oh, good, you got him.'

'Let me go, pig! My family won't let you do this!'

'They don't seem to be stopping us just now,' Lexi said.

'So you should cooperate,' Finn said. 'Get in the car.'

'I can't tell ya nothing anyway! They'll kill me.'

Lexi smiled coldly as she held the door open. 'It'll hurt more if I do it.'

'You don't know what pain is, lady, not yet! But I'd be happy to show you.'

'Yeah? And I'd be happy to hide your dead body in the boot of my car and help the cops look for you.'

'Bullshit!'

'It's really not,' Finn said with a smirk as he helped Jason into the car and secured his seatbelt. 'You drive,' he told Lexi. 'I'm going to sit in the back and keep an eye on him until we can transfer him into the wagon.'

Lexi belted herself in and adjusted the rear-vision mirror. He gathered it was so she could see Jason, who scowled back at her.

'Juicey didn't know you were a cop, did he? Now he does, he's gonna come after you.'

'It's sweet you're concerned,' Lexi said, 'but I think you've got enough of your own problems to worry about.'

Finn worried, though. He'd have to remember to ask her about any possible fallout with Juicey and what that might mean for her safety.

'You don't know anything!' Jason spat.

'I know you and your brother have been dealing Crystal Gold. You've been replacing that tag the cops keep getting rid of because that's how people find you to buy your stuff. The night Sergeant Rico and I found you out by the tunnel, your brother ran in there to dump the drugs so we wouldn't catch you with them. The thing is, the next night when we went back to find them, Rico was murdered. Since you're such a sook, I'm thinking it was by your friend with the teardrop tattoos. You know, the one who also killed your brother. What's his name?'

'Dunno!'

'Are you sure?' At Jason's stoney silence, she shrugged. 'Fine, let's call him Tears for now. Once you're in the interview room you're going to need to tell us about Tears so we can decide if you're an accomplice to two murders, or a stupid kid who needs protection.'

Jason hesitated, stammered a bit, then said, 'I'm not either!' His head hit the back of the seat with a thump. 'Aden's death was an accident. He just ... he gets a bit carried away with his habit. He's not careful. We lost our stash because of you! So ... *Tears* roughed him up a bit. Told him how we can't be making mistakes 'cause some dickhead is after the family. Aden was smashed, mouthed off at him and there was a bit of pushing and shoving.'

'Yeah, into the path of a train. You really want to protect that guy?'

'I told ya, it was a fucking accident! Train was coming so Tears tried to grab him 'cause Aden was out of it, not seeing straight. But I reckon Aden thought Tears was coming at him to smack him and he stepped back. Right into the fucking train.' Jason choked up.

'So this Tears. Is he the cook?'

Jason pulled himself together, sat straighter. 'Dunno.'

'So you're trying to tell me you don't know who this guy is or where he comes from. He just gives you drugs and kills people.'

'Dunno,' he said again.

'And the cop you bashed—Constable Hadley?'

'Dunno.'

'Too much mind-altering crap or are you naturally stupid?'

'Maybe we had a stack of gear on us! Couldn't let no cop catch us with it. Maybe we had no choice.'

'Right.'

'But maybe we didn't do it, either. I want my lawyer.'

'What's going to happen is you're going to sit tight while we work out what we're going to charge you with,' Finn said. 'Then we'll call your lawyer.'

'I want my phone call.'

'Yeah. Yeah. To Grandpa Raymond, right?' Lexi said sweetly. 'You think he's going to bail you out?'

Jason's eyes widened, then some of that shiftiness came back. 'You're not gonna mess with them. They'll get ya for this,' he spat. 'You're dead.'

'So seriously,' Finn said to Lexi as he hung around the interview room waiting for Jason's lawyer to finish speaking with his client, 'is this Juicey guy going to retaliate?'

'For what?'

'For you being a cop and not telling him.'

'I have no idea. I didn't tell him I was a cop. I don't think it came up. I walked in, Jason spotted me and bolted. I threw the cash at Juicey and followed. As far as I know it all went down perfectly.'

'But surely Juicey would have spied us getting him in the car.'

She shrugged. 'Maybe.'

'Does he know where you live?'

'Do I look like an idiot?' she asked wearily.

'No, but you take too many chances.'

'And look at the progress we're making!'

'Your life is more than one case. If you—'

'Sorry,' Rachael said, powering towards them. 'What are we up to?'

'Still waiting on the lawyer to finish with his client,' Finn said, deciding to drop his conversation with Lexi for the time being.

'So what do we know?'

'Our POI with the tear tatts is producing the meth the boys have been distributing. Meaning, of course, he works for the Hamills. Aden's death was an accident. He was toasted on meth and stumbled in front of the train while he and Tears were having a disagreement.'

'Not a bad morning's work,' Rachael said. 'Well done.'

'Did you discover anything of value from Kirsten's autopsy?'

'There was already quite a lot of damage to the body from being in the water—'

'No kidding,' Finn and Lexi said in unison.

'—but it looks like she was beaten and strangled.'

'Strangled? Not drowned?' Finn asked.

Rachael shook her head. 'Body went into the water after death. Divers said she was attached to an old wire crab trap that in turn was partially caught under some other metal rubbish that looked like pieces of discarded railway line and barbed wire. It appears the act of tossing her body off the jetty submerged it enough to get caught up much as Lexi did.'

'So he wasn't trying to hide the body,' Lexi said.

'Unless she'd gotten loose from some other weighting method we missed, then no.'

'It's not like he bothered to hide Latimer's body either, assuming Mark Bradley's responsible,' Finn reminded them.

'On that, there was no evidence of any of Kirsten's blood on the shirt recovered from their home, only Latimer's. But as we didn't recover his jacket, and Daisy said he had it done up when he got off the train, that may have protected the shirt.'

The interview room door opened to reveal a big man who looked like he'd be more at home in the boxing arena than in the expensive suit he was wearing. But Finn knew how deceiving looks could be. Especially in the case of Stewart Diggens. The man rarely lost a case and charged enough to warrant his reputation. The Hamills weren't cutting corners with their grandson's future.

'Are we ready to begin?' Rachael asked.

'Yes, yes, inspector. After talking to Jason, I'm positive that you'll see this is all one big misunderstanding.'

'I'm sure,' Rachael said dryly. Then she turned back to Lexi. 'Are you coming in?'

'Yeah, okay.'

While Rachael set up the interview, Finn stared hard at Jason. The teenager looked more like a lost, angry kid than anything else. Being born into that sort of family hadn't given him many options. He could almost feel sorry for him. Almost.

'So, Jason,' Rachael began, 'we're looking into two murders. We're not here about the drugs. You can chat about those with Inspector Slavek later. All we want to know about is what happened to Sergeant Rico and to Aden. I'm going to give you a chance.'

Jason briefly glanced her way. He seemed to be having trouble sitting still. 'To what?'

'Talk to us. To tell us your side of what happened before we catch up with our suspect with the tears tattoos. I'm very sorry about Aden. Let's get both victims some justice.'

Jason looked at Diggens, who said, 'Mr Hamill is exercising his right to silence.'

'It really is in his best interest to talk to us. So what do you say, Jason?'

Another glance at Diggens's set face had Jason looking down at his hands. 'No comment.'

'I hear there's a few members of a rival family in Silverwater detention centre that would like some time with one of Raymond and Lena's grandkids. That's where you're headed right after this interview. I can make sure you don't end up with them.'

Diggens sat straighter in his chair. 'I shouldn't need to tell you, inspector, that you can't threaten or bribe a witness!'

'I'm doing neither of those things,' Rachael said coolly. 'I'm genuinely concerned for his welfare. I'd really like to make sure you're safe, Jason. We know what some of those inmates are capable of. But you need to give us something in return.'

'I'll be fine,' Jason murmured.

'Come on, Jason,' Finn said. 'Are you flat out stupid?'

Jason's hand slapped the table. 'No!'

'You're going to risk being put in a cell with people who want you dead to protect the identity of the man who killed your brother? You really think he'd do the same for you?' Finn saw the doubt so kept pushing. 'Raymond can't help you once you're inside. All the dirty money in the world won't protect you in there. So be smart! If we can prove you weren't involved in Rico's death we can take murder off the table. All you've got to worry about is some minor league drug charges.'

Jason seemed undecided. He bit on his lip as though wanting to speak. Then his hand went to his head, the heel of it rubbing his left eye. He gave a frustrated growl. 'You think I'll dob him in? I'm not gonna do that to him! I can't!'

''Cause, what? You'll hurt his feelings?' Lexi asked from the corner of the room.

Jason's expression turned hateful. 'Fuck off, bitch.'

'You think those tears he wears signifies he's a cry baby? Seriously?'

'No!'

'He killed Sergeant Rico!' she snapped.

'I know!'

'And if he's happy to kill Rico, why wouldn't he kill you?'

'He wouldn't dare!'

'Because he's just the cook, and cooks can be replaced, right?'

'Damn straight!'

'What's his name, Jason?' Rachael pushed, keeping the pressure on. 'Just a name, and your future looks a hell of a lot brighter.'

'I …' Another glance at his lawyer.

Diggens cleared his throat. 'My client has said no comment, detectives. Will that be all?'

Rachael took a deep breath and looked at Finn. He shook his head to let her know he had no more questions. They'd already gotten more than they'd dared hope for and she had a feeling the Hamill laywer would have been strictly instructed to make sure Jason didn't say anything helpful.

'Thanks, Jason. That's all we need for now.'

'But what about remand?'

'Good luck. If you change your mind about identifying our suspect we'll take another look at your prison conditions. Talk soon.'

'Well done!' Finn told Lexi as soon as the door closed. 'Kid didn't know what he was saying.'

'So we now have confirmation Tears killed Rico and accidentally killed Aden,' Rachael said.

'More than just those two, judging by the number of tears,' Lexi said.

'It's likely,' Rachael agreed, 'but although multiple teardrops can indicate how many victims the wearer has murdered, my understanding is the symbolism varies. In some cases, it's symbolic of killing someone, in others, of losing someone to crime. It could mean murder or attempted murder … there's a few possibilities.'

'Regardless, we need to get this guy off the street,' Finn said, 'unless the Hamills take him out for us. I can't imagine they'll be too happy about Aden's death.' Then to Lexi, who was staring into space, he said, 'What are you thinking?'

'Tears was accessing the station by boat, so where was he coming from? He has to have a place with boat access and it has to be somewhere on the river because that little boat he had isn't doing trips into open water.'

'No, but he might have a bigger boat he travels there in,' Rachael said. 'Only using the dinghy to come ashore.'

'And this Bradley guy. He's been meeting a woman in a boat out there every Friday night; that's the same night and the same place Tears was delivering to the twins. Almost the same time. You don't think that's an odd coincidence?'

Rachael shook her head. 'I don't believe in coincidence.'

CHAPTER TWENTY-NINE

'Cass, where are we with the Latimer accounts?' Rachael asked. She finally had everyone around the table and didn't want to waste any time. Lexi sat at the end of the table. This wasn't the case she was here to assist with but Rachael couldn't shake the idea there could be a connection, so she was happy to have Lexi on board.

'We've worked out the rejected scaffolding ended up at an intermediary company before being picked up by Latimers, who paid top dollar for it.'

'That's strange,' Finn said. 'A man in Bradley's position must have known it wasn't up to scratch.'

'What is this company?' Rachael asked.

'That's the thing. It's called the Building Supplies Contractor. The website claims it's "the easy way to do business". You fill in a form of what you need for your project, they do all the searching and, for a small fee, source your materials from all over the place at the best possible price. Except they don't. A closer look revealed it's a shell company with a bank account and address in Panama.'

'A shell company?' Lexi asked.

'It's a company that only exists on paper,' Rachael explained. 'No employees or offices, sometimes used for tax evasion or money laundering.'

'Yeah, I know, but I mean, this company that you say doesn't actually exist purchased unsafe scrap scaffolding and sold it on to Latimer Developments for a large profit.'

'What if ...' Rachael chewed her lip as she frowned. 'What if Bradley created the shell company as a way of embezzling from Latimer?'

'How exactly would that work?' Cass asked.

'Easy. Part of Bradley's job was to source and purchase materials on behalf of Latimer Developments. So he sets up this pretend company to send jacked-up quotes. He accepts the quote on behalf of Latimer, then when Latimer's funds land in his company's account, he secures the materials for the lesser price and pockets the rest.'

'That's ... clever,' Cass said. 'And that profit could potentially be huge. From what I can see, hundreds of other transactions have gone through.'

Rachael nodded. 'But we're speculating. Cass, can you access Bradley's bank accounts and find out if there's any transactions connected to that shell company?'

'I'll see what I can find.'

'Bingo!' Linc said. 'I have a possible match on our Tears guy.' He tapped on his laptop and a picture appeared on the wall screen.

'Yeah, that's him,' Lexi said, her face darkening.

'His name is Ian Clarke,' Linc said. 'He's got an impressive rap sheet for robberies and drug offences. Spent most of his young life in and out of juvie, and is currently wanted in relation to a spate of armed robberies on the coast four years back, one of which ended in the death of a security guard.'

'Good work. Get that information out. You know what to do.'

'How can I help?' Lexi asked.

'Ah, Linc, do you need any assistance?'

'Not with Clarke, but I have a ton of CCTV footage to get through from Friday afternoon. I'm trying to trace what happened between Mark Bradley leaving the site of Latimer's death and when he got on the train.'

'Can't you trace his movements through his phone?' Lexi asked.

'I have that data on my desk. But we want to know what he was doing in those locations. Whether he purchased anything, met with anyone, that sort of thing.'

'Then I guess I've got something to do.'

Linc moved some of his things, clearing Lexi a space. 'We're good,' he told Rachael.

'I'm sure,' she said. 'Craig will be interviewing Jason at the remand centre soon. I'm going to watch on in case he gives anything else up. I'll be back shortly.'

Rachael made the interview just in time and sat through twenty minutes of Jason refusing to cooperate before Craig gave up and ended it.

'We don't have much on him,' Craig said, leaving the room. 'He's already been fined for possession, he's not admitting to bashing Hadley and we can't prove he was dealing. We know he was associated with Clarke and witnessed his brother's death, so we can possibly throw hindering a police investigation at him, but we need a stronger case.'

'That witness Lexi brought in, Lochie. He's willing to testify that Jason and Aden were dealing, isn't he?' she asked as they headed down the corridor.

'Of course, but it wouldn't hurt to have more than one witness. That Hamill lawyer will rip Lochie's credibility to shreds in seconds.'

'What about Elias? How did that go?'

'He's not saying any more than his son. But we've charged him with murder and he's been refused bail.'

'Did he give you any idea of why he turned himself in?'

Craig stopped walking, sighed. 'Do you ever wonder if Lexi's giving you the full story?'

'Occasionally, but I can't see how she could convince Elias to turn himself in. Why?'

'I can't come up with any reason Elias would hand himself over to police other than to get Adam off the hook, and the only person I know of who knew Adam had ordered the hit *and* had the evidence to manipulate him was Lexi. I could be completely on the wrong track but I sometimes get the feeling she's working with us but not *with* us, if you get what I mean.'

Rachael nodded slowly. 'She hates what the Hamills did to Rico, what they're doing to all the vulnerable kids they use and abuse. She has this idea of working her way up that pyramid of hers, putting them all away because the only way to get to Raymond is through the others. Then she's hoping Raymond will give up Debbie to save himself. But as I've told her, she's not involved in that investigation. Or in the one the Feds are running on Reynolds and Vaughn. I brought her in on Rico's murder. That's it. She might know of another witness we can round up to testify against Jason.'

'Worth a shot,' he said, stepping out of the way of a couple of passing guards. 'But, Rach, I'd be happy for Lexi to be involved in the Hamill investigation. I'd be stupid not to have her onboard. Would that be a problem?'

She considered that for a moment. 'Lexi has her own take on the rules, a very limited amount of experience on the job, little to no sense of self-preservation and a serious grudge against the Hamills. Let's get Rico's killer dealt with first, see how that all pans out. Then, if you involve her, you keep her safe, keep her out of trouble.'

Craig pressed his lips together against a smile. 'Or I'm dead. Got it.'

Satisfied, Rachael returned to homicide and found Lexi and Linc still working at his desk, Finn and Cass nearby sorting through Latimer files. 'How'd you go?' she asked Linc.

'Excellent,' he said. 'Lexi found some footage of Kirsten Bradley before she boarded the train.'

'I spotted her getting out of her car at a nearby shopping centre,' Lexi said as Linc brought the footage up. They watched the CCTV footage on screen as Kirsten got out of her car in the well-lit carpark. She swung a bag over her shoulder and locked up, then strode towards the station. She looked around, over her shoulder, down both sides of the street.

'Is she looking for someone or is she worried she's being followed?' Rachael asked.

'Can't be sure,' Linc said. When Kirsten disappeared from the screen, he stopped the recording.

Lexi shifted in her chair. 'Okay, I know I've watched that a few times now, but can you zoom in on that bag again? Something's bugging me.'

'Yeah, hold on.' He brought Kirsten's image back into view and enlarged her image.

'What is it?' Rachael asked.

'I can't be certain, but I have a faint memory of seeing a bag that had a buckle like that in a rubbish dump out at Wondabyne. Finn, do you remember? Down in the shallows of the inlet.'

'I know the spot you mean but I didn't see a bag,' Finn said.

'You saw a handbag out there and didn't think to check it?' Cass asked Lexi.

'You have no idea what that little rubbish pile is like,' Finn said. 'Old clothes, linen, gumboots, pieces of fibro, some sort of artwork and even an old dishwasher. It's a mess.'

'If her bag is out there it could contain the phone she was going to confront Bradley with,' Rachael said. She glanced at the time. 'I don't think we can get out there this afternoon. Are you busy tomorrow?' she asked Lexi. 'Can you go back out there with Finn?'

'You know I'm not busy,' Lexi said. 'I'm in.'

'I'll get it sorted,' Finn said.

'I should come too,' Linc said. 'Nine years on the water police. I can drive the boat. It'll be easier than trying to organise a patrol to take us out.'

CHAPTER THIRTY

Friday, March 11

'I see it!' I tell Finn, pointing. We've been back at Wondabyne since way too early in the morning and after scanning the rubbish for several nervous moments I was beginning to think I'd imagined the handbag and wasted everyone's time. But as it turns out, the bag has moved, pushed further out into the middle of the debris, perhaps by the movements of the tide washing in and out through a drainage pipe under the tracks.

'I don't,' Finn says from a few feet further along the lagoon. 'Where?'

I swat at a random bug that's landed on my arm. 'It's there,' I say, doing my best to point. 'About five feet out. Kind of half-submerged under the— What is that big rusted box?'

'Oh, that? I think it could be an old washing machine.'

'Even if squatters were living out here, what would they do with a washing machine?' I shift my feet further back from the water's edge. It's getting sloppy.

'It probably pre-dates the squatters. I see the bag. It looks like it could have been in there as long as the washing machine. You sure that's it?'

'Nup. But if you were dumping something out here to get rid of it, you'd want to cover your tracks and poke it in there a bit.'

Finn's clearly not convinced. 'Even if the phone's in there, it's probably wrecked.'

'Well, go on then. Only one way to find out. In you get.'

He turns and I get the look I'm expecting. 'You want me to go in there?'

'How else are we going to get it? Linc's minding the boat, remember?'

'How about you go in? You're half my weight. You won't sink as far in the mud on the way in.'

'I can't go in. I'll get my stitches wet and then they'll get infected.'

'Oh, how convenient.'

'It is, isn't it?' I say, not bothering to hide my smile this time.

With obvious reluctance, Finn takes off his shoes and socks.

'Are you sure that's a good idea?' I ask. 'You might step on something nasty.'

'I've already ruined a pair of shoes this week,' he says. He shoves his socks in his shoes and rolls his pants above his knees. His second step into the mangrove-speared mess has the mud seeping dangerously close to the material.

'Can you see a long stick somewhere? I can't get in any further.'

'It'd need to be an entire tree to reach that far.'

'So go get a tree!'

I chuckle, enjoying myself. 'Strip down and wade out there.'

'In this mud?'

'It's clear further out. If you get the bag and keep going over to the other side you'll wash off. It's rocky over there.'

'I love it when you're helpful.' He's still eyeing the bag and weighing his options. He drags his leg out of the black mud. The move makes a sucking sound, then a squelch as he tries a different spot with the same result.

'You're going to ruin your pants,' I warn him.

'Well, I'm not going to strip down in front of you, am I?'

My laughter burbles out. 'Don't mind me. I've seen it all before.'

'Not mine, you haven't! And like you said, who knows what's in that rubbish?' He's clearly not impressed. 'Go back to the boat. Tell Linc to get his arse over here in case I get stuck.'

I know it's not fair that I'm finding this so funny, but I can't help it. The big bad detective is shy. I head back out to the rail line. Finn's completely out of sight when I throw back a wolf whistle. I get a 'You'd better be gone!' in response.

I make my way back to the boat still stupidly chuckling, until I reach the jetty and my humour fades. I can't help but take a look down at that one spot in the water I'd desperately attempted to avoid when we'd arrived. But there's nothing down there. Not anymore. It's as peaceful as the rest of this place.

Linc jumps out of the boat. 'That where you went in?'

'Yeah.'

'Bound to give you the heebie-jeebies for a while.'

I lift my gaze to meet his cheerful one. He's cute when he's trying to help. 'Finn asked me to get you. Follow the train line until you see a naked guy taking a swim. He had to go in to rescue the bag and he might need some help.' The idea a train might pass occurs to me. Finn's gonna kill me if it does.

'Naked? Did you pinch his clothes?' Linc asks wickedly.

'I wasn't allowed to hang around.'

'I honestly don't know what's wrong with that guy.'

Amused, I sit in the skipper's chair and spin it around so I'm facing the broad expanse of creek, rather than the jetty. Deciding to keep my mind busy, I pull out my phone to call Rachael. There's no answer but she calls straight back.

'We just got word a local fisherman has seen a houseboat on the water regularly on Friday nights. He said he's noticed a dinghy going between the boat and the jetty a few times, but he's hazy on details. The houseboat is usually still there when he calls it a night around two, but it's gone the next day.'

'So we're looking for a houseboat? Do you know how many houseboats there are on the Hawkesbury River?'

'It's not much to go on, but the boat is predominantly white, not too flash and has a name scrawled across the back that our witness could never read in the dark. We'd have to be lucky to get something from that but I've got the guys on the water heading over to Brooklyn to check out the marina and all the mooring sites and chat with whoever's around. If they don't have any luck they'll cruise the river, take a look at what's on the water. How are you going?'

'We found the bag. Finn's retrieving it now.'

'Excellent. Keep your eyes open on your way back for that boat.'

'Will do. Finn and Linc have just come back into view. We'll see you soon.' I end the call and watch the men. Finn looks sticky and uncomfortable, but has the bag in his hand.

'How was the water?' I ask as they step on board.

'Same as it was two days ago when I saved your arse.'

'Got it. I'll play nice,' I say. 'Find the phone?'

'I found two phones, one's no doubt Kirsten's. The bag was zipped shut, so we'll see. They're soaked but remarkably not muddy. Neutron might be able to work his magic for us.'

'Right, let's get this thing moving,' Linc says and starts the engine. We head out of the creek and rejoin the Hawkesbury River. There's a settlement of houses lining the mountain to our right, with long wharves poking out from a maze of mangroves that reach far into the river. I catch glimpses of a few boats in the small harbours made by the twisty, woody shrubs, but the majority are at least partially hidden from view. No sign of any white houseboat, but that doesn't mean one's not hiding in there.

'Can we get in closer to those wharves?' I ask Linc.

'That's Cogra Bay. Why?'

'Oh—right. We're looking for a houseboat. White, not flash, some name scrawled along the back. Rachael asked me to keep a look out.'

'Then of course.' He sweeps the boat around and after a couple of minutes of scanning the shoreline, I catch the briefest hint of a large vessel before a long stretch of mangroves reclaims it. 'Can we get closer to that wharf over there? I thought I saw a houseboat. It's difficult to see a lot of the moorings among the mangroves.'

'No problem.' Linc takes us in. He cuts the engine as we close in and the boat slows. 'Where do you think you saw it?'

I point. 'Through there. We might have to drift around a bit more.' A few seconds pass before I see another glimpse of the boat. 'That kind of fits the description of a white, not flash houseboat, doesn't it?'

Finn considers that as he gets a better look. 'It's a houseboat, right colour, so yeah, possibly. But water police have been door knocking around here. They would have spotted it already.'

'They didn't know what they were looking for then. We should check this out.'

'We'll let Rachael know and find out a bit more about the property owners.'

'You sure?' Linc says. 'We're right here. Only take a minute.'

'Forget it,' I reply. 'Captain Sensible here will not be swayed.'

'I've allowed myself to be swayed before!' Finn objects over Linc's snort of laughter. 'You nearly got my head blown off!'

I think back to the time I convinced him to check out a cabin belonging to a would-be murderer after the damn television had us thinking someone was being attacked. 'Oh, there, there. I saved you, didn't I?'

'Just. Got a hammer on you this time?'

'A hammer?' Linc asked with a laugh. 'Seriously?'

'No hammer or cattle prod this time. But I'm adaptable.' Then I say, more seriously, 'Why don't we get a couple of photos to show the witness? He can verify if it's the same boat and if so, we can do the research and come back.'

'What do you want to do?' Linc asks when Finn doesn't immediately answer.

'The photo idea has merit,' Finn says after a moment. 'Pull in at the end of the wharf, I'll grab a couple and we'll take off. Let me know if you spot anyone.'

'You got it.' Linc swings the boat in gently against the wharf with the ease of a pro and Finn steps off. I jump out behind him, cop a frown.

'What?'

'Is there any point asking you to stay in the boat?'

'Nope.'

'Then stay close.'

We walk down the wharf far enough to get a proper look at the houseboat. On the mountainside above at the end of way too many stairs, a fancy corrugated iron home comes into view. No movement, no sound comes from it.

'Tripping,' I say.

'Huh?'

'The houseboat. The writing along the back says, "Tripping".'

'Apt name if it's our boat.' He takes three or four quick shots with his phone. 'Right, let's go.'

I hear a crack, but it isn't until Linc ducks from his standing position on the boat that it makes sense. I have time to be relieved the bullet has hit the engine rather than Linc before a figure emerges on the next wharf across, blocking our path back. It's Clarke. This is not good. Linc is now hidden mostly below the side of the boat but I hear him get off a shot. A second bullet hits the boat engine. A hint of flames begins to lick at it.

'Lexi, get down!' Finn orders when I just stand there, everything happening too fast to process. We duck for cover as Finn gets on his radio for assistance. I risk another look at the water and see Linc leap over the side of the boat, a lifejacket in one hand.

'I think the boat's on fire. But Linc's okay.'

'Great. We're not. Move!'

I'm towed to the end of the wharf and along the bank. Another shot, this one at us. The bullet glances off the houseboat as Finn manages to put it between us and Clarke's line of sight. I'm now being pushed along, this time towards the cover of the mangroves, then behind an old red gum that's leaning over the shallows.

'Well, that was close.' I look at Finn and notice his 'I told you so' expression. 'What, we're gonna do this now? Really?'

'Every time!'

'You're not dead. Yet.' Then I spot the woman on the balcony. 'Duck!'

'Where?'

'Balcony!' I risk a better look. 'Hey, that's Josie Hamill!'

'Great, I'm more worried about the one I can't see. Keep your eyes open.' A voice over Finn's radio confirms police backup is on the way. He turns the sound off. 'Do you know how to swim?'

'Of course I know how to swim! Why?'

'I want you to get under the wharf. Keep to the cover of the mangroves and get as far away as possible. I'll draw fire. You ready?'

It takes a moment for that to sink in.

'Lexi! Are you ready?'

'What—no! You think I'm going to take off while you wave yourself around as bait? I'm not going anywhere!'

'I'm not going to get shot.' Another bullet, then another and another in rapid succession from two different directions. 'There's Clarke.'

He's moved off the wharf and is walking along the shoreline, shotgun pointed in our direction. The only way to go is towards the house and Josie Hamill. Finn points to some cover behind a tumble of large boulders on the mountainside. I nod. We run, then lunge behind it as more shots ring out.

'Not a good idea to pop in unannounced around here!' Clarke calls out.

'Drop your weapon!' Finn orders. 'This is the police!'

'No shit!' comes the reply, followed by another shot.

'Yeah, he doesn't care,' I say.

'Hey, darlin'! Reckon you can get 'em from there?' Clarke calls.

'Can't see 'em!' Josie calls back. I hear her steps on the balcony, then, 'Oh, wait. There they are.'

'Move!' Finn orders and shoves me out of our hiding place as it explodes into chips of sandstone. Then he drives me up some steps tight against the side of the house.

'Josie—'

'She went in—probably reloading. Go faster.'

I'm puffing as I look up, see that there's way too many stairs to go. 'How about this,' I say, trying to ignore the fact that not even adrenaline can stop the pounding in my ribs. 'You shoot them and we don't have to climb the mountain.'

'Keep going.'

'And what if Josie's moved around the back of the house?'

'Yeah, right,' he mumbles but he's still driving me on, trying to keep sight of Clarke through the trees that are somewhat protecting us from view. 'Under the rail,' he orders when we are almost at the top. 'Head into that bush. Keep low.'

I try to do as I'm told but my feet are slipping on the steep, leaf-littered mountainside, slowing me down and forcing me to use my hands. Finn surges ahead, then my arm is taken in a tight grip and I'm dragged onto firmer ground. We keep going, past the house and into the bushland beyond.

'Finn!' I hiss and point. Through the trees ahead is a large shed. Two men are smoking nearby and, obviously alerted to our presence, are scanning the trees. I can't see any weapons. One turns in our direction. I step back and slip, sliding down the bank, my feet unable to get any purchase in the leaf litter. I hit something solid. Shaken and sore, I look up. My breath stops.

'Well hi there again, darlin'.'

Clarke has me lined up, shot gun inches from my face.

Heart racing, I attempt to scramble away in a kind of backwards crab walk, my eyes glued to the gun. But the hill's too steep. I'm not getting anywhere.

'Put it down!' Finn thunders.

Clarke smiles slowly, then with a jerk of the rifle, gets a shot off at Finn, forcing him back. Clarke lowers his gun back to me. His finger is on the trigger.

When the gunshot echoes off the mountainside I wonder why nothing hurts. Almost simultaneously, I see Clarke flinch and stumble until a young gum tree halts his progress. He manages to half fall, half shuffle behind it, the barrel of his gun just visible.

By the time I can react, Finn's already behind me and dragging me out of sight.

'So the gun does work,' I say.

'Smartarse.'

'Thanks for not letting him kill me.'

'You're welcome. Stay put.' Finn cautiously moves around the tree.

'Is he dead?'

Finn extends his arm, probably checking for a pulse. 'Yeah.'

'Dead?' Josie screams from somewhere above us. Then she's on her way down, her eyes glued to Clarke.

'Don't move!' Finn calls, gun trained on her.

'I'm not armed!' she wails, lifting her hands before reaching Clarke and sliding down beside him, sobbing hysterically.

I get my shaky legs under me and walk cautiously down.

'Who else is on the property?' Finn asks Josie.

She launches a tirade, moaning and crying and clinging to the dead guy but not telling Finn what he needs to know.

'That's a lot of carry on!' It's Linc's voice. He's at the bottom of the stairs, leaning heavily against the wharf railing and dripping water all over the deck. I see a thin line of watery blood trickling from the hem of his clinging pants and realise he's favouring the leg.

'What happened?' Finn calls.

'First bullet went right through the engine and grazed me a bit. No drama.'

'Got any cuffs on you?'

'Always.'

Finn turns his radio back on and we immediately hear Rachael's voice.

'Yeah, hi,' Finn says.

'You called for backup. What's happening?'

'We, ah ... found Clarke. He's unfortunately deceased. We also have a female Lexi has identified as Josie Hamill. Linc is injured, but he's being a smartarse so I think he'll survive. There's at least two more POIs in the bush somewhere behind the property.'

'Property? What property? Where are you?'

'I don't know exactly. Cogra Bay ... somewhere.' We all duck instinctively as something on the police boat blows up. 'I think if reinforcements follow the burning boat they'll find us.'

'I—you're serious?'

'Would I be game enough to joke about something like this?'

'My God. I don't even know where to start! I'm on my way.'

Finn looks at me and his face has 'we're in trouble' written all over it. 'Now can I do the I told you so?' he asks.

'I'm going down to check on Linc.'

'There's still more guys out there.'

'They bolted!' Josie cries, eyes full of wet fury. 'I went to get them and when I told them you were cops, they took off!'

So that's where she'd gone, not to reload but to get backup.

'We all go together,' Finn orders. 'Keep your eyes open.' He drags Josie to her feet. 'Move.'

'I'll go first,' I say when he has trouble removing Josie from Clarke's body.

'Be careful.'

'Good plan!' I start down the mountain. It's much easier making my way down than it was going up under fire.

Linc has sunk to a sitting position but he smiles when I reach him.

'You sure you're okay?' I ask, probably stupidly.

'Yeah.' He reaches under his sodden jacket and locates his handcuffs, then hands them to me.

I take them to where Finn has sat Josie on the edge of the wharf. He cuffs her to a pole attached to a rail that runs the length of the wharf. 'He's still bleeding,' I tell him. 'I should look in the houseboat, see if I can find a first aid kit.'

Finn's gaze moves up the hill and I know he's still worried about the other POIs. 'Keep an eye on Josie. I'll take a look.'

I sit out of range of the crazy person and watch Finn examine Linc's calf until Josie's sniffing eventually drags my attention back. She's sitting with her knees bent, crying and banging her head against them.

'Sucks, doesn't it?' I say.

'You think?' She gives me a disgusted look. 'He's dead!'

'Yeah, well, shoot at the cops, they're gonna shoot back. Eventually,' I add with a pointed look towards Finn.

'He was a human being, you know!'

'Yeah, so was my partner.'

She thinks about that for a few seconds before it clicks. 'The cop in the tunnel?'

'Rico. His name was Chris Rico. He was a human being too. A good one.'

'It wasn't personal.' She rolls her shoulders around and groan-yells in frustration. A ziplock bag with three rolled joints pokes out of her hoodie pocket, falls to the ground. She stares at the joints longingly.

An idea comes to me. It's probably not the best one I've ever had but it could work. 'Hey, Finn, I need the key to the cuffs.'

He's just climbed onto the houseboat and stops to look around. 'Why?'

'She's gonna hurt herself. We need to cuff her hands round the front.'

Finn assesses Josie's jarring movements. 'She'll be fine.'

'No, really, come on.'

He seems annoyed but gets off the boat and comes over, hands them to me.

'All right, turn around.' I pause with my hand on one cuff. 'See the big guy behind me? If you try anything it's not gonna end well. Got it?'

'Yeah, fuck, just get 'em off!'

I undo one cuff, lock it back around the pole in front of her. She's rubbing at the nasty mark she's made on her wrist from all the squirming. As Finn is on his way back to the boat, I pocket the keys.

Josie's still looking at the joints. 'So can I have one or what?'

'Sure.'

She pounces on them, awkwardly fishes a lighter out of her pocket. I probably should have searched her for any potential weapons. Oops.

The click of the lighter has Finn's attention back on us. His eyes bulge. 'Lexi, what the?'

'You just killed my fucking boyfriend!' Josie explodes after taking a long drag. 'Fuck, man, I need it.'

'Yeah, Finn,' I repeat, hoping my eyes will do the talking for me. 'Give her a break.'

He's not going to. He's already on his way back over. Then he's distracted by the radio but I get a filthy look.

Josie's staring at me. 'What kinda cop are you anyway?'

'One that likes the occasional joint and has trouble following the rules.'

'Well, thanks.'

I let her get in another couple of drags. 'Finn didn't want to shoot Clarke. He wouldn't have if he could have avoided it.'

'He wasn't a bad person.'

I force down my opinion on that. Right or wrong I'm glad the bastard is dead. That we've got some justice for Rico. I do my best to keep my tone even. 'Guess he killed lots of people, though. The tatts, right?'

'Only four.' She looks towards Linc. 'Nearly five. And only when he had to.'

'Does that include your cousin Aden?'

'That was an accident! A fucked-up accident.' She bangs her head again.

'So why did he turn up while the cops were there after the accident?'

'He never had a chance to leave. The train stopped. There were guards and off-duty cops on it. He was stuck. Had to hide. Wait them out.'

'Jason got away.'

'He took off on foot. Easier. But Ian was worried they'd check the rego on the boat, maybe wait him out. So he had to take the best chance he could. The cops went to the cottage. He saw some woman sitting on the jetty and thought no big deal so he made a dash for it, but then it went to shit.' Another drag and a pause then, 'There were a lot of you guys out here for one kid.'

'We've also been looking for Mark's wife,' I say, testing out the theory that the cases could be connected. 'We're trying to figure out what happened to her.'

She laughs a little. 'Guess you know now. You guys found her, right?'

'Yeah. Me personally, actually. I got pretty close.'

'Wow, no shit? You were the one that went in the water? Man. That's bad.'

'Worse for Kirsten.'

Another laugh. Then she drops her head back to stare at the sky. 'Man, we didn't see that coming.' She pauses, says more quietly, 'Though maybe we should have ...'

My mind is scrambling to keep up. Josie knows Mark Bradley, knows about Kirsten. 'You didn't think Mark had it in him?' I press. 'He got Latimer.'

'That was so stupid. He had the north run. Fucked up everything.'

He had the north run. Bradley was the other dealer? And then I use what I know of the description of the supposed lover and superimpose it over Josie. It matches.

'You know what's funny? Everyone thought he was meeting you every Friday night because you were lovers.'

Her eyes bulge. 'Mark? Fuck, no. Business only.'

The sound of a boat approaching has her shutting up. She takes one more desperate drag then tosses the remains of the joint into the water to watch the boat. 'You know, I didn't do any of that shit. It wasn't me.'

A million retorts spring to my lips, but then Finn's back and pulling her to her feet.

'Get up,' he says. 'You can tell it to a judge.'

CHAPTER THIRTY-ONE

Finn watched Josie Hamill be taken away by police boat as another two arrived. Drug squad. The noise was all but drowned out by two choppers overhead, brought in to search the bushland for the remaining POIs. Rachael and Craig were directing police and Lexi was sitting on the wharf, watching the comings and goings with a bored look on her face. He decided to join her.

'How are you holding up?'

'Yeah, fine. Good. Bored.'

'Your arm is bleeding through the bandage.'

She looked at it in surprise. 'I think I banged it when I slid down the hill.'

'It doesn't hurt?'

'Only now that I'm looking at it. My ribs have even stopped aching. Maybe I inhaled a few of those pot fumes.'

'Yeah,' he said with a sigh. 'We need to talk about that. You can't give out joints to people in custody.'

'Because they shouldn't have joints or because they're in custody?'

'Um, both?'

'Well, anyway. Thanks for saving me. Again. And for getting Rico's killer.'

'You're welcome. Again.' The last thing he'd wanted to do was kill the man. No matter who that man was, taking a life was extreme. Then he remembered the moment Lexi had slid down the embankment, the sight of Clarke levelling his gun on her, his smile as he sat it on his shoulder, finger adjusting to fire. He'd had no choice. 'I should have stopped him before your life was at risk. I hate using my gun.'

'I know. You should. That's okay.'

'But he was going to kill you.'

'No question.'

'So.'

'So,' she repeated, then she bumped him amiably and got up. 'Come on, looks like Rachael's finally got time to kill us.'

From the look on Rachael's face as she approached them, death would not be swift.

'Are you both all right?' she asked, looking them over from head to toe.

'Yep,' they said in unison.

'Handy, because this would want to be good.' She folded her arms. 'Let's have it.'

'You asked us to keep a look out for the houseboat,' Lexi said before Finn could begin. 'We found it. The plan was to take a couple of quick photos to show your witness and head straight back. We were literally a minute, if that, but bullets started flying. Linc was in the boat, the boat's engine caught fire and we had no choice but to head for cover. Lots more bullets later, I slid down the mountain, Clarke lined me up and Finn had to shoot him.'

'I see.'

'Or Clarke would have killed me.'

'I gathered that.'

'Then Josie came running down the hill, totally distraught, to fall all over her dead boyfriend and Finn arrested her.'

'Distraught? She seems quite calm about it all now. Anyone know what she's on? Drug of choice around here seems to be meth but Linc mentioned it smelled like cannabis.'

Finn exchanged glances with Linc, who winked before his attention returned to Rachael.

Lexi cleared her throat. 'As I let her smoke one of the joints she had on her I can positively say it was cannabis,' she said.

Rachael's stare was cutting. 'Don't say another word.'

'But you asked.'

Rachael held up a finger at Lexi but was now glaring at Finn like it was his fault.

'I assumed it was to garner information, so I allowed it,' he said in explanation.

'And I was complicit,' Linc said happily, limping over, though Finn doubted Linc was having all that much fun. He was deathly pale and had to be in pain. Trust him to be too worried about impressing Lexi to admit it.

'Just get on the boat,' Rachael said.

'We're leaving?' Finn asked.

'I've had radio confirmation we've captured the two other POIs, forensics are still about forty minutes off and the drug squad are taking over the rest. So, yes. There's transport waiting at the wharf to take Linc in to get checked over and you two can wait for me at headquarters. We'll discuss what I'm going to do about you when I've cleaned up this mess. Go.'

Finn gladly complied, following Lexi and Linc onto the police boat.

'Still okay?' Lexi asked Linc as the boat got going, bouncing around on the choppy water. 'You don't look all that great.'

'Pissed off I didn't get to play hero,' Linc said with a wide grin, 'again.'

Lexi frowned. 'Why would you want to do that?'

'To show off, of course. I haven't been in this much trouble in ages. May as well look good doing it.'

'I seem to have a habit of getting people into trouble,' Lexi said, but it wasn't quite the throwaway comment it should have been.

She was thinking about Rico, Finn realised. 'You got to jump out of a burning boat after taking fire,' he told Linc. 'Surely that's heroic enough for one day.'

'I suppose that'll have to do,' Linc said. Then to Lexi, he said, 'Is that enough for a drink?'

'I was under the impression you had hordes at your disposal for that,' she said with a slightly forced smile.

His grin only widened. 'Sounds like someone's been spreading jealous rumours. How about this: the offer's open. You feel like a night out, you let me know.'

'Did you get anything useful out of your stoned friend?' Finn asked Lexi.

'I totally did. Mark is the Hamills' other top dealer. He covers the northern end of the coast.'

'Josie told you that?'

'She did. See? Cannabis has its uses.'

'Save it for Rachael,' he says. 'You're going to need all the ammo you can get.'

'Thanks for the lift back,' Lexi said as Finn pulled in to her driveway. By the time Rachael had gotten back to headquarters, there'd only been time for a quick debrief before she'd sent them home.

'No problem.' His attention was caught by three rough-looking types out the front of Dawny's old place blasting out a Skid Row tune. 'New neighbours?' he asked with a frown.

'Yeah. This place gets better and better.'

He wasn't going to argue. He glanced at his watch and, damn it, he was going to miss the story.

'What's up?' Lexi asked.

'There's a report airing on Bradley in about ten minutes. I wanted to try and catch it.'

She pushed open the car door. 'So come in.'

'Yeah. Okay. Thanks.'

'Ooh, look!' one of the morons called out as Finn stepped out of the car. 'Lexi's got herself a bloke!'

'Have another beer, Trev!' Lexi called back. 'Put the last of those brain cells out of their misery.'

'Aw, c'mon! What's he got that I haven't?'

'Mate, I don't have all day.'

'I'll take ya out, what d'ya say to that?'

She dug her keys from her bag. 'Honestly, I don't think I could laugh that hard and still say anything.'

'You're breaking my heart!' the one she called Trev said over his friends' laughter. 'What's a guy gotta do?'

Lexi paused by the door and considered him. 'Would you go to the ends of the earth for me?'

He burped loudly. 'You know it, baby!'

'And stay there?' she asked just as nicely.

Finn locked the car to a chorus of 'Oohs' and more laughter from Trev's mates. This was ridiculous. He stared hard at the trio while Lexi unlocked her front door.

'Got a problem, mate?' one called out.

Finn felt a tug as Lexi caught his arm and pulled him towards the door. 'Not by your standards!' she yelled. Then to Finn, she said, 'Don't engage. You'll never dig yourself back up from their level.'

'How often do you have to put up with that?' he said, following her inside.

'Alcohol helps.' She kicked off her shoes and turned on the television, put it on mute then went into the kitchen and poured herself a JD.

'You want me to have a serious word with them?'

'Somehow I don't think that would help.' She tossed her drink back and poured another.

'Maybe you should have hung around for that drink with Linc,' he said.

'Why? I'd rather come home and drink. It's cheaper. You want one?'

'No, thanks. You know he didn't want a drink for the sake of it, right? He was asking you out, like on a date.' He felt silly for explaining it when he saw the humour in her expression.

'Ha. You're right, maybe I should have. I've never been on one of those.'

He couldn't help the surprise in his tone. 'You've never been on a date?'

'Why would I date? Look what I did for a living. It'd be like going home from work and ... working. But, like, pro bono.' She shuddered.

'No, it wouldn't. It would be going out with someone because you enjoy their company. Because you want to spend time with them.'

Lexi's nose crinkled. 'Doesn't sound like me, does it?'

'Not when I say it out loud, no.'

She laughed.

'But seriously, if you find the right person it can be very rewarding having a partner in your life.'

'You're so sweet and idealistic, Finn.'

'Oh, shut up,' he said without heat.

'Hey, speaking of the rewarding nature of partnership, did you figure out how to save your house?'

'My loan was approved.'

'Great!'

'But that doesn't change the fact I can't afford the repayments.' He nodded at the television. 'There it is.'

Lexi grabbed the remote and turned the volume back on.

'Details are emerging tonight of a cold-blooded killer on the loose on the state's Central Coast. Mark Bradley, a forty-nine-year-old construction foreman and drug dealer with suspected ties to the notorious Hamill crime family, murdered his employer after being caught embezzling from the company. It's also alleged he lured his wife of almost fifteen years out to a secluded location and murdered her, dumping her body in a creek near the tiny station of Wondabyne. Todd Newman has the story …'

'Was all that okayed?' she asked. 'We haven't proved that yet.'

'Yeah. It's all in the "alleged". We need everyone looking for him so Rachael gave it the go-ahead.'

Lexi carried her computer to the lounge and sat beside Finn, opening it up. It immediately pinged several times. She hit a button he assumed silenced it while they watched the news story through.

'What's that about?' he asked when the story ended.

'Checking in with my dodgy ties. I'm curious to see if the story sparked anything. How about being helpful and getting me a drink?'

'You—sure.' He felt like a coffee, so he made two and placed one in front of her.

She looked at the mug, at him. 'Did you make me *coffee*?'

'Yeah, I—'

'Pfft. Top shelf.'

He huffed out a laugh in resignation but poured her another JD. She looked at it, did a double take in disgust at the single finger and tossed it back. 'I can't see anything suggesting anyone's particularly interested in Bradley.'

'Do you think it's wise to be drinking when you're dealing with these people?'

'It's this or Mojo.'

He glanced across to the window where Lexi's cannabis plant stood. 'I can't believe you still have that thing.'

'I told you, Mojo's a pet.'

'Another thing you and Linc have in common.'

'He does not have a pot plant!'

'No, but he's all for legalising it. And if he thinks it'll impress you, he'll tell you all about its medicinal properties.'

'They're very real.'

'Yeah, but you're not sick.'

'No. See? Wonder plant.'

He shook his head, but grinned. 'Maybe you're right for each other. You know he'll keep going out of his way to make sure you end up with a crush on him.'

'I don't do crushes! Crushes are for kids. You want to talk about crushes, talk to your daughter.'

'Ava? Why? She doesn't—she's too young to have crushes. Did she say something to you? She didn't. Did she? Who? When? What's funny?'

'You. Calm down. Seriously. She's eleven. Of course she has crushes.'

'She didn't tell me!'

'I wonder why?'

'She told me she's been talking to you.'

Lexi nodded over another sip. 'FaceTime. I have all the inside goss. There's stuff a girl just doesn't discuss with her parents.'

'You're giving her good advice, right?'

'Fully versing her in the birds and the bees and the danger of boys thinking they need extra large condoms.'

He stared at her until all that computed. 'See, I know you're joking. But when you joke it's because you're changing the subject. You're not telling me something.'

'For fuck's sake, she's hardly sleeping around! She's enjoying being a preteen. Doing normal preteen girly stuff.'

'Which is?'

'Liking boys because it's fun to like boys. It's cool to have crushes. It's cool to find out everyone else's crushes and hassle them about it. Total rite of passage.'

'Right.'

'I can't wait to see what you're like when she really starts dating.'

'Right,' is all he can think to say again.

CHAPTER THIRTY-TWO

Saturday, March 12

'Good morning,' Rachael says to the room.

I take the spare seat next to Finn. We've just come from Rachael's office, where she made it clear she's still not happy about yesterday's events. I mean, yeah, she would have liked to have been informed before we stepped foot on the property, made the call whether we were to proceed or not, but come on, that's getting pretty close to needing a permit to use the toilet. At least Linc seems okay this morning, with barely even a limp from his injury.

'You should have heard by now about yesterday's successful raid on the Cogra Bay property.' There is applause, but honestly, Rachael doesn't look in the mood to enjoy congratulations. 'We are in the process of dismantling a large drug lab complete with raw ingredients. We've seized hundreds of thousands of dollars in methamphetamine, several illegal weapons and tens of thousands in bundles of cash.' More clapping and congratulations.

'We get in trouble, she gets a pat on the back,' I mutter to Finn.

'Shh,' he warns as Rachael looks our way.

'Ian Clarke was unfortunately killed in a shootout with officers, and Josie Hamill and two POIs involved in production are in custody. We've also discovered a solid link between Mark Bradley and the Hamills. Bradley is a dealer for the Hamill drug operation. Jason told us he and Aden were supplying the south end of the coast and we now know Bradley was supplying the north end. There was no secret lover at Wondabyne. The woman Bradley was meeting was Josie Hamill, Ian Clarke's partner, to collect the drugs. So with Sergeant Rico's killer dead, the drug operation shut down, and the Hamills responsible under arrest, we have one target: Mark Bradley, who we need to bring in on serious drugs charges and suspicion of two murders. We can't assume the Hamills don't have him stashed away somewhere, so we'll be putting plenty of pressure on there. Do we have any updates?'

'Yep,' Cass says. 'Fifty grand from that shell company account we discovered found its way into Mark's account on Friday afternoon and ten thousand was withdrawn at the Commonwealth Bank at Tuggerah on Saturday morning.'

'He's managed to grab the money before the hold went on his account,' Rachael says. 'Okay, that sighting could suggest he's staying somewhere local, so we need to make sure hotels, motels and the like on the northern end of the coast are aware to look out for him. All the local police in the area need to be updated. He can't hide forever.'

'Will do.'

'Anyone else?' There's a few head shakes and when no one speaks, Rachael gives them a nod. 'Okay, thanks, everyone. Let's get on with our day.'

The drug squad guys move off with Craig while the rest of us stay put. I can't help but think back to my conversation with Josie. Something's niggling at me as I replay it in my mind.

'You didn't think Mark had it in him? He got Latimer.'

'That was so stupid. He had the north run. Fucked up everything.'

Why would killing Latimer ruin Bradley's work with the Hamills? Because he had to disappear? Or something else? I'm wary of opening my mouth again but I think I have to.

'Something's still off,' I say, chewing at my lip.

'What do you mean?' Rachael asks.

'Just ... something. I don't know yet. Are Latimer's financial records on that computer you brought in?' I ask Cass.

'I've got that under control,' Cass says in her snappy way.

'Have you got something else, Cass?' Rachael asks.

'I've made printouts.' Cass pulls several sheets of neatly stapled papers from a plastic wallet. She hands out copies with a list of payments, some highlighted. 'I've been looking at the payments made into the Latimer accounts. Among the legit payments and projects, there's fake ones. The private buyers and companies don't exist, yet there's payments going in to the tune of hundreds of thousands of dollars.'

'The money has to be coming from somewhere,' Linc says.

That nagging thought takes form. What if the shell company isn't Mark's? I skim down the page and land on something ridiculous, and everything begins to make sense. 'Er, can I interrupt?'

'Go on,' Rachael says.

'You know when you think you have an idea but it's really something you've heard and filed away, you've just forgotten where from?'

'I suppose. Why?'

'Last page, last line.'

I wait while everyone flips pages.

'A half-million-dollar private residence construction for a client by the name of Sherman,' Rachael reads out.

'Yeah. P. Sherman,' I say, waiting for that to sink in.

Finn swears under his breath. 'P. Sherman. 42 Wallaby Way, Sydney. You've got to be kidding me.'

'I can't believe I missed that,' Cass admits.

At Rachael's and Linc's blank stares, I sigh. 'Oh, come on! Even Dory managed to remember that one! Nemo, people!'

'Perhaps he's been watching too many movies with the nephews,' Finn says, 'or—wait. This entry went in *after* Latimer's murder. Why would he bother to enter fake project payment details after he'd killed Latimer and taken off?'

'My first thought would be so the business was exposed as a sham,' I say. 'We know Bradley was involved with the Hamills. What if the Latimers are too?'

'Go on,' Rachael says.

'After I … helped Josie calm down, I mentioned Mark killing Latimer and she said he was stupid for doing that. At the time it sounded like she meant he'd stuffed up his job by bolting, but it could also mean killing Latimer had stuffed up the business arrangement between the families.'

Rachael nods, her eyes still on the paperwork. 'So this isn't embezzling—it's money laundering.'

'Can we prove it?' Cass asks. 'All we're going to get from Carole Latimer is she doesn't know anything.'

'Well, yes, I think we can,' I say, 'assuming you'll share the damn records so I can trace the shell company back to its owner. So, are we going to work together?' I smile nicely.

'Absolutely not.'

'Oh, go on, lower your standards a little. I did.'

'I've already looked into that!' Cass says. 'There's no way to get those details.'

'Maybe there's no way for *you* to get them,' I say.

Rachael clears her throat. 'Cass, give Lexi the computer.'

Cass is not impressed but she slides the laptop across the table.

'Am I going to have to bypass the passwords?' I ask.

'Neutron reset them to zeros.'

I jump in, then hesitate. 'Just checking I don't need one of those politically correct procedural boxes ticked before I do this?'

'You're good to go,' Rachael assures me.

I get to work, eyes glued to the screen. 'Okay, so I have the—I can't pronounce that—offshore company in Panama the shell company is registered to and the associated bank account—'

'Yes, but the problem is it's all anonymous,' Cass says. 'We can't find out who owns it. All we know is Mark was paying them.'

'Pessimist.' What I want isn't here but looking at a former network connection gives me an idea where it might be. 'I'll take a look at Carole Latimer's personal computer while I'm here. Okay?'

'The warrant we have will cover it, but we don't have it here,' Rachael says.

'Well, you're gonna have to give me a minute. I don't have magical powers.' How am I going to trick Carole into letting me in? I'm considering that when Rachael's phone rings.

'Langley.' A moment later she's scooping her things into her bag. 'Finn, Cass, Linc. Bradley's been spotted. Let's go.'

I watch them all race out the door, then get back to work. I know Carole's playing games with the police. We've already proved her 'poor little naive me' character is at least partly a sham. I need to find the proof I'm right.

I find her email address then send her a spoof email from the shell company provider, telling her there's been a possible data breach and to change any passwords associated with her account, then I add a malware-infected link with a keylogger back to their site so I can see what she comes up with. I wouldn't mind going a step further. It's a Saturday morning so I'm not hopeful, but I try Neutron.

'Lexi? Hey. How are you?'

'Great, where are you?'

'At work.'

'Excellent. I was counting on you not having a life. Do you mind if I use that little data-copying program of yours?'

'I've upgraded that, actually.'

'Can you come and show me what you've got?'

'Where are you?'

'Homicide.'

'So no life either?'

'Did—did you just insult me?'

'What? No!' he stutters. 'I meant—it was a joke!'

He's so damn cute, I can't help the laugh. 'I'm messing with you. When can you get here?'

'Give me five minutes.' He sounds more than happy to oblige so I don't feel bad about getting him to trek over. Maybe I'll make him a coffee.

I sit back and wonder what else to do while I wait. It occurs to me I haven't tracked down Lochie's friend yet so I look into it and discover Stubby's not too difficult to find. I send him a message on one of the chatrooms Lochie mentioned and get one almost straight back.

Thought you were never gonna contact me.

Rude. Never mind. Also, *How did you know I was?*

Lochie told me. He wanted to make sure I knew you were legit. Didn't want me to miss my chance to get out.

Damn it. So much for listening to me. *Well I'm here now so this is your chance.*

You're going to help me like you did Lochie?

I'll do what I can, which was all I could promise Lochie.

Okay. Shit, that'll have to do. There's a meeting set for tonight. We're supposed to pick up a shipment of weapons pinched from the cops that were marked for destruction.

Tonight? Was that enough time? *Okay. I need more details.*

They're gonna be in the back of a Mitsubishi EX4 marked with RH tool shop ads on the sides.

Got it. Where and when?

There's a long, long pause. Then, *If I get locked up with these guys, I'm dead. I need some kind of assurance.*

I get it, I do. But there's not much time. I type in Craig's mobile and hope he doesn't kill me for doing it. *This is the guy in charge and what he says goes. He'll help you.*

How do I know you're telling the truth?

You're gonna have to trust me a bit or this isn't going to work.

How do I say I got his number?

Tell him ... Shit. I'm not giving this guy my name. *Tell him Elsa told you to call.*

You've got to be shitting me. I thought it was Sam.

Yes, but then Craig won't know who sent you! *It's a codename. Don't pass it around.*

Right. Thanks. Elsa.

And shit again, I can almost hear the tone. I can't believe I did that. *Good luck*, I type, then sign out. I jump back onto my emails as Neutron appears at my desk.

CHAPTER THIRTY-THREE

'He's on the top of the building,' the security guard said as Rachael and the team pulled up at the site of Latimer's death. They got out of the car and looked up.

Rachael couldn't see anything. 'Is anyone still in the building?' she asked.

He shook his head. 'No. I got them all out.'

Three more police cars pulled up. 'Linc, Cass, get a perimeter set up. I need the place surrounded.' As Rachael spoke, she caught sight of Mark Bradley peering down from the top of the building before disappearing again. The glimpse showed an untidy appearance and a strained expression. A handgun.

Rachael stepped out as far as she dared onto the road, which was being blocked off by officers. 'Mr Bradley!' she called.

A head appeared again, disappeared. Reappeared. 'She's dead! It's over! It's fucking over!'

'Cass!' Rachael called. Cass jogged over. 'We need a chopper up there so we've got eyes on him. Try and keep him talking for me. I need him distracted. Finn, I want to go up. Grab Linc and some vests. Can we get up there without using the lift?' she asked the security guard.

'There's scaffolding stairs at the side of the building. But you're not supposed to use it. The whole lot needs to be taken down. It's not safe.'

'Noted,' she said, then took the vest Finn offered and slipped it on. 'Okay, let's go.'

They moved as slowly and quietly as possible on the aluminium steps. Cass was doing her best to talk to Bradley but wasn't getting much in return.

When they reached the fourth floor, Finn stopped and pointed upwards. 'Above us,' he mouthed.

She listened, heard Bradley's feet resume their pacing on the floor over her head. She nodded, adjusted her grip on her weapon and waited. A minute passed before the footsteps retreated to a safer distance and she nodded again to get them moving. She took the last few steps between Finn and Linc, closely huddled so that they reached the floor at the same time. Bradley was around ten metres away, looking over the edge.

'Put the gun down!' Finn ordered.

Bradley spun around. The man was highly distressed. His face was red, eyes swollen. His jerky movements told Rachael he was not likely to be rational. He took two steps closer and again Finn barked orders. Bradley's gun hand lifted but only to scruff over his dishevelled hair.

'I saw her on the television!' he said. 'You think I did all those things. But you're wrong! I didn't want her dead, I wanted her safe!'

'Mr Bradley, if you put the gun down we can talk to you,' Rachael said calmly.

He looked at the gun as though he'd forgotten he was holding it. As though he didn't know what to do with it. 'I was getting threats. My wife was being turned against me. Didn't trust me. I didn't know why. We had a couple of huge fights. Then the phone calls started. Threats, crazy shit, telling me I was about to lose everything. I didn't know what to do. I—I needed time to figure something out.'

All the movement was making her nervous. Finn risked a quick glance, for instruction. She shook her head.

'Mr Bradley, I think you just want to tell us what happened. Am I right?'

'I—it doesn't matter now.'

'It does. I want to hear what you have to say. It's important. But you're waving that gun around and that's not safe for anyone. Please put it down.'

He looked around, took a few steps away, then lowered the gun to his side. 'I went to Latto and I told him I couldn't do the pick-up. I had to go away for a bit. I had to get Kirsten somewhere safe. He should have understood! He should have helped! But he said no, I wasn't getting out. I was desperate!' He swiped his gun arm across his eyes.

'I understand. We can help make this right, I promise. I will listen. But it's not safe—'

'I told him if he didn't let us go I'd go to the cops—blow their whole operation! He was furious, but I didn't care. I had to go. I tried to leave, that's all! But he grabbed me and … and I punched him, I think I broke his nose. He shoved me towards the edge and I got him in a headlock but he was dragging us both out here, right to the edge.' As he spoke he walked towards it, touched the broken railing. He swiped the gun across his face again. He was drenched in perspiration. 'We fell against the scaffolding and it gave way. I didn't throw him off! He fell through. I didn't know if he was dead, but I knew if I hung around to find out I would be. I panicked and ran.'

'Okay, I believe you,' Rachael said soothingly. 'These things happen. It's terrible, but it was an accident.'

'It was!'

'And we know you weren't stealing from the Latimers. We know you were only doing what the Latimers asked you to do. We know what it's like once you get in over your head with these people.'

'But you don't. You don't know half of it.'

'Okay, so let's go down to the station and talk it through.'

'I'm not going anywhere!' Bradley was at the very edge again.

'Okay! I'll listen from here. Come back from the edge a bit though, okay?'

He took a step away. 'I tried to convince myself no one would know I'd had anything to do with it. That he'd fallen. It sounds stupid now.'

'I think that's a very normal reaction.'

He looked lost for a moment, then nodded. 'But just in case, I thought I should do the drug pick-up. If it went bad I could go to the cops, hand in the drugs, maybe do a deal to keep Kirsten safe from the Hamills. So I got on the train as normal, but there was a woman, sitting downstairs. I could only see part of the back of her head but I could have sworn it was Kirsten. I spent most of the trip to Wondabyne telling myself I was being silly but then she turned her head and it was her. I went down there to see what was going on and she told me she found a phone and what it had on it, that the latest message had said I was meeting this other woman at Wondabyne that night. Even what train I'd be on. I swear I've never seen that phone in my life! So I told her what I was really doing. What caused all this in the first place. She was mad but scared enough to listen.'

'So she went with you,' Rachael prompted when he stopped to stare out over the edge.

'I made her stay on the platform while I got on the boat with Josie. I told her we were both dead if she followed. We were twenty minutes, maybe twenty five, tops. But when I got back, she wasn't there. I thought she'd changed her mind and gotten on another train. I went home to see if she was there, but she wasn't. I cleaned up because I had blood all over my shirt from when I punched Jeremy's nose, then I left. I didn't know what else to do. Then I saw the news. That she was ... She was right under my feet as I got off that jetty. She was dead and I didn't know.' He began crying, racking sobs.

'All right, Mr Bradley. I need you to come with us so we can sort this out. So we can find out what happened to Kirsten.'

His head shot back up. 'I know what happened! It's my fault. I should never have gotten wrapped up with the Hamills. First Anna, now Kirsten. I didn't mean it. I never took that shit again! It was a terrible thing to do but she wasn't meant to die. I didn't kill her.'

'I believe you.'

'Think what you like. I don't care. What's left to care about?'

'Mark, please. Let us help you,' Rachael said.

'You can't help me. But you'd better find Mike. Warn him.'

Mark Bradley flipped over the rail and disappeared. Almost instantaneously there were shrieks from below. A sickening crash. *He's landed on a car*, Rachael thought.

Finn and Linc moved together, looked over. She didn't need to follow them, just waited, then read their faces.

CHAPTER THIRTY-FOUR

I can't quite believe how easy it ended up being. Carole Latimer doesn't know it yet, but she's currently enjoying her last moments of freedom. I've been filling in time waiting to hear from Rachael but when I spot her, she's leading what looks like a funeral procession.

'What happened?' I ask.

'He jumped,' Rachael says.

'As in committed suicide?'

'Yes.'

'Oh.' Unlike everyone else in the room, I'm finding it difficult to care. But I can understand their devastation. It can't have been easy watching someone jump from a building. 'Did he say anything first?'

'Yes.' Rachael lets out a long breath and takes a seat. 'He was adamant he didn't kill Kirsten. That Latimer's death was an accident. We told him we'd help him and he jumped anyway.'

'He didn't kill Kirsten? Do you think he was telling the truth?'

'Why bother hanging around to make up a story and then jump anyway?'

'Maybe he believed jumping was better than what the Hamills would do to him.'

'Valid concern. Damn.' Rachael drops her head back to stare at the ceiling.

'On a more positive note,' I say brightly, 'you can go and arrest Carole Latimer any time you feel like it.'

Rachael sits up in her chair. 'You got her?'

'Neutron and I got her. Everything we needed to prove the shell company and bank accounts belong to her family was on her laptop.'

'Family?' Finn asks.

'It was strange the Hamills would work with or for anyone else, right? They just don't. They have their own businesses. So I dug a bit further back into Carole Latimer and found out she used to be Carole Greentree, as in, the daughter of Raymond Hamill's sister.'

'How did we miss that?' Linc says, lightly slapping the table.

'Well, I wasn't here for that part,' I joke, because Rachael still looks like death warmed up.

'Are you suggesting we can't function without you?' Cass snaps.

Oh for fuck's sake. 'I was just answering the question put to me. Any inferences are all yours.' I manage to leave the word *bitch* off the end of my sentence. 'That does beg the question, though. What was Bradley and Latimer's argument about?'

'Bradley said he and his wife were being threatened by someone,' Rachael says. 'He asked Latimer to let him take some time off and inferred Latimer should have understood and let him go, but apparently he refused. It got heated, they wrestled and Latimer fell.'

'It's getting stranger by the minute. Maybe Carole can shed some light.'

Rachael nods. 'One way to find out. Cass, Linc, go get her.'

'Yes, boss,' Linc says happily.

'Are you okay?' I ask.

'Yes,' Rachael says, rubbing her forehead. 'It's shit, but we did all we could. Kirsten was dead and nothing we could say could change that. He was devastated. He said something about an Anna and to warn someone else ... I don't know. You can listen to the recording. It didn't really make sense.'

'Yeah, okay. I will.'

'Hey,' Craig says, winding his way into our pod. 'I heard what happened. Sorry.'

'Thanks,' Rachael says.

'I'm afraid I've got some more bad news. Elias Hamill was just found hanging in his cell.'

'Another suicide?' Rachael asks wearily.

'Doubt it. Not with the number of people in there that would have wanted him dead.'

'Wasn't he in protective custody?'

'He refused it, said he didn't want any favours from the cops. We're looking into it but either way, he won't be telling us anything.'

'He probably wouldn't have anyway,' Rachael says, then her face brightens a touch. 'But in better news, Lexi and Neutron found the evidence we need to tie Carole Latimer in to the Hamill business. You want to talk to her?'

'Yes, but not right now. Because I, too, have some better news. Thanks to Elsa,' he says with a grin in my direction, 'we've got a takedown to plan. I just found out about an upcoming weapons deal. But next time don't give out my number, okay? I have to change it now.'

I grimace. 'Sorry about that. It seemed time sensitive. I wasn't sure what else to do.'

'What weapons deal?' Finn asks.

Craig perches himself on the edge of Linc's desk. 'Robert Hamill has a deal going down at a warehouse in Blacktown this evening. We're going to be there to interrupt.'

'Like dominos,' I say happily under my breath. Stubby didn't back out and now it's all coming together. I'm getting ever closer to Raymond.

'The guy wants you there,' Craig tells me. 'Said you're insurance. He doesn't trust us, but you got Lochie out, so he wants you in the cop car when we take them all down. You in?'

'I really don't think—' Rachael begins.

'Of course!' I cut over the top of her. 'Did he give you any more details?'

'Yeah. Goods will be packed inside plastic-wrapped tool boxes. There's several pallets of those mixed with other legit stock. Time is up to the Hamills, but they like between six and nine, before the roads get too quiet. Robert reckons it's less conspicuous than late night.'

'Stakeout. Cool.'

'We'll sit you at the Macca's around the corner,' Craig tells me, 'then bring you round once we've made the arrests and secured the scene so you can take your latest rescue back to the station.'

'Oh, come on! I only get to do the boring bit? Really?'

'I'll have someone wait with her,' Rachael says. She seems relieved. 'To make sure she stays put.'

'Oh, good, a babysitter. Do I get to choose?'

'No,' Rachael says.

'I'll leave you to sort that one out. Thanks again, Lexi. Rachael, let me know how you go with Carole Latimer. I'll have a chat with her tomorrow.'

I have to wonder why she thinks I need a babysitter. We're making progress based on a lot of what is my work and right now she's looking at me like I'm some problem she has to deal with. One she probably doesn't need after the event she just witnessed. Still, I can't quite help my tone. 'You know, if I'm such a pain in the arse, I can go home instead,' I tell her.

'I never said you were a pain in the arse.' Rachael presses her fingers to her eyes. 'You have the brains and the guts to be an incredible cop but you don't have the hours behind you. You haven't even done as many weeks on the force as everyone else here has years. While you're there tonight, pay attention to how everything runs. Look at the cohesion within and between the teams, how everyone communicates and works together. That's the part you need to understand before I directly involve you in something like this.'

'Uh-huh. And ... how am I supposed to do all that from McDonald's?'

'Now you're being a pain in the arse.'

I can't help the grin that creeps onto my lips at her tone. It stretches when I see the sadness in Rachael's expression lift a little to return it. 'All right. So what now?'

'Now we interview Carole Latimer. You can help Finn and me prepare.'

Carole Latimer sat in the interview room with Rachael, Finn and Lexi in a teary, confused mess. She'd been crying gently into a tissue since the evidence had first been put to her. The fact she'd called on the same lawyer the Hamills used hadn't escaped anyone.

'I just don't understand this,' she told Rachael. 'I've cooperated fully with everything you've asked. I have nothing to hide.'

'Let me explain all this to you, Mrs Latimer,' Rachael said, and took her through some of the evidence once more.

'Mark is a liar and a fraud and he's set us up!' Carole sniffed as she scanned the paperwork again.

'It's all right, Carole,' Stewart Diggens told her gently. 'We'll get this sorted out. Try not to worry.' Then turning his attention to Rachael, he said, 'Surely Mrs Latimer's been through enough. Whatever this man made up in order to make himself look innocent is just that. Made up. He's simply trying to shift the blame in an attempt to get out of the charges he's facing. I'm gathering you have Mr Bradley in custody?'

'I'm afraid we don't have Mr Bradley in custody,' Rachael said. 'Mark Bradley took his own life after speaking with us earlier today. There was nothing for him to gain by giving his account of recent events.'

It took Diggens only a moment to change strategy. 'That's terrible, of course, but the man was clearly unstable. You can't possibly take his word on these matters.'

'I'm afraid it's gone a bit beyond that. We've obtained texts and emails as well as files pertaining to a shell company in Panama from Mrs Latimer's computer.'

'You can't have,' Carole Latimer said, looking confused. 'You don't have my computer.'

'We accessed your computer remotely,' Finn said. 'There's more than enough evidence of your involvement in the Hamill family drug manufacturing operation and the money laundering done through your construction company.'

Carole stared open-mouthed at Diggens. 'Can they do that? You can't do that!'

'I'm afraid we can and we did,' Rachael said brusquely. 'Mrs Latimer, we're charging you with—'

'This is bullshit!' the woman shrilled, surging to her feet. 'You'll pay for this, you dumb slut!' She poked a finger at Rachael's face. 'You'll be dead before morning! We'll kill you and your family and every fucking friend you've got and burn your fucking houses down around you!'

Finn jumped up and wrestled Carole's hands behind her back and cuffed her.

'Lock her up until she calms down!' Rachael said over the racket. 'We'll explain her charges when she's finished with the tantrum.'

Finn handed Carole Latimer to two officers who hovered by the doorway. Without another word, her lawyer slipped out behind his loudly objecting client.

Rachael followed them out then paused when she noticed Lexi and Finn had stalled by the door to watch Carole's exit. 'What are you doing?' she asked them.

Lexi shook her head in disbelief. 'Wondering if I should call an exorcist.'

'What a temper,' Finn said.

'It wasn't far below the surface,' Rachael agreed. 'Let's go,' she ordered, and led Lexi and Finn back to Cass's and Linc's desks to update them.

Linc spotted them first. 'Was she a big sobbing mess on the floor?'

'Not exactly,' Rachael said.

'She morphed,' Finn said, 'into a big, crazy Hamill.'

'Picked it!' Cass said, wiggling her fingers. Linc groaned and slapped a ten-dollar note into her palm.

'Hey, it's almost stakeout time,' Lexi said, checking her phone.

'What stakeout?' Linc asked.

'Hamill weapons deal,' Rachael explained. 'It's technically Craig's area but because of the crossover with cases and Lexi's involvement, we're assisting.'

'Lexi's involvement?' Cass asked.

'The informant wants her there. Lexi's going to be around the corner at the McDonald's until we've sorted it. I need someone to stay with her.'

'I have to shoot home but could be there by seven,' Linc offered.

'Okay. Finn will be on scene. He can fill in until you arrive.'

Finn groaned. 'Fine. I'll download a book or something.' Then, at Lexi's raised eyebrow, he said, 'I don't know why you're so excited. It's boring.'

'Do you need me to be there?' Cass asked Rachael.

'No, you may as well head off now. I know you have things to do with your son.'

'Thanks.' Cass gathered her belongings. 'I'll see everyone tomorrow. Good luck.'

CHAPTER THIRTY-FIVE

'Whoa, what's going on there?' I ask as Finn turns into the designated McDonald's. A swarm of teenage boys in oversized jerseys is spilling out of the restaurant. Every seat is taken, every parking space full. The noise level is not for the faint-hearted.

'Some sort of basketball win or something?' Finn guesses.

'Hmm. You really want to go in there?'

'Do you have to ask?' he says, cruising slowly through the carpark. 'We'll drive thru for a coffee. Hang in the car.'

'Good plan.'

He puts the car in line. 'You want something to eat?'

'Nah. Linc will no doubt be hungry later and I'm not eating two meals here.'

'Fair enough.'

The drive thru is about as slow as expected considering the chaos inside, but once served, Finn parks on the street. 'Okay, stakeout time.'

'It's not really a stakeout though, is it? I mean, I just sit here until it's all over. That's different.'

'Close enough. You'll hear it go down over the police radio.' He takes a sip of his coffee and settles back in his seat.

'Mmm. Exciting. You know, even as a probationary constable I got to do a proper stakeout once.'

'Oh, yeah? What was that about?'

'An underwear thief.'

'Seriously?'

I nod. 'Serial offender. I chased her down the street and onto a bus. She didn't want to be caught with the stolen goods so she started chucking undies around. One pair landed flush on Rico's face as he came in behind me and he's blind, just about falls into an old lady's lap!' My laughter fades as the familiar pain of Rico's death hits me in the chest.

'Tell me about him?'

'I don't really want to talk about it.'

'Yeah, but you should. What was he like?'

'He was a good guy. A great cop to be partnered with. He taught me a lot. I don't really know what else to say.' Finn doesn't immediately say anything and while I know it's a deliberate tactic to keep me talking, damn it, it works. 'He was a lot like Linc, I guess. Not physically so much, but that same, I don't know ... indomitable, positive, happy attitude.'

'You were fond of him.'

'Fond?' Through the lingering ache of sadness I manage a laugh, because who says that? 'Yeah, I was.'

'Like Linc, huh? So did he want you to go out with him too?' he asks in an obvious attempt to lighten the mood again.

'Well, duh,' I say, playing along.

'And ... did you?'

I glance at him sideways. 'No. I've never dated anyone, remember?'

'Right.'

Right? I can't quite help my quizzical smile. 'Why?'

After wrestling with his words for a moment, Finn shrugs, 'I didn't know Rico, but I know Linc. He's a great cop. And a good mate. But he's not very good at meaningful relationships.'

My expression turns to complete devastation. 'Oh, damn. And I'm so desperate to settle down.'

'Smartarse.'

I ruffle his hair. 'You're so sweet.'

'Get off,' he says with a grin, flicking my hand away to tidy his hair in the rear-view mirror. As he does, the smile drops.

'What is it?' I ask.

'Probably nothing.' But his eyes are pinned on something. 'Cancel that. That's our van.'

'Already? It's not even six!'

'You really want to go argue that out with the Hamills?' He radios the information and the next few minutes are tense, while precise orders are transferred to the various tactical and drug squad members. Then nothing. The radios are completely silent. We wait. Listen.

There's an eruption of sound as the team go in shouting commands. An officer reports they have the POI but on top of that there's another message. A body. Something's not right. A loud crash, more shouting, gunshots. Automatic weapons and handguns. Calls for reinforcements, confusion. Chaos.

'What's going on?'

'Something not good,' Finn says and starts the car, spins it in a U-turn and makes the block in a few seconds. 'Stay there!' he orders as he jumps out.

'But—'

'Stay there, Lexi! I mean it!'

I stay put, craning my neck to catch sight of what's going on, but we're about two cars too many behind the action so I can't see much. Cops are swarming into a large concrete building from everywhere. Calls for ambulances over the radio become more desperate. If nothing else, I should be out there helping out any injured cops, surely? All that first aid stuff I had to learn isn't helping anyone from here.

I have my hand on my seatbelt when, almost as quickly as it started, it stops. Finn jogs back and opens my door, tilting his chin to tell me to get out.

'What happened?'

'I think the Hamills figured out they had a rat.'

Stubby? My stomach sinks, but I make myself walk towards the large open roller door. As two officers step past me, I walk in and catch a glimpse of the mess hanging from a beam in the high ceiling. Nausea rises to the back of my throat as I squint in horror. It used to be a person, but there isn't much left that resembles one.

Craig appears through the crowd. 'Lexi! That your guy?' he asks me. I drag my eyes off the remains to Craig. He looks like he's been in a war zone, but he's alive. As I take in more of the scene around me, I notice some others aren't that lucky.

'I don't know who that is. What happened?'

'We came in focused on the van, no one else in sight except the driver, who seemed surprised to see us. He put his hands in the air in surrender, so my men went in to get him, then noticed the body. At the same time a dozen or so men burst from the back of the van like out of a damn Trojan horse, guns blazing.'

I step out of the way of two paramedics wheeling out a dead body. I can't tell if it's one of ours or one of theirs. 'Is this my fault?'

'No, of course not. All you did was turn him over to me. I set this up based on Stubby's information. If it's any consolation, it doesn't look like he double-crossed us,' he tells me, with another glance at the body in the rafters. 'The Hamills must have somehow figured out what he'd done. They've been tight on security. They probably tapped his phone.' He rubs the back of his neck as he looks around. 'Damn. What a mess.'

Craig is called away and my attention returns to what was left of the man who was probably Stubby. But was it? I step closer, stare. I don't know what Stubby looked like, but I do know what …

I move around the remains. My mind tries to reject what my eyes are seeing. Light brown hair. That face. There was enough still recognisable …

No. No it *can't* be.

I feel a hand on my shoulder, hear Rachael's voice: 'Are you okay?'

'I think—I think it's Lochie. He was safe! I …' I hear my voice crack and swallow, try again. 'He was supposed to be safe! Why wasn't he safe?'

'Okay, come away.' She tries to turn me around but my feet won't cooperate. 'Let me talk to Craig.'

Two cops block my line of sight, leading Robert Hamill past us.

'Inspector Langley, we found this,' a uniformed cop says, handing Rachael a wallet and ID. Robert's head whips around. He stops walking and stares, ignoring the officers attempting to move him on. His eyes narrow in on Rachael.

'Langley. The big shot, pain-in-the-arse homicide detective?'

Rachael steps forward, eyes as cold as his. 'Something you'd like to say?'

'You had no business fucking with Carole.'

'Her husband was murdered. The investigation into Carole Latimer was simply an extension of our enquiries. But rest assured, your family is getting the best of both the homicide and drugs and firearms squads—and a few others. We're very thorough.'

'You're very dead,' Robert tells her quietly. 'You just don't know it yet.' He glances at the body, back to Rachael, then smirks nastily. I take an unconscious step towards her and he spots me. His smirk grows, then he winks and is finally pushed past me, strolling away like he's somehow won.

I want to claw his eyes out. I want to tear him to pieces. The effort not to has me shaking on the spot. My eyes return to the remains. Maybe I'm wrong, I tell myself desperately. Maybe it's not the same young man full of hope of a reunion with his parents and a second chance at university. The one who cared enough about another human being to risk his own safety to help. I need to take a better look.

I can't bear to.

I spin on my heel and stride outside, stare in silent rage as Robert is loaded into the wagon. He's driven away and another wagon approaches. Another Hamill thug is led out. This one's battered and bleeding, limping heavily and … he's younger than I realised. Probably because he's built and tall and kinda looks like *a big, tough guy*. Lochie's words echo in my head. The guy's swollen eyes bounce off mine for a split second and the 'Stubby?' falls out of my mouth. He cranes his neck around as they keep him moving.

'How the fuck do you—' His eyes go round. He stops dead, fighting against the pull of the two officers flanking him. 'You?' he asks. I don't answer but he barrels on anyway. 'I'm sorry! They were in my phone! They knew I'd been talking to him and they did this to me! They would have killed me! It was me or him. I panicked. I—I had no choice!'

'Lexi!' Rachael says, catching up. 'Are you—'

I hold up a hand. Stubby's words have confirmed what I was so desperately trying to deny and I can't keep the rage and devastation inside me. I can't. 'He was clear!' I scream at him. 'He was free and clear and he put his life on the line. For you! And you do that?' I throw my arm out to point back to the warehouse. 'You fucking traitor!' I don't realise I'm striding towards him until I plough into Rachael as she steps in front of me.

'They made me pretend I was on the run. That I needed to know how to find him. Find safety. I had a gun to my head! He shouldn't have told me anything. He shouldn't have told me where he was!'

I step back from Rachael to stare at Stubby in shattered disbelief. 'You're blaming him? You piece of shit!'

'Get him in the wagon and wait for further orders!' Craig calls out from somewhere behind me. 'Don't put him anywhere near any of Hamill's men, understand?'

'I'm sorry!' Stubby cries again as he's wrestled inside the wagon. I can see the tears streaming down his face. Hear the choked sob. He's a victim too, I know he is, but Lochie's terrible death is too raw.

'So if you didn't catch it, that was Stubby,' I hear Rachael tell Craig. 'The guy hanging in there was Lochie.'

'Shit, was it?' Craig strides back inside, pulling out his phone and ordering more cops to a location I guess is where Lochie's supposed to safely be in hiding.

Everything that's happened in the last week hits me all at once. 'I thought he was safe,' I tell Rachael. 'But the cops couldn't stop them getting to him, couldn't prevent him being tortured and murdered ... and that bastard! That smug, winking bastard just strolls away.'

'In handcuffs.'

'But Lochie's dead!'

'And if we do nothing, then what? They run riot? Do as they please? Kill even more kids?'

'And now they're coming after you.'

'He's just posturing. Lexi, snap out of it. You want to be a cop, these things are going to happen. There are times when things are the cops' fault, we're all human, but this is not one of them. Even if it had been, even if this had been the result of something you personally had stuffed up, you'd need to be able to get past it and do the job. Otherwise you don't get to wear the badge. Understand? Lochie made the choice to contact Stubby. That's not on you. As for the rest, Craig set this up. He sent his men in. Look at him. He's not feeling sorry for himself, because he knows. He knows everything I said is true and he accepts that. He gets on with the next part, and the next, because his team needs him. So help or leave. Your choice. But I don't have time to stand here making you feel better.'

On top of everything else, the lecture almost leaves me in a heap. I feel as lost as I ever have. What am I doing? I see Rico dying in my arms, Aden's remains being picked up off railway lines, Kirsten's body floating in front of me, Lochie's destroyed remains hanging from the rafters. Now Robert has the rest of his fucked-up family coming for Rachael?

'Well?' she asks.

I walk back inside and make myself take one last look at Lochie, silently tell him I'm sorry, that they'll pay. Then I turn around and walk out.

'I have to go.'

They're not getting her. No fucking way are they getting Rachael. The Hamills are evil. They're fucking done. But I need to do this on my terms, not the cops' way. The Hamills don't play fair. Why should I have to?

CHAPTER THIRTY-SIX

Monday, March 14

Finn strode into homicide at eight on Monday morning and went straight to Rachael's office. As he'd expected, she was already in.

'Morning.'

'Morning. How was your day with Ava yesterday?'

'Fine. Great,' he said, because it had been both of those things and the odd day off during a major investigation was a plus, especially after Saturday night's events. 'Have you heard from Lexi?'

'No. Why?'

'Because I tried to call her last night to see how she was, and I didn't get an answer. I should have dropped in this morning.'

'What's bothering you?'

'What's bothering me is the way she walked out after you yelled at her at the crime scene,' he said with a touch of irritation.

Rachael frowned. 'I would have called it more of a pep talk and she needed to hear it.'

'Was it? She was as upset as I've ever seen her and then you let her leave. I don't even know how she got home. If she did.' He heard the anger in his voice and calmed it down. 'What if she doesn't come back?'

'She will.'

'She's coped with more in the last week than many cops do in their entire careers. She's still raw over Rico. Now Lochie. I'm just saying—'

'I know what you're saying, Finn. But think about this: because she's so good at what she does, she's going to keep getting in the way of the worst of the worst. When's going to be the right time to learn to cope with that? I'd say the sooner the better, and a few scares will actually do her good.'

'But—'

'She's getting hurt!' she said over him, and he saw the worry. 'Too often and too much. I'd rather she take some time out and rethink things than charge ahead and die.'

'Ah, do you mean that?' Craig asked, appearing from behind them. Finn noted the drawn look to his face, the deep shadows.

'Hey, how are you holding up?' Rachael asked him.

'We lost Carter. Two more in ICU. Petrie looks good, Donald not so much.'

'Sorry, man,' Finn offered.

Craig dragged in a deep, not quite steady breath. 'We're remaining hopeful they'll make it. Everyone else got away with minor injuries. Robert Hamill is, of course, not talking. But we've got more than enough on him to put him away for decades. We took out seven of his men, three are in hospital with less serious gunshot wounds, the one who knows Lexi was helping Lochie is being held in a separate facility and leaking like a sieve, and we grilled the other two for whatever we could get for most of yesterday.'

'No offence, but I can tell,' Rachael said. 'You need to get some rest.'

'Yeah, I will. But I need to talk to you about something.'

'Sure, take a seat. Would you like a coffee?'

'Nah, I'm already wired on caffeine, but thanks.'

'Do you need me to step out?' Finn asked.

'No, you can hear this. Elias Hamill's wife Leila handed herself in about an hour ago.'

'Another one?' Rachael said, stunned.

'She's pretty distraught. She believes the family forced Elias to turn himself in in order to protect Adam and are therefore responsible for his murder in custody. On top of that, there was the incident with Clarke that led to her son Aden's death and she doesn't believe Raymond will be able to prevent Jason's murder in custody either. There's plenty of people he's about to be put away with that will be looking forward to it. She's pleading with us to make sure that doesn't happen.'

'She wants protective custody for her son,' Rachael said, nodding. 'What's she prepared to give us for it?'

'She said she's not privy to everything within the business and I believe her, but she knows enough to be useful. She's validated our story on the Latimers and on Mark Bradley's part in the business. She doesn't know anything about Kirsten. She's willing to assist with and testify in our case against her family.'

'That's huge—and suicide.'

'Unless we can bring them all down pretty fast, probably. But we'll do our best to protect her. She doesn't care about the repercussions to herself. She's only worried about her remaining child.'

'Congratulations,' Rachael told Craig.

'Yeah, but there's more. You know there's been talk of someone bothering the Hamills? Since the reward went out on Debbie, a few self-professed bounty hunters have been giving them some trouble, but they've been knocking them off. A couple of our recently discovered tortured bodies are a result of that. But Leila says they're worried about one, someone they're taking very seriously. They're blaming him for all of their recent trouble and they're pissed off. They're beginning to wonder if it's the same person who helped Lochie and tried to help Stubby. They've put their own reward out and it makes Debbie's look like pocket money.'

'As long as Stubby doesn't get a chance to talk to the Hamills about Lexi, there should be no problem,' Rachael said.

'Nothing could be further from his mind. He hates the Hamills and is in a bad place over Lochie. We've got him on suicide watch. But back to Lexi. Our intelligence has so far flagged thirteen aliases that have been in regular contact with the guys from Lexi's pyramid in every dodgy area of the web you can imagine. Each one of those is totally untraceable. Complete ghosts. I don't know about the Hamills, but we think they are all one person.'

'And you think that's Lexi. I'm sure she'll tell you if you're right. Look, she's had a lot to cope with recently and she—'

'The thing is, the Hamills have people on this, people Leila says know what they're doing, and my team thinks Lexi's at risk of standing out because she's too good. We need her to back away immediately. I wouldn't put it past them not to take on a false identity of their own—if they haven't already—to try and lure her out of hiding. Pretend to be a Lochie or a Stubby wanting help.'

'Got it. I'll talk to her. Thanks.'

'I'll keep you posted,' Craig promised, getting to his feet.

Rachael and Finn followed him out then joined Linc and Cass in the meeting room.

'Hey,' Linc said. 'I heard about Carter. That's tough.'

'It's a sad time,' Rachael said. 'However, we need to see this through, so here we go. We know that Mark Bradley worked for the Hamill drug operation. That Latimer Developments was a front for laundering Hamill drug money. We know the real reason Bradley was going to Wondabyne each Friday night was to pick up the drugs, not to meet with a mistress. We know Bradley accidentally killed Latimer during an argument over Latimer refusing to allow Bradley to take time off to protect his wife from an outside threat of some kind. That threat is what we need to focus on now. Who made the threatening phone calls to Bradley? Who planted a phone full of messages about an affair in Bradley's pocket for Kirsten to find? If we believe Bradley did not kill his wife, we have to assume that whoever was sending those threats is responsible. We'll be talking to Josie Hamill this afternoon. Up until now she's refused to answer any questions but we'll keep pushing. See what we can get.'

'Lexi should talk to her,' Finn said.

'Anyone got any more cannabis on them?' Cass said snidely.

Rachael glared at her. 'Damn it, this is not a joke!'

'Kind of feels like one,' Cass shot back. 'Lexi's not a true team player and it's affecting the entire team!'

'Cass—' Finn cut in.

'No, that's fair,' Rachael said. 'Lexi's not always great at working as part of a team and it does affect how we operate. That comes from having to do things for herself for so long. It's frustrating for both sides but it takes time to unlearn the habits that kept you alive from an early age. She's still a very junior police officer who is going to make mistakes.'

'Okay, then what about learning some consequences?' Cass continued. 'She killed a man when she was ten years old, attempted to kill another. Then you got her immunity from prosecution for the crimes she committed during the Spider case. She recently got her partner killed chasing a vendetta, put Finn and Linc in extreme danger out at Cogra Bay and then there was Saturday night's disaster. She breaks the rules and she gets away with it time and time again. And why not? There's never any consequences. If she stays on this team, I can't help but wonder what disaster awaits us all next!'

The look Rachael sent Cass could have cut her in two perfect halves. 'Saturday night's raid was done by the book.'

'It was a last-minute rush job, based on bad intel.'

'Intel that a more senior officer than you made a decision to act on,' Finn reminded her, his own temper building. Rachael didn't need this right now. She was doing her best to juggle Lexi's inexperience against the valuable intel she was providing. 'So unless you want to take up that argument with Craig, maybe we should stick to the current problem?' He just didn't understand it. Cass could be harsh but he'd never seen her like this. It was almost as though she felt threatened. But why?

'Finn, I'm sorry if you don't like what I'm saying but I—'

'It's not what you're saying, Cass. It's your high and mighty judgemental attitude that's pissing me off. You look at Lexi like she's some sort of inferior peasant and she's not the only cop I've seen you do it to. Right now it's pissing me off enough to tell you that if you ever accuse Lexi of being responsible for Rico's death again, especially in front of Lexi, one of us is going to have to swap teams. Clear? Now, if you don't mind, we have a case to solve.'

A heavy silence stretched while Finn and Cass stared each other down.

'Where is Lexi today, anyway?' Linc asked.

'We don't know,' Finn said when Rachael didn't answer. 'I'll give her a call.'

'No,' Rachael said. 'I'll go get her. I need to talk to her privately. Cass, talk to Kirsten's sister again, see if she's remembered anything that could be useful. Linc, chase up the latest on the second phone we found in Kirsten's bag. We need to see those messages. Finn, ask Craig to let you see the interviews he's just completed with Hamill's thugs in case you catch anything that's relevant to our case.'

'Will do.' He grabbed his coffee, not unhappy to leave Cass alone until he cooled down. 'Bring her back, Rach,' he said. 'We need her.'

CHAPTER THIRTY-SEVEN

I'm sitting in my office messaging Raymond on the phone. I haven't checked it for too long, because once on the official investigation, I'd been trying to do things the way I knew Rachael wanted them done. Deciding I don't need to worry about that is quite freeing. And already working.

I'll pay you to go away, Raymond tells me.
I don't need money.
One million.
Nope.
Two.

Oh, hell, two million dollars. Two. Million. Dollars. I briefly wonder if I can figure out a way to get the money and Debbie. What good that could do towards rehabbing kids like the ones the Hamills fucked up. But there's no time. *Nope.* That hurt. *I want Debbie.*

I can't give her to you.

Bullshit, I type, snarling. *I'm through playing.* Because I really am. *Adam's next.*

'And then you, you bastard.'

'Who's a bastard?' Rachael asks.

I jolt. I had a suspicion she still had a key but I should have heard her come in.

'Hi. Come on in,' I say, hearing the sarcasm in my tone.

'What are you doing?'

'Nothing you need to know about.'

She pins me with one of those damn stares of hers and asks again, '*What* are you *doing*?'

'What I've been doing all along. I'm taking apart the Hamills.'

She takes the phone I've been messaging Raymond on. 'Is that why they're throwing money at you?'

Oh, what the hell. 'I'm blackmailing them.'

Rachael sinks into the spare chair. 'Oh my God. Lexi. You're joking.'

'Why would I joke? I told Raymond to hand Debbie over, he told me to get stuffed. So I told him I'd come after every single one of them and take the family apart piece by piece until the day she was in custody. Just like I told you I would.'

'So this has never been about simply keeping an eye out for news on Debbie or saving the necks of a few low-level drug dealers. From the outset you've been demanding the Hamills give her up. You're the one they're looking for.'

'It's been about all of those things,' I object. 'And what do you mean?'

'These are some of the most dangerous people in the country we're talking about. Leila Hamill has come forward. She says they have a price on the head of the person who's causing them so much trouble. They're looking for you. They want you dead.'

I shrug. 'They have to find me first. All they have is a few untraceable texts.'

'Leila told us the Hamills know the person blackmailing them is probably the same person who helped Lochie and Stubby.'

'Well, I didn't exactly help Lochie, did I?' I say and turn back to my computer.

'You're not listening!' she says desperately. 'They're hunting you.'

I spin back around. 'I am listening! But what choice do I have? Rachael, the Feds aren't getting anywhere fast enough. Vaughn is out there right now, making bucketloads on child pornography and murder! Imagine how easy it must be for him in some of those overseas countries where they don't have the same child protections in place as we have here. He has access to countless children and he knows how to keep hidden on the web. I can't stand the thought of more kids going through that kind of terror and torture and not do everything I can to stop it. I have to find Debbie and make her talk!'

In contrast to my raised voice, Rachael's is quiet. 'What Vaughn does is not on you.'

'Yes, it is! Because you chose to save me over stopping him before he got the chance to bolt! I'm eternally grateful, but he needs to be found *now*! The look on his face when he had Finn's daughter, it was … God, Rachael, he's so, so sick!' I take a much needed breath and lower my voice. 'It's eating away at me. Every day. I *need* to stop it. I *need* to feel like I'm doing every single thing I can to stop him. I don't care about me. I care about this.'

'I see.'

'And it *is* about saving guys like Lochie. The Hamill bastards are destroying lives left, right and centre. No one cares about these young people dying because they assume they're bad, but they're not! They're kids who make one silly mistake and then they're reeled in and they're dying. I figured out a way to kill two birds with one stone, to make a large dint in the Hamill operation and get Debbie. How could I not take it? Besides, Robert threatened you.'

'You think I don't get threats every day?' She pushes back to her feet. 'We need to go.'

'I'm not going anywhere. I quit. I need to get this done fast and I can't do that following your rules.'

'Resignation refused.'

'You can't refuse!'

Rachael's arm is extended, gesturing to the door. 'We'll argue that out later.'

CHAPTER THIRTY-EIGHT

'Got a minute?' Rachael asked at the doorway to Craig's office.

'Yeah, of course, come in. Take a seat, ladies,' Craig said, glancing from Lexi to Rachael. 'What's up?'

'Lexi's just told me she's been attempting to blackmail Raymond into giving up Debbie Reynolds from the get-go,' she said. 'I tried to explain the danger but she's not listening to me. She might listen to you.'

Craig leant back in his chair and laced his fingers behind his head. 'I guess I could start with ... you know it's illegal to blackmail people, right?'

'It's a deal,' Lexi said. 'They're business people and I'm offering them a deal.'

'Keep talking.'

'Look, Debbie was adopted out, only came back into their lives as a young adult, attracted by the money and stuff, right? She agreed to become a cop to give them some leeway with the police and when she failed, she bolted. How much could she possibly mean to them? More than each other and their entire empire? I very much doubt that. So, I told Raymond if he handed her over I'd leave them alone. If he didn't, I'd take the rest of the family apart. Rachael doesn't like it, but I'm not going to stop. So I quit.'

'No, you won't be doing that,' Craig said dismissively.

'It doesn't seem to have occurred to either of you that I totally can! It's not the damn army.'

'It's not going to happen, Lexi,' he said. 'Not mid-case.'

'But—' Whatever she was going to say changed when Craig started humming that *Frozen* tune under his breath. 'Seriously?' Lexi objected, but Craig's unusual way of diffusing the tension seemed to have worked, at least to some degree. Rachael wasn't sure she didn't almost see the hint of a smile.

'Okay, okay,' Craig said affably, obviously nowhere near as upset as Rachael was. 'I can't stop you from quitting, but before we discuss that any further, is there anything else we don't know about what you've been doing?'

Lexi stared at the wall, a frown marring her brow. 'No, I don't think so. Lochie gave me Jason and Aden. Getting Jason meant I was able to infect his phone with spyware that in turn got me into Elias's phone, which contained the hit-and-run video I sent to Adam in order to bribe him into handing over Elias.'

'A-ha!' Craig crowed. Then to Rachael, 'And you said she couldn't have done it.'

'Hmm.'

'So as you also know I gave Lochie the video to get him the deal. Then you know about Aden's death. And you know I gave Juicey some cash to keep an eye out for Jason and some more when he found him for me. Lochie gave me Stubby and that's how we got to Robert. That's it.'

'Okay. How have you been talking to Raymond?'

'I got a prepaid phone and mailed it to him. Simple.'

'And how is he supposed to hand over Debbie?'

'He has to leave her in a car, restrained, then message me with the location for pick-up. He thinks I'm after the million-dollar reward.'

'Raymond offered her double that to stop,' Rachael added.

'And how did you explain not taking it?' Craig asked.

'I've led him to believe I'm working for someone else—a rival family—and that I'd be dead if I did a deal with him.'

He dug through some files on his desk. 'These men—' he dropped crime scene photos in front of her, '—thought they could mess with the Hamills and find Reynolds.'

Rachael hoped she'd see some shock, some horror on Lexi's face. She needed to realise what she was up against. Instead, Lexi looked bored. 'Yes, I know. Raymond told me. Had me look one up.'

'Raymond Hamill told you.' Craig shook his head. 'I can't get over the fact we can't get within sight of this guy and you've been having conversations about hits with him.'

'Texts. A few texts, that's all. Can I go now?' she asked, getting to her feet.

'Well, yes, you could,' Craig said, 'but then you'll miss out on some big news.'

Lexi visibly struggled with that for a moment before dropping back into her chair with a heavy sigh. 'What big news?'

'This is highly confidential.' Craig handed Lexi a document.

'What's this?'

'Read it.'

She skimmed over it, her expression turning to surprise. 'The Hamills *are* still in contact with Debbie!' She turned the page to read a set of text messages. 'It's travel plans, arrangements. These are dated three weeks ago. She's back in the country?'

'We believe so.'

'This is what you couldn't tell me?' Lexi asked Rachael. 'Why can you share this if she couldn't?' she asked Craig.

'Rachael had me speak to some people, explain the value of sharing that information with you. So there it is.' He linked his fingers under his chin and leant his elbows on his desk. 'Look, we all know the toll the Spider case took, so I get why you went after Raymond. You were out of the loop with the investigation and desperate to locate Vaughn and Reynolds. With your past being your past you dived right in the way you'd always done. I even get this anger over Lochie and worry over Rachael driving you back to what you know, what you believe works. But that has to end now. If you really want to help, if you really want to make a difference, we need you working with us.'

'You're good, Lexi, but you're one person,' Rachael said. 'Everyone else around here works as part of a team, which is part of a larger team connected to a whole lot of other teams. That's why it works! You know this!'

'Sorry to interrupt,' Finn said. 'Oh, Lexi, hi.'

'Hi, Finn.'

'We're going to have to get going if we're going to talk to Josie today.'

'We'll have to finish this later,' Rachael told Lexi. 'I want you to go with Finn and talk to Josie Hamill. She'd suggested when you spoke to her that she might be familiar with more details surrounding Kirsten's murder. I want to see if you can get anything else out of her.'

Rachael waited for Lexi to respond, determined to win the silent battle of wills.

After several seconds, Lexi took one last glance at the papers Craig had given her and stood up. 'Sure. Why not?'

'She's determined. I'll give her that,' Craig said when Lexi and Finn left.

Rachael sighed. 'She's so damn difficult sometimes.'

'Really, the only part of that whole story she didn't share as it unfolded was the bit about contacting Raymond. It was a ballsy move and, yes, reckless, but she's got them on their toes. That's not a bad thing. I think some of your anger is about you wanting to protect her, but I say we help her finish what she started. If you really want to keep her safe, the last thing you want is to alienate her into quitting and carrying on off-books. Keep her onside, okay?'

Rachael sighed. 'Well, she didn't take the two million.'

'And that's why I know she doesn't really want to quit.'

CHAPTER THIRTY-NINE

'That was a waste of time,' I say as we head back to headquarters after attempting to interview Josie. 'Why do they get away with the whole no-comment thing anyway? They're criminals. Why do they have more rights than we do?'

'What extra rights do you want us to have?' Finn asks.

'How about one where we can shove their "no comment" up their arse? That just cost us two hours. How much time do you think police everywhere waste attending interviews with criminals each year only to have them legally refuse to talk?'

'A lot. Anyway, what was the chat with Rachael and Craig about?'

'They've gone all dramatic because I've been blackmailing Raymond Hamill.'

He leans on the brake as he stares at me.

'Are you trying to cause an accident?'

He glances in his mirror and resumes driving properly. 'Jeez, Lexi! How could you not say anything?'

'You know everything I've been doing! The only part I left out is that after a Hamill is taken down, I message Raymond, reminding him I'll stop if he hands over Debbie. Totally minor point.'

'Depends on your perspective. So ... what's he like?'

'Not very chatty. But he did offer me a couple of mill to stop.'

'Two million dollars?'

'Yeah. But I reckon he's got twice that on my head. Instead of copping crap from Rachael, I could have stashed that money somewhere untraceable, reinvented my identity and disappeared. I could be set for life and living it up overseas. But no. Here I am.'

'Because you're too good a person to profit from the proceeds of crime.'

'Or I'm not as smart as everyone seems to think I am.'

'That could be true,' he says, pulling into the headquarters carpark. 'Taking on the Hamills without telling anyone.'

'The less people know, the less people die. Once I get enough on Adam, Raymond will cave. I know he will.'

'We've already got enough on Adam. We just can't find him.'

'Yeah, well, I can. I'll keep using my sources, putting the pieces together. It won't take long.'

Finn turns the car into a space. 'As long as we find Adam faster than the Hamills find you. Is Craig going along with this?'

'I think so. They won't let me quit.'

'Why would you quit?' he demands, looking at me like I've grown another head. 'You're not quitting!'

'So I'm told. And told. And told.'

We've only just walked back in to homicide when Rachael snags us.

'How did you go?'

'Don't get her started,' Finn says with mock desperation. 'We were stonewalled.'

'Not unexpected. Still, worth a shot. Right, let's go.'

'Where?' I ask.

Rachael guides us back to our pod, where Cass and Linc are working. 'We're all going to sit down together and get everyone up to speed, then we're going to work out how to proceed.'

'Sure,' I say.

We've only been at it five minutes when Craig appears.

'Lexi.' He dives onto a spare seat, eyes pinned on mine. 'How do the Hamills know what car you drive?'

'What?' I ask, genuinely clueless. Unwelcome fear edges in. 'I have no idea.' How have I slipped up?

'After what you told me earlier, I decided I should send a couple of my guys out to push Leila for more info on this troublemaker they're worried about. She remembered overhearing Karl telling Raymond they had the plates of a woman who'd been helping Lochie. That maybe this woman was the source of their problems. Raymond apparently said he'd have someone look into it. That was several days ago.'

The car chase! I close my eyes on a nasty curse. How could I have been so stupid not to think of that?

'What?' Rachael asks.

'Lochie had been hiding out in a dump of a place at Narara, which is where I picked him up from to bring him into the station. Except when I arrived a couple of thugs Lochie assumed the Hamills had sent after him were already there. We got away but they chased the car for a bit.'

'Yet another little stunt you failed to mention!' Rachael says sharply.

'I was helping out a friend! I wasn't even officially on the case back then!'

'Do you think that makes any difference? They have everything they need to ID you!'

'Okay, then I need to hurry this along.' My mind is racing. 'I think I have enough on Adam to—'

'No. Just stop,' Rachael snaps. 'It ends. Now.'

'What's that supposed to mean?'

'Rach—' Craig interrupts, but she's not listening. She's suddenly about as pissed off as I've ever seen her.

'It means you're out! It means you go to a safe house right now and stay there under police protection until we get this sorted.'

'No.' Is she kidding?

Rachael's eyes bulge. 'Excuse me?'

'No. I'm not stopping. You think I'll be safe? You told me Lochie would be safe!'

'That's not fair and you know it. He chose—'

'To be a decent human being! Besides, how long am I going to sit around for? The Hamills won't give up and they won't forget what

I've done. I've destroyed half their family and a major drug operation and I'm this close to bringing down the rest. If I can get Adam, Raymond and Lena are screwed. They know that. They won't risk it. I can almost guarantee they'll hand over Debbie with a bit more pressure. They've already brought her back into the country. This is working! Once we have her we'll round up the rest. I can do this, Rachael. Trust me!'

'You're not listening!' she explodes. 'You're going to give us everything you have and I'm putting you under police protection so we can save your life. That's it.'

'You can kick me off,' I say, voice shaking with anger, 'but you can't force me to sit around, locked up somewhere like a fucking prisoner.'

'Don't test me, Lexi,' Rachael warns, deathly quietly. 'Finn will take you home. I'll have backup meet you out there in case the Hamills have somehow gotten their hands on the information they've already had days to find. You're going to dismantle that office so there's no evidence for them to find when they turn up, because they will. Then you're going to make sure every single device you have hidden around your house is handed over to me, along with whatever the rest of the team need to know to gain access to it.'

If there was ever a way to tip me over the edge, that was it. Take my computers? Was this actually happening? 'Oh, you have fucking lost it. No *way*!'

'Do I need a warrant?'

'Hell, yes!'

'Linc, organise it. Finn, get moving.'

'I'm not going anywhere!' I reiterate.

Rachael's eyes flash in fury. 'I *will* arrest you if I have to.'

'For what!' I stalk over to the window because I'm too furious to stand still or do what I'm told. What is wrong with her? One little threat from the Hamills and she's locking me up?

'About time, if you ask me,' Cass murmurs.

I spin, see Cass take a couple of steps towards my computer and take one very menacing one towards her. 'I dare you.'

'Let's all just ... calm down,' Craig says, stepping into the standoff.

'I will *not* back down to that cyborg!' I tell him. 'If you want to start, start,' I tell Cass, 'but you'd better be ready to fucking rumble.'

'Lexi.'

'What?' I snap at Finn, eyes still on Cass.

'Let's go, okay? Come with me.'

Cass picks up my computer and it's either physically take her out or relent, and as satisfying as it would be to do the former, that might be taking things too far. Craig catches my eye and nods towards Finn. 'Fine. But that's mine,' I say, pointing to my computer. 'It better not disappear.' To Rachael, I say, 'You just lost your best chance of pulling this off.'

I head for the lift, Finn behind me. He doesn't say anything. I don't want to talk to anyone anyway.

'She's petrified,' Finn finally says when we're on the road.

I look out the window at the busy streets and wonder why I didn't take Raymond's money. I still would have brought them down, but afterwards I'd have got my arse out of the police force as quickly as possible and had money to live on.

'She's not petrified. She's pissed off and pulling rank.'

'That's Rachael being petrified. She doesn't do scared, she just annihilates people. She's protecting you.'

'No, she's not! She's treating me like I'm an idiot.'

'Well, to be fair, you treat us like idiots every day.'

I look at him, stunned, because— 'I do not!'

'You need to trust us enough to work with us, not just alongside us, throwing us scraps when you feel safe enough to pass them on.'

'I'm sorry, Finn. I never looked at it that way. But Rachael is seriously overreacting.'

'Okay, but what would you do if you knew a group of desperate criminals with a history of torturing and murdering their enemies was coming directly at Rachael?'

'They could be! Robert told her she was dead, she just didn't know it yet. And the answer is ... whatever I had to do to stop them getting their hands on her,' I answer reluctantly. 'Even today. Probably.'

'There you go.'

'Don't "there you go" me. I get what you're saying but like hell I'm going to sit in some room being supervised while she takes my computers! I can do this!'

'You have no idea, do you? You've been under her wing for so long you don't even see it. She's bent so many rules for you, stood up for you countless times, and sometimes that puts her in some pretty difficult situations. She doesn't tell you about them, barely sets you any boundaries because she knows you have good reason to work the way you do. She knows that because she wasn't able to save you as a child you had to learn to do things your way, on your own terms, and she pushed you to join the force because she also knows what an asset you can be to the police. She truly believes it.'

'I hear a but.'

'But she didn't get to be in her position by being a softie. Rachael can be as hard as nails and completely uncompromising. And she doesn't make idle threats. She wants you under twenty-four-hour protection so you will be. She wants your computers, so she'll take them. She wants access to them, so you'll give it to her. It's that simple. She's not doing this to you, she's doing it *for* you. Someone comes after you and she's like a rabid mother hen.'

'I don't think hens can catch rabies.'

'She wants to get Reynolds and Vaughn as much as you do. We all do. But she's not willing to risk your life to do it.'

'Change her mind.'

'No.'

'Come on, Finn! Nothing's going to happen to me!'

'Right.' He takes his eyes off the road long enough to pin me with a meaningful stare. 'Because we're not going to let it.'

I shift to look out the window. 'I don't need looking aft—'

I barely have time to register the truck but I feel a split second of complete terror before it ploughs into us. There's an intense jerk, an explosion of pain, an ear-splitting eruption of noise. The car is spinning. I can't tell up from down or control my body as it's flung around within the confines of the seatbelt. Airbags mean I don't see whatever we hit next before we come to another painfully abrupt stop.

The car is motionless but everything is still spinning. Every movement hurts. I manage to turn my head far enough to see Finn. He's squinting as though trying to focus against the obvious bang to his head.

'Lexi? Lexi! Are you okay?'

I can hear him but I can't organise my words to reply. My door rattles, the car rocks. I hear him swear under his breath, struggle to reach inside his jacket. The door is ripped violently open. Finn's free hand rises to push me forward as the other reappears with a gun. 'Down,' he rasps.

Confused, I try to turn to look but my body isn't cooperating. He fires.

What is going on? Nothing makes sense. The window behind Finn smashes. He makes some sort of noise as whatever smashes it cracks him in the head. I think I'm going to be sick, but before I am, I slip into a painless darkness.

CHAPTER FORTY

The banging of Finn's head against something solid brought him around. His head was splitting. An attempt to shift position was hampered by his hands cuffed to a rail. He looked around. He was in some sort of small delivery van. The space was a bare box, save for the rail on each side. From the dried bloodstains on the walls and floor, the van had seen a lot of action. Something bumped his leg. Lexi. She was unconscious, being tossed around by the bouncing and swerving of the stripped-out van. Glass littered the left side of her face, her already injured arm was bleeding through her shirt and she had who knew what other injuries from taking the brunt of the crash.

This had to be the Hamills' doing. They wanted Lexi. So why hadn't they killed him at the crash site? Maybe they intend to play Finn and Lexi off against one another? Whatever they were going to do, it was going to be bad. He felt a sharp stab of real fear. Because he knew. He knew exactly what they were going to do to Lexi.

And he might not be able to stop it.

He swallowed the panic and tried to focus on thinking like a cop. Two men sat up front. They were laughing over something, the stereo pumping out an old Guns N' Roses tune.

All he could see through the windscreen was trees and sky. He needed to try and stop them getting to where they intended on taking them. Because that would be the end.

He took a look at the rail he was cuffed through. It was tekscrewed in place. Whoever had been in here last had had a good go at prying the screw loose from its fixture, and enough force might pull it out. But could he do it without drawing attention to himself? He quietly slid around, timing his movements with the radio noise and chatter from the men.

A phone attached to a holder between the men rang. As the passenger turned to grab it, Finn caught sight of his face.

Adam Hamill. Here in person. This was *really* not good.

'Yeah,' Adam said into the phone. 'We're about twenty minutes out. Went off like clockwork. Guys did a good job. Yeah. See you soon.'

'This bitch is gonna scream,' Adam told the driver on a laugh. 'Karl reckons he's taking a finger off for every Hamill she's messed with—to start. Maybe send some bits back to that Langley cow.'

'Kinda a waste though,' said the driver. 'She's one sweet-looking little bitch. Reckon we could … have a go at her first?'

'Mate, you want to hold up the Butcher?'

'Don't think I'd be game.'

'He's my brother and I don't reckon I am either.'

More laughter. Finn planted his feet on either side of the rail, gripped it in his hands. As the car turned off the smooth road and began bouncing onto a rougher one, he braced himself and pulled hard. Nothing. The men were still none the wiser. He tried again. This time he was pretty sure he felt it give. Another attempt made a screeching sound that had Adam turning around.

'Hey! What the fuck!'

Heart pounding, Finn tried again, again. On the third desperate attempt, the bar gave way and he slid his cuffed hands free to lunge at Adam, who pointed a gun into the back. Finn pushed the weapon up, managed to get his cuffed hands around Adam's throat and, bracing his legs against the front seat, pulled back hard.

The driver swore and undid his seatbelt, flinging one arm back. His hand connected with Finn's face, thumb digging into Finn's eye. Finn adjusted position and kicked out at the driver but didn't dare let go of his grip on Adam as the van lurched again. Another kick connected with the driver's jaw. The van swerved violently and slammed into a tree. The impact sent the gun's aim high and a shot blew through the roof as the driver hit the windscreen. Finn hit the back of the passenger seat, his chest colliding with the headrest with enough force to knock the wind from his lungs, leaving him stunned.

The driver groaned and got a hand on the door, snatching at the gun before tumbling out. Finn untangled himself from Adam, not sure if the man was passed out or dead. He climbed over, spotted the driver stumbling, disoriented, into the bushes. A quick glance back at Lexi showed her body had been thrown into a different position but her hands were still attached to the wall and she was still out. He checked Adam's pockets for the key to the cuffs but couldn't find them, so he took the car keys and went around behind the van to open it up.

A bullet lodged in the van an inch from his head as the door swung open. He ducked back around the side and checked the front again, hoping for another weapon. Instead he found Adam's phone on the floor. He picked it up and dialled Rachael's number.

'Rachael Langley.' She sounded stressed. Well, so was he.

Finn threw himself onto the ground as another bullet whizzed past his head and the phone fell, bouncing into the long grass under the van. Another bullet meant he couldn't go back for it. He was set to try again but was forced to scramble as another car came flying along the trail and hit the brakes hard. Finn recognised the man in the window—the Butcher, Karl Hamill.

Karl stepped out of the car. He was tall, lean and muscular. His hair was greasy, too long, so was his stringy beard. He looked … insane.

The driver appeared from behind a nearby cluster of bushes. 'Thank fuck!'

'What the fuck has happened here?' Karl asked.

'That cop!' the driver called. 'He got Adam.'

'Serious?' Karl's smile vanished as he moved to the front of the van and stepped back a few seconds later with a wild growl, clutching his hair. Finn presumed that meant Adam was dead.

'Where is he?'

'He's round here somewhere but he's not armed.'

'Detective Carson!' Karl screamed. 'You fucking coward! Come out here!' He looked around as though waiting for a response. 'You left the girl here?' With another growl, he kicked the van hard enough to dent it. 'You know what happens to people that mess with us!' Then, 'Davey, mate, unlock the cuffs.'

The driver got into the back of the van. A moment later Karl appeared, dragging Lexi out by the hair.

'What are you doing?' Davey asked. 'Aren't we going back to—'

'We're fucking doing it here!' Karl roared. 'Where the coward can watch!' He released Lexi's hair and her head hit the ground. Then he walked to his car and came back with a black metal box. He dropped it beside her. 'Let's wake this bitch up!'

Finn felt his blood run cold. He tensed, mind racing.

Karl pulled a pair of secateurs from the box and held them in the air as he snapped them open and closed, turning a full circle to ensure Finn could see him. 'Hold her up, Davey.'

Davey dragged Lexi to a sitting position, pinning her limp form between his knees while Karl picked up her hand.

'What finger doesn't she need?' He examined her fingers, turned her hand over a couple of times. Her hand looked so small and delicate in his. 'How about we start with the little one?'

Finn knew if he surrendered they would lose their only chance. He had to sneak around behind these guys, try and take the gun from Davey. But that would take time. And that meant he had to switch off to whatever the Butcher did to Lexi until he could take the guy down. He felt nausea rise in the back of his throat under the pure panic lodged there.

'Ah, fuck it. Let's go the thumb. She's not gonna need any of 'em, is she?' Karl laughed and looked at Davey, who laughed back as though it was expected. The Butcher slid Lexi's thumb between the blades. 'Wonder if I can get it off first try.' He clamped down. Blood spilled to the ground. The Butcher grimaced and dragged the blades around the finger. 'They're a bit past blunt.' He tossed the secateurs to the ground. 'Fuck this.'

He went to the box again, came back ripping open a scalpel. 'Might go an ear.'

When the Butcher brought the blade to Lexi's ear, Finn's vision swam.

'Stop!'

He stumbled out from his hiding spot, hands raised. Either Rachael found them in time or they were dead. He couldn't stand by and watch Lexi be taken apart while he hid in the bushes. Whatever happened to him might at least give Rachael more time to find them, and Lexi time to wake up, maybe escape. If neither of those things happened, all that was left to hope was that she wouldn't wake at all.

CHAPTER FORTY-ONE

'Hello?' Rachael said a third time. 'Hello?'

'What is it?' Linc asked.

'I don't know,' she said. 'Finn, Lexi?' Nothing. To Linc, she said, 'There was some static on the line, maybe the crack of a phone falling. I think I can hear voices but I can't make out what's going on. Keep it open and have someone trace the number in case it's Finn or Lexi trying to contact us.'

'On it.'

People all over headquarters were working at full speed but it wasn't fast enough. There were cars swarming the roads. Why had no one found them yet? She scrubbed her hands over her face. She'd put them in that car together. If anything happened to either one of them, she'd never forgive herself.

'Where are we on traffic cams?'

'Still searching,' the officer in charge of CCTV said.

'Cass, how are you going with Lexi's computer?'

Cass tossed her hands up in helplessness. 'Rachael, I don't have a hope. I don't even know what this security is.'

'Get Neutron!'

Cass scrambled for her phone.

'Rachael,' Craig said, puffing as though he'd been running. 'We found the SUV that took them from the crash site. It's just off Henry Lawson Drive but they're not in it.'

'Damn it!'

'But there's been a report that someone saw two people being dragged from that SUV and put into the back of a white delivery van before it headed south.'

'Okay,' she raised her voice to the officers working the surveillance, 'we're now looking for a white delivery van heading south on Henry Lawson Drive.'

'Plenty of traffic cams out that way. We're on it,' came the response.

'They're going in the direction of the Hamills' place,' Cass said.

'No, they won't go there,' Rachael said. 'They know we'll be swarming that place in no time. Somewhere else. Somewhere remote enough that—' Her mind didn't want to go there. 'That they can make some noise without drawing attention.'

'There's plenty of bushland out that way,' Craig said. 'I'll have some of my guys head out to Silverwater to talk to Leila Hamill. Find out if she has any ideas.'

'I'm here!' Neutron said, running into the room. He slid into a seat as Cass passed the computer to him. He opened it then paused, took the sort of breath an athlete would before a race and looked at Rachael. 'If I can get into this thing, what am I looking for?'

'If?'

'Honestly, I wouldn't be surprised if she has it rigged to self-destruct.'

'Neutron, I'm in no mood for jokes.'

'I wasn't exactly joking.'

'I need you to find out if any information on that thing could lead us to where the Hamill family has taken Lexi and Finn to torture and murder them!'

'No pressure,' he mumbled, as his fingers gingerly touched Lexi's computer. A distinct sheen erupted on his forehead.

Five minutes passed, ten.

'Neutron.'

'I'm trying!' In that short time, he'd become a sweaty, shaking mess. 'I did it!'

'And?'

Neutron dropped back in his seat, hands clutching in his hair as he stared at the screen. 'Shit. Shit! I should have known it wouldn't be that easy.' His face was agonised as he looked at her. 'I'm sorry, Rachael, you know how good she is. Everything's locked up in vaults … I'll keep trying but—'

'Keep trying.'

Linc returned. 'Phone's a burner so no name attached. It's going to take some time to trace it. Everyone's busy.'

'I can do it!' Neutron said. 'Something I can do that's actually helpful. I'll get straight on it.'

'Thank you.' Rachael placed a hand on his shoulder. 'It's a lot of pressure. I'm sorry. You're doing great.'

'It's Lexi and Finn.'

'I know.' She turned and willed the tears sitting behind her eyes to stay there. She would never let her team see her as weak. She had to keep it together. But damn it, she had overreacted with Lexi. The more she tried to keep her safe, to fit her into a mould, the more Lexi got hurt. But that didn't change the fact that Lexi didn't have the experience to be making decisions during these sorts of investigations. The only real answer was to let her finish her years on general duties, let her do her detective training before bringing her back in on any more cases. But if Lexi lived through this, how on earth could she stop her looking for Vaughn? Rachael would need a much clearer, calmer head to work that one out.

Right now she had to concentrate on how to save their lives.

CHAPTER FORTY-TWO

The pain is the first thing that registers. It travels up my hand, my arm, then dulls to an intense throbbing that matches what's going on inside my head. What happened? I can hear birds. I'm outside. The late afternoon sun is in my eyes. I inhale sharply as something stabs into my cheek when I move my head. From a view partially obstructed by the open door of a van I can see two holes in the ground. Not holes—graves. I recognise the long black trousers and realise Finn's still digging the second one.

Why?

I get my answer by turning my head and seeing a pair of boots standing over him, the tip of a gun dangling lazily by a leg.

'Can you take any fucking longer? We can't start on the real fun until you've done all the hard work.'

'The earth is like concrete,' Finn says.

I sit up in stages, then look through the back of the van and see a figure slumped in the passenger seat. A tree has carved its way into the windscreen. My hand is killing me. I lift it to look at why and the swollen, bloodied injury turns my stomach. Most of the skin is detached from my finger.

I can hear my heart beating in my ears as the possibilities race through my mind. We're in the bush somewhere, Finn is being forced to dig holes in the ground by someone with a gun.

I try to move as quietly as I can. The pain almost floors me. As Finn bends down to lift a rock from the hole he spots me, pretends to fumble the rock in order to duck down again. His eyes move from mine to the bush, back again. *Run.*

First of all, that's not going to happen. My body isn't capable. Second, the bump I can now see on his head must be bad if he thinks I'd leave him in this predicament. I can't physically take them on. Not even if I was feeling a whole lot better than almost dead. So what next? *Use your head, Lexi.* But the physical mess I'm in seems to be inhibiting my ability to think.

'Hey, Davey, toss me the smokes.'

I see movement in the other vehicle, hear the snatch as the gunman catches the packet. Did he say Davey? My mind struggles to place him. Then it hits me. Adam's right-hand man. Adam's buffer between his brothers and getting his hands dirty. Davey had organised that weapon drop for Robert, had some tie or other to Elias's drug business, though I wasn't sure what that was.

Doesn't matter. That could work. That could be enough. If there's one thing the Hamills have got to hate more than me, it'd be a traitor. All I can do is hope I can turn these two against each other and give Finn a chance to get us out of this.

I clumsily get my feet underneath me and take several moments to steady myself as the world spins. My hand goes to my face and comes away with a piece of glass. Ow. Standing also has the blood rushing down to my injured hand and I grit my teeth against the pain. It really is going to have to be Finn who gets us out of this. I swallow, hope I don't pass out again and limp into view.

'You have got to be shitting me!' I say as angrily as I can.

I see Finn's face reflect that same thought at my apparent stupidity.

'Awake, sweetheart?' Karl Hamill says with obvious happiness.

'You, shut up!' I order, pointing at him as I limp on to face Davey. 'This is not what we agreed, Davey! This is so fucking far from what we agreed you'll be lucky if the deal still stands!'

Davey is scowling. 'Did you bump your head too hard?'

'And the rest! I never agreed to being hit by a freaking truck, he—' I say, pointing at Finn, '—wasn't supposed to be involved and now we're who knows where, did I mention I have one hell of a headache and … what the fuck is this!' I add, holding up my thumb. 'We shouldn't have paid you a fucking cent!'

'What is she talking about?' Karl asks in a voice that's about as scary as it gets.

'She's fucking lying, man!' Davey spits. 'Jeez, see through the bullshit. She's desperate.'

'I'm not desperate, I'm fucking furious! I could have died! Did you really think giving us the location on Clarke and the meth lab was going to be enough to seal the deal when this went south? I mean, using Stubby for that tip-off on Robert didn't go down all that well, but this is a joke. So what have we got here, a pathetic little double-cross, or just a cop-out because I was knocked out and you turned to chickenshit? What excuse could you possibly have cooked up in that teeny brain of yours for Inspector Langley?'

'You're a fucking liar!' The terror written all over Davey gives me a boost and keeps my legs working a bit longer.

'She's about two minutes away so you'd better hurry and get this under control! Why the hell aren't you pointing a gun at this guy?'

'You did a deal with her?' Karl asks, hand changing grip on his gun.

Davey doesn't seem too sure where to point his gun. 'No!'

'Of course he did a deal with us. You're all going down and we offered him a way out, just like we did Lochie and Stubby. But screw that, my thumb is hanging on by a thread! Check his phone, it's got a tracker in it,' I tell Karl. 'Check his bank account. We paid him for this. He was supposed to lead you on right up until the moment you were surrounded by cops so you couldn't escape, only it's my personal opinion that having my friend dig our graves in order to lead you on that bit longer is one step too far.'

Davey is backing away. 'This is bullshit! I didn't!'

Finn is edging closer. His grip on the shovel has changed to that of a baseball bat.

'Show me your phone!' Karl erupts.

'She's lying!'

'Give it to me!'

'I ...' Davey starts fumbling. 'It's in the van.' He moves closer to me than I'd like in order to check but I hold my ground. 'It—it's not here. I don't know where it is!'

'Yeah, right,' I mock, thanking the universe for the unexpected assistance. The far-off sound of sirens catches our attention. I can barely hide the enormous sigh of relief. 'Lying, am I?'

'You bastard!' Karl lifts his gun at Davey.

Finn uses that moment to smash Karl in the head with the shovel. Davey bolts into the bush while Finn picks up Karl's gun and points it at the dazed Butcher.

'Please tell me you were bluffing,' Finn says.

'Totally bluffing,' I reply, leaning against the van and dropping my head in an attempt to stave off the black dots hazing my vision. When it mostly clears, I limp over to him. 'I wanted to give you a chance to save us. Wanna tell me how Rachael knew where to find us?'

'I grabbed Davey's phone from the front seat after the crash, called her.'

'That worked out well. But I was beginning to wonder how long it was going to take you to get around to tackling this guy.'

'You see the size of him, right?'

'Yeah.'

'I had to make sure he was close enough for that swing to count.'

'Understood.'

A car pulls up, pluming dust. Rachael springs from it and runs ahead of the other police. Looks at us in equal parts relief and horror.

'Oh my God. We need those ambulances!' she shouts back as other cars come in at speed. 'How are you two on your feet? Sit down!'

My 'Yep' and Finn's 'Absolutely' come out at once. We ease onto the edge of one of the holes he's dug. Well, technically, I fall in, but manage to right myself before I'm lying in it.

'Ambos are on the way. Just hang in there.' Rachael grimaces at the graves before dropping down beside me and examining my left cheek with a tight expression. At the risk of shocking her more, I hold up my thumb for a closer look. I'm really not sure why it's not falling right off.

'Can you tell me what happened to this?' I ask Finn.

'Karl was gonna cut it off but the blades were blunt.'

'Oh, well, then … hmm. How did you end up being the centre of attention?'

'He was preparing to cut off your ear. I decided I'd better distract him.'

'Appreciate that.'

'You were supposed to run,' he complains.

'You were digging graves at gunpoint. I decided I'd better distract him.'

'Are you two delirious or did they give you something?' Rachael asks with genuine concern.

Finn grins at me and he does look a little delirious. Maybe it's just my blurred vision. 'Appreciate that,' he tells me as Linc reaches us.

'Hey,' Linc says, squatting down. 'Glad you guys are alive. Can you make it back to the ambulance or are we stretchering you out?'

'Nah, I'm up,' Finn tells him.

'Me too,' I say and hold my undamaged hand out so Finn can pull me to my feet. 'Are we leaving the armed man hiding in the bush?'

'Are we—what?' Rachael's hand goes automatically to her weapon.

I shrug. 'I'm pretty sure he's running for his life.'

'Lexi convinced Karl the guy was on our side,' Finn tells Rachael, then with a bemused frown at me, says, 'We probably should have led with that.'

'Blame the near death experience.'

'That'll do it.' He gives my hand another helpful tug as I step out of the shallow grave. 'You know, it's quite terrifying how convincingly you can come up with absolute bullshit on the spur of the moment. Even under pressure of death.'

'I had the research to back it up. The research that I did on my computer. That I got in trouble over. That saved our lives …'

I don't finish because Rachael is striding away to get a manhunt underway.

My attention is drawn to a commotion where three officers are wrestling to keep Karl under control. 'Hey, our friend woke up.'

Karl is raging. Another two police jump in to help.

I smile in satisfaction. 'We got the Butcher.'

'Yes, we did. And Adam, he's the dead one in the van.'

'Ooh, I want to hear *that* story.'

'Bring the wagon up!' Rachael calls.

As Karl is brought forward, he spots my grin and his face contorts. 'You're fucking dead, sweetheart! I'm going to hurt you in ways you didn't know were possible!'

'Sorry, I've moved on,' I reply. 'It's Raymond's turn.' I allow the gentle pressure on my lower back from Finn to guide me towards the ambulance.

'Fuck you!' the Butcher roars.

I'm battered, bruised and bleeding, but I can still do smug. I look back over my shoulder. 'Get in line, *sweetheart*.'

CHAPTER FORTY-THREE

Wednesday, March 16

Finn sat at Rachael's desk at headquarters keeping an eye on Lexi while Rachael recovered Lexi's things and got the police apartment organised. In his mind, this was Rachael's code for take it easy. He'd spent the night after their run-in with the Hamills in hospital, then come in yesterday to witness Rachael charge Karl Hamill with everything she could throw at him. There'd been a lot of cops waiting in line to chat to The Butcher. He was never going to breathe free air again.

Lexi had stayed on in hospital another night after having surgery to repair her thumb, then had checked herself out just before lunch that day. While he was still dazed from the headache that had yet to give him a break and felt about as uncomfortable as one would expect to after being in a couple of car crashes, Lexi—in his opinion—had no business being anywhere but in bed on plenty of painkillers. But here they were. Her determination to catch the last of the Hamills was currently the most powerful drug in her system and cuts and bruises and a minor surgery were apparently not going to sway her from that goal.

'I don't see why you don't have to be locked up if I do,' she told him, draining her coffee.

'Raymond is after you, remember?'

'If they didn't want some sort of revenge on you too, why didn't they kill you and leave you at the crash site?'

'I think the idea might have been to torture me into making you talk before he started on you.'

'Pretty big assumption that I'd spill my guts to save you an appendage.'

'Glad to have both ears, are you?'

She grinned. Grimaced. They'd removed several pieces of glass from her cheek and forehead. 'Okay, maybe I would.' Then more genuinely, she said, 'Thanks.'

'You can thank me by not giving Rachael a hard time.' His phone buzzed. Vivienne. 'Yeah?'

'I need you to be at the house at eleven tomorrow to sign the contracts.'

'Wait, what? You accepted an offer?'

'Yes, didn't I tell you? Sorry, the last couple of days have been hectic. Anyway, it's a great offer, Finn. There was no way I couldn't accept it.'

'A couple of days ago?'

'The agent warned us the market is showing signs of slowing down. Besides, the bridging loan is crippling us. We need the money and it's exactly what I was hoping for.'

'But ...' After the last twenty-four hours, he was right in the mood to tell her he had run out of flying whatevers about their bridging loan and making sure Vivienne got exactly what she was hoping for. As usual. 'Honestly, Viv, right now is not a good time. Let me call you back, okay?' He needed five minutes to get his head in the right space.

'Oh sure, Finn,' she spat. 'I knew you'd sabotage this! You don't want to sell the house so you're going to mess around until the offer falls through. You're so damn selfish! You—'

'Selfish? You can call me whatever you like, Viv, but never selfish. I've just about bankrupted myself to pay for everything over the last few years so you don't have to work.'

'That's for Ava's sake! You don't care about Ava?'

'Full child support and then some, all Ava's expenses, her school fees, all the house expenses, rates, electricity, water, repairs, your car, my own rent so you could live there and now I'm selling the place I poured everything into holding on to because you gave me no time to organise the funds to buy you out. Don't you *ever* call me selfish! And just try telling me again that I don't care about my daughter!'

He ended the call and took several deep breaths.

'Wow,' Lexi said quietly.

He rubbed at the frown between his eyes. 'I know. Damn it. I shouldn't have lost it.'

'I disagree. Were you drunk when you married that bitch?'

He managed a small smile. 'Young and hopeful? In love? I don't know. It's not normally like this. I think Louis is in her ear over everything.'

'You really pay for all that stuff?'

'I do it for Ava.'

'You're a good guy, Finn.'

'I don't think Viv would agree. She's accepted an offer and had contracts drawn up. She just … forgot to tell me. Now she wants me to drop everything and be there tomorrow morning to sign the paperwork.'

'Rachael said if they'd given you a few months to get it sorted you could have bought her out.'

'Rachael spoke to you about this?' he said, not sure he was happy about his finances being discussed.

'A bit. We used to be friends.'

'You dork. You still are.'

'Dork? Really?'

He huffed out a laugh. 'I'll sign the papers but the time might have to change if Rachael needs me to be here.'

'Mmm.'

'Mmm, what?' he asked.

Lexi shook her head. 'Nothing. I think I'm still a bit zonked.'

'I know that feeling. Here she is.'

An officer wheeled in a trolley containing three suitcases. Rachael came in behind with another trolley piled with cardboard storage boxes. 'Right. I think I've packed everything you need.'

'You think?' Lexi asked in surprise. 'I didn't know I had this much stuff. How long do I have to be away?'

'We don't know yet. But I brought everything that looked like it might be important, because if Raymond Hamill sends anyone over I can't guarantee what might happen to it.'

'Everything from my office?'

'Is in these cartons here. That's staying put.'

Finn watched the dynamic between the two with interest. They were conversing like they'd forgotten how to be comfortable with each other. Almost walking on eggshells.

'How far from HQ is this place?'

'Right next door. Does it matter? You need to rest.'

'I will. Once we have Raymond Hamill in custody. I want my computer back.'

'What for? You've just had surgery on your hand. Let it heal.'

Lexi lifted her heavily bandaged hand. 'I don't need this one to type. Finn's back at work.'

'He doesn't look like an extra from *The Walking Dead*.'

'You watch that?' Lexi asked doubtfully.

'I've seen the ads. Finn's in better shape.'

'He had five stitches in his head and concussion.'

'Yes, you'd know all about those since you've had two recently. Stop arguing.'

'I'm not arguing.'

'Oh? What would you call it?'

'Helping you see why I'm right.'

Finn's chuckle attracted both sets of eyes.

'What?' they asked in unison.

'You two kickarse personalities tiptoeing around each other. You know what? Never mind.'

Rachael's smile was reluctant, but it broke some of the tension. 'I'll think about it.'

'So, while you think about it, can I ...?' Lexi wiggled her finger at the boxes.

Rachael sighed. 'What for?'

'You don't want to know if Raymond has made contact?'

Rachael's brow rose. 'Maybe we already know. I gave Neutron your computer.'

Lexi laughed dryly. 'Rachael, no one got into my computer. No one.'

'Neutron said you probably had it rigged to self-destruct.'

'Maybe I did.' She got up and shuffled to the boxes. 'Ah … by the way, what happened to Mojo?'

'Nothing,' Rachael replied.

Lexi's mouth fell open. 'You left him at the house? If Raymond's guys do break in they'll pinch him for sure! He's like a pet to me.'

'Then, hopefully, like a pet, he'll guard the house.'

'That's not funny,' Lexi said then muttered something unintelligible as she opened the top box and dug around in it one-handed. 'Not what I was after but …' She slid out the pyramid poster and pinched a pen from Rachael's desk. She used it to put an X through Davey's, Adam's and Karl's names. 'Board's rapidly shrinking,' she said with satisfaction, then dropped the pen into its holder and dived back into the box. She pulled out three different phones and read the names on the back before finding the one she was after.

She turned it on and waited for the phone to come to life. 'There's a new message. It's just a phone number. Do you want me to call it?'

'Not yet!' Rachael said. 'We'll run the number first on the slim chance we can trace the owner. Talk to Craig about how we're going to proceed.'

'So does that mean I'm … back on the investigation?' Lexi asked cautiously.

Rachael stared at her so long Finn wasn't sure she was going to answer. Finally she said, 'I'm not letting you out of my sight again until this is done. So you're in. But so help me if you even breathe without my permission—'

'I can live with that,' Lexi cut in. 'Should we talk to Craig now?'

'We'll get things moving now, yes.' Rachael already had her phone pressed to her ear. 'It's Rachael. Raymond has given Lexi a phone number to call.' She listened, then ended the call. 'It'll take a bit of time to get set up. In the meantime, let's get to work. Can you walk to the pod?'

'I got this far, didn't I?' Lexi said, shuffling to the door. 'Just a little stiff.'

'Hmm,' Rachael said, and Finn noted she walked much slower than usual to accommodate Lexi.

'Morning,' Rachael said when they found Cass and Linc at their desks.

'Wow,' Linc said, taking a good look at Lexi. 'Should she be here?'

'She,' Lexi said, 'could still kick your arse. Just—' she grimaced, '—slide me that chair.'

'Right,' Rachael began as Linc sprang up to move the chair, 'with everything that's been going on we haven't had time to look into something Bradley said before he died. He told us to warn Mike. We still don't know what that means.'

'Can I hear the playback?' Lexi asked.

'Wait, she's back in?' Cass asked Rachael in disbelief.

'We've reached an agreement,' Rachael said. 'And yes, regarding the bodycam. I think we should all refresh ourselves on it. Linc?'

'Yep, I'm just pulling it up.' A moment later Rachael's and Mark Bradley's voices echoed through the room.

'All right, Mr Bradley. I need you to put that gun down and come with us so we can sort this out. So we can find out what happened to Kirsten.'

'I know what happened! It's my fault. I should never have gotten wrapped up with the Hamills. First Anna, now Kirsten. I didn't mean it. I never took that shit again! It was a terrible thing to do but she wasn't meant to die. I didn't kill her.'

'I believe you.'

'Think what you like. I don't care. What's left to care about?'

'Mark, please. Let us help you.'

'You can't help me. But you'd better find Mike. Warn him.'

Rachael leant over Linc's computer and stopped it there. She didn't want to hear the crash and the screams.

'First Anna,' Lexi said. 'As in Anna Hamill?'

'Charlie Hamill's wife,' Rachael said. 'Charlie murdered her. He's doing life in prison.'

'"First Anna, now Kirsten. I didn't mean it",' Finn said. 'It almost sounds like he's responsible for both their deaths.'

'Except he said he didn't kill Kirsten. He was adamant.'

'He also said he should never have gotten wrapped up with the Hamills. What if he or he and the Hamills did something that indirectly caused both women's deaths?' Cass said.

'But Charlie was convicted.'

'Linc,' Lexi said, 'would you mind if I borrowed that laptop for a sec?'

Linc glanced at Rachael, who nodded, so he slid it in front of her. A frown marred Lexi's forehead as she typed with one hand. 'So the victim was found in the water. She'd been incapacitated by an impact to the back of the skull before being beaten and strangled.' She paused, did some more typing. 'The victim was found in the water ... incapacitated by an impact to the back of the skull before being beaten and strangled.'

'What are you getting at?' Rachael asked.

'The first time I was talking about Anna, second time I was talking about Kirsten.'

'They died exactly the same way?' Finn asked.

'Pretty close. There's some variation in the bruising patterns caused by the beatings but, otherwise, yes.'

'Charlie couldn't have murdered Kirsten, he's still in prison. Did he confess to that crime?'

'No,' Cass said, then read from her screen. 'He swore he was innocent. He was caught after an anonymous tip-off to police. They were on holiday at The Entrance at the time when Anna died. The police found methamphetamine in his system and argued he was too affected by drugs to remember the crime. Anna's skin was found under his fingernails and matching scratches were found on her scalp, maybe from him picking her up by the hair ... Lots of damning evidence including a detailed report by a guest who was in the room next door. She said she heard a loud argument between the Hamills over another woman.'

'What about Clarke? Could he have been responsible, simply imitated Charlie's act?'

'Maybe. What happened to the phone we found?'

'It was too damaged,' Linc said. 'We've got nothing.'

Rachael stood. 'I think I'd like to talk to Charlie Hamill.'

'But he's in supermax in Goulburn, isn't he?' Lexi said.

Finn got to his feet. 'Not a problem. I'll see if we can organise a video link.'

*

'I wasn't having an affair!' Charlie Hamill told the team an hour later via the video link-up. 'There was no other woman.'

'We have phone records from a second phone you kept which proves otherwise,' Rachael told him.

Charlie lifted his hands over his head then threw them down as though he wanted to throttle someone. 'I don't know where that phone came from!'

'Did you kill your wife, Mr Hamill?'

'No!'

'But you were fighting the night she died?'

'So we had a fight! It was over the damn phone. Someone was screwing with us. We were happy until then. Anna had been so thrilled to win that weekend away.'

Rachael's gaze narrowed. 'You won it? How?'

'I don't know. It was Anna. She was part of some online cosmetics club and they sent her a prize for being a loyal customer or something. We should never have fucking gone. But I'd had some calls on my regular phone, some fuckwit threatening to make me pay for something, dunno what, and Anna picked it up one day, got all freaked out. The weekend was supposed to take her mind off all that shit.'

'Do you know who the phone calls were from?'

'If I did, do you think they'd still be breathing? The voice was altered, one of those cheap download jobs.'

'I see. Are you familiar with a Mark Bradley?'

Charlie seemed to calm a bit and sat back. 'Heard he knocked off his wife and killed himself.'

'We don't believe he killed his wife. We're speaking to you because Kirsten was murdered the same way Anna was, after Bradley had received similar phone calls. Could you shed any light on that?'

'How could I? I'm in here!'

'Mr Hamill, if you didn't kill your wife, would you have any idea who did?'

'No.'

'Not Clarke?'

'Why would he kill Anna? The family would have slaughtered him. He had a good deal going with us.'

'Did he know her?'

'Not especially. No.'

'Mr Hamill, I'm inclined to believe you didn't kill your wife. But I need you to help me prove it.'

He sat up straighter, leant towards the screen hopefully. 'Yeah? How?'

'I need you to tell me who Mike is.'

Every ounce of energy seemed to drain from his body as he slumped back in his chair. 'No idea.'

'Are you sure? Before he died, Mr Bradley mentioned him. His words were, "first Anna, now Kirsten", then he told us we'd better warn Mike.'

'I told ya, I don't know. Is that it?'

'I would have thought you'd be more interested in clearing your name,' Rachael pressed.

'What's the point?'

'Funny, Bradley said that, too.'

Hands on the table, Charlie pushed to his feet. 'Thanks, anyway.'

'Interesting,' Finn said as they ended the link.

'Yeah,' Rachael said. 'He shut down at the mention of Mike. He knows more than he's saying. He, Bradley and this Mike must have been in on something together. This whole thing screams payback. Sorry,' she said as her phone pinged.

'Anything important?' he asked.

'Craig's ready to go on that phone number Lexi got from Raymond. He wants us over there.'

CHAPTER FORTY-FOUR

'All right,' Craig says to the room. 'Everyone ready?'

I'm sitting at a desk in cyber trying to stay awake. I'm not in quite as much pain as I probably should be, but the drugs blocking those pain receptors aren't helping with alertness. Rachael and Finn are hovering and the phone I use to contact Raymond is in front of me, the number he sent on the screen. At Craig's nod, I press dial. The room echoes with the ring tones projected through the specialist equipment, once, twice, but on the third ring the call cuts out.

'Well, that's disappointing,' I say.

Then the phone pings. I read the message on the screen. 'Uh oh.'

'Uh oh, what?' Rachael asks.

'I don't know, that's what it says: uh oh. Hold on … There's a video. It could be dodgy, but there's nothing on this phone he could hack. Should I open it?'

'Go for it,' Craig says.

I tap the screen, my face screwing up in confusion. 'It's my place. What—' I jump as my home explodes, chair screeching back as I watch the windows shatter, the roof collapse. Smoke, fire, dust. The place is a disaster. Then the screen goes black. I look up, helpless as to what to do.

Finn snatches the phone.

'Lexi's house was just blown up!' he announces. 'It's impacted the townhouse next to hers. We need emergency services out there now!' Several people scramble for phones at Rachael's and Craig's direction.

I don't move. That was my house. My house is ... gone. It's rubble.

'Lexi, I'm sorry,' Finn says.

It could be worse, I tell myself through the shock of it. I could have been in there. I swallow to return some moisture to my mouth and try to shrug. 'It was just a place to live. I'll find another one.' But my voice sounds thick and strained even to my own ears. Because another thought sneaks in, and it's not about me. It's so much worse than that.

'We'll get him. Okay?' Rachael tells me, planting her hands on the desk. 'Raymond has lost almost everything. He's flexing. He wants to upset you. He wants to make you pay. He won't get the chance to get near you again.'

'No, he won't. You'll sort it.'

'We have early reports that everyone got out of Lexi's building. No casualties,' Linc calls.

'Great, thanks,' Rachael says with obvious relief. Then to me, she says, 'Try not to worry. We'll take care of it.'

Everything hurts and I'm dizzy. But it's the fact I've been kidding myself that hurts the most. 'You were right.'

'What?' Rachael asks. 'Me? How?'

'Isn't it obvious? If I'd've had that phone on me earlier today, while all you guys were running around, being involved, being at my house, it wouldn't have occurred to me to do anything other than call the number and find out what whoever was behind it wanted me to know. You were at my house, packing my things. The only reason you didn't die today was because I didn't have that phone on me alone earlier.'

'That didn't happen.' Rachael's expression softens, but I don't want sympathy. I deserve a slap.

'Everything you said about working in a team was right. I'm sorry. Maybe I'm not cut out for this.'

'Because you can't predict the actions of animals?' Rachael asks quietly, below the general noise of the room. 'You've been on the force for five minutes. You're still learning. I keep trying to explain this to you. With what you're involved in there's no time to coach you with baby steps. We're going to butt heads from time to time because there are situations where I need you to listen to me, trust me and do what I need you to do. And you're not always going to want to do that. And quite honestly, if it took blowing up your house for you to understand the difference between working with a team and working as part of one, then it was a worthwhile explosion.'

I'm not sure whether I want to laugh or cry. But fuck, I need to pull it together. 'Just don't get any ideas for the future. First time is always the most effective.'

'There's another message,' Finn says.

Rachael takes the phone then hands it to me.

You think we're done? We're not.

Rage sweeps through me. 'What do you want me to say?' I ask Rachael.

'What do you want to say?'

'That he's done. That if he doesn't turn Debbie over by the end of the week, I have everything I need to destroy him once and for all.'

'Do you have enough?' Craig asks.

'I haven't checked Adam's phone yet, but there's a good chance I—we—can get enough to make a decent start.'

Craig exchanges glances with Rachael. 'I'm good with that. Let's give Raymond one more serious push. Call his bluff.'

'Okay. Do it,' Rachael tells me.

'How about I type it?' Finn offers. He sends the message.

After several minutes of no reply, Rachael sighs. 'Right, we'll keep an eye on that. Lexi, I think you've dealt with more than enough for today. I'm going to make sure we're good to head over to the apartment we've set up for you.'

I get up again and notice Cass's eyes on me. 'Oh, go on, you're dying to say something, aren't you?' I ask tiredly.

'I'm not going to lie, I disagree with you being here,' she says. 'But right now I'm wondering how you're still on your feet.'

So am I. 'Well, thanks for the honesty. See ya.'

Finn follows me out as I head for Rachael's office. 'That was almost a compliment.'

'And so warm,' I enthuse. 'I *really* should have taken the two million.'

'And yet you turned it down without a thought,' Finn reminds me.

'I wouldn't say without a thought,' I admit. 'There was a definite moment of "damn it".'

'You could have used your powers as a criminal. Very lucratively. Probably on a regular basis, if you chose to. You didn't. You don't. That was a choice. You chose cop.'

'But I did,' I admit. 'Before. That's where I learnt it.'

'Ah, the born out of necessity mystery job,' Finn teases. 'You know, you never got around to telling me what that was.'

'It was anything but lucrative. At least, for me,' I say as we reach the office.

'Right,' Rachael says, spotting us. 'We're good to go. I'll grab some officers and take you over. Finn, would you mind dropping in on the crime scene? Check it out?'

'Of course.' To me, he says, 'I'll see you tomorrow.'

I manage a smile. 'See ya. Thanks.'

'Come on,' Rachael says. 'I want to get you settled in over there.'

'Okay, but can I please have my laptop back?'

Rachael hesitates, then moves behind her desk and unlocks a drawer. She takes it out, holds it against her chest. 'Lexi, promise me.'

'You want me to swear on something? I nearly got you blown up. You're gonna have to believe I'm not in a hurry to go there again.'

Rachael puts the computer with my other things. 'Okay, let's go.'

As it turns out, my temporary home is down one elevator, a one-minute walk into the next building and up another. Handy, because, though I wouldn't admit it, I'm dead on my feet.

'Here we are,' Rachael says, unlocking a door at the end of a very ordinary hallway eight storeys up. The apartment is simple but comfortable enough, a tiled, open-plan space with lots of light and a balcony.

I head for it and look out. 'Nice view of headquarters. There's no door to the balcony.'

'Security measure,' Rachael tells me, letting in two officers with my things. 'That glass is bullet proof and one way. No one can see in or get in. We keep this apartment for just this sort of thing. It has every safety precaution possible.'

I stick my head in the bathroom. 'There's no cameras in the shower, right?'

'Of course not. But there is an emergency switch in every room. We'll have cops on the door at all times both here and in the lobby.'

'Doesn't that draw attention to the fact I'm here?'

'This is Raymond Hamill, Lexi. We're not taking any chances. Kitchen's fully stocked but if you need anything else, call the number by the phone and someone will get it for you.'

'Room service. Yay. That's great, but I can't just sit here the rest of the day and night and do nothing.'

'How about you see what you can dig up on this Mike person for me?'

'Really?'

'Don't make me regret it.'

'Okay. Got the wifi?'

As soon as Rachael leaves I unpack as little as possible and meaning to just lie on the bed for a minute or two, end up sleeping for three hours, only waking when Bailee calls to check on me. After reassuring her I'm fine, I attempt a shower with my hand stuck out of the screen. At least the stiches from the water incident and the damaged thumb are on the same side. I manage, just, then debate whether the JD Rachael by some miracle packed me or the prescription drugs are going to do a better job of keeping me going while I look into Mike. I decide on the JD first, because I know more meds are going to knock me out again.

I open my computer, prepare to get started. But where? Mike. It's not much to go on. There's no one within the Hamill circle I can find by that name. I widen the search to social media profiles. There's a few Mikes and Michaels so I note them down, but it's not an uncommon name. I access the Latimer company computers next, go back ten years. A few more Michaels crop up to look into but none seem like they had any close ties to Mark Bradley. I throw back another shot of JD. I didn't expect this to be easy. I know

Cass has been working on it and anything obvious would have been discovered.

I refill my glass then log in to the police database, scroll through Charlie Hamill's records. Bradley had no prior convictions and looking up a Mike would be a waste of time. There was bound to be thousands.

There's not too much on Charlie but what's there ranges from first degree murder down to minor vandalism. I click on each conviction and, when nothing springs out at me, start on the rest of the records because what have I got to lose? One involves illegal shooting in the national park. There was no conviction recorded, but thanks to the police policy of keeping records of all arrests and official interactions regardless of whether the person is found guilty or not, there are lots of minor incidents like this one to dig through. The complainants' names mean nothing to me, but their address catches my attention. It looks like the couple were caretakers of the Wondabyne railway cottage twelve years ago. Could that be relevant? I read on.

Charlie had been shooting in the area and a bullet had gone through the cottage window. They'd gotten a photo of him and a local cop had recognised him, tried to charge him, but Charlie didn't have a gun registered to him, no gun could be located and the cop couldn't prove anything other than that he was in the area. What a joke. As if any of the Hamills would bother registering a gun. I wonder if Charlie might have been living in the Cogra Bay home where we found Josie at the time.

I click on the next record and the caretakers' names pop up again. Charlie had gone back a few days after the initial incident and terrorised them for an evening, no doubt in retribution and this time with friends. When the cops managed to get out there, they saw three men take off into the bush but were unable to catch them. The couple moved out shortly after the incident, but not before—

I sit straighter in my chair. What the hell?

CHAPTER FORTY-FIVE

Thursday, March 17

'The explosives were in the roof cavity,' Rachael told Lexi. It was still early but Lexi had been ready when she'd arrived. 'The damage is not quite as extensive as it looked in the video but the building is still a write-off. Most importantly, we've confirmed the early report that no one was in the adjoining home.'

'Well, of course not,' Lexi said with a wry grin. 'The Parkhursts are indestructible.'

'Finn said they've decided you must have had a drug lab in there that blew up.'

'Not bad,' Lexi said. 'I can live with that.'

'At least we got most of your stuff out.'

'Yeah. Most of it,' Lexi said.

Rachael caught the sulky glare. Honestly. Lexi couldn't possibly have believed she'd bring a cannabis plant to headquarters! 'Anyway, the type of explosives used and the way they were rigged points to a pair of contract killers we've been on the trail of for a few years. We can't prove Raymond hired them yet, and Raymond and Lena have gone completely off radar. But we're working on it. Craig's organising a raid on the Hamill property. It'll take a few days to ensure everything is absolutely spot on by the book and all the legal is in place. We can't risk something like this going wrong and having them walk on some technicality.'

'Okay, so can we get back on with the rest of the case now? I found Mike. And I think I know what's going on.'

'Already? How?'

'You packed my JD. I do my best work on the stuff.'

'I knew there had to be a higher power at work that made me throw that in. Okay, hold that thought. You can fill in the whole team at once. I'll carry your laptop for you,' she said, putting it in its case and zipping it up. 'Need anything else?'

'Nah, thanks. I'm guessing we're not coming and going on our own?'

'No.' Rachael tried for her most serious tone. 'Or your next arrangements will be protective custody in Silverwater.'

'Oh, ouch. You really are mean in the rabid mother hen role.'

'The what?' Rachael asked, genuinely startled.

Lexi chuckled. 'Just something Finn—never mind.'

'Finn called me *rabid*?'

Lexi's face was pure innocence. 'No, of course not.'

'Hmm.' She led Lexi into the hallway where a uniformed cop was waiting. 'We're heading over, Ted.'

'Yes, ma'am.' He got on the radio and let the officers in the lobby know.

'Do do, do-do, do do, do-do …' Lexi starting on the *Mission: Impossible* theme was too much.

'Would you please take this seriously?'

'I am! But there's only so much serious I can take. Take a breath, Rach.'

'Okay,' she said, relieved they were getting back on a comfortable footing. 'Let's get over there.'

'You know, why not set me up in one of the offices in HQ?' Lexi asked. 'It'd save a lot of time and drama. Plus whatever all this is costing.'

'Can't do that. Regulations. Besides, you need your own space. Time away from the case.'

'I'd rather just get it done. I'm not the type to be locked in a room.'

She sighed. 'I've got you in the apartment to ensure your safety when you're alone, that's all. You're still part of the investigation. As long as you're with us when you're out and about, you're free to help us get on with ending this.'

'You know, I'm probably a lot safer now most of the Hamills are in custody or dead.'

'Raymond blew your house up. Don't underestimate him, especially when he's backed into a corner. Besides, where would you go?'

'Well, an idea kinda popped into my head late last night,' Lexi said as they stepped out of the lift.

'Can't wait to hear this one.'

'I'm going to need a place to stay now I don't have a home for the foreseeable future. And Finn's got a spare.'

Rachael stopped. 'What?'

'Finn said he could afford the loan repayments on his house if he didn't have the apartment to worry about, right?'

'Yes ...'

'Dawny left me some money. I could use it to pay Finn for the bond and remaining months' rent. Then I could get out of protection prison and he could get his house back.'

'Okay. That's a nice idea. But let's not get you or his place blown up by getting ahead of ourselves. For the time being, you're staying put.'

They made their way to the meeting room for the morning briefing while Rachael turned Lexi's idea over in her mind. It could just be the perfect solution.

'Hey!' Finn said, spotting them first. 'How you feeling today, partner?' he asked Lexi.

'Better than you look,' Lexi teased. 'You?'

'Back at you. How's the thumb?'

'I presume it's still attached in here ... somewhere,' Lexi said, eyeing her bandaged hand.

Rachael supposed it was good they could joke about it. She wasn't quite there yet. She sat and put Lexi's computer down on the desk next to her. Lexi opened it. 'Right, we have progress,' she said, moving them along. 'Lexi?'

'Okay. On to mysterious Mike. Twelve years ago, a couple staying at the caretaker's cottage at Wondabyne had a run-in with Charlie Hamill. He's a keen shooter and put a bullet through their window one afternoon while illegally hunting. They managed to get a photo of him and called the cops, who gave him a bit of grief, so in true Hamill fashion he retaliated by going back a few nights later with some friends. They trashed the place around the terrified couple, who again called the police. As you know, it takes some time to get to the cottage. By the time police arrived, the men were charging off up the hill. The couple said the men had worn balaclavas but swore one of them was Charlie yelling out that they should have kept their mouths shut.

'Working on the statements from the couple, who told him they regularly heard shooting on Friday evenings, Sergeant Luke Jenkins took a few men out there the next Friday evening and ran into a group of men shooting. They were charged for being in possession of unregistered weapons but again, there was no proof they'd terrorised the caretaker couple so that was dropped. The three men were Charlie Hamill, Mark Bradley and Mike Smith.'

'Sounds promising,' Rachael said.

'Wait for it. After all this Hamill shit, the caretakers understandably had had enough. They were in the process of leaving when their adult daughter disappeared. They were packing their things onto a barge, so the daughter took her child for a walk to get her out from under their feet. She never came back. The little girl did. She was hysterical. She told them that three bad men had taken her mother. That they did bad things to her and they put her in the water.'

Linc uttered a curse. 'I'm guessing at least a couple of those bad things involved hitting her over the back of the head and suffocating her before putting her in the water?'

'And the child couldn't identify them?'

'She could only say they had "black things on their heads".'

'Balaclavas,' Rachael said. 'Like in the previous attack. Did they find the mother?'

'Nothing. Apart from the fact she was gone, there was no evidence of any foul play. The child was too traumatised to give them any clear description of events or lead them back to where it was supposed to have happened. The police conducted a search but there was no body found in or out of the water and no evidence of who might have been behind it. Charlie and his friends were obviously checked out but were all apparently somewhere else and provided reasonably loose alibis. A missing persons report was filed but that was all that could be done. There wasn't any proof.'

'You spoke to this Sergeant Jenkins?'

'Yeah, last night. It was late but he didn't seem to mind. He retired five years ago but said he'd love to see it resolved. He's happy to help if we want to speak to him again.'

'So it was Mike ... Smith?' Cass asked. 'I'll pull him up on the system, track him down.'

'Already done,' Lexi said. 'He never got in trouble with the police again, seems to be living a fairly ordinary life. He lives in Wyong, is married and recently became a father. He plays in the local all-age men's soccer team, works at Bunnings in the paint section, and is on shift there from one till nine today.'

'Great, if we can't get him at home we'll get him there,' Rachael said. 'Finn, are you right to come?'

'Yeah, I need to be up that way to sign the house contracts anyway.'

'Can I come?' Lexi asked.

Rachael hesitated. 'Okay, but just to be extra cautious, you ride in the back and keep your head down. Finn, you're still loaded on painkillers. I'll drive.'

Rachael got them on the road and as promised, Lexi kept her head down until they were far enough away that Rachael deemed it safe they hadn't been followed. They'd reached the coast and had just turned off the motorway when Finn's phone buzzed.

'It'll be Viv making sure I'm going to be there on time to sign,' he muttered.

Lexi cleared her throat, prompting Rachael to say, 'There's another option.'

Finn flicked her a glance. 'What's that?'

'Lexi needs somewhere to live.'

'I do,' Lexi echoed from the back. 'Once I'm out of jail.'

'You ... you're not buying my house.'

'No,' Rachael said, 'but she's willing to sublet your apartment.'

'I can pay three months up front, along with the bond, which means you can afford the repayments to buy out your house,' Lexi clarified.

Finn turned in his seat. 'You're kidding. Can you afford that?'

'I can. I mean, I don't know the exact rent but I'm guessing it's not exorbitant ...'

'And as her house was blown up in the line of duty, I think I can wrangle some extra support,' Rachael said.

Finn was silent for several seconds, letting it all sink in. 'I haven't finalised the loan.'

'But it's been approved,' Rachael reminded him.

'You're sure about this?' Finn asked, looking from one to the other.

'Hundred per cent,' Lexi said. 'I mean, I've gotta live somewhere. At least temporarily. And as I'll no longer have the pleasure of living across the drive from Trevor, it's win-win.'

Finn stared off into space then nodded slowly to himself. Smiled. 'I'll call Viv back.' He tried. 'She's not answering. Probably on her way over.'

'So call the bank, and let's get over there and tell her the good news,' Rachael said enthusiastically.

CHAPTER FORTY-SIX

At five minutes to eleven, Rachael pulls the car up in front of a solid slate grey fence. Open gates stretch back to twice the width of the driveway to show off a neat and tidy home: white render, grey roof, a small second-storey addition over the garage. A veranda runs along the front, bordered by nondescript shrubs. Behind the house, thick trees and shrubs continue into the hillside.

'Hey, this is nice,' I tell Finn.

'Thanks. I haven't seen it looking this good for years. But it's been for sale so they've put some effort in.' A family parks on the opposite side of the road. 'I'm guessing that's the buyers. I need to talk to Viv privately before letting them know.'

'Of course, go ahead,' Rachael says.

Vivienne and the real estate agent appear on the veranda to meet the family.

'I'm sorry, if you could give me a minute,' Finn tells the man who has emerged from his car, wife and two boys in tow.

'What's this about, Finn?' Vivienne asks.

'I need to talk to you inside.'

He steps through the front door and Vivienne and the estate agent follow, leaving an awkward silence outside. There's no way this could go wrong now, surely? So why am I nervous?

'This is a really nice place,' I say to Rachael. 'I didn't expect it to be so big.'

'The house sits on almost half an acre of land. Extends into the bush.'

'And the park's right across the road. I can see why there's so much interest.'

Raised voices float out the front door. Rachael grimaces. 'It doesn't sound like it's going too well in there.'

'She can't make him sell it.'

'No, but if this turns into a bidding war, Finn's going to struggle.'

'What? How?'

'Finn says he has this much, the buyers say they can offer more, Viv plays the "I'm entitled to half what we can get for it and now it's worth this much" card … '

'That can't be right.'

'If she fights him over it, there'll be legal costs. Finn can't afford that.'

'Well, that's shit. Imagine both of us losing our houses in the same week …' I chew on my lip as an idea occurs to me.

'What?' Rachael asks.

'Nothing,' I murmur. But an idea is forming.

'Don't give me that. I know that look.'

I get out of the car and Rachael follows me. 'What are you doing? Stay in the car!'

'I'm stiff. I need to stretch,' I tell her, catching the eye of the father. He takes the opportunity to come over. Excellent.

'Excuse me, could you tell us what's going on?' he all but barks at me.

'Oh, hi. You're buying this place?'

'We're supposed to be signing right now. Who is that man?'

'That's Detective Sergeant Finn Carson. He owns the house with Viv.'

'Does he have a problem with the sale?' the wife calls out from the other side of the road where her kids are playing.

'Oh, I'm sure they'll sort that out,' I say carelessly. 'Honestly, after recent events, I'm surprised you want it. But good for you. You're braver than me.'

The couple exchange looks. 'What do you mean, braver?' the man asks. I hear the wife tell the kids not to leave the equipment before she crosses the empty road.

'You don't *know*?' I glance at Rachael. 'Aren't these sorts of things supposed to be disclosed?'

'I would have thought so.' Rachael's clearly not sure what to say.

It's more of a question than a statement, but I push on. 'Finn's involved in a very serious case against a Sydney crime family. They've already made one attempt on his life.'

'Okay ... so?' the husband prompts.

'His colleague's house—mine—was blown up a couple of days ago.'

'What?' This from the wife, who eyes my bruises and bandages with new interest. 'Wait ... the one at Ourimbah? The one on the news?'

'That's the one. And look, I don't know if they'll target this place or not. Maybe they won't. And I know you had nothing to do with any of that, but I'm not sure those sorts of people are going to knock on the door and check who they're killing.'

'How did you get the ...' The husband waves his finger around my face.

'A guy called the Butcher tried to torture and kill me,' I tell them, holding up my damaged hand. 'Same case.'

The husband and wife exchange glances and go back over the road, talking between themselves. I hear the wife say, 'We should make an offer on the other house. It's just as lovely with a full acre of land. It's not that much further from your office ...'

'There's no evidence Raymond Hamill has any interest in coming after Finn's house,' Rachael says.

'There was none that he was coming after mine. Finn killed Raymond's favourite son. If Raymond can gather the resources there's got to be a solid risk he'll be after retribution. I'm only telling these people the truth. And if they decide to pull out there's no chance of the stupid bidding war you're worried about.'

'Uh oh.'

'Uh oh? Really? Great choice of words, Rachael.' But I look back to the house, notice the husband striding towards the front door while the wife bundles the kids into the car. She looks around nervously before dropping into her own seat. The husband knocks, lets himself in.

'There's no way this is going to come back to bite me, is there?' I ask.

'Whatever goes down, you're going down with it.'

'Thanks.'

'But I'm on your side.'

'That actually makes me feel a lot better. He's back already.'

The husband strides out the door and heads for the car. He spots us watching, changes direction. 'Thank you,' he tells me. 'At least there's still some honest people in the world.' He nods and heads for his car.

As the family drives away, the real estate agent emerges. 'That looks like a man who just lost a hefty commission, doesn't it?' I mumble.

'Yes, he does.'

Raised voices, one Vivienne's, one Finn's, creep back up in volume as the estate agent slams into his car and reverses out of the drive.

'Let's go,' Rachael orders.

'Where are we going?'

'To see if I can calm things down. Right now, Viv's blaming Finn for that. Knock, knock!' she calls before entering. I follow her through a large living area decked out in neutral tones, stairs to the right, open-plan kitchen and dining ahead. Black and white with hints of grey that tie it to the rest of the house. Beyond the kitchen stretches an undercover entertaining area. I had assumed that the house would have an old feel to it, but everything is modern and light.

'They pulled out!' Vivienne complains as we reach the kitchen. 'They found out about Lexi's place and think I'm luring them into some death trap!'

'Oh, that's shit,' I say.

'Yes! That was low, Finn.'

'It wasn't me!' he objects.

'No, it was me.' I spot a basket of goodies on the dining table. 'This is cute.' I sit and poke through it.

'I bought it for the new owners,' Vivienne says, glaring at me in disbelief.

'The information needed to be disclosed. Chocolates, yum.' I pin the box under my injured arm and rip the lid off, then offer one to Rachael.

'Are you right?' Vivienne snaps.

I look innocently at Finn. 'You don't mind, do you?'

'What's it got to do with him?' She looks ready to gouge my eyes out. But whatever.

'As Finn's buying you out, he's technically the new—even though he's also the existing—owner. I didn't think he'd mind.'

'But I liked those people! They were a lovely young family!' Vivienne's glare has returned to Finn. 'The house would have suited them down to the ground!' She sighs. 'Anyway, the house should go to the other family who offered the same amount. They were only a day late. You don't need such a big place and I bet they'll raise their offer.'

Finn is shaking his head. 'I'm not selling the house now that I can afford to pay you out, Viv.'

Vivienne's face turns dark. 'This was nothing but a low trick! You're costing me money by not giving the other potential buyers a chance to counter-offer. I'm entitled to half of what we can get and I won't be bullied into this. I'll fight you all the way!'

I catch Rachael's *I told you so* look.

'I can give you exactly the same amount you were contractually willing to accept less than two minutes ago,' Finn told her. 'There's nothing to fight.'

'That's not the point!'

'Then what is?'

I swallow my chocolate, lick my fingers. 'It's simple. She doesn't want you to have your house back.' I look up from checking out the white wine to see Vivienne's hard stare so I add, 'Am I wrong?'

'Lexi,' Finn warns.

'Nup.' I slide off the stool and dust off my good hand. 'I'm sorry, I know I should stay out of it, but this is total bullshit.' Then to Vivienne, I say, 'You need to back the fuck up, lady. You're out of control.'

'How dare you!' Her fists clench in rage.

'How dare I what? Call it like it is? Finn's tolerated this crap for too long because he doesn't want Ava to have to choose sides or be upset by any friction, and you're damn lucky on that front, but I digress. This is Finn's house. It's always been Finn's house. The law entitles you to half its value and that's what he's giving you. So fucking take it and quit lording it over him like you're somehow in charge. Because you're kidding yourself, princess. He's keeping it.'

Mouth open, Vivienne looks from me to Finn before landing on Rachael. 'Can you believe this?'

Rachael shrugs. 'Honestly, I think that about covers it.'

'Rachael!'

'What you're legally entitled to is yours fair and square. But Lexi's right. You don't just want the money, you want Finn to lose the house. You know how much it means to him and yet you're making it as difficult as you can for him to buy you out. You're not a bad person, Viv, so I don't really understand the way you're behaving, but that's the truth of it and that's why I'm done.' She walks to the table and snatches the hamper. 'We appreciate the gift basket.'

I follow Rachael out and send Finn a look that suggests he'd want to come too.

'I'll have my lawyer draft the paperwork,' he tells Vivienne as we leave. Outside, he says, 'I hope you two feel better, because I don't like my chances of shuffling weekends and extra time with Ava for the foreseeable future.'

'Sorry, Finn,' Rachael says, 'but that woman is …'

'Taking the piss?' I suggest helpfully.

'Yes. That. Since Viv's been with Louis she's been all sorts of nasty and she needs to be called out on it. She's not going to stop you swapping weekends and giving you extra time because one, it suits her to have you run around after Ava when she's supposed to and two, because of all the extra stuff you pay for.'

We reach the car but rather than get in, Finn leans on the door, staring thoughtfully at the road. 'Okay. You're probably right.' He looks at me. 'And you. You told the buyers some crazy house-destroying crime gang is after me? Then you let Viv have it?'

'Well, the crazy, house-destroying crime gang is the straight-up truth. And so was what I said—' I decide to change tack. 'You know, in my defence, I could have *really* let her have it. I don't get anywhere near enough credit for the things I manage *not* to say!'

As he's begun grinning like a mad person, I gather he's not too pissed off. 'Thank you.' He opens his door. 'You two just saved my house.'

'We'll have to celebrate later,' Rachael says, getting in. 'We have to pick up Mike Smith, remember?'

'Then what?' Finn asks.

'We'll take him to Wyong Station. Interview him there and get his wife to safety as fast as possible.'

CHAPTER FORTY-SEVEN

Finn stepped out of the way of a tradie carrying a ladder and looked around. Bunnings was packed with its usual array of home renovators, DIY builders and plant lovers. Men and women in red work polos with the company logo scurried around like ants in the fray, halted regularly to answer yet more questions and point down aisles.

'You think it's always this busy or did we just hit the worst possible time to arrive?' Lexi asked.

'Not sure,' he answered, unconcerned. Nothing was going to dampen his mood this afternoon. He did wish things hadn't had to turn bitter with Vivienne, but Lexi and Rachael were right, she seemed hell bent on making sure he wasn't able to buy his house back. He couldn't understand it.

'I'll go find someone to help us,' Rachael said, and approached a stocky checkout operator wearing a tired but polite smile. She spoke to the woman and a moment later a call for Mike Smith came over the loudspeaker.

It took almost ten minutes and another announcement before a tall, middle-aged man with messed-up dark hair and a paint-splattered apron appeared, his name tag declaring he was, indeed, the man they were after.

'Mike Smith?' Rachael asked, intercepting him from his beeline to the register.

'Yes?' The professional smile wavered as he took in their suits.

'Mr Smith, we're arresting you in relation to the murder of Amelia Davidson. You do not have to say—'

'What? Hang on!' he said, taking several quick steps backwards.

'Mr Smith, if you want to make a scene in front of the entire store that's up to you,' Rachael said, then finished reading him his rights before slipping the handcuffs on and leading him out without further protest.

He didn't speak again on the way to the station except to request his lawyer, who was almost magically able to arrive at Wyong Station for the interview before they did. That was almost unheard of, but it was a good day, Finn reminded himself.

'You can take lead on this one,' Rachael told him.

'I'll grab us some coffees,' Lexi offered.

Finn got the interview underway, but Mike Smith was not going down without a fight.

'I told you. I don't know this Amelia woman!'

'Mr Smith, we can keep playing this game all day,' Finn said, 'but regardless of whether you want to cooperate with our investigation or not, I need to know where your wife is.'

Mike had been staring at the table for the last ten minutes but his head came up at the mention of his wife. 'Greta? She left me a week ago. We've just had a baby and she thinks I've been having an affair. I've never cheated on her once, but she doesn't believe me. She's taken our child away from me.' He looked absolutely gutted.

'Let me guess, she found a phone. It was full of messages between you and the mystery woman that implicated you in an affair.'

'Yes! That—that's what Greta said. She reckons one even suggested me and this chick had plans to knock her off, but she wouldn't show it to me. She said it's evidence for court. I didn't believe her at first. I thought she was feeling insecure and trying to trip me up. I don't have another phone! But then I got a few nasty phone calls and I wondered if someone was screwing with us. I tried to tell her but she wouldn't listen. She left and I don't understand it.'

'We believe you,' Rachael said. 'And that makes things much more urgent. Where is your wife?'

'Why? What's urgent?'

'Charlie Hamill's and Mark Bradley's partners both found a phone containing messages like Greta did. Both are now dead. There's no reason to believe the person responsible won't come for your wife next.'

'Oh my God!' Mike put his head in his hands and dragged the heels of his hands across his eyes. 'Who's doing this?'

'We can't be sure of that yet. We do, however, believe it could have something to do with what happened to Amelia Davidson.'

His face reflected his shock, then turned to desolation. 'Okay. Okay. Damn it. Look, it was an accident. And it wasn't me! I didn't kill the woman!' He began to shake, his hands jittery on the table before moving back to clutch his hair. 'It was stupid. It was so stupid!'

His lawyer leant in and spoke in his ear.

'What happened, Mr Smith?' Finn prompted.

'No comment.'

'We don't have time for these games, Mr Smith!' Rachael raised her voice. 'We need to have all the facts in this case so we can protect you, Greta and your baby! They are in serious danger!'

Again his lawyer mumbled something. Mike looked around the room as though struggling to know what to do.

'If you care about your wife …' Finn said.

'I was nineteen years old!' Mike blurted. 'A brickie's labourer without the physical stamina for the job. I was on the brink of being fired when we did a job for Latimer Developments. I was taking speed to help keep me going. Mark Bradley was on site one day—'

'So Bradley and Latimer knew each other that far back?'

'Longer than that. Mark told me they'd studied construction together before Lato even met that crazy wife of his. When he married Carole, Lato was given money by Carole's family to start the construction business and he put Mark on as his right-hand man.

The payback to that was the Hamills could use that business to clean their drug money.'

'And how did you get involved?'

'Mark caught me doing a line of speed. I copped it for taking it on the job and I told him not to worry about dobbing me in, that I was gonna lose my job anyway. He pulled me aside the next day and offered me a new job. That was working in the Hamill drug lab. Crazy, I know, but I needed the money and the meth.'

'Go on,' Finn said.

'Charlie was running the place at Cogra Bay at the time. He was living out there and he liked to take drugs and go shooting. He invited me to go out with him and Mark occasionally. Told me he'd teach me to shoot. I was quite a bit younger than them and I was equal parts in awe of and scared of the bloke, so I went along. That day, we were all as high as kites. We'd been out for a while. Charlie bagged a couple of wallabies, chased an injured one down towards the creek.' He dragged in an unsteady breath. Released it slowly. 'There was a kid. A little girl. He got so excited and pretended like we were going to bag the kid. Mark got nervous. I don't reckon he was as into the shooting thing, just went along, you know, like me. It was fun because we were high, but not serious, you know? Then Charlie's stalking this kid and we got freaked.'

'Keep going.'

'So he's off after this kid and she spots him and screams out for her mum and the next thing, the mother's there. Charlie lined the gun up at the kid, and the mother whispered something in her ear and the kid bolted. I don't know why the woman didn't bolt too. I think she wanted to give her daughter time to get away. She was standing between the kid and Charlie's gun.'

Mike stopped. He was crying now, head in his hands, swiping at his eyes. A loud sniff had Rachael sliding him a box of tissues.

'And then?'

Mike took a few noisy breaths. 'He raped her. Told us all to have a go.'

'And did you?'

He dropped his hands out, palms up, as if pleading for understanding. 'You don't say no to Charlie, and it didn't seem like such a big deal, because we were off our heads. A bit of fun. But even so, I knew it was wrong. I went along with it. She fought back. It was rough, ugly. We heard voices on the water, there was a barge taking all the furniture from the house away. The woman wriggled free but Charlie caught her and covered her mouth to stop her screaming out, but the voices went on for ages and his hand was so big and the more she struggled the tighter he held on. None of us realised he was covering her mouth and her nose. She couldn't breathe. We didn't know, I swear! She dropped like a stone when he let her go. Smashed her head pretty hard but didn't move. Charlie was like, well, fuck me, she's dead.

'Then we heard someone else close by. It was the kid. She hadn't run. She kind of cried and Mark stepped towards her. Charlie told him to grab her but she was quick and little and after a few minutes of looking we were getting too close to the station, so we went back to the body. We stashed it in the old railway dam.'

'Railway dam?' Rachael asked.

'It's a bit south of the caretaker's cottage, up the hill a bit. Used to store fresh water for the steam trains. It's mostly mud these days so we had to go back to the house and get shovels and dig her down into it. Then Charlie told me and Mark to forget it.'

'It's not a memorial,' Lexi told Finn. 'It's a grave.'

'Memorial? Grave?' Rachael asked.

Finn nodded. 'We've been there. Someone's been taking flowers and candles to the site.'

'But who?' Lexi said.

'We'll worry about that later,' Rachael said.

'I'm sorry, I'm so sorry.' Mike was sobbing now.

'And your wife? Where can we find her?'

'She was staying at her sister's place, but I went over there yesterday and they're gone. I called Greta's mum but she said they've taken off for a few days to get away while she gets her head around things.'

'I'll need her mother's number,' Finn said.

Mike gave it to him. 'You know, Amelia's dad. He knew we did it. I had to move a couple of times because he kept after us. Said he'd never give up until he found his daughter. Then he'd make sure we paid for it.'

'I see,' Rachael said. 'Stay put for us for a moment please, Mr Smith.' She gestured for Finn and Lexi to follow her out.

'No wonder Charlie didn't bother to talk to us once we mentioned Mike,' Finn said. 'He and Bradley were both right. What was the point of being cleared of killing their wives if it meant going up on charges of raping and killing Amelia?'

'Let's update the others,' Rachael said. 'I want everyone working on this.'

CHAPTER FORTY-EIGHT

'So it's the same set of circumstances we met with the other two murders,' Rachael told the team back at headquarters. 'Mike's wife thinks there's another woman. They've both received texts to that effect. Mike's received threatening calls and his wife has left him. Greta's taken off with the sister to get away from Mike and their mother's sticking to the story that she doesn't know where her daughters have gone. She tried calling them for us, but apparently the sister made Greta leave her phone at home because she needed a break from Mike's harassment. I'm guessing Greta did too.'

'At least we now have a solid possible motive tying together Kirsten's and Anna's murders,' Cass said.

'But why the cheating?' Finn asked. 'How does that part play into it? There's nothing in Mike's confession that has anything to do with a cheating spouse.'

'It could be nothing more than a ruse to cause conflict,' Rachael said. 'If you want people to believe a husband has killed his partner you want them to believe the marriage was under pressure. This isn't something that's been thought up overnight. Our POI has been following and studying these couples for quite some time, manipulating them over weeks or months. We know Kirsten got a message telling her when and where to be on the night of her murder and I wouldn't mind betting that prize Anna Hamill received in the mail didn't come from a cosmetics company. This is a long game. Based on what we've learnt, I think we should start by looking at Amelia's father. Lexi, how are you feeling?'

'Good enough.'

'Then I need you to find me everything you can about Amelia's family.'

'I already have the case files and a bunch of notes Sergeant Jenkins emailed this morning,' she said, opening her computer. 'According to these files, Amelia's parents, Paul and Vanessa Davidson, took over care of the little girl, Jessica, after Amelia went missing. They moved to Woy Woy, set Jessica up at the local school and got on with their lives. Vanessa is a painter. She runs a small home business dealing in local artists' work. Paul ... okay ... he's an interesting character all right. He did some time in the army straight out of school before getting out on his thirtieth birthday and taking on work for the railway. After Amelia's disappearance, he lost the plot. Was very aggressive towards police, accusing them of being in Charlie Hamill's pocket when they were unable to charge Charlie and his mates over his daughter's disappearance. He contacted the media, the government, and when he wasn't getting anywhere, became increasingly hostile. He was charged for throwing a rock through a police station window after a heated exchange. His behaviour caused the railway to let him go.

'After that he seemed to have calmed down. From what I can see, he dedicates most of his time to his rock-sculpting hobby. His wife's website sells some of his pieces for quite a lot of money. I'm not sure a lot of this isn't out of date, but it gives us a general idea.'

'Ex-army rock sculptor with a murdered daughter and a grudge against police. Yeah, that gives us a very good general idea,' Rachael said. 'Make sure the address on them is still current. We need to talk to him. Cass and Linc, I need you working on finding Greta.'

It was approaching late afternoon as Finn steered the car towards the Davidson place. 'What a day!' he said with a yawn, glancing in the back at Lexi. 'I can't believe you insisted on coming out again.'

'Well, I wasn't hanging around to work with Cass.'

'We're almost there,' Rachael said. 'Number twenty-seven.'

He slowed the car to check a letterbox number before pulling off the road in front of an older-style weatherboard. Two cars were in the drive. 'Looks like they're home.'

'Bonus,' Lexi said.

They walked to the Davidsons' front door, where two Maltese terriers barked loudly from behind the screen.

'Shut up!' came a man's voice.

Rachael rang the doorbell. The dogs exploded into more noise.

'Whitey! Champ! Come here!' It was a woman's voice this time, and she came shuffling up the narrow hallway in a pink tracksuit and slippers. 'Can I help you?' she asked as she gently shoved the dogs out of the way with one foot.

'Mrs Davidson? I'm Detective Inspector Rachael Langley and these are my colleagues Detective Sergeant Finn Carson and Constable Lexi Winter. May we come in?'

'Paul! The police are here! It's not Jess, is it? Nothing's happened to—'

'No, Mrs Davidson, we're not here about Jess.'

The woman visibly relaxed.

A burly older man in overalls appeared in the hall behind her. 'Are you gonna let them in, Nessa?'

'Oh, of course. Come in.' Mrs Davidson stepped back against the wall and held the door open.

'Thank you.'

They were led to a sunroom at the end of the house, which looked over a small reserve and a private wharf stretching out into Brisbane Water channel. The walls were covered in framed photographs of Amelia. More sat on top of an old piano and a photobook on the coffee table carried her name. It was ... shrine like.

'What a lovely spot,' Rachael said.

'Neighbours are a bit annoying, but the view is nice enough,' Mr Davidson said. 'Sit down, please. How can we help you?'

Finn and Lexi took a two-seater floral lounge opposite Mr and Mrs Davidson, while Rachael sat in a matching chair. 'Mr and Mrs Davidson, I'm sorry if we're opening old wounds, but we're looking into Amelia's death,' Rachael said.

'You really think that wound ever closed?' Mr Davidson growled. 'That the damage a murdered child leaves ever heals?'

'Paul,' Mrs Davidson said quietly.

Her husband took a breath and nodded. 'I apologise.'

'Have you found her?' Mrs Davidson asked in a thin voice.

'No, I'm sorry, we haven't. But we have some new information that might lead us to her,' Rachael said carefully.

'What information?' Mr Davidson asked. 'Who came forward?'

'I can't disclose any details to you yet, I'm afraid. But I was hoping you could take us through the events of that day in your own words. Often the official reports don't shed the same light.'

'All right.'

Mrs Davidson got to her feet, her hands wringing a handkerchief. 'I'll make some tea,' she offered, and hurried from the room.

'It was that damn Hamill bastard,' Mr Davidson began. 'But no one would listen.'

Rachael made a few notes as he relayed his story. When Mrs Davidson put a tea in front of each of them on the coffee table with a small jug of milk and some sugar cubes, Finn kept his black and sipped at it, even though he never drank the stuff. Then he sat back and listened to the slow burning rage in Mr Davidson's voice as his story continued. Saw the desperate sadness in Mrs Davidson's eyes.

'And everyone just forgot about it,' Mr Davidson finished. 'Like it never happened.'

'Mr Davidson, the police reports noted several incidents of abuse; on one occasion you threw a rock through a station window,' Rachael said.

Mr Davidson thumped a forefinger on the coffee table. 'Imagine losing your child in the most horrific way possible. Imagine holding your granddaughter every night while she wails for her lost mother and shakes uncontrollably from the nightmares. Imagine you know who is responsible for that. Imagine the people who are meant to protect society, who at the very least are meant to provide justice, shrugging their shoulders, saying, sorry, can't help you. Times all that by weeks, months, years, and tell me that the grief and frustration wouldn't eat you up from the inside out. I broke some glass, inspector, when I wanted to break heads. The cops did more about me breaking a window than they did about Amelia being murdered.'

'I can't imagine how difficult it must have been for you, but I assure you, what looks like a very thorough investigation took place. The officer in charge has never forgotten Amelia. Never. He's assisting us now.'

'Hmph.'

'Have you had any contact with any of the three men you believe were responsible since that time?'

'I kept tabs. I know Charlie Hamill is in jail for killing his wife. No surprise there. And I saw that Bradley arsehole was wanted for something or other, but I couldn't tell you more than that.'

'And I'm sorry to have to ask, but could you account for your whereabouts on these dates please?'

Mr Davidson looked at the dates she handed him. 'Why? You think I did something?'

'This is all just part of the investigation.'

'I can check,' Mrs Davidson offered, taking the piece of paper and walking down the hallway.

'Enough bullshit,' Mr Davidson said. 'What's going on? Did that Hamill prick finally admit something?'

'No, but we do have someone in custody who is assisting us with our enquiries.'

'So you found Bradley? Or is it the other one, Smith?'

'I really will tell you as soon as I can,' Rachael said as Mrs Davidson reappeared with an open wall calendar.

'These times of night we're generally always home, detectives,' Mrs Davidson said. 'We certainly were on the first date. But Paul and I hosted a small exhibition in Byron Bay a couple of weeks ago as part of an arts festival. On that second date we were up there. I hope that helps.'

'It does. Thank you, Mrs Davidson. We appreciate your time. We'll be in touch.'

'Please do let us know,' Mrs Davidson said. 'The idea we might still find justice for Amelia is ...' She dabbed at her wet eyes with her handkerchief. 'I'm sorry, please just do it. Please make them pay. I'll ... try and let Jess know. She'll want to know. It might make a difference.'

'What do you mean, try and let her know?'

Mrs Davidson glanced at her husband.

'We didn't just lose Amelia through all of this, detectives,' he said. 'Jess wasn't the same after what happened. Doctors, teachers, psychologists ... none of it really made a difference. We thought she was coping for a while. Then she hit her teens and discovered drugs. In and out of the house like it was a motel, stealing money, occasionally even Nessa's jewellery to pay for her habit. She was bringing all types in and out until I had to make a stand. Then she stopped coming round at all.'

Mrs Davidson went into the next room and returned with a photograph. 'No father, her mother taken from her so young. Witnessing the murder. It's too much for a child. We could never heal that all the way.'

'May I ask what happened to her father?' Finn asked.

'Oh, he was a lying, cheating sack of shit,' Mr Davidson growled. 'No way he was getting custody. Wanted Amelia to get an abortion. Lost interest in her once she started to show. Started fooling around with whatever tramp would have him. Then Jess found a bunch of disgusting messages to and from various women on his mobile phone and that was that. She told him to piss off. Never even laid eyes on Jess.'

'It was a silly thing to do but we promised our granddaughter those men would get what they deserved,' Mrs Davidson said. 'But they never did. Now they might. We have her phone number. We'll try that. Maybe she'll answer. This was Jess the last time we saw her, just after Christmas.' Mrs Davidson handed Rachael the photo. Rachael's mouth thinned as she turned it around, showed Lexi.

'That's Daisy Mackenzie,' Lexi said in surprise.

'Well, not really; her mother called Jess her little daisy girl because she was always picking the wild daises by the railway tracks at Wondabyne. Her real name is Jessica Mackenzie Davidson. But ... how did you know that?'

'Like we said,' Rachael told them, 'we're looking into the case.'

'But—'

'Would you mind if I copy this photo?' Rachael barrelled on.

'No, that would be fine, I suppose.'

'Thank you. We'll be in touch shortly.'

'Why didn't you tell them about Mike?' Lexi asked Rachael as they climbed into the car. 'He's admitted to what happened and been charged for his involvement.'

'Because I'm concerned about Mr Davidson's possible involvement in what's happened since. I'm sure we can all agree there's no way Jess coming in to report the incident between Bradley and his wife under a false name was coincidental to this case. But is Jess in this alone? If Mr Davidson's involved and he knows we have Smith, there's no telling what he'll do, but it could be to go after Greta immediately to ensure we don't reach her first. If he's not involved but manages to tell Jess before we find her, she could do the same. Either of them may already know where Greta is and we don't. We need time with the team to catch up. I'll organise a car to sit on the Davidson property tonight, make sure Mr Davidson doesn't go far while we track down his granddaughter and Greta Smith.'

Finn walked in the door and snagged a beer before falling onto his lounge. Long day. No doubt another long one tomorrow. He had a couple of missed calls on his phone so he checked them out, listened to a message from the bank asking him to sign some paperwork, another from his solicitor wanting to talk to him about the house contracts. He had no idea when he'd have time to do either. But he was getting his house back. The relief was enormous.

The cat appeared and hopped up beside him, rubbing his face against Finn's arm and purring, demanding a pat. He'd taken to calling it Gizmo because he still thought it looked more like a Mogwai than a cat. 'Hey, how's your day been, huh?'

He heard the knock on the door and swore under his breath. Who could that possibly be? The list was short.

After getting up to answer it, he wasn't entirely happy to see Vivienne on the other side.

'What are you doing here?' he asked resignedly.

'I just need a minute.'

If she'd looked angry or riled for a fight, he probably would have closed the door. But she seemed tired and sad, and he wasn't a complete arsehole, so he opened the door to let her in. 'Do you want a drink or something?'

She shook her head. 'I wanted a chance to explain.'

'Okay.'

She sat at the table so he sat opposite.

'I don't hate you, Finn. If I'm honest, it still burns that you chose work over me but—'

'That's not what I did. Viv, we've been over this. And there was never an affair.'

'I know. I know. I was lonely. I had a small child. I know the job was difficult at times but I felt you weren't there for us enough.'

'And I'm sorry for that. But why are you bringing this up now?'

'I'm saying I still resent that sometimes. I still get angry sometimes, but not so much now, not since I've met Louis. And I don't hate you.'

'Well, thanks for letting me know.'

'I know it must seem that way, what Lexi said. But … ' She sighed. 'Ava doesn't want to live in the new place. She's been on and on about moving in with you for ages and I thought that if you kept that house, that'd be the last straw. She'd never want to come with us. She loves you, resents Louis, loves living in your house, all her friends are close by. What chance do I have?'

Finn frowned. '*That's* why you didn't want me to have the house? That's why I nearly lost the place?' He couldn't help the bitterness in his voice. 'You've got to be kidding me.'

'I panicked! And Louis was so keen on this other house because it's close to work and the beach and everything. I got barrelled along in his plans and I didn't want to lose her.'

'Viv, the court orders say Ava stays with you.'

'Because you agreed that was best. But that means nothing if you challenge them!'

'I'm not going to. I love Ava. I love every minute I get to spend with her. But I also want what's best for her and that's the stability you can give her. My hours are all over the place. You know this.'

Vivienne stared at the table. 'I'm sorry. I spent a whole lot of time storming around over what Lexi said this morning and the more the words sank in, the more I realised how I was coming across. I can't hold a grudge against the woman who saved Ava's life. And Rachael's always fair, so that sealed it.' She looked up. 'I appreciate all the extra support, Finn. I don't take it for granted. I'll sign my share of the house over for whatever you think is fair.'

'Price will stand,' he said. 'But I appreciate that.'

After he let her out, he downed the rest of his beer and returned to the lounge with the cat. It yawned, stretched and walked onto his lap. He pushed the fluffy tail from his face and absently stroked it once it settled. 'Well, Gizmo, we still have a murderer to track down, but overall, today really was a good day.'

CHAPTER FORTY-NINE

Friday, March 18

'Good morning,' Rachael said, walking into the meeting room with Lexi and taking her seat. 'Our obvious priorities today are locating Jessica Davidson and Greta Smith,' she told the team. 'So as a young child, Jessica Davidson—' she stuck the picture Mrs Davidson had given them to a whiteboard, '—was witness to her mother's rape and murder by Charlie Hamill, Mark Bradley and Mike Smith. She was left severely traumatised and allegedly turned to drugs as a teen before taking off from her grandparents' home. In the last year, both Charlie Hamill's and Mark Bradley's wives have been murdered following a similar pattern of events, allegedly by their husbands.'

She watched Lexi open her computer as she spoke, her right hand flying over the keys. Rachael paused. Lexi might know these details already, but it was always good to talk through the case with the team each morning in case any questions or insights resulted from the revision.

Lexi looked up and stopped. 'Sorry. Go.'

'In the first instance, the murder was called in anonymously. The report says the voice sounded "young and female". In the second, Jessica Davidson turned up at Wyong Police Station where she reported an incident between Mark and Kirsten Bradley on the train under a false name, returning later to identify Mark Bradley from a picture on the news. She seemed surprised we hadn't found a female victim at the time. Possibly because Kirsten had remained submerged by accident.

'Now we have Mike Smith in custody telling us of a similar set of occurrences to those that led to the previous murders and we can't contact his wife. So what does that mean? Do we presume Jess is responsible for the murders? She's twenty years old. Do we think she could be pulling this off, and if so, is she doing it alone?'

'What about the parents?' Cass asks.

'Mr and Mrs Davidson,' Rachael said with a nod. 'Their house was a shrine to Amelia. It's no wonder Jess couldn't recover; being in that environment, she never had the opportunity to. Linc, did you confirm Mr and Mrs Davidson attended an art festival at Byron Bay on the night of Kirsten's murder?'

'Only just,' he said. 'But yep, they were there. Motel confirmed it and social media photos from the event place them at the venue.'

'Okay, that seems solid. Cass, did you request information on Jess's phone number? I'm especially interested in any communications between Jess and her grandparents, and, though I doubt she would be silly enough to use the same phone, if she's sent any texts that might tie in with those received by the victims.'

'Yes, but I doubt it will come through before nine. Neutron's already in. He's trying to track the phone now.'

'Good work,' Rachael said. 'Next, we need to find Mike's wife, Greta Smith. Repeated attempts to call the sister, Abigail Speers, last night or trace the phone have failed. Greta's phone was left behind due to receiving unwanted calls from Mike. I'm gathering her sister's phone is off for the same reason. I know we have Mike in custody so our POI isn't going to be able to pull off another identical murder scenario, but if Jess's grandparents have managed to contact her, she might panic and do something rash.'

'I've got them,' Lexi said, eyes back on her computer.

'You're joking. How?' Finn asked.

'Abigail is a social media nut. I'm talking the type that tells you what she eats for breakfast every morning kind of nut. She hasn't posted for a couple of days because of that whole phone-free thing, but from her various profiles I did get that she loves the beach, relaxed holiday parks and supporting local businesses. So I shot out an official sounding police email to all the holiday parks on the coast last night on the off chance I was right and sure enough, the manager of the Lakeview Tourist Park in Long Jetty has just gotten back to me, confirming they're staying there.'

'Lexi, that's excellent work,' Rachael said with relief. 'Go out there with Finn and pick Greta up. But remember to watch your back. Don't forget Raymond Hamill is still out there.'

'Right,' Finn said, getting to his feet. 'Let's get going.'

While Finn steps into the tourist park office, I hang outside and take a good look around. From my vantage point outside reception, I can't see much more than neat rows of caravans and cabins, but I know from the drive in that next door is a very large, very cool-looking park and plenty of lakefront reserve. I'm tempted to go for a quick wander around, see if Greta is close by, but I've only taken a few steps when Finn comes back out.

'Cabin six,' he says and, leaving the car where it is, heads in the direction I assume he's been pointed.

We walk along a short row of white cabins and Finn knocks on the door of the one we're looking for. It's opened by a blonde woman in jeans and an oversized jumper. Behind her on the floor is an assortment of baby equipment.

'Hi. Abigail, isn't it? We're looking for Greta?' Finn asks.

Abigail doesn't look particularly pleased to see us. 'Who are you?'

'I'm Detective Sergeant Finn Carson and this is Constable Lexi Winter. Could you tell us where she is, please?'

She eyes his credentials. 'Why?'

'We have concerns for her safety and we've been unable to reach either of you on your phones.'

The woman's face relaxes. 'She's fine, detective. She's sick of Mike calling her so she left her phone behind, that's all. And I never pick up mine for an unknown number. It's generally scammers or sales people. Or Mike calling on a different number to trick me into answering the phone.'

'We did leave messages.'

A flicker of annoyance touches her features. 'And I would have gotten around to checking them. Look, we just wanted a couple of days of peace and quiet. She's fine, okay?'

'I understand. However, we really need to know where she is.'

There's a pause as she stares at them tight-lipped for several seconds before answering. 'She's taken the baby for a walk.'

'Any idea where she's likely to have gone?'

'No.' Her eyes narrow. 'Is it Mike? Did he send you guys out here because he wants to see the baby? She's not going to stop him, she just needs a chance to get her head around what he's done without him bombarding her every five minutes.'

'Again, I understand. We're not here about that. We'll take a look around, but if she gets back in the meantime, could you ask her to call me, please? It's urgent.'

'All right,' she says, taking his card. I can see that she wants to ask more, but she doesn't.

'Thanks for your help.' Finn walks away from the cabin.

I open a map on my phone. The park and reserve cover a large area, lots of trees, a BMX track, playground, carpark, waterfront. 'I think we should split up.'

Finn looks over my shoulder at the map. 'Agreed. If you want to start heading this way, I'll go over there.'

'Got it.'

'Remember, there's no reason to believe she's in imminent danger and I can't see any of Hamill's thugs finding us out here but be aware. Keep your eyes open, okay? If you're the least bit concerned call me and head back in my direction.'

'Got it.'

I head back out to the main road that borders one side of the tourist park and cross a much quieter road, continuing along one of many paths that lead into a playground area. There's a scattering of small kids around—I'm guessing most are at school at this time of day—and it's anything but peak tourist season. There's a light breeze coming in off the water but it's not warm.

I keep going, past some picnic tables and barbecues, until I see a walking bridge, but there's no sign of Greta and her baby. I walk along the waterfront, follow it for a bit while my damaged body starts to ache from the exertion. I don't see anything, but I hear a commotion beyond a stand of casurina trees and as it's clearly two female voices, I decide to investigate.

'Please! I don't know what you're talking about! Just let me go!'

Okay, that doesn't sound good. I message Finn then sneak around the trees. A woman is on the ground with a head wound, one hand in the air in a weak attempt to stave off another blow. Jessica Davidson is standing over her holding a crowbar, about to take another strike. A pram with a sleeping baby stands nearby.

'Jess!' I say, walking into view. 'Wait!'

Jessica's head spins around, her arm still hovering threateningly over Greta. 'You don't understand!'

'I do,' I tell her calmly. 'I understand exactly what happened. But you need to put that down.'

'I can't! Don't you have a mother?'

'I don't honestly know. She's not the sort of mother you'd bother tracking down.'

'Well, mine was! I miss her every day!'

Greta attempts to shuffle back and Jess's hand tenses on her weapon. Greta freezes.

'I know. You found the place they buried her, didn't you? The flowers, the candles. They're lovely.'

Twin tears roll down Jess's face. 'As a kid, I couldn't lead the police back there. It was too confusing, I was too upset. Everything looked the same. But I started seeing it a couple of years ago, in dreams. I started to remember, so I went out there. I covered every inch of mountainside. I knew the place as soon as I stumbled across it. I remembered. I remembered what they did to her, I remembered following them because I wanted my mummy. I remember them covering her in smelly black mud. I remember the laughing, the sick comments. So I didn't tell the police I'd found her. How could that ever be enough? I had to make those bastards pay!'

'What happened was terrible. Evil. We have Mike in custody. He admitted everything.'

'No!' The tears fall faster now. 'I sent him a text. He's supposed to be coming! It's all planned! Don't you see? She walks off alone with the baby, he comes here and finds it. Then she turns up dead and he's been on the scene. He's got the kid. Let's see him explain that!'

'He's not coming, Jess. He's not going anywhere. He's been charged.'

'That's not enough!'

I risk a step forward. 'You just got through telling me how great your mum was, how much you miss her. Do you really want to be responsible for taking this mum away from her baby? Look at that baby, Jess. He needs his mum! You're not a bad person. Don't be responsible for that!'

I catch sight of Finn running towards us. So does Jess. She lets out a scream of frustration then looks around wildly, kicking the pram before bolting in the opposite direction towards the cover of the reserve.

'My baby!' Greta is slipping and sliding as she tries to get up. The pram hurtles across the path and down the slope of the boat ramp to the water. I run after it. I'm still four or five strides away when it hits the water and tips into the lake. I reach the pram and use my good hand to drag it up far enough to see the baby isn't inside. The water is murky and the blankets spreading out in the water block my possible view. I drop to my knees and plunge both hands in to push the blankets out of the way. How long does it take for a baby to drown?

I fumble desperately around and the seconds feel like minutes. Then I feel him, scoop him up awkwardly with my good arm, my heart in my throat as the weight of his sodden nappy and clothing has him almost tipping from my hold. Is he moving? I know that just one breath of water could be fatal. For a second I'm not sure, then he's coughing and screaming, his little face screwing up and turning bright pink in the throes of a tantrum. His tiny fists rub at his face and punch the air.

Finn reaches me and takes the baby before Greta throws herself at us in an attempt to gather him up.

'Thank you,' she says, her own sobs joining the little boy's. 'Thank you so much. Thank you.' She's cuddling the baby close while blood drips down her face and neck from the blow.

Finn helps me to my feet. 'Jess?' I ask, looking around.

'I had to let her go,' he says. 'I was worried you wouldn't be able to get the baby out. I'll call some police out here to get a search going, but we need to take Greta and her baby to the hospital.' He looked down at my soaked bandage and grimaced. 'And you'll need that dressing changed. I'll get the car, wait here.'

'Why don't you sit with him?' I ask Greta over the screams of the baby. I'm worried the poor woman will fall over.

'I—okay,' she says, and drops to the ground to sit. 'I'm a bit dizzy.'

'That's a nasty gash, but you'll be okay.'

Greta spends a minute or two calming the baby then asks tearily, 'Why did she do that? Was it to do with a lover? He was cheating on me. That's why I left him. That girl said she lost her mother?'

'He wasn't cheating on you,' I tell her, relieved that the baby's screaming has dulled to an unhappy cry. 'For what it's worth, I think he really does love you.' I see Finn's car, see another following that I think is the sister's. 'But he made a mistake a very long time ago. A bad one. And you very nearly paid for it.'

CHAPTER FIFTY

Saturday, March 19

I haven't been on a train for a while, so I don't really mind the trip out to Wondabyne, but request-only stations are weird. I remembered to let the guard know where I needed to get off, then sat close to the rear exit to make sure he didn't forget to tell the driver to stop. Of course, the guard does this every day and the train stopped exactly to plan. So here I am.

It's a nice morning and I do my best to shove images of Aden and Kirsten from my mind, readjust the flowers I've brought with me in the crook of my arm and begin the trek to Amelia Davidson's final resting place. No, not final. We're not letting her stay in that disused dam forever. A specialist team will be here in a few hours to recover her remains.

I'm tempted to take my time, but this is a train line, not a bushwalk, so I move at a reasonable pace. I turn onto the little trail that goes around the inlet, can't help but check the rubbish for anything fresh. Then I push through the heavier bush, protecting the flowers as best I can until I reach the dam.

The bunch that had graced the wall last time Finn and I were here is gone and a bright new bouquet sits between the candles. I add mine, lay them gently down, then step back. 'We know you're in there, Amelia,' I tell the swampy mess. 'And you don't deserve to be. You died protecting your daughter from monsters and there's going to be a whole team of people here soon who are going to find you so we can take you somewhere lovely. Somewhere you can rest in peace.'

I wait, silently. Then I hear a footstep behind me, the crack of a twig.

'Why did you do that?' Jess's voice.

I turn slowly. 'Because it was the right thing to do.'

'Are there really going to be people out here? They're going to find her?'

'Yes. They're really coming. We're not leaving her here. Not where that terrible thing happened.'

Her eyes fill with tears and her face contorts in anger. 'That's why the men who did that to her had to suffer! It was the right thing to do.'

'Maybe, but what about the innocent wives?'

'They weren't innocent! How could anyone innocent be married to trash like that? Besides, how else would those men know what it's like to lose someone they care about? They needed to *feel* it. To know someone they loved had died horribly. That it was their fault! They needed to be held accountable and they needed to pay, if not for Mum, then for someone else.'

I sit on the edge of the dam, cross my legs at the ankles. 'Does it make you feel better?'

Jess looks away. 'I feel better that Mum has been found,' she says quietly. 'I feel better that those men have been caught for what they did.' She pauses, then approaches her makeshift altar and touches the flowers I've brought. 'I feel better that you did this for me. For her.'

'But what about the women you killed?'

She sighs and sits beside me. 'They didn't go through half of what Mum did. I knocked them out first. Mum didn't get that mercy.'

'The third one, Greta. She's left Mike. She can't forgive what he did. She's going it alone. Their lives together are ruined, and that's his fault. He's lost her and he still has to pay for what he did. You got them all, Jess. One way or another.'

'That's something. How did you know I'd be here?'

'This is the anniversary of that horrible day. I had a hunch you would be.'

'I wanted it all over by today. That's how I planned it. So I could come back here and tell Mum it was done.'

'It must have taken a lot of planning.'

'It took months.' She drags her fingers across her eyes. 'Stalking them, learning their routines, finding out enough about them to make those fake phone texts seem legit. Manipulating them. The Charlie and Anna thing fell into place easier than I thought. I was pretty confident after that. Then Kirsten surprised me by getting off the train with Mark. I thought she was just going to watch him get off the train to meet that woman. Get her proof. But he spotted her and they got off together ...' She shrugged. 'It didn't matter.'

'But weren't you worried about being caught out? How did Mark not see you on the platform?'

'Huh? Oh. Even if he did, he wouldn't have given me a thought. I'd gotten off at Wondabyne Station when he did lots of times. I'd always head straight for the caretaker's house like I belonged there, then I'd find some cover and watch what Mark did, how long he spent out there. He and Kirsten were totally wrapped up in whatever they were talking about that night, weren't paying attention. Then the boat came in and he left her there.' She stares off into space. 'It was like a gift.'

'And Greta?'

She shrugs. 'Same deal. Follow, watch, learn. Plant the phone. Create an opportunity ... But you stuffed that up,' she says, gaze returning to mine. 'So what now?'

'I think you know that. Just like you made them answer for what they did, you're going to need to answer for what you did, too. You can't have it both ways.'

The 'Couldn't agree more' comes from somewhere behind Jess and is followed by a gunshot. Jess's face reflects shock, then goes blank as she slumps backwards into the dam.

'What the hell?' slips from my lips as I spin around and face Debbie Reynolds. What? How? It takes me a moment to speak through the shock, then, 'Why did you shoot her?' I demand. 'You didn't even know her!' I desperately want to see if Jess is alive, if I can help her, but I can't take my eyes off Debbie and that gun.

'She got in my way. Like you keep doing. And you're right—you need to answer for what you do. This is the second time you've ruined everything. You're not going to get a third chance.'

CHAPTER FIFTY-ONE

'Move!' Finn heard Rachael order over the radio, but he was already running from his location on the hillside. This was supposed to have been a relatively safe and straightforward exercise. Lexi had wanted to give Jess the chance to tell her story and turn herself in. She'd wanted Jess to have one last moment with her mother.

It had been a risk, but Lexi had been adamant Jess wouldn't hurt her. So she'd been dropped off by police at Hornsby Station and Rachael had had the team in place close by in case Lexi was wrong, and to make sure Jess didn't escape.

But this? This was something else entirely. He knew that voice. Debbie Reynolds was a whole other breed of criminal. He leapt over a fallen tree, nearly rolling his ankle as he hit uneven ground on the other side, and charged on.

Damn Lexi and that soft bloody heart she'd never admit to possessing. It was going to get her killed.

'How did you find me out here?' he heard Lexi ask Debbie. Stalling, he realised, as in his other ear Rachael called for paramedics.

'You think I didn't know the cops have had you stuck in that tower?' Debbie said. 'That I haven't been waiting for them to cut you loose? I followed your ride to the station, watched you buy the damn flowers. I did wonder what you were up to, but then, you're always up to something, aren't you! I'm so fucking sick of you getting in the way!'

'Well, technically, today, you got in the way. I was—'

'Sneaking straight out here underneath the cops' noses to have a heart to heart with a fucking psycho. Let me guess ... the cops were after that one, right? But you wanted to single-handedly bring her in on your terms. Be the hero. That's how you work. But you ruin things, Lexi. You almost ruined everything with Vaughn! Now you've ruined my family! We had support, ties, cover. It's all gone!'

'May as well turn yourself in, then.'

Finn slid a few feet down a steep boulder to save some time and knew he was getting close, moved more carefully, pitting his need to get there fast against giving his position away and causing Debbie to panic.

'You know they were actually going to hand me over to the cops because of you? My own parents were going to turn me in. That's on you! So is the fact they're dead.'

'You killed Raymond and Lena?'

'Are you not listening?' Debbie demanded, her voice increasing in pitch. 'They were going to put me in handcuffs and leave me somewhere for you to pick up! What choice did I have? Of course I killed them! Bastards! So much for their fucking family loyalty bullshit!'

When he could hear Lexi's and Debbie's voices close by rather than just over his earpiece, Finn slowed, made his way around behind Debbie, cursing every noise his feet made in the leaf litter.

'Maybe their loyalty simply lay with other family members first,' Lexi said.

'There were none left! Just those two old fuckwits looking out for themselves. Wait ...' Debbie continued, suspicion leaching into her tone. 'If you didn't know Raymond and Lena were dead, why did the cops let you go?'

'Because I'd had more than enough of playing pretend prisoner,' Lexi said, not missing a beat. 'Most of the family is dead or in custody. You think I was scared of a couple of senior citizens?'

'That blew your house up!' Debbie reminded her. 'Whatever, now I get to kill you and Vaughn and I have come into a lot more money. Couldn't get much better than that. I only wish I could make this slow and painful.'

'That's exactly what it'll be for you if you pull that trigger,' Finn warned. 'Put it down!'

Debbie turned and fired sightlessly in his direction. He ducked low, saw her turn back around at Lexi, but Lexi had gone for cover. A second later, Cass and Linc appeared, then Rachael, surrounding Debbie from all sides.

Debbie spun slowly, gun still extended, as Rachael ordered her to put the weapon down.

A wild, panicked look came over Debbie and her head shook from side to side. 'Nup. No. No way.' She turned in a circle again, firing randomly, unloading every shot. Finn's joined those that rained back.

As soon as Debbie fell, Lexi was at her side. 'Where is he? Where's Vaughn!' she demanded.

Debbie's smile was full of blood. 'Closer than you think.'

'Where!'

'You beat him. He can't handle that. It's eating him up. Don't … need to … look. Soon enough … he'll find … you.'

'Lexi, move back,' Rachael ordered, assessing Debbie's wounds.

'Don't let her die!' Lexi pleaded. 'We need her alive!'

Finn jumped knee deep into the mud of the dam and checked on Jess, but he knew immediately it was too late. She lay dead in this awful place, like her mother.

'Finn?' Lexi asked.

He looked up and shook his head and her face fell.

'She would have handed herself in.'

'I think you're right. And I think it was good, what you did for her today. But don't forget what she did.'

'She was a victim of the trauma she suffered as a child, of the Hamills … and the drugs probably screwed her up even more.'

'And Anna and Kirsten were victims of Jessica. Where does it end, Lexi? How long can we make excuses for people who use their own pain as an excuse to hurt others?'

'I feel sick.'

He dragged himself out of the mud and went to her side. 'You should sit down. You shouldn't even be out here with those injuries. You've been doing too much. We'll get you checked—'

'It's all this death! Do you ever get used to it?'

'Not yet. I hope I never do.'

Lexi looked back to where Rachael and Linc were performing CPR on Debbie. 'She's not going to make it either.'

'You don't know that.'

'Four bullets in the chest. She's done. We needed her alive.'

'We needed us alive more,' he said, earning an almost-grin. 'You've nearly died way too many times lately.'

'Yeah, this cop stuff is great,' she said. 'I need a drink.'

Finn took a sip from his water bottle as the back doors on the forensic van slammed shut with a sense of finality. The Hamill property was crawling with police, busily dismantling Raymond's empire while his and his wife's bodies were being taken away for further examination.

'Thanks, Finn, we're off now,' Steven Van Zettan called from the van as two other forensics vehicles pulled away. Finn raised his hand, then spotted Rachael. She was exiting the main residence behind a line of uniformed police carrying evidence, so he strode over to talk to her. 'How's it going?'

'We're working on the office. We've got multiple computers and phones, a police tracker, an old-fashioned filing system with some interesting names in it. Books and books of evidence of illegal activity going back decades. I only wish Raymond and Lena were still around to answer for it. How are you going?'

'Steven's got the bodies. Should be pretty straightforward. Fatal gunshot wounds and Reynolds admitted to the murders so he's not expecting any surprises.'

'Anything else?'

'Yeah, you should see the blue shed at the back of the property. There's enough weapons and explosives to arm a small country. Craig's having a field day.'

Rachael stepped out of the way of an officer wheeling out a filing cabinet. 'It's going to take weeks to untangle all of this.'

'At least.'

'Inspector!' An officer jogged over holding one of the confiscated phones. 'There's a message.'

Rachael looked at it. It read *Rachael Langley*. Almost as soon as the phone was in her hand, it shrilled. Rachael looked at Finn, then slowly lifted it to her ear.

'Yes?'

'Where's Lexi?'

The voice chilled her.

'Vaughn,' she mouthed to Finn, putting the call on speaker before answering. 'She's not here.'

'But alive.'

'Why wouldn't she be?'

'Deb went a little off the rails. I was … concerned.'

'Yes, she did. But your girlfriend's the dead one, I'm afraid.'

'Oh, shame.'

'I agree. We had more questions. Where are you?' She and Finn scanned the area.

'Look up. A little to your right. That's it.'

She spotted a camera, one of many dotted around the property.

'Tell Lexi I miss her. I've got a few things to take care of first, but I'm looking forward to a catch-up.'

The call cut out.

Finn's jaw clenched as he stared hard at the camera before ripping it down.

'Finn!' Rachael said in surprise, but he ignored her and stalked away, then changed his mind and turned back.

'He's not done with Lexi? How much more does he intend to put her through?'

Rachael's face was grim. 'It's all a game to him. He doesn't care, as long as he's entertaining himself. But he's made a mistake. He told us he's coming back for her.' She walked a short distance to where another camera peered at them and stared coldly into the lens. 'Bring it on, you sick bastard. But don't expect a prison sentence at the end of it. If Lexi doesn't kill you, I will.'

CHAPTER FIFTY-TWO

Monday, March 21

As the crowd that had gathered for Rico's funeral wander away, I stay put, staring at the coffin, needing a bit more time. I have no idea what happens when you die. I don't usually think about it. But I'd like to think there's maybe something else. I hope Rico can hear what I'm telling him in my head. I hope he saw all the people here. I hope he heard all the stories. I hope he knows how much he was loved and admired. He deserves that.

'He thought very highly of you, Lexi,' Rico's father, the Major, tells me quietly. 'Both as a friend and rookie cop.'

'He was a good friend. I'll never forget him.' *I can do better. I can do better than that for Rico's father.* I look the Major in the eye, try again. 'He made a difference in his job. Every day. Everyone loved him. He was kind and compassionate and funny. Nothing and no one ever broke his positive attitude. He put himself between me and danger countless times but he also taught me how to stay alive. He taught me how to be the best cop I could be. How to really make a difference, like he did. I'll carry those lessons, those memories, with me for the rest of my life. I'll treasure them.'

The Major draws in a steadying breath and blinks against the tears sitting in his eyes. 'Then Rico's final student is a success. Thank you, Lexi. I'll carry *those* words with me for the rest of mine. And I'll treasure them.' With a tremulous smile, he takes one last look at the coffin, nods, and walks away.

I draw in a steadying breath of my own. I *hate* this emotional shit.

I turn at the hand on my shoulder and realise it's Finn.

'Are you ready to get going?'

'Yeah.'

We catch up to Rachael and Ed, who are standing by their car. 'We'll pick Ava up from school and see you at your place with food,' Rachael tells Finn.

'Thanks,' he says, checking his watch. 'The removalists are probably already waiting for me.'

'No problem.'

'You still feel like coming to my house? I understand if you'd rather give it a miss.'

The smile I send him is a bit forced, but it's there. 'You think I'd miss the big move? Besides, the faster I get you out, the faster I can move in!'

'Great, because I need the extra hand,' he teases, but his eyes carry sympathy.

I dig my keys from my pocket. 'I'll see you soon.'

'I'm not sure how I got roped into all this one-handed manual shit,' I say an hour later, taking my end of a small table and backing inside to deposit it in the kitchen.

'That's the last of it,' Finn says.

'Right. Who wants a drink?' Rachael asks. She's at the kitchen bench pouring red wine through some sort of glass contraption.

'What are you doing?' I ask, curious.

'Aerating the wine.'

'Why?'

'Because it makes it taste better.'

I watch as it gurgles into the glass. 'You're suggesting I've gone through my entire life thinking wine tastes like shit because I don't pour it through that thing?'

Rachael's lips twitch in amusement. 'You never know.' She hands me the glass. 'Why don't you find out?'

'I had the obligatory glass of champagne when we walked in.'

'So?' Rachael's grin spreads. 'You're eyeing it off like a poisonous snake. Try it.'

I sip it, taste the tartness. It's probably good. And yet. 'Mmm ... I s'pose.' I take another sip. 'It's not JD.'

Finn reaches over from behind me and takes my glass from my hand.

'Hey!'

'If you're not going to enjoy a hundred-dollar bottle of wine, I'm drinking it.'

'I didn't say I wasn't.' A glass of ice lands in front of me followed by a bottle of Jack Daniel's. 'You bought me this?'

'It's a thank-you.'

I wedge the bottle in the crook of one arm so I can get the top off and pour myself a glass while Finn drinks my wine. I take a grateful sip and sigh. 'Good old number 7.'

'What's that about?' he says, looking at the label.

'No one knows.'

'Someone must know. It's on the label!'

I shake my head. 'Nope.'

'I don't believe you.'

'Look it up!' I grin at him when he does, because I know I'm right. 'I live for ridiculous facts.'

'You need to spend less time on your computer.'

'It's my fifth limb. I don't enjoy it being cut off,' I add with a mock glare at Rachael.

'Okay, that's my cue to find something else I need to be doing,' Finn says, taking his glass and walking into the lounge, where Ed is setting up the television.

'I'm sorry,' Rachael tells me. 'I know I overreacted. I was worried about you and I sent you off and you nearly died. I—'

'It's fine. Besides.' I take another sip. 'It's difficult to hold it against you when you were right. Also, you're scary when you're pissed off.'

Rachael's stricken look dissolves. 'Scary?' Then she raises her voice enough to carry into the lounge area. 'I believe the word was *rabid*.'

Finn makes a strangled noise. 'In the context of the conversation it wasn't an insult!' he calls back.

'Anyway, that's behind us,' Rachael says, sipping her wine. 'You're a team player now.'

'In my defence, there was no team. Not when I started this. My current rank has its limitations.'

'But it's also good training. Experience on the street makes you a better detective.'

'You're talking as though it's a given I'll pass the exams.'

Rachael's brow lifts. 'You're top of your class at the academy. You've already assisted with two major cases, you're a wizard behind a computer and, between Ed, Craig and me, you have at least three high-ranking officers behind you. You'll get there.'

'Eventually.'

'It'll go fast. We've got Vaughn to find. I'll pull you into that, of course. And anything else I think you should be involved in.'

'So ... the task force on the Vaughn case is kicking off again? Debbie said he was close. Surely that means he's back in the—'

A look comes over Rachael's face that I know means she's not telling me something. I pounce on it.

'What else do you know?'

'We'll talk about it later.'

'Oh, come on! Tell me!'

'We may have reason to believe he is back. Nothing's concrete yet.'

'What reason? When did this happen? Does Finn know?'

'We'll talk about it later,' he says, mimicking Rachael and making me wonder why we were raising our voices. He can obviously hear us.

'But—'

'You'll be involved,' Rachael promises.

I huff but relent, because Ava has appeared and she's carrying a very fluffy cat.

'Hi, sweetie. I wondered where you'd gone.'

'This is Gizmo.'

I look at the cat being held in my direction. 'Hey, cat. What happened to your face?'

'See?' Finn says to Rachael, coming back to the table with Ed.

'Pat him,' Ava says with a laugh.

'Um ... okay.' I give it a go.

'See, he likes you. He's purring.'

'Right.'

Gizmo starts squirming. 'I'd better put him back in the spare room. He doesn't know where he lives yet.'

'Thanks for introducing us.'

'He's a nice cat,' Rachael says. 'Placid.'

'I don't really get the pet thing. You take an animal home, spend a heap of money on it, feed it and clean up after it for a few years, and then it dies. I mean, what's the point?'

'I guess you've never had a pet,' Finn says.

'I *had* Mojo. Now I'm going to have to adopt another one. Won't be the same though.'

'A cannabis plant is not a pet,' Rachael says in amused exasperation. 'Also, if you get caught with any of that stuff in your system while you're working you're in serious trouble. Do you really need the JD *and* drugs?'

'What can I say? I'm a work in progress.'

'I feel the need to sit out on the deck and admire my backyard,' Finn says, changing the subject. 'Anyone?'

'Sorry,' Ed says, draining his glass and reaching past Rachael to snatch one last piece of cheese from the platter on the table. 'We've got to get moving.'

'Right then, we're off,' Rachael says, standing. 'Ava!' she calls.

Ava runs out. 'I was still playing with Gizmo!'

'You've got all of next weekend,' Finn promises and gives her a tight hug. 'I'll see you then.'

'Bye, Dad,' Ava says, squeezing him back tight before landing a kiss on his cheek. 'Love you. Bye, Lexi!'

'See ya, kid.'

We walk out the front to see them off.

'Enjoy your house,' Rachael tells Finn, giving him a goodbye peck on the cheek. I haven't seen that before. I guess at work it's not appropriate.

Rachael turns and, after the briefest hesitation, goes through the same ritual with me. 'I'll see you tomorrow. Help you get settled into Finn's old place.'

I'm taken aback by the simple gesture and the offer, manage an 'okay'.

I guess it feels nice to be included.

'Oh, I forgot. I got you something.' I walk onto the lawn with another wave as Rachael, Ed and Ava drive away and take the present from the back seat of my car. I find Finn inside refilling our champagne glasses. I glance longingly at my empty JD glass but say nothing.

'Here, happy housewarming.' I hold the gift out.

'Ah, thanks.'

'It's called a ZZ plant, which sounds pretty cool, but I really only got it because they're apparently next to impossible to kill.'

'Only next to?' he says, admiring the plant with a cute amount of enthusiasm.

'You did once tell me you toppled a plastic plant with dust.'

He put it on the table. 'Should I water it?'

'Less is more. It's more likely to survive if you mostly forget about it.'

'Then it'll enjoy a long, happy life here. Thank you.' He hands me my champagne glass then picks up his and the bottle. 'Let's go outside.'

I follow him out the back onto the veranda that looks over the enormous sunny backyard.

'There's lots more plants out here.'

'Yeah, but they're in the ground and they survived Viv, so they're obviously pretty self-sufficient. She hates gardening.'

'You know, it's hard to believe you two were ever compatible.'

'We were happy for a while.'

'When?' I ask with a laugh. 'Before you met?'

'Smartarse.' He takes a sip of his champagne and sighs. 'You know the number one reason for divorce?'

'Marriage?'

'*Such* a smartarse. Infidelity. I was working day and night to claw my way up through the ranks and she decided I was out with other women.'

'Probably easier on the ego to think other women rather than work.'

'I guess it's not easy being married to a cop.' He looks at me with curiosity. 'Are you going to let Linc take you out?'

I make a dismissive noise. 'Nope.'

'Why not?'

'For one, I can't be bothered with the awkward conversation.'

'Which one is that?'

'Seriously? It starts with "So tell me about yourself", and is followed by "In my younger years I was a child porn star who shot her father dead before going on the run from the police. As I grew up on the streets, I graduated from petty theft to prostitution and cybercrime" to which he responds … well, no, he's probably already left the building.'

Finn chuckles. 'He already knows all that.'

'It still doesn't make good small talk. Anyway, I prefer my own company. I don't feel the need to sit around with a man socialising for the sake of it.'

'And yet here you are.'

'Yeah, I am, aren't I?'

'Cheers to that,' he says and touches his glass to mine. Then his eyes crease with amusement. 'But only because you want to grill me about Vaughn.'

'He's going to come after me!' I say. 'I have to know.'

'Not today.'

My phone rings. A glance tells me it's an unknown number so I mute it. 'But—'

'Not today.' He drains the last of the champagne into our glasses and sits back to look over his backyard.

'Okay, fine. Not today,' I concede, because he has this goofy, happy look on his face and I don't want to spoil his moment.

I've settled back to take another sip of champagne when I get a voicemail alert.

'Someone really wants to talk to you,' Finn says.

'Ugh, fine,' I groan and hit the button.

'Lexi, dear, it's Dawny. I'm afraid Desmond and I have gotten ourselves into a rather urgent little pickle.'

ACKNOWLEDGEMENTS

There are so many incredible people who helped bring *Retribution* to life.

Nicola Robinson, you're simply brilliant. Thank you for all the time and effort you put into Lexi's stories. And speaking of brilliance, Annabel Blay and Kylie Mason, thank you for helping to making the story the best it can be. Thanks also to the outstanding design team for my amazing cover and to the fabulous sales team who take my books out into the world.

Another huge thank you to all my police and former police friends who generously share their knowledge and experience, with a special shoutout to my new volunteers Sergeant Danny Jackson, OIC Strahan Police Station and Steve Apps, retired Inspector, QLD Police, for their valuable assistance.

Tea Cooper and Charlie Smith, thanks as always for your brilliant critiquing and treasured friendship.

Thank you to my agent Clare Forster, my family and all the friends without whose support I wouldn't be able to write.

And last by not least to all my readers. Thank you for reading, sharing and reviewing my books. Your support means so much.

Don't miss the next suspenseful Lexi Winter thriller ...

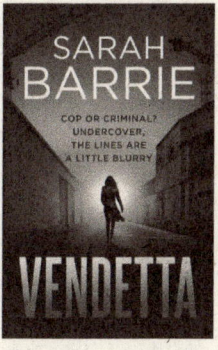

VENDETTA

by

SARAH BARRIE

Available November 2023

PROLOGUE

Ten years ago

Laura clenched her jaw tight in an attempt to stop the desperate sob escaping her throat. Her body hurt. Her head ached. She needed to be sick. To fall apart. The constant beep, beep, beep in her ears wouldn't leave her alone.

Her son sat on her lap, playing cars on the table. He wore his cartoon pyjamas adorably askew, the buttons out of place. Mikey insisted on doing them himself. They're allowed to be cute at three, aren't they? Like the time he wore his undies over his shorts for a week because he'd made the mistake once at daycare and the kids had picked on him, so his teacher had told everyone he was a trend-setter. None of the kids had had any idea what that meant, but her praise had given him some serious cred in the pony room. Made him feel good about himself, rather than silly. Mrs Mayes was a lovely teacher.

She breathed in the sweet scent of his Minions shampoo as he twisted around to snuggle that beautiful baby face into her neck, still clutching his red and yellow Matchbox cars in his tiny hands.

He was tired, needed a nap. But he never slept well without Goatee, his favourite stuffed brown goat. And Goatee wasn't here. She swallowed another sob, bit down hard on her lip. It wasn't fair, this wasn't his fault.

'Mummy, why are those men meanies?'

She struggled to find her voice, make it normal. 'They're mad, baby.'

'You had tears.' He drew a line down her cheek with his finger. 'If I was big I would protect you. Like Superman.'

Her soul shattered. She was big and she couldn't protect him. 'They didn't hurt me. Not really.'

'They're mad at Daddy.'

'Yeah, at Daddy.'

'I'm hungry. I miss Daddy.'

He own stomach churned, but not with hunger. 'If you could have anything in the world, what would it be?'

'Ice cream!'

She pressed her lips to the top of his head and cuddled him close, ignoring the pain every movement his small body caused her broken one. 'Double scoop?'

'Yeah!' he said and bounced on her lap. 'Ice cream forever! Can we have some soon?'

Her eyes welled again. This time there was no stopping the tears from sliding down her cheeks. 'I hope so, baby. I hope we can have ice cream. All the ice cream ever.'

'It's hot, Mummy.' He shifted on her lap and tried to get more comfortable, his forehead dotted with sweat. 'Do you think we can we go soon?'

The hope in his voice was too much. Just too much.

'Yes, we'll go. Soon.' Her voice choked and her arms trembled around him as she watched the bomb's timer.

5 … 4 … 3 …

Oh, God. No. *No*. 'I love you so much, baby.'

His eyes beamed back at her out of his flushed little face and his arms snaked around her neck. 'Love you too, Mu—'

CHAPTER ONE

Monday, March 21

I flatten the accelerator to get around a P-plater in a beaten-up work ute and my tired little Civic revs hard. I swerve into the next lane, have to brake quickly to avoid rear-ending a Lexus before the gap increases. I pass two more cars before diving back across. I have a vague recollection of some weird dream about a car accident last night, have to hope it's not prophetic. I take a chance anyway and put my foot down again, slide into a rudely tight gap and earn a beep from the car I cut off. Whatever. The M1 motorway is slow with peak-hour traffic and I need to get through.

I see a sign for the Morisset exit and swing back into the left lane to take it, following three other cars onto the offramp. In the fast-dying light, the horizon stretches into a sea of dense bushland forming shadowed, rolling mountains. I turn right onto a single-lane road. Where is all this traffic going? Am I still on the Central Coast? I'm pretty sure I won't be by the end of this. I spot some light industrial buildings, signs to suburbs I've heard of. Shops. There's life out here. The knowledge is reassuring as the phone message plays over and over in my head. 'Lexi dear, it's Dawny. I'm afraid Desmond and I have gotten ourselves into a rather urgent little pickle. Now, try not to worry too much, but I'd appreciate it if I could meet with you. Just you, please. Now would be good. So no one dies. I'll text you the address. Ta-ta.'

My fingers catch painfully in my hair as I sweep some stray black wisps from my line of vision. *Urgent little pickle.* I can only guess what that could possibly mean. Coming from Catherine Dawn Delaney, the sweet old pie-making, dodgy-kneed lady who once helped me stash a body in a freezer, I'm guessing it's nothing minor. I haven't seen her for more than a year, and as her plan was to stay gone with that gangster-style husband of hers, I'm intrigued. I'm also very nervous and hoping the 'so no one dies' part includes me.

I glance at my phone to see I'm still seven minutes out. More, probably, because the old twat in the funny hat in front of me doesn't seem to be able to do over fifty in the eighty zone. I'm trying not to sit on his arse. There's got to be somewhere I can overtake. I hope Dawny doesn't have a gun to her head or something.

My phone rings and I hit the button. 'Yeah?'

'You didn't take the apartment keys,' Finn tells me. Finn Carson, friend and temporary landlord, is subletting me his apartment and I'm moving in tomorrow.

'Oh, right. I'll ... get them later.'

'When you tell me what's really going on?'

I'd been last to leave his housewarming party, sitting on his back veranda trying to pry information on a current case out of him when Dawny's message had come through. I'd gotten up as casually as I could and made what I thought had been a reasonable excuse to take off. But being that he's a detective sergeant—and a pretty good one—I'm not surprised he saw through me.

'Can't believe I forgot those keys. I'm looking forward to moving in. You said the cleaners would be out before two? I'm sure that's when my furniture is supposed to arrive.'

'It was Dawny on the phone, wasn't it? I heard her voice.'

'I mean, Tom's great and I thought a night or two staying in a room at his pub while waiting to get into the apartment might be fun. But no. No, it's not. Way too noisy!' An overtaking lane opens up—yes!—and I jump into it, put my foot down.

'You know the dead giveaway here is the small talk, right? You don't do that. Ever.'

Smartarse. 'I'm evolving.'

'Do you really think you should be rushing off on some Dawny-style mission? You're not fully recovered from our last case.'

He was right. The thumb that had been sliced to the bone is still bandaged, I have a chest full of not-quite-healed ribs and my face looks like a slowly fading war zone. But what can I do? I was the one stupid enough to join the police force. 'You've got to be shitting me!'

'Why would I be—'

'Not you! Turbo here!'

'Sorry?'

'The old snail in front of me who suddenly got a rocket up his arse when the overtaking lane began. For fuck's sake!' I lean on the accelerator and end up having to do twenty over just to edge ahead before the lane closes. I glare as I pass but the gaze of the dick straining to see over the steering wheel never shifts from the road ahead. 'You know, I'm a police officer. There should be some way to arrest people for that shit.'

'Yeah, like we do with people who drink and drive.'

Drink and—What had I had to drink? A Champagne, a JD, another couple of sips of Champagne. Shouldn't be over the limit, should I? Maybe. A headline flashes in front of my eyes LOCAL PROBATIONARY CONSTABLE FIRED FOR DRINK DRIVING ON HER WAY TO AID AND ABET A FORMER FELON AND HER WANTED HUSBAND.

Damn it, Dawny. 'I'm not over. I barely drank any of that second Champagne.' Even though I've eased up on the speed, Turbo's rapidly losing ground, trapping the cars still behind him as the lanes merge back into one. Poor bastards.

'*Where* are you *going*?'

'I told you.'

'You told me you were going home. Home was a half-hour ago. You're still driving.'

'You're using your fancy detective skills on me now?'

'You get a phone call with a mysterious message then all but sprint to your car with the lamest excuse I've ever heard and tear out of my street at light speed. It doesn't take much in the way of detective skills. Nor does knowing that, whatever this is, you shouldn't be doing it.'

'Don't be dramatic.'

'I'm being anything but dramatic. You know how this goes. You get into trouble, then I nearly die stopping you from dying.'

I want to argue, but it's a valid point. 'Can't you just be grateful I'm not dragging you into it then?'

'No, because I'm bound to be dragged into it. It's only a matter of when.'

'I could say the same about you and Rachael not telling me everything you know about Vaughn's next move,' I say of the murdering arsehole I've been hunting for more than a year.

'Can we deal with one thing at a time, please?'

I see the road I'm looking for and make the turn. It's a quiet enough street lined with narrow, small-acreage blocks stretching back to what looks like a lake. Pretty. There's a large brick fence hiding the number I'm looking for and I pull up in front of it. 'I've got to go.'

'Lexi—'

'I'll call you as soon as I know what's going on. Bye!' I want to push out of the car, hurry to reach Dawny, but I force myself to wait. Look around. Listen. There's no traffic on the street. Lights are on in homes and someone in the house over the road has a monster TV with the nightly news showing. I hear a kid squeal, another shout and laugh. Otherwise, all is quiet. Seems safe enough.

I get out of my car and lock it. Then on another thought, I type Dawny's address into a message to Finn. Anything goes wrong, I just have to hit the send button. I open the gate and am faced with a very ordinary eighties brick home with a serious security system: one of those military-grade screen doors, cameras, warnings of a potential guard dog on duty. Shit. Really? Where?

I step around two Harley Davidsons parked by the front step. One's an old shitbox, the other is a seriously nice bike. I bang on the door, hope for the best.

'Dawny?'

Nothing. I bang again. 'Hello!'

A curtain moves and I get the fleeting impression of a round, hairy face in the window before I hear a snapped, 'What?'

'I'm looking for Dawny?'

'Why?'

'Because she asked me to come.'

'Who are you?'

'My name's Lexi.'

'Lexi who?'

I growl impatiently. I didn't bolt over here to play knock-knock with some random arsehole. 'Winter! Is Dawny there or not?'

'Strip down.'

'Ask me that again. I dare you.'

'I need to know you're not armed!'

Oh, for fuck's sake, who are these people? I pull off my jacket, do a spin. 'Happy?'

A dog barks and I freeze in fear before deciding it's behind next door's fence. My nerves are returning. What's taking so long? Maybe I should call Finn.

Maybe I should toughen the fuck up. 'Look, I'm not leaving until I've seen Dawny.'

'You'll do what you're fuckin' told, bitch or else.'

'Or else *what*? I kick this door off its hinges, smack you over the head with it and use it for your fucking headstone? Where's Dawny!'

'Lexi! Better late than never. You can let her in,' I hear Dawny call out.

'I'll do more than let the bitch in!'

I hear three locks click over; the door opens an inch. A shotgun barrel emerges, pointed straight at my head. Before I can process more than an initial flash of *Oh shit!*, I'm shoved sideways and a large figure barges past into the house, pointing the gun barrel skyward and sending its hulk of an owner back several steps into the room. The door slams back against the wall with a crack.

'Don't move!' Finn demands, now in possession of the gun and pointing the barrel at the hulk.

For a moment, I'm as stunned as the hulk. Then, 'You *followed* me?' I ask stupidly.

'What's going on?' Finn says, ignoring me.

'Oh, Lexi, dear! How lovely to see you ... eventually.'

I spot Dawny and another arsehole, younger and weedier, in the doorway to the kitchen. Dawny hasn't changed much, she's still dressed like a street kid, but her Clairol brown hair now sports a purple streak. Other than looking a little dishevelled, she seems unharmed. 'And you brought that big, bad boyfriend of yours. How's business, Finn? I hear the body count's going up? No need to be taking anyone out tonight though, please. How about we all sit down, eh? Have a nice calm chat.'

I take my eyes off Dawny and flick a nervous glance around. Black leather lounge, old carpet, smart TV, coffee table. The stink of cigarette smoke and old beer courtesy of an overloaded ashtray and half-a-dozen empty beer bottles. Beyond is a hallway with an older-style kitchen to the left. More mess.

'Great idea,' Finn says, then, 'Sit,' he orders, waving the gun towards the lounge.

The hulk is probably fifty-something, dressed in ripped jeans and a stained tee with a patched leather bikie vest, big boots and a chilly expression. He does as he's told.

'You too,' Finn tells the tattooed and multi-pierced weed standing next to Dawny.

Dawny hobbles in behind the weed on the knee that's been dodgy as long as I've known her. My gaze returns to hulk's vest, the patches. The ones I'm most interested in tells me he goes by Woolly and belongs to the Chaos Reigns Motorcycle Club. He's a full member. I check the weed. Just a prospect. I'm not familiar with this MC, but they're both displaying one-percenter patches.

'Dawny,' Finn says. 'Are you hurt?'

'Oh, no need for all that drama, dear,' she says with a casual wave of her hand. 'I'm perfectly fine.'

Finn shoots me a glare and I aim my own at Dawny.

'You're perfectly fine?' I say, before placing my hand to my head. 'That message you left on my phone suggested you were about to die!'

Dawny's eyes crinkle with amusement. 'If I ever am, I'll call someone who drives a bit faster.'

'Okay,' I say, because honestly what's the point? 'You said, "urgent little pickle".'

'Well, it is rather,' Dawny says, taking a seat in an armchair across from the lounge. 'I need you to sort something out for me. Nothing major, I'm sure you'll be fine.'

I'm not fooled by the conversational, all-the-time-in-the-world speech. Nothing fazes this woman. Nothing. Armageddon could be imminent.

Her gaze moves over my bruised face and she grimaces. 'Although from the looks of you, I might have overestimated things slightly.'

'Can we get to the point?' Finn prompts.

'Ah, yes. Desmond's depending on us, so we'll push on.'

'Fine,' I say. 'Let's get out of here and you can tell me about it.'

'She's not going anywhere till we got proof!' Woolly snaps, folding his arms and glaring at Dawny.

'You're not exactly in any position to call the shots,' Finn reminds him.

'Oh, he is, dear,' Dawny says. 'At least, as long as I want to see Desmond alive again.'

My stomach sinks. 'Desmond's in trouble?' I ask. 'What do they want proof of?'

Dawny sighs dramatically. 'A very desperate young fellow bailed up a few of the members last night at gunpoint.'

'Where is Desmond?' Finn asks.

'Not here, unfortunately.'

'Is he injured?'

'Oh, please, dear. Desmond just gave this young fellow a bit of a bop on the head and that was that. Turns out the young fellow wasn't supposed to be where he was and it all got a bit out of hand and ... these things happen. Anyway, someone needs to see this young fellow and we need you to get him for us.'

I shift my weight onto my foot closest to the door, as though by backing up I can lessen the impact of the drama I know I'm about to be hit with. 'Why call me?' I ask suspiciously. 'You don't know where he is?'

Dawny pulled a face. 'Well, that's the problem, dear. We do.'

'So ... he doesn't want to come in?' I ask.

'Oh, I don't think it would bother him too much to be honest.'

'Dawny.' I hear the exasperation in my tone, but seriously. 'What's the problem then?'

'Ah, well, Desmond didn't realise the boss would need to see this fellow and he'd already ... removed the evidence.'

'Evidence?' I stare at her for two seconds. Three. Then it hits me. 'How hard was that bop on the head?'

'And where is this young fellow?' Finn demands.

'Oh, just off Patonga Wharf. It's not deep.'

'He took him all the way out to Patonga?' Is that even really the question I should be asking? 'Why?'

'Supposed to be lots of sharks.'

If Finn clenches his jaw any harder he's going to break teeth. My gaze shifts to Woolly just to make absolutely sure no one is taking the piss. He certainly seems serious enough.

'We need to know he's dead,' Woolly tells me. 'Make sure Desmond hasn't jumped ship. Changed sides.'

'Sides of what?' I ask, but the look on his face tells me I don't need details.

'I can't believe this,' Finn mutters to the ceiling. Then to Dawny, he says, 'You called Lexi here to dive into shark-infested waters to recover a murder victim to prove Desmond is loyal to a motorcycle gang.'

'You need to relax, dear,' Dawny soothes, 'you'll give yourself a migraine.' Then to me, she says, 'And yes, please. It's a bit past me, I'm afraid. In the dark would be best. Shouldn't take you long.'

Like fuck. 'Dawny, I am absolutely not—'

'I know it's not a glam job,' Dawny hurries on, 'but I'll make sure you get your normal fee. And you don't even have to kill anyone! It's your lucky day, I'd say.'

Normal fee? Kill anyone? I'm trying to keep up but I've got nothing.

'Right, that's enough,' Finn says, and I can see he's done with whatever game this is. Fuck. I need to manage this. 'You're both—'

'Okay! Fine!' I cut in loudly. I'd rather he didn't tell these guys we're cops. 'But only because we owe you a *serious* favour,' I add to remind Finn that Dawny and Desmond once helped save his daughter's life. 'We'll get your proof, but nothing better happen to Desmond in the meantime,' I say with a glare at Woolly. 'What do you need?'

Finn takes his eyes off Woolly long enough to give me the sort of *what the fuck?* look I've become accustomed to. I pretend not to see it.

'Photos. Video. Whatever. Just some general proof. Once we know he's dead, they're both off the hook,' Woolly tells me.

'Oh, we have until tomorrow night.' Dawny adds.

'Then what?'

'Then we stop being nice,' Woolly says with a mean smile.

'Dawny, you're coming with us,' Finn orders.

'Oh, no, dear—'

'That's non-negotiable,' Finn tells Woolly, 'You've got Desmond, we get Dawny. That's the deal.'

'Fine! Take the old bat. She's as annoying as fuck anyway.' Then to me, he says, 'You send the proof to this number I'm gonna give ya. You don't come through, Desy's getting some dentistry, a solid meal and a long cruise.'

The prospect sniggers like he's sharing some private joke. Half-wit. Still, the idea Desmond might have his teeth removed and concrete poured down his throat before being dumped far enough off the coast to never be found is not a nice one.

'Won't be a problem, dear,' Dawny promises. 'These two are very dependable. What's the number?'

Woolly reads it out and I store it in my phone. 'Got it.'

'Right. Go,' Finn tells me. 'Get Dawny out of here.'

'Give me my damn gun back!' Woolly demands as Finn follows us out.

'Not going to happen.'

'There'll be hell to pay!' Woolly growls.

'You're right on that,' Finn mutters. But I'm pretty sure he's talking to me.

CHAPTER TWO

'You followed me!' Lexi hissed as they reached her car. 'I can't believe you were talking to me on the phone while you were behind me the whole time!'

Finn barely took his eyes off the house as they went through the gate. All quiet. 'I think the words you're looking for are "Thanks, Finn".' He paused when they reached Lexi's car. His was right behind it. 'Get in. I'll follow you back to the pub with Dawny so you can leave your car there. I'll call Rachael, let her know what's happening, then you can come with me for whatever we do after that.'

Both women looked set to argue, so he added, 'Or I do this the traditional way, call it in right now and bring those two with us for questioning.'

Lexi pressed her lips together over whatever she wanted to say and exchanged looks with Dawny. He noted the slightest shake of Lexi's head before she silently opened her door and slipped into her car. He watched her pull out onto the road before going to his.

'You may as well know now,' Dawny said when they were on the road, 'I won't be setting foot inside one of those police stations tonight, dear. I want to get Desmond out of this alive and that's not the way to go about it.'

'Desmond murdered a man, Dawny. And if you had anything to do with it, you're an accessory.'

Dawny barked out a laugh. 'Desmond didn't kill the poor fellow. Where'd you get that idea?'

'You said he bopped the guy on the head and dumped him at Patonga.'

'Ah, well, he did, but he didn't kill him.'

'Just ... hold on.'

'What are you doing?'

'Calling Rachael.'

'Rachael? You mean that inspector lady?'

'That's the one.' He hit Rachael's number, had to wonder if his aunt and the leader of his homicide team had even made it home to Sydney from his housewarming yet.

'Hi, we just got in,' Rachael said, answering his question. 'Everything okay?'

'Not exactly. What's the chance you could get divers out to Patonga Wharf within the next twenty-four hours to recover a body?'

A pause, then, 'I'll find out.'

'Thanks.'

'I'll call you back after it's sorted and you can fill me in.'

'Will do.' He hit the end button.

'Finn, dear,' Dawny says. 'No disrespect intended of course, but if you get the police all tangled up with this—'

'The police are already tangled up in this,' he said. 'Lexi and I are police. You called Lexi for help.'

'What?' she squawked as her face went blank with shock. 'Lexi joined you coppers? When did that happen?'

'You've been gone a while.'

There was some unintelligible muttering out the window before she said, 'I *knew* she had too much fun catching that Spider pervert.'

'I wouldn't have called the Spider case fun.'

'I thought she had more sense,' Dawny complained. 'I'm guessing this police business is why she looks like she's gone ten rounds with Mundine. I thought more of you, Finn.'

He glanced at Dawny in disbelief. 'I'm not the reason she looks like that!'

'No, of course not. I'm sure you had nothing to do with it.'

'That's right. Thank y—'

'Even though you should have had something to do with it. Something that involved keeping her safe. I never pegged you as inadequate. I hope you can live with yourself.'

'I—' He bit back his reply and answered his phone. Rachael.

'We'll have a team in the water at first light. Cass and Linc will head out there to oversee the recovery.'

'Oh, that's wonderful news!' Dawny gushed in a sudden and complete change of tone. 'He's just off the front of the wharf. We'll need some photos of the unfortunate fellow, please.'

'Dawny?' Rachael asked in surprise. 'Is that you?'

'Oh, it's Dawny all right,' Finn answered.

'He's a bit cross,' Dawny told Rachael. 'Think I might have hit a nerve when I asked him why he let Lexi cop all those terrible bruises. Do you think the police divers can go in without too much fanfare? I'm a little bit worried they'll be spotted and things won't end well.'

'Do the divers have anything to worry about?' Rachael asked sharply.

'Oh, no, dear. Of course not. But it'd be much better for Desmond if no one knows the police are looking for that body.'

'Would someone care to fill me in?' Rachael said weakly.

'Desmond's being held by two men belonging to a motorcycle club called Chaos Reigns,' Finn said. 'They want proof of death on that body. Dawny called Lexi earlier to get it, not realising she was now working for the police and it's just gotten more ... interesting from there. We need to check ownership of the house at an address Lexi will be able to give you and I have a gun belonging to the more senior member of the club called Woolly that we should be able to get some prints off for a more accurate identification.'

'You didn't arrest them?'

'I did say it got more interesting. Dawny's given us alter egos and it seemed important for Desmond's longevity to keep them.' He glanced at Dawny almost threateningly. 'Temporarily, at least.'

'So who did they think—actually, never mind,' Rachael said. 'Bring Dawny down to headquarters. You can fill me in and Dawny can give us a statement.'

'No offence, dear, but you can sit me in that place all night. Until you find that body, I've got nothing to say.'

'That'd be a first,' Finn muttered.

'Let's aim for a cup of tea and a chat tomorrow,' Dawny said, ignoring him. 'Once you've found that young fellow and we clear Desmond. Okay then?' Dawny said. 'Ta-ta.' She reached forward and pressed the end button on the screen.

'Dawny!' Finn snapped.

'Oh, weren't you finished? There's another call coming through.'

From Lexi, he saw, and pressed the button. 'Yeah?'

'I have questions.'

'Don't we all.'

'Like why don't we need to kill anyone and what's our regular fee?'

Dawny chuckled. 'The young fellow's already dead, isn't he? And your regular fee is for cleaning up. I have no idea what cleaners charge these days.'

There's a huff from Lexi, before she says, 'I get cleaner, Finn gets hitman?'

'You're right, dear. No one who saw your house would believe that. I meant one that takes care of sensitive messes. The kind we don't want police nosing in on. No offence,' she said for the umpteenth time as she shot Finn a look. 'And I told you to come alone. Remember? I had to come up with something spur of the moment. Thought the hitman tag looked good on Finn. Might hold some sway. And what better partnership? Finn kills 'em, you clean up the evidence. Very clever, actually, when you think about it.'

'And you just assumed we'd go along with it?' Finn asked.

'Not everyone could pull off a successful hitman. Those big, broad shoulders of yours are still looking pretty good,' Dawny said. 'I'll make you a pie, just as soon as Desmond's released.'

'What do you mean "still"? And as I'm so *inadequate*, are you sure you want us getting Desmond out of this?'

'Inadequate?' Lexi cut in.

'Well, anything's possible,' Dawny rolled on. 'The fact you didn't mention you were with the coppers is miraculous in itself. Desmond would be dead for sure if you'd given that away. They'd be after us, too. I'd never be able to show my face again!'

'Who's the victim?' Lexi asked.

'I suppose it depends on your point of view. Desmond was only trying to help and—'

'The dead guy, Dawny. The one in the water. What's his name?'

'Oh, I wouldn't know.'

'And those men?'

'You already know the big one goes by Woolly. The skinny one with the funny haircut is Skink. Skink told me all the noms are given terrible nicknames.'

'Noms?' Finn asked.

'A club prospect, dear. Nice enough kid, actually. Had a bit of a bad time of it growing up. Had a lovely chat. Much nicer than Woolly. Did you see the size of Woolly's ears? Kept wanting to call him Dumbo. It was bound to have slipped out if you'd taken much longer. I—'

'Is Desmond in the MC?' Lexi cut in.

'Oh, no, dear. He just does odd jobs for whoever needs them done. Jobs that aren't advertised on regular channels. Because he's good at minding his own business, you know. Which is why this is all so ridiculous.'

'What job was he doing?' Finn asked.

'He picked up some work doing deliveries from the Newcastle docks, oh, probably going on six months now. Never had any trouble until yesterday. That young fellow has turned out to be quite the headache.'

'Yes, poor Desmond,' Finn muttered sarcastically. 'Rachael's calling back, I have to go,' he told Lexi.

He ended Lexi's call and answered Rachael's. 'Yep.'

'This MC is flagged on the system with the Organised Crime Squad. I messaged Chad McCabe. He's asked for an early meeting before proceeding. That's at seven. Dawny, I'm going to assume for this evening that you're an innocent party in all this, but I need you on standby to come in as soon as the victim is located. If you don't show I'll put a warrant out for your arrest as a possible accessory after the fact to murder. That's jail time. Are we clear?'

'That's very understanding of you. People give coppers a bad rap, don't they? But you don't *all* deserve it, that's what I say. I'll be in for that evidence when you find it. Don't you worry about that.'

'Then I'll see you both tomorrow.'

'Do you need me to stop anywhere to pick up some things?' Finn asked Dawny after ending the call. 'Where have you been staying?'

'Here and there, and never mind that. I'm sure I'll survive a night. Lexi will put me up.'

He doubted it would be just one, but they could sort that out later.

'She's staying at her friend's pub in Gosford. Her house was destroyed during our last case.'

Dawny's mouth fell open, her eyes wide. 'She's been beaten up *and* had her house destroyed? And you lot put her in a *pub*?'

'She's been in a great apartment under protection—'

'Well that obviously worked.'

'—which she hated and because she's moving into my place—'

'She's moving in with you? Maybe get her a German shepherd. Something that can actually protect her.'

'Not *with* me, I have a new place …' Why was he bothering to explain? 'You know what? How about we focus on this latest disaster. Are you sure there's nothing else you can tell me?'

Dawny stared out the window as he took the onramp to the motorway. 'That's the problem with the police these days. Always looking for someone else to do their job for them.'

He bit back the retort and concentrated on merging. He might owe this woman, but he had a feeling by the end of this that favour would be well and truly repaid.

talk about it

Let's talk about books.

Join the conversation:

 facebook.com/harlequinaustralia

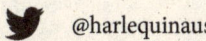 @harlequinaus

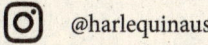 @harlequinaus

harpercollins.com.au/hq

If you love reading and want to know about our
authors and titles, then let's talk about it.